"I LOVED Katie!"
—LUCY KNISLEY, *New York Times* bestselling author of *Stepping Stones*

"…-girl comic to …courage adventure, entrepreneurship, and excellent, pun-filled pet names."
—*The Bulletin of the Center for Children's Books*

KATIE THE CATSITTER

"The new Feline Queen of All-Ages Superhero Comic Books. A . . . universal story about growing up."
—ComicBookResources.com

"Super fun and utterly delightful!"
—GENE LUEN YANG, creator of *American Born Chinese*

"A winner!"
—NICK BRUEL, creator of the Bad Kitty series

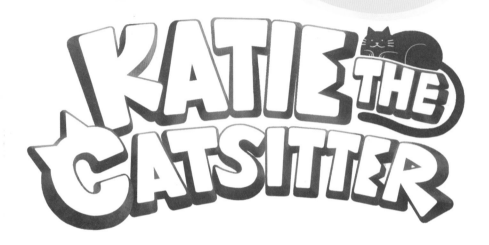

Read all the Katie the Catsitter books!

#1 *Katie the Catsitter*
#2 *Best Friends for Never*
#3 *Secrets and Sidekicks*

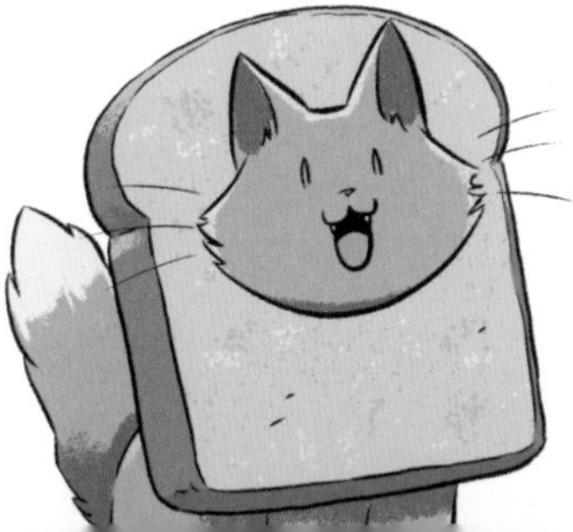

KATIE THE CATSITTER

SECRETS AND SIDEKICKS

Colleen AF Venable

ILLUSTRATED BY
Stephanie Yue

WITH COLORS BY
Braden Lamb

Random House 🏠 New York

With grateful thanks to Shasta Clinch for her invaluable feedback.
Special thanks to color assistants Shelli Paroline and Sam Bennett

Visit us on the Web! rhcbooks.com

Educators and librarians, for a variety of teaching tools,
visit us at RHTeachersLibrarians.com

Library of Congress Cataloging-in-Publication Data
Names: Venable, Colleen A. F., author. | Yue, Stephanie, illustrator.
Title: Secrets and Sidekicks / Colleen AF Venable, Stephanie Yue.
Description: First edition. | New York : Random House Children's Books, [2023] | Series: Katie the
catsitter; #3 | Audience: Ages 8–12 |
Summary: "Still training to be a sidekick, Katie protects the city against mysterious robot
attacks—while trying not to feel like an outsider within her own friend group"
—Provided by publisher.
Identifiers: LCCN 2021043969 | ISBN 978-0-593-37970-7 (library binding) |
ISBN 978-0-593-37972-1 (paperback) | ISBN 978-0-593-37969-1 (hardcover) |
ISBN 978-0-593-37971-4 (ebook)
Subjects: CYAC: Graphic novels. | Supervillains—Fiction. | Pet sitting—Fiction. |
Friendship—Fiction. | LCGFT: Graphic novels.
Classification: LCC PZ7.7.V46 Se 2023 | DDC 741.5/973—dc23 eng/20220107

Book design by Stephanie Yue and Juliet Goodman

MANUFACTURED IN CHINA
10 9 8 7 6 5 4 3 2
First Edition

To all the volunteers, especially
the crew at Bunnies and Beyond and
Animal Care Centers of NYC
—C.A.F.V.

To Fidget, Ruby, Yoli, Dash, and Fred,
who is not actually a cat
–S.Y.

CHAPTER ONE

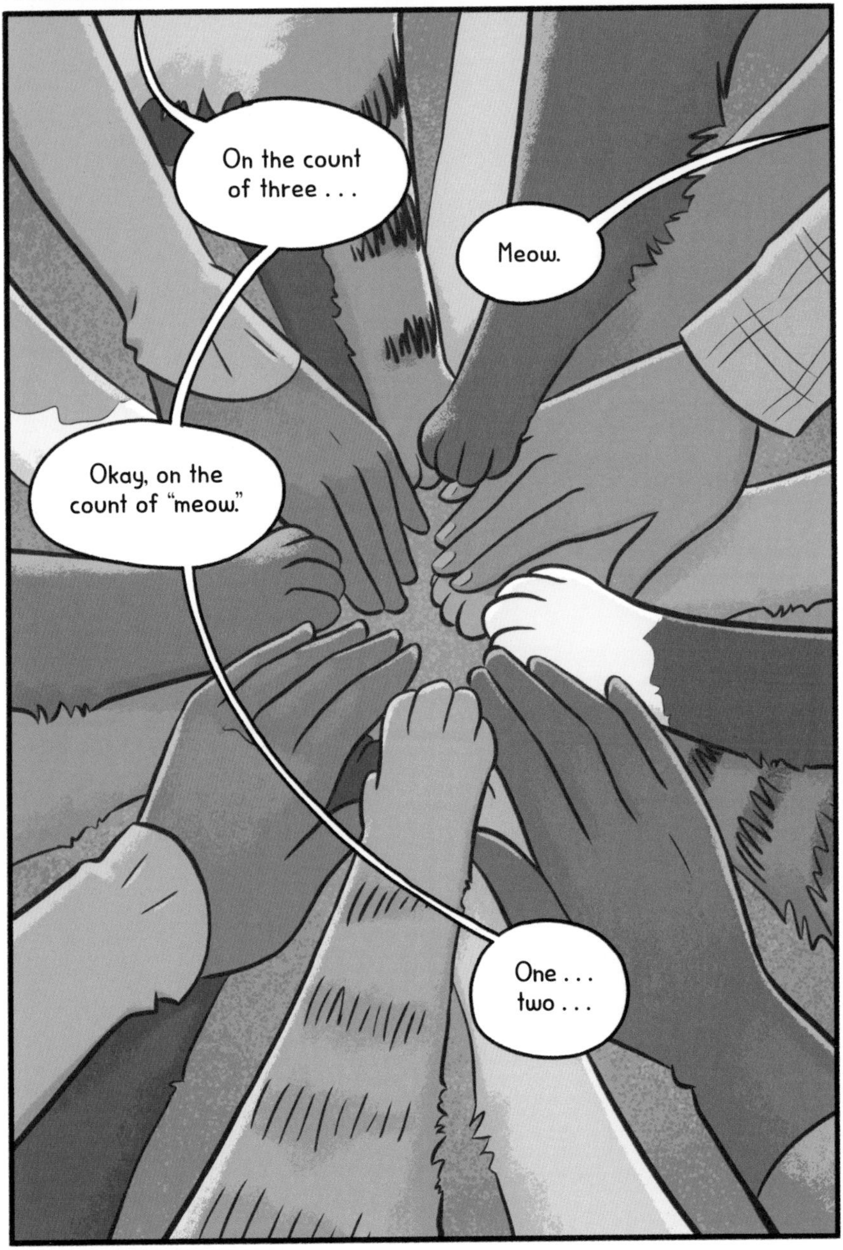
On the count of three . . .
Meow.
Okay, on the count of "meow."
One . . . two . . .

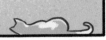

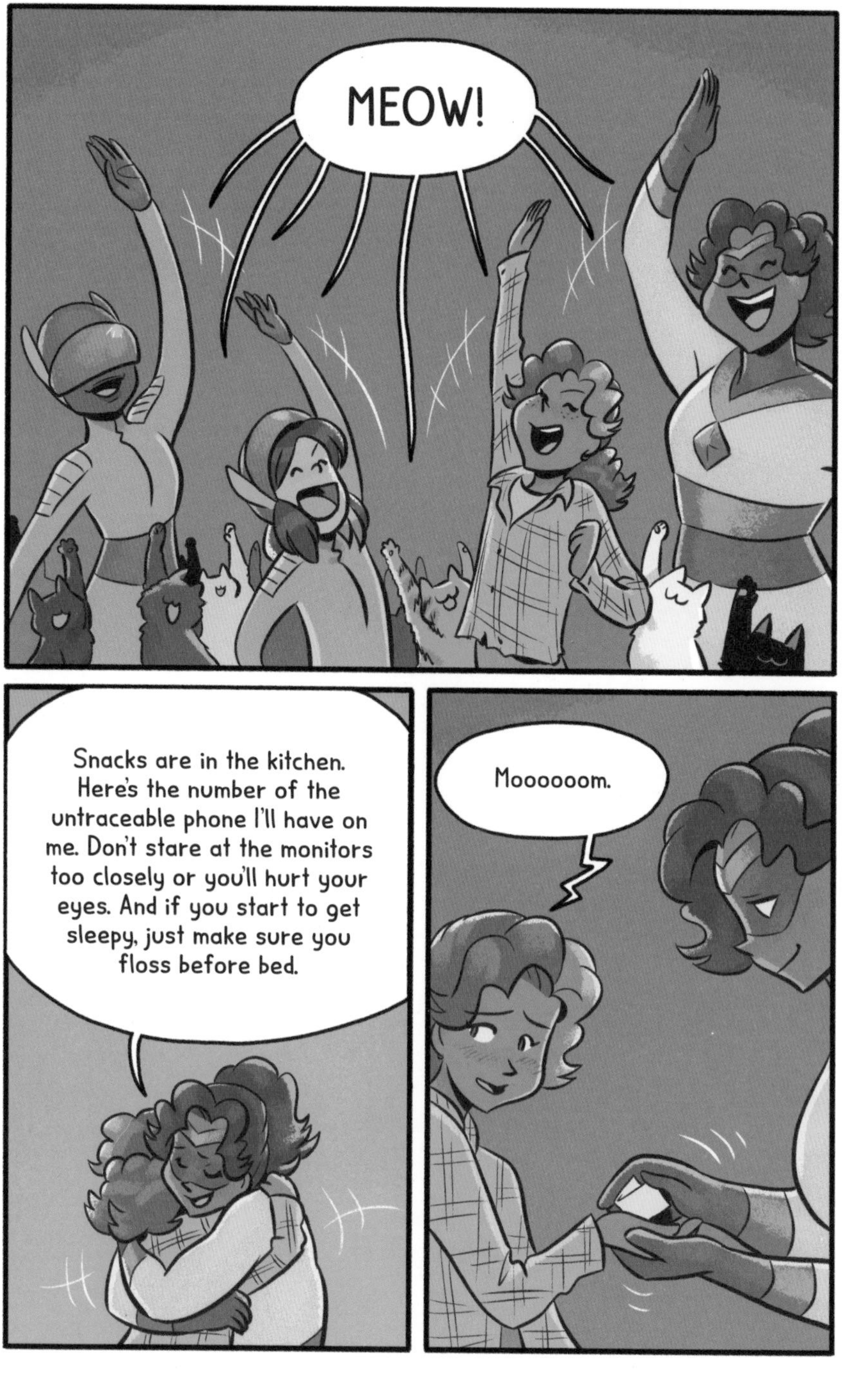
MEOW!
Snacks are in the kitchen. Here's the number of the untraceable phone I'll have on me. Don't stare at the monitors too closely or you'll hurt your eyes. And if you start to get sleepy, just make sure you floss before bed.
Moooooom.

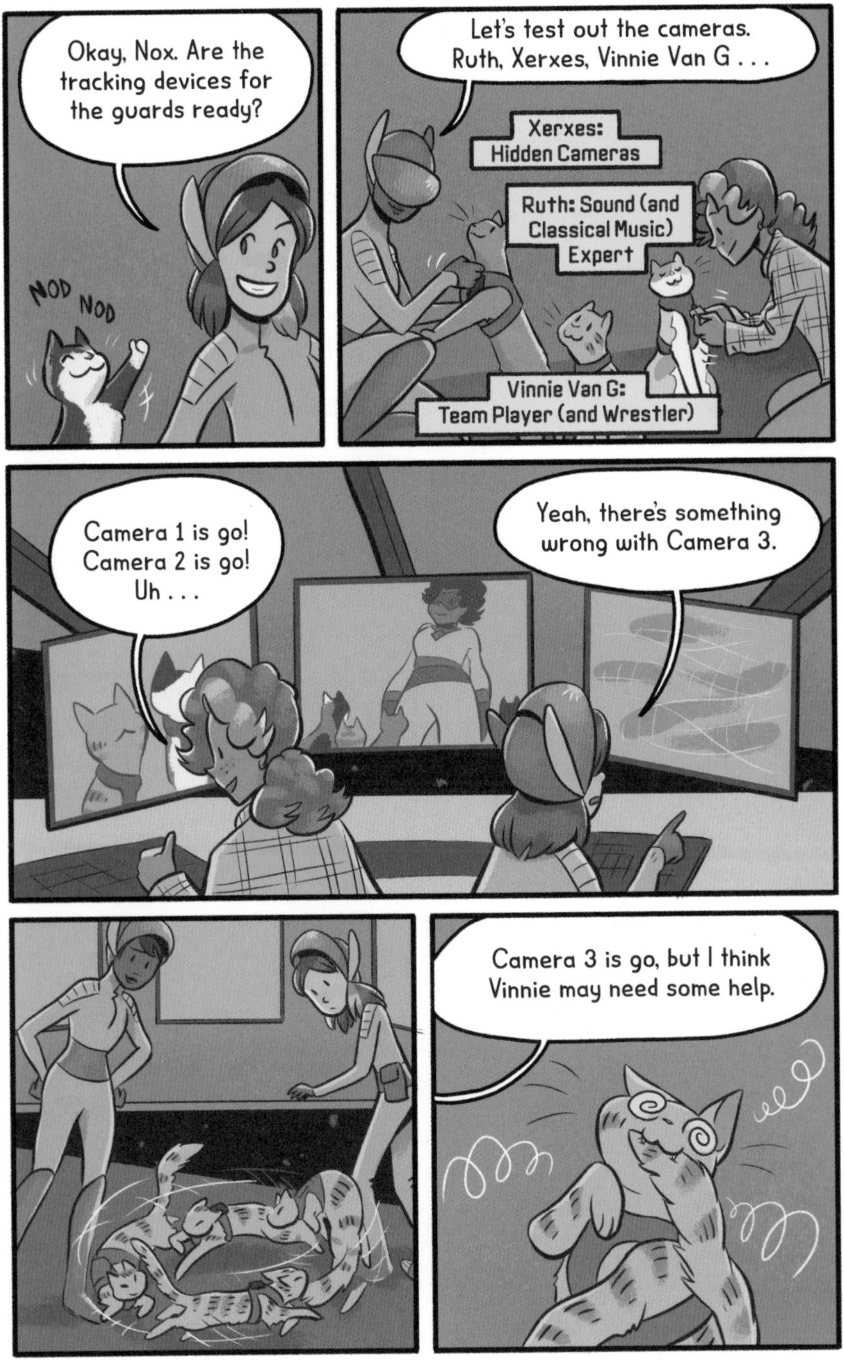
Okay, Nox. Are the tracking devices for the guards ready?
NOD NOD
Let's test out the cameras. Ruth, Xerxes, Vinnie Van G . . .
Xerxes: Hidden Cameras
Ruth: Sound (and Classical Music) Expert
Vinnie Van G: Team Player (and Wrestler)
Camera 1 is go! Camera 2 is go! Uh . . .
Yeah, there's something wrong with Camera 3.
Camera 3 is go, but I think Vinnie may need some help.

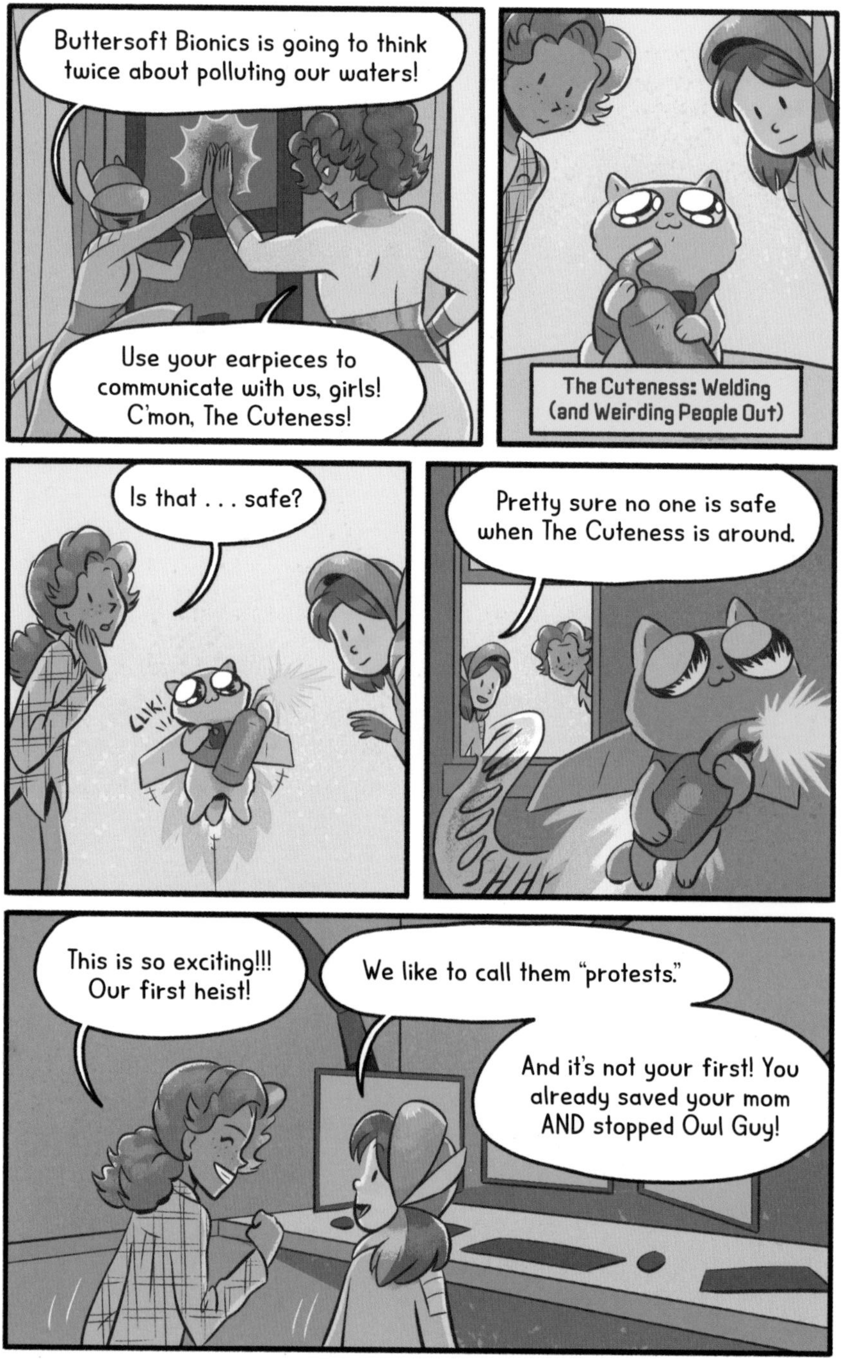
Buttersoft Bionics is going to think twice about polluting our waters!
Use your earpieces to communicate with us, girls! C'mon, The Cuteness!
The Cuteness: Welding (and Weirding People Out)
Is that . . . safe?
CLIK!
Pretty sure no one is safe when The Cuteness is around.
This is so exciting!!! Our first heist!
We like to call them "protests."
And it's not your first! You already saved your mom AND stopped Owl Guy!

Okay, Madeline, Miles has turned off the security system.

Wonderful.

Nox placed the trackers on the guards.

Excellent.

Now we take a few minutes to study their surveillance route patterns.

TWO MINUTES LATER

FIVE MINUTES LATER

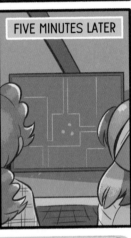

Ruth, can we get eyes on the guards?

Yeaaah, I don't think we have to worry about the guards.

How much birthday cake did they eat?

Operation "Hey, Buttersoft! Let's see how you like it!" is GO!

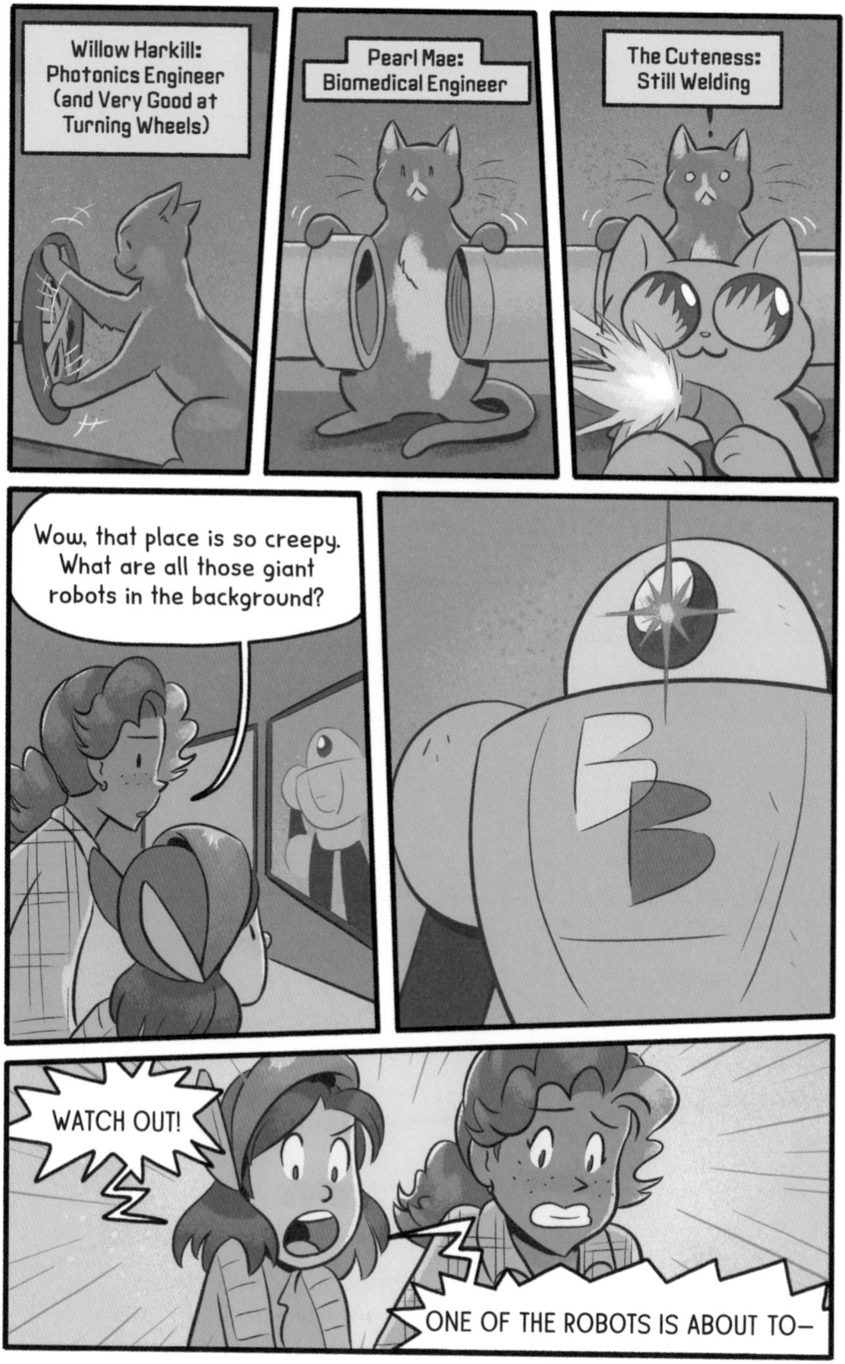
Willow Harkill: Photonics Engineer (and Very Good at Turning Wheels)
Pearl Mae: Biomedical Engineer
The Cuteness: Still Welding
!
Wow, that place is so creepy. What are all those giant robots in the background?
WATCH OUT!
ONE OF THE ROBOTS IS ABOUT TO—

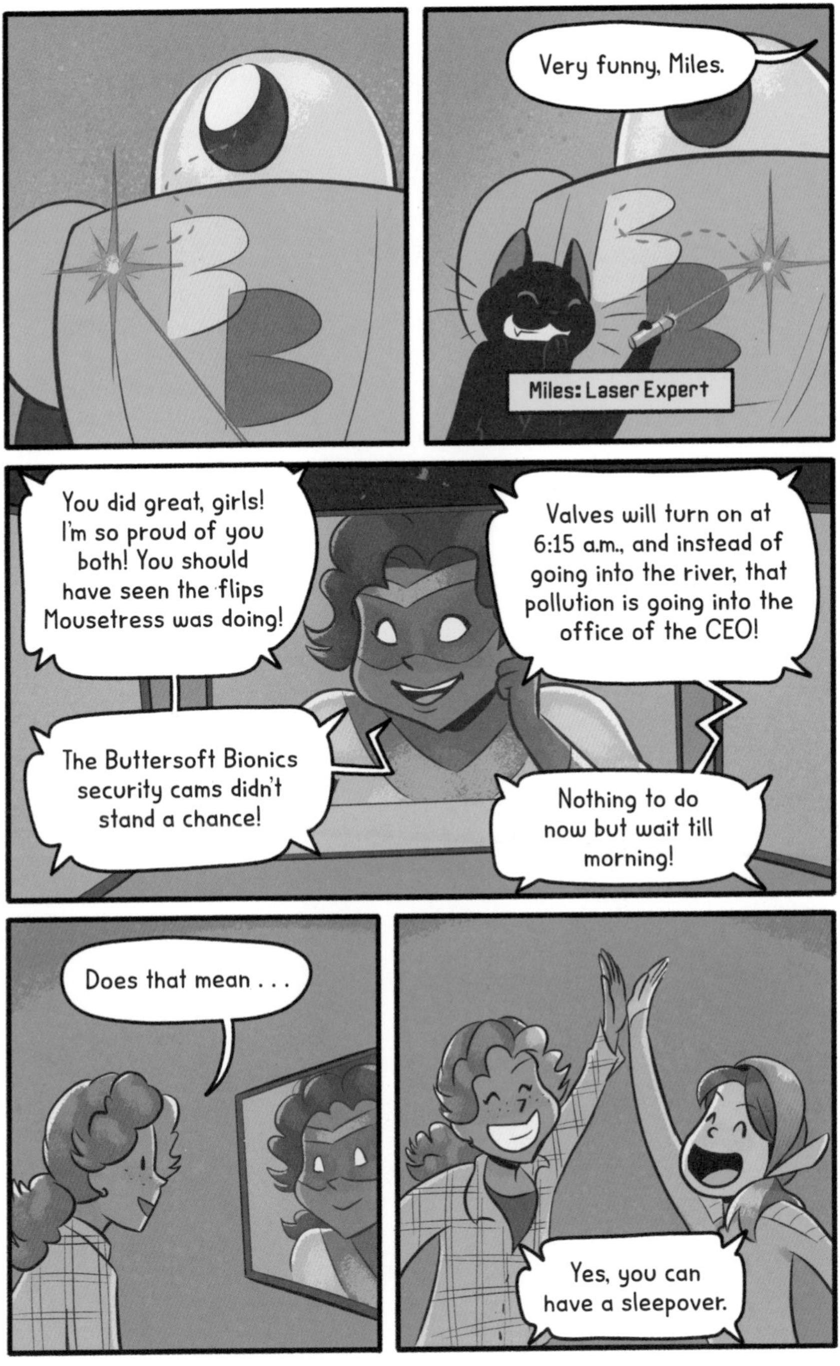
Very funny, Miles.
Miles: Laser Expert
You did great, girls! I'm so proud of you both! You should have seen the flips Mousetress was doing!
The Buttersoft Bionics security cams didn't stand a chance!
Valves will turn on at 6:15 a.m., and instead of going into the river, that pollution is going into the office of the CEO!
Nothing to do now but wait till morning!
Does that mean . . .
Yes, you can have a sleepover.

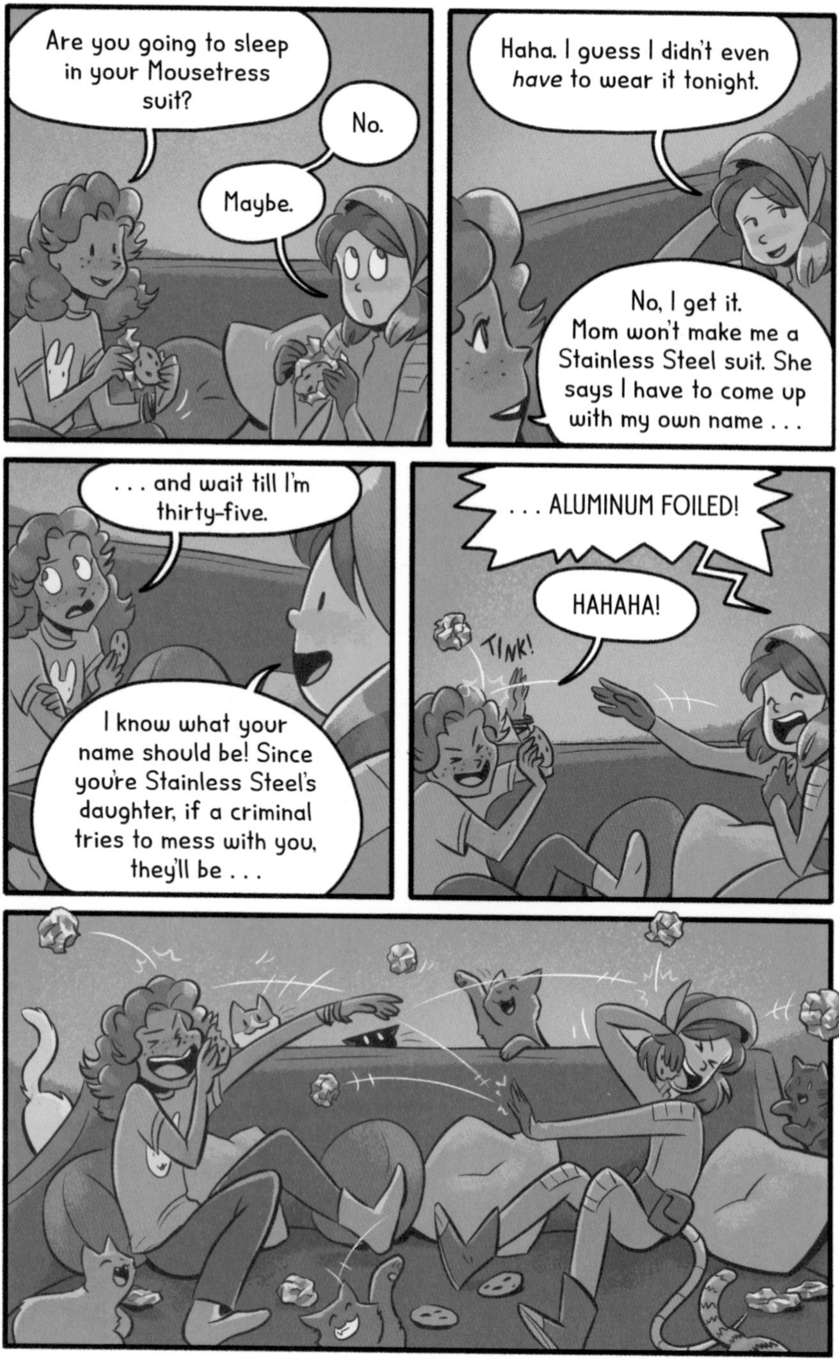
Are you going to sleep in your Mousetress suit?
No.
Maybe.
Haha. I guess I didn't even *have* to wear it tonight.
No, I get it. Mom won't make me a Stainless Steel suit. She says I have to come up with my own name . . .
. . . and wait till I'm thirty-five.
I know what your name should be! Since you're Stainless Steel's daughter, if a criminal tries to mess with you, they'll be . . .
. . . ALUMINUM FOILED!
HAHAHA!
TINK!

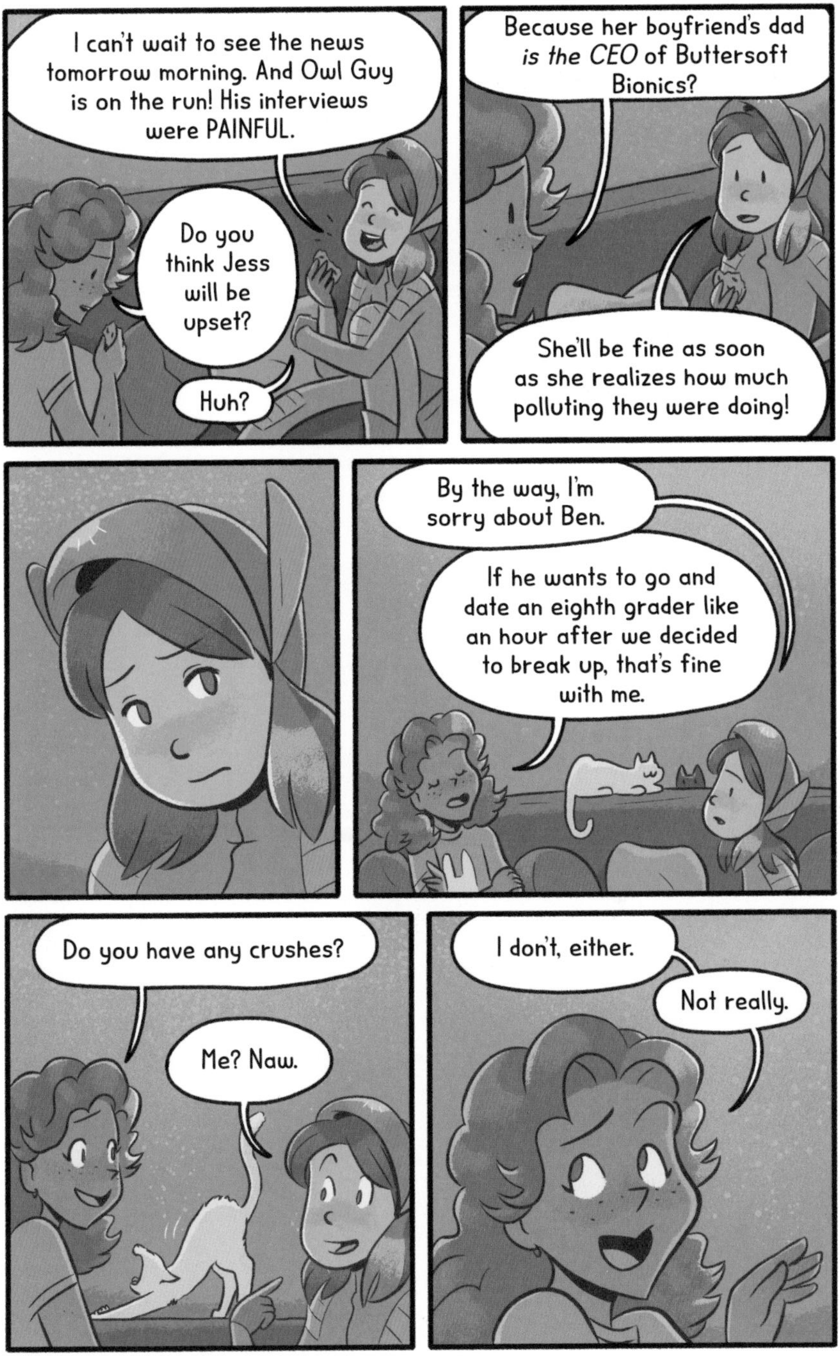
I can't wait to see the news tomorrow morning. And Owl Guy is on the run! His interviews were PAINFUL.
Do you think Jess will be upset?
Huh?
Because her boyfriend's dad *is the CEO* of Buttersoft Bionics?
She'll be fine as soon as she realizes how much polluting they were doing!
By the way, I'm sorry about Ben.
If he wants to go and date an eighth grader like an hour after we decided to break up, that's fine with me.
Do you have any crushes?
Me? Naw.
I don't, either.
Not really.

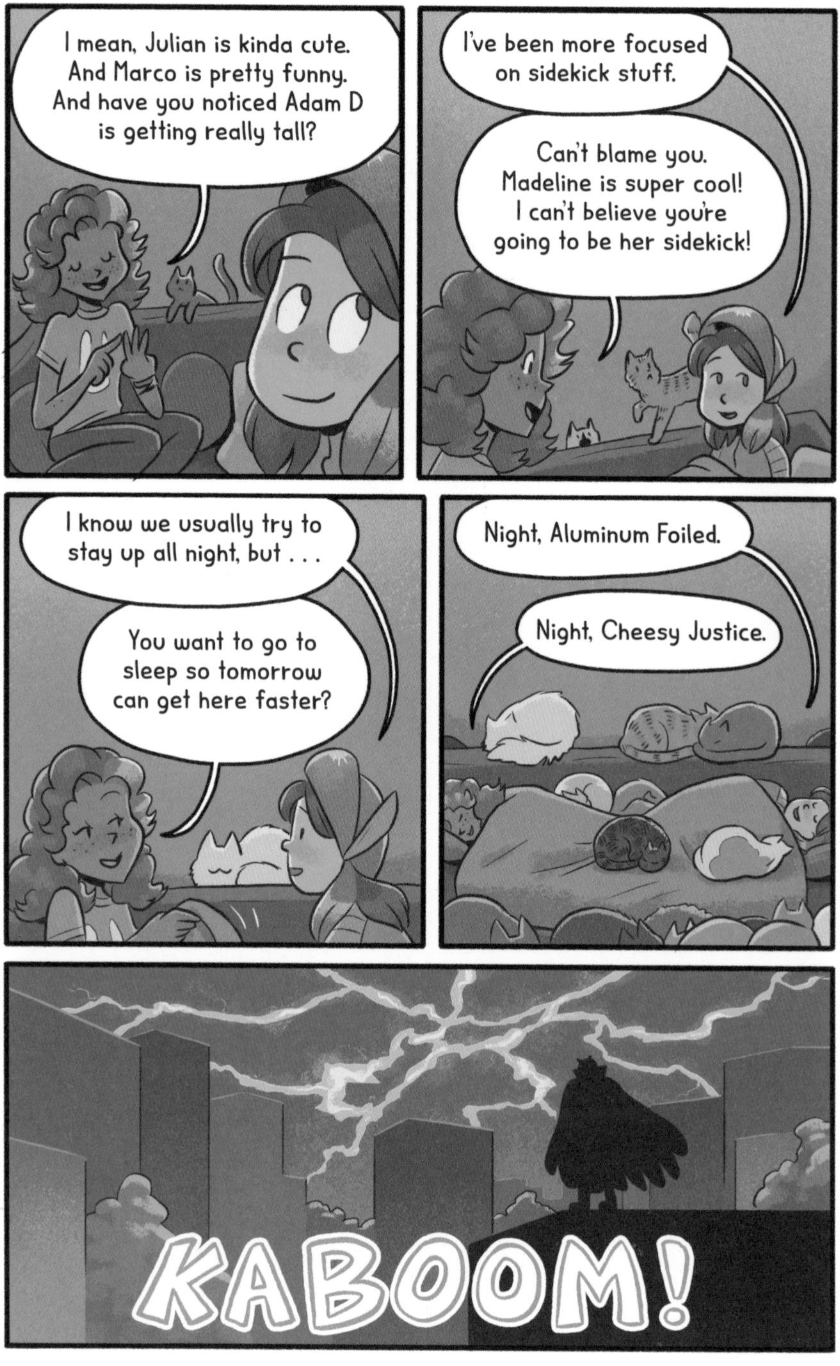
I mean, Julian is kinda cute. And Marco is pretty funny. And have you noticed Adam D is getting really tall?
I've been more focused on sidekick stuff.
Can't blame you. Madeline is super cool! I can't believe you're going to be her sidekick!
I know we usually try to stay up all night, but . . .
You want to go to sleep so tomorrow can get here faster?
Night, Aluminum Foiled.
Night, Cheesy Justice.
KABOOM!

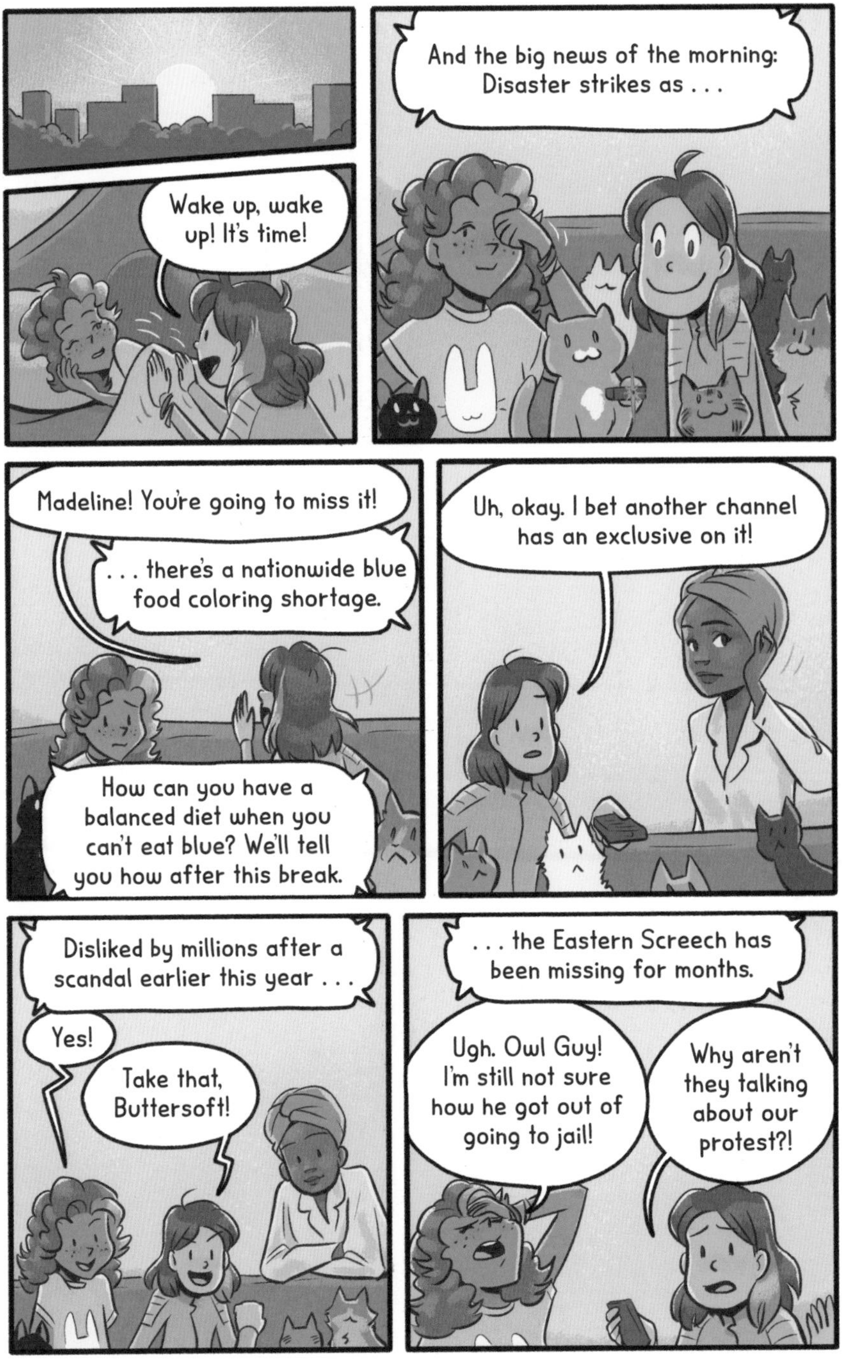
And the big news of the morning: Disaster strikes as . . .
Wake up, wake up! It's time!
Madeline! You're going to miss it!
. . . there's a nationwide blue food coloring shortage.
How can you have a balanced diet when you can't eat blue? We'll tell you how after this break.
Uh, okay. I bet another channel has an exclusive on it!
Disliked by millions after a scandal earlier this year . . .
Yes!
Take that, Buttersoft!
. . . the Eastern Screech has been missing for months.
Ugh. Owl Guy! I'm still not sure how he got out of going to jail!
Why aren't they talking about our protest?!

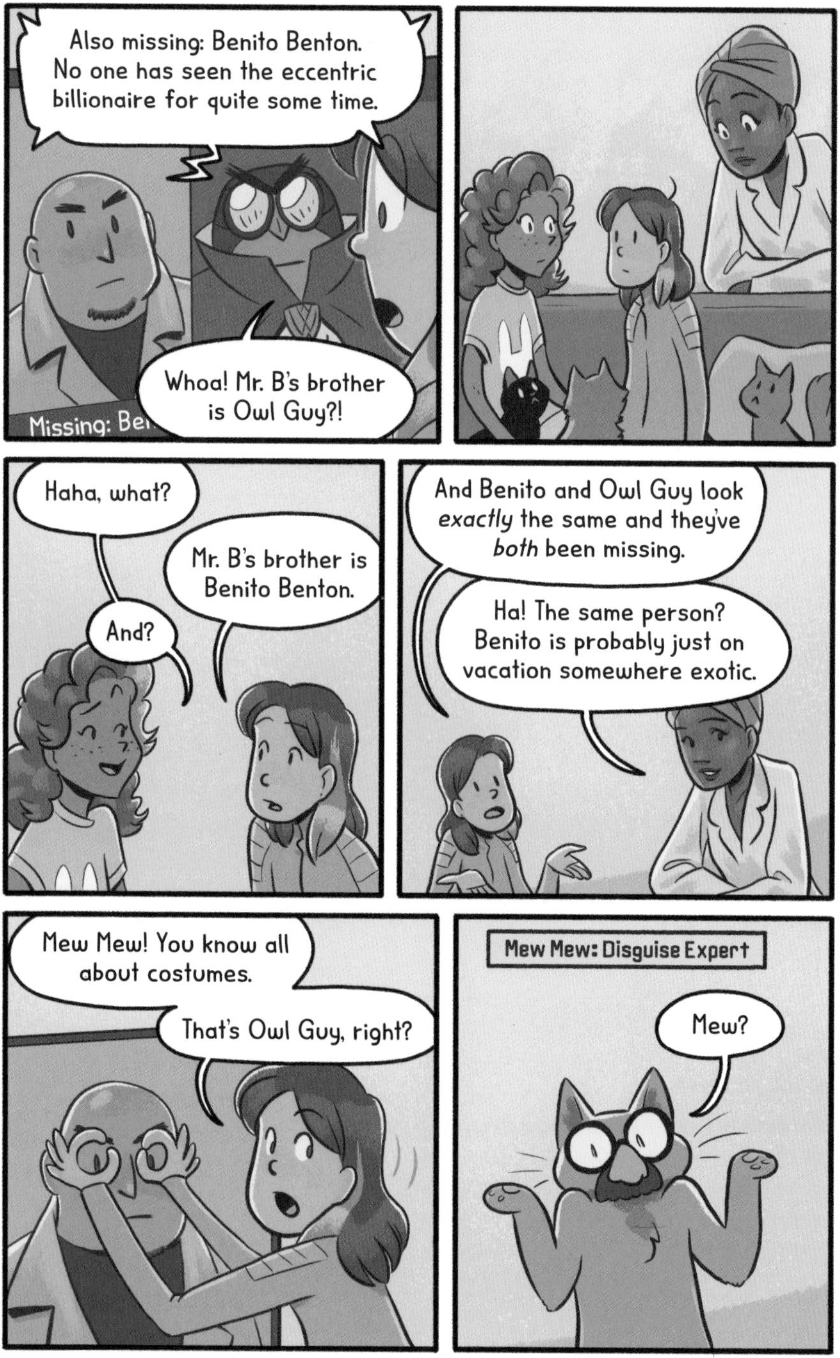
Also missing: Benito Benton. No one has seen the eccentric billionaire for quite some time.
Missing: Be
Whoa! Mr. B's brother is Owl Guy?!
Haha, what?
Mr. B's brother is Benito Benton.
And?
And Benito and Owl Guy look *exactly* the same and they've *both* been missing.
Ha! The same person? Benito is probably just on vacation somewhere exotic.
Mew Mew! You know all about costumes.
That's Owl Guy, right?
Mew Mew: Disguise Expert
Mew?

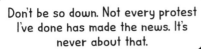
Don't be so down. Not every protest I've done has made the news. It's never about that.

The important thing is that Buttersoft realizes how many pollutants they've been dumping and what that does to those innocent animals.

Yeah, I guess.

I know what will cheer you up.

You know how you keep saying that I haven't taught you any fancy superhero moves yet?

We're going to start sidekick physical training this week.

YES!!!

WOO!!!

Oh, I'm so sorry, Beth. I just meant Katie. Your mom doesn't want you training.

Last night was a one-time thing.

Sigh. I know.

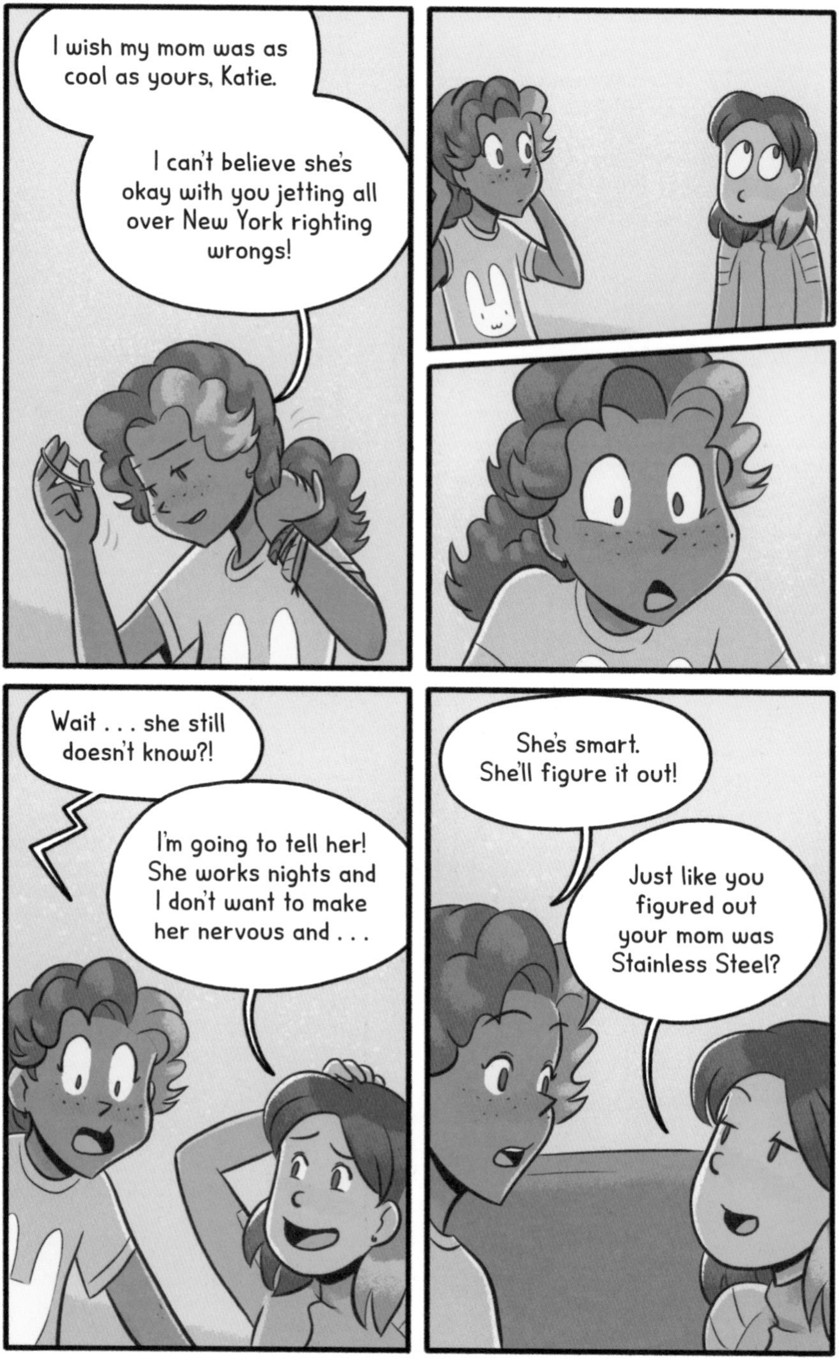

I wish my mom was as cool as yours, Katie.
I can't believe she's okay with you jetting all over New York righting wrongs!
Wait . . . she still doesn't know?!
I'm going to tell her! She works nights and I don't want to make her nervous and . . .
She's smart. She'll figure it out!
Just like you figured out your mom was Stainless Steel?

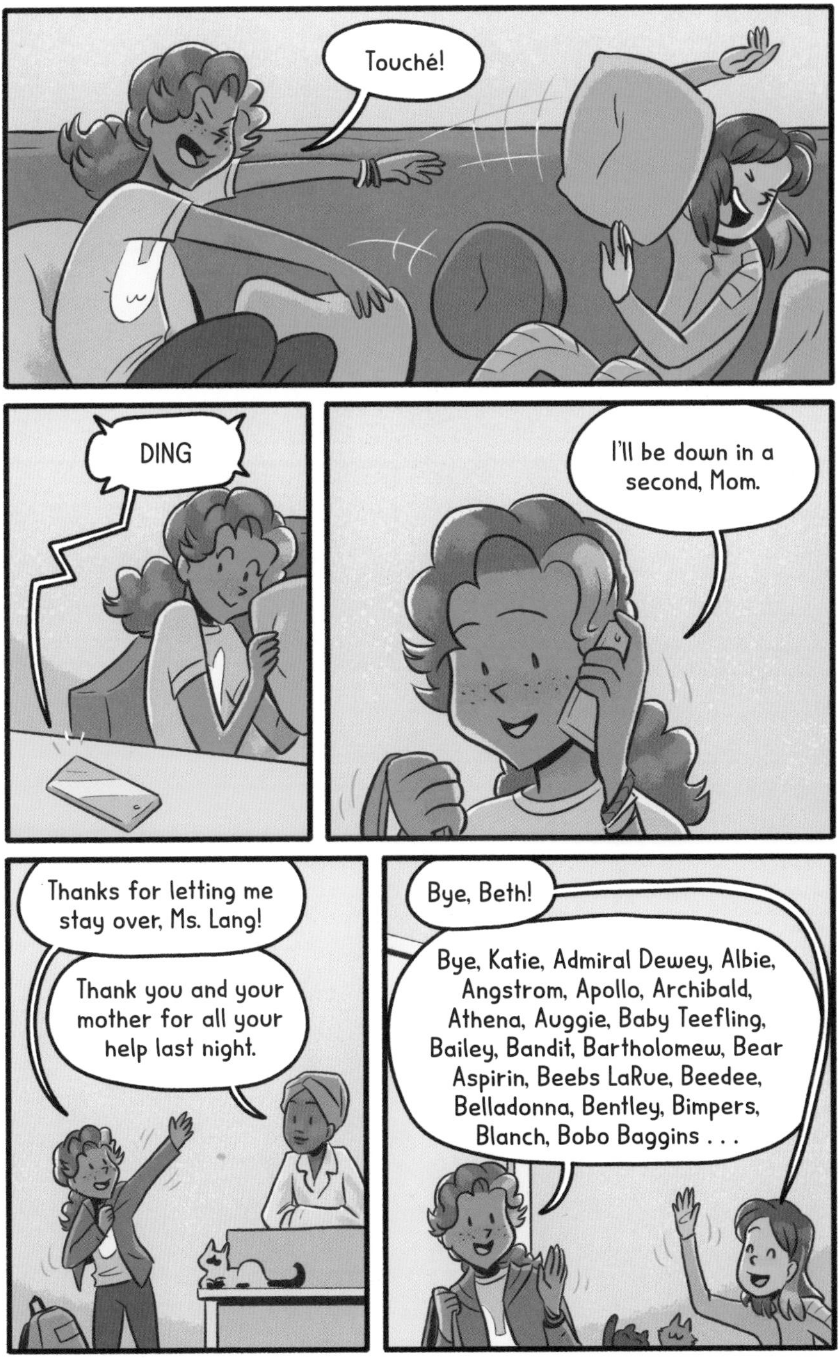
Touché!
DING
I'll be down in a second, Mom.
Thanks for letting me stay over, Ms. Lang!
Thank you and your mother for all your help last night.
Bye, Beth!
Bye, Katie, Admiral Dewey, Albie, Angstrom, Apollo, Archibald, Athena, Auggie, Baby Teefling, Bailey, Bandit, Bartholomew, Bear Aspirin, Beebs LaRue, Beedee, Belladonna, Bentley, Bimpers, Blanch, Bobo Baggins . . .

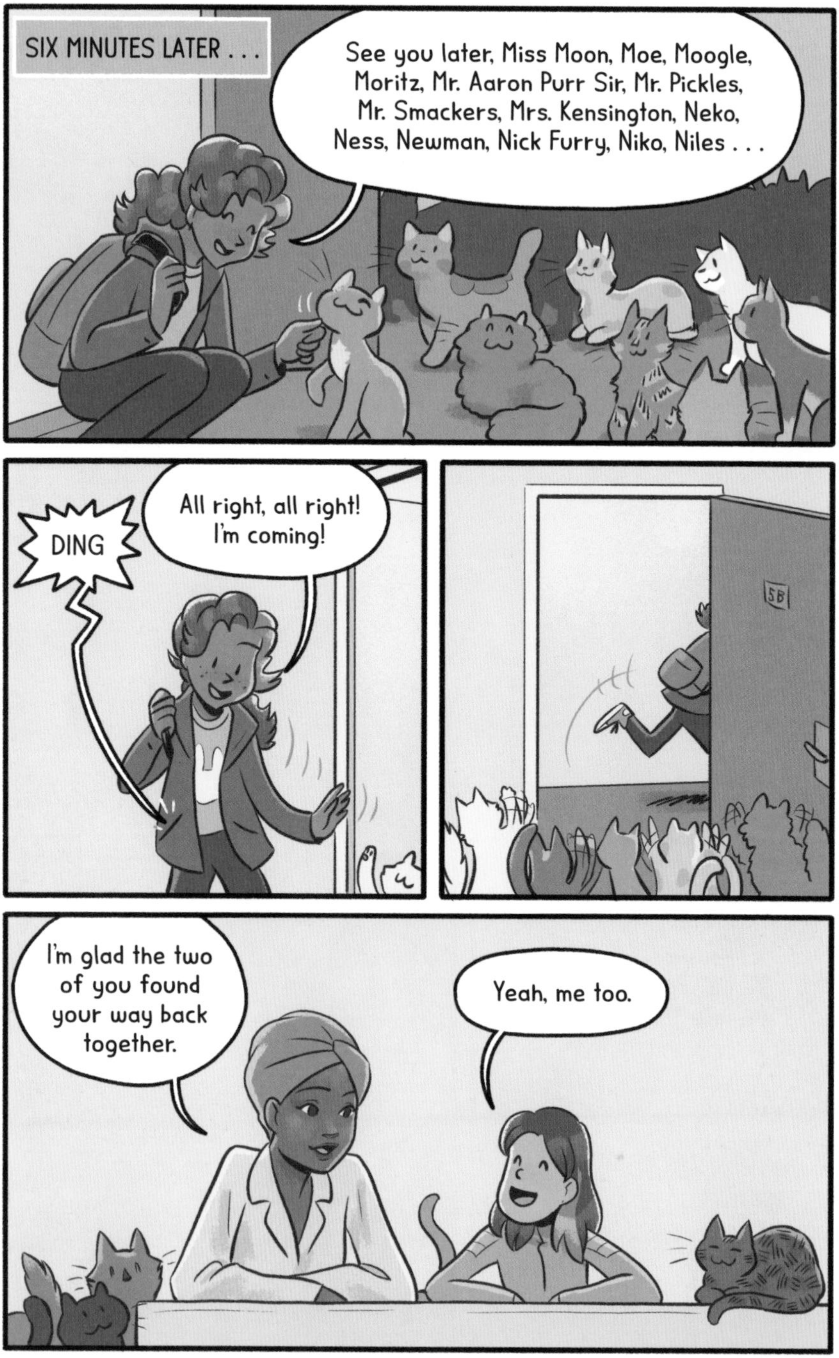
SIX MINUTES LATER . . .
See you later, Miss Moon, Moe, Moogle, Moritz, Mr. Aaron Purr Sir, Mr. Pickles, Mr. Smackers, Mrs. Kensington, Neko, Ness, Newman, Nick Furry, Niko, Niles . . .
DING
All right, all right! I'm coming!
5B
I'm glad the two of you found your way back together.
Yeah, me too.

CHAPTER TWO

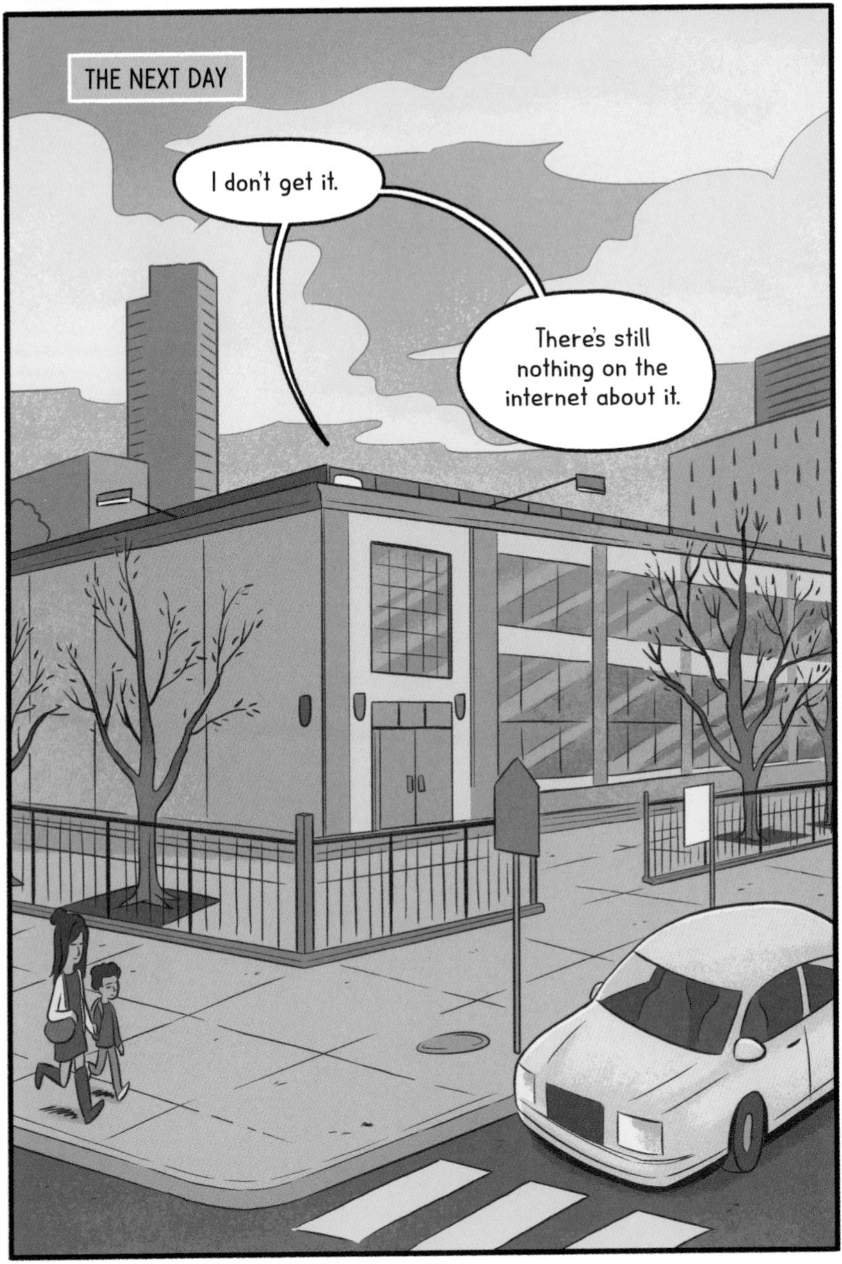
THE NEXT DAY
I don't get it.
There's still nothing on the internet about it.

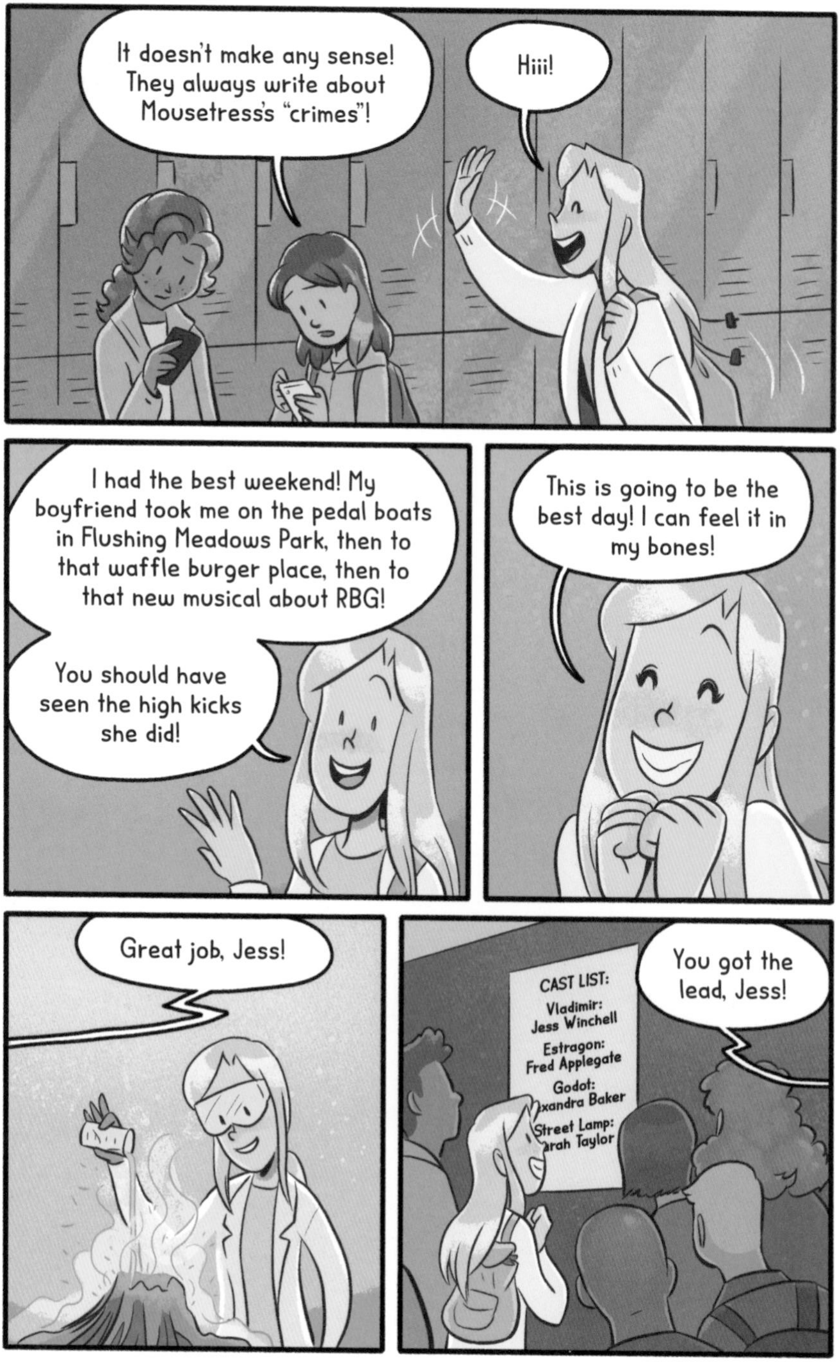
It doesn't make any sense! They always write about Mousetress's "crimes"!
Hiii!
I had the best weekend! My boyfriend took me on the pedal boats in Flushing Meadows Park, then to that waffle burger place, then to that new musical about RBG!
You should have seen the high kicks she did!
This is going to be the best day! I can feel it in my bones!
Great job, Jess!
CAST LIST:
Vladimir:
Jess Winchell
Estragon:
Fred Applegate
Godot:
Street Lamp:
You got the lead, Jess!

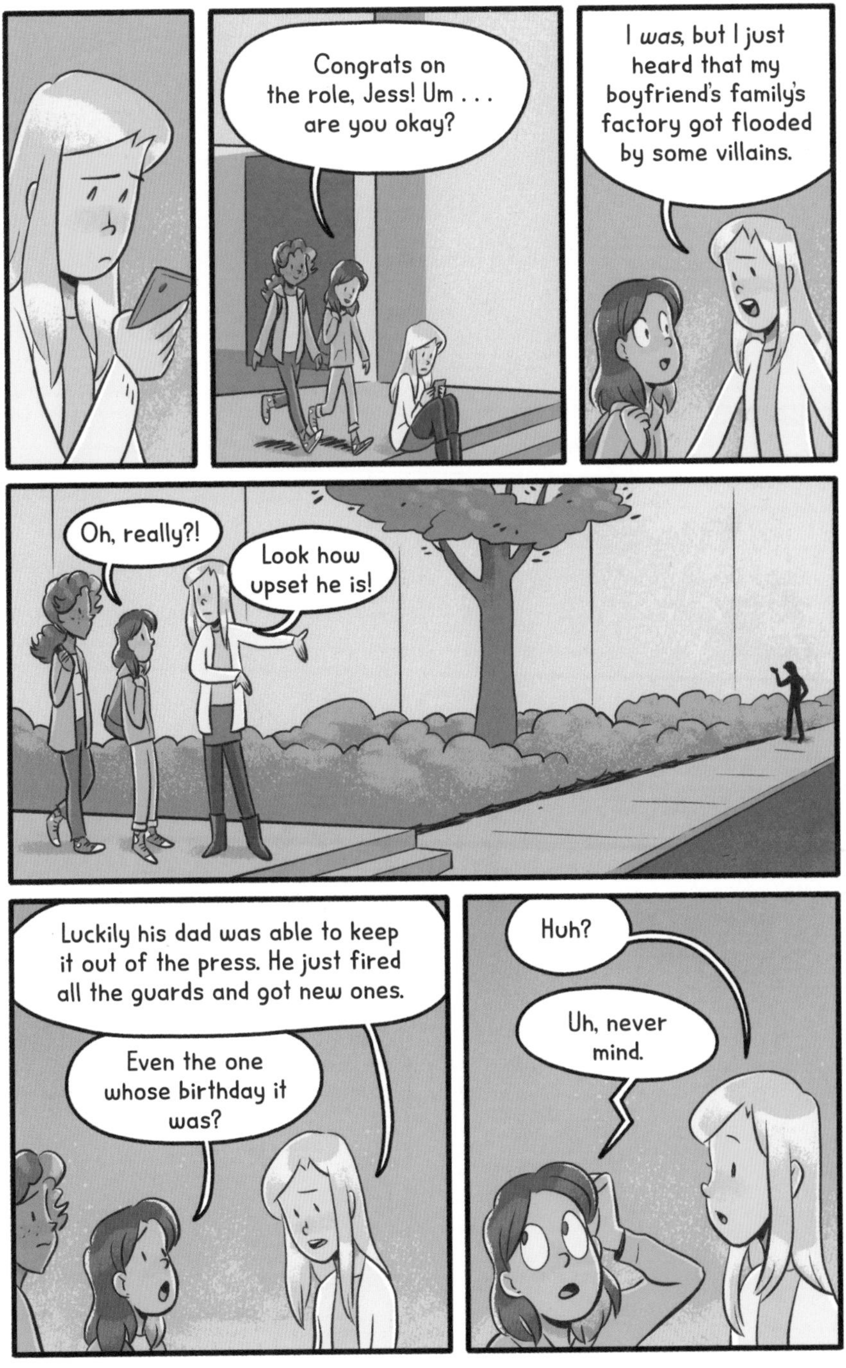
Congrats on the role, Jess! Um . . . are you okay?
I *was*, but I just heard that my boyfriend's family's factory got flooded by some villains.
Oh, really?!
Look how upset he is!
Luckily his dad was able to keep it out of the press. He just fired all the guards and got new ones.
Even the one whose birthday it was?
Huh?
Uh, never mind.

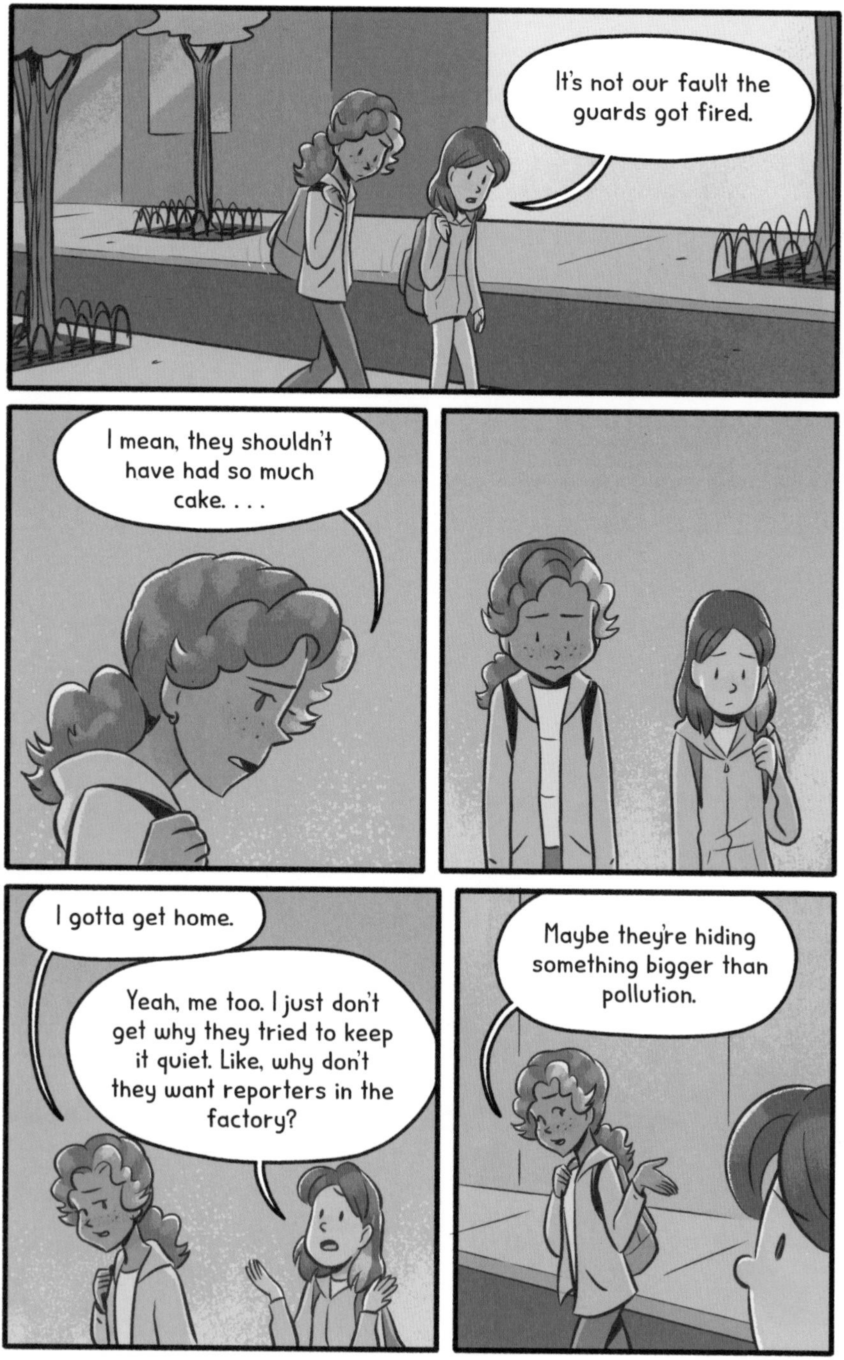
It's not our fault the guards got fired.
I mean, they shouldn't have had so much cake. . . .
I gotta get home.
Yeah, me too. I just don't get why they tried to keep it quiet. Like, why don't they want reporters in the factory?
Maybe they're hiding something bigger than pollution.

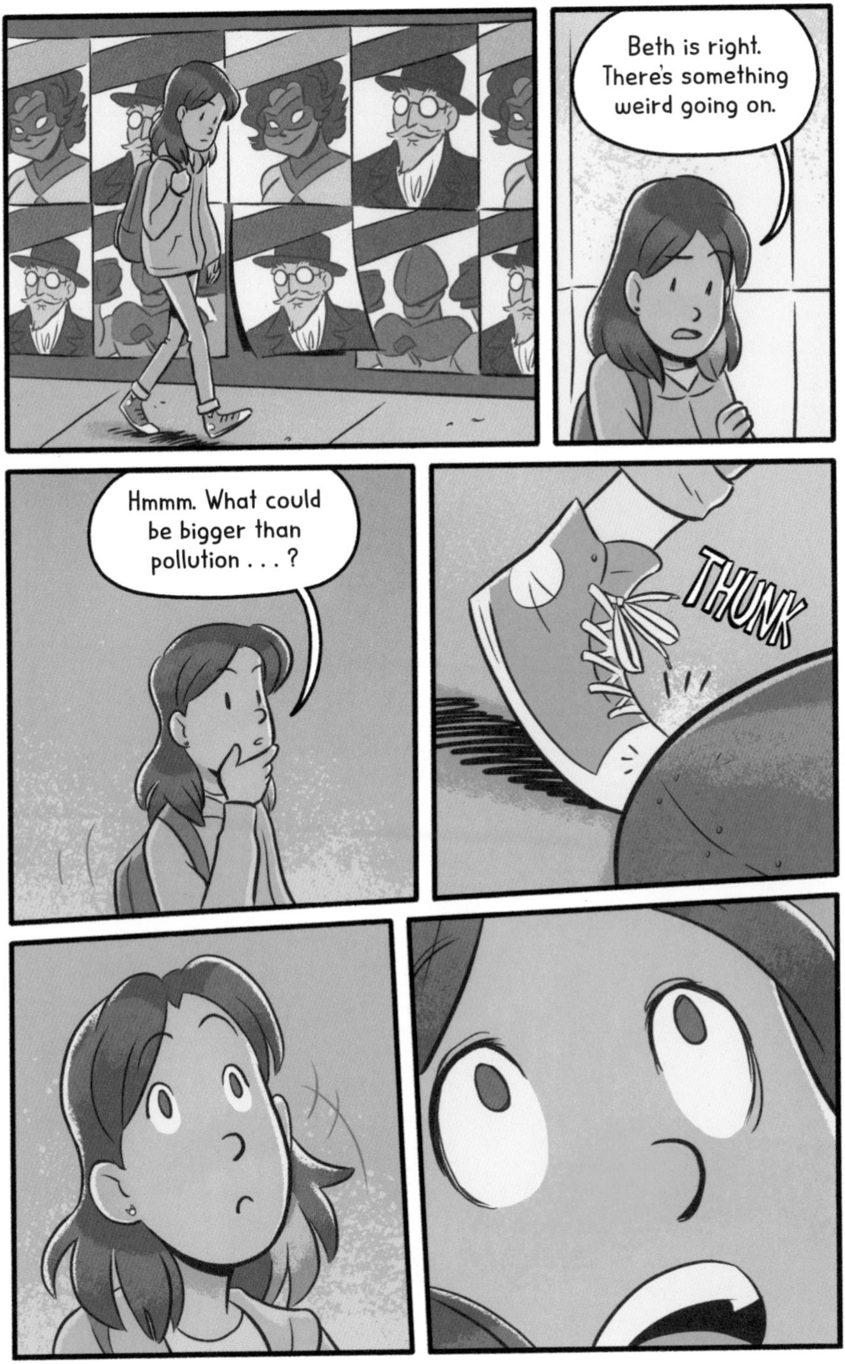
Beth is right. There's something weird going on.
Hmmm. What could be bigger than pollution . . . ?
THUNK

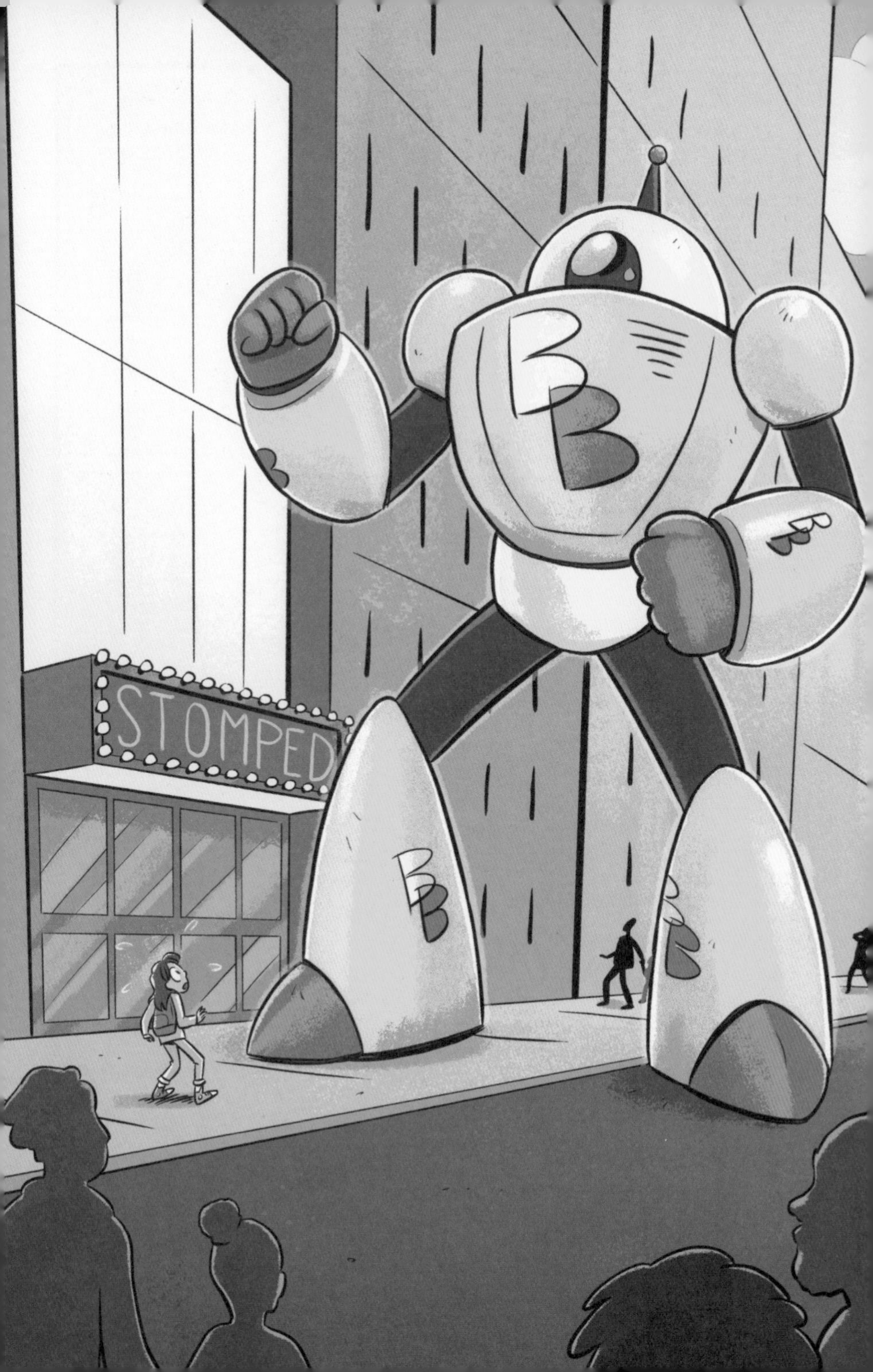
STOMPED

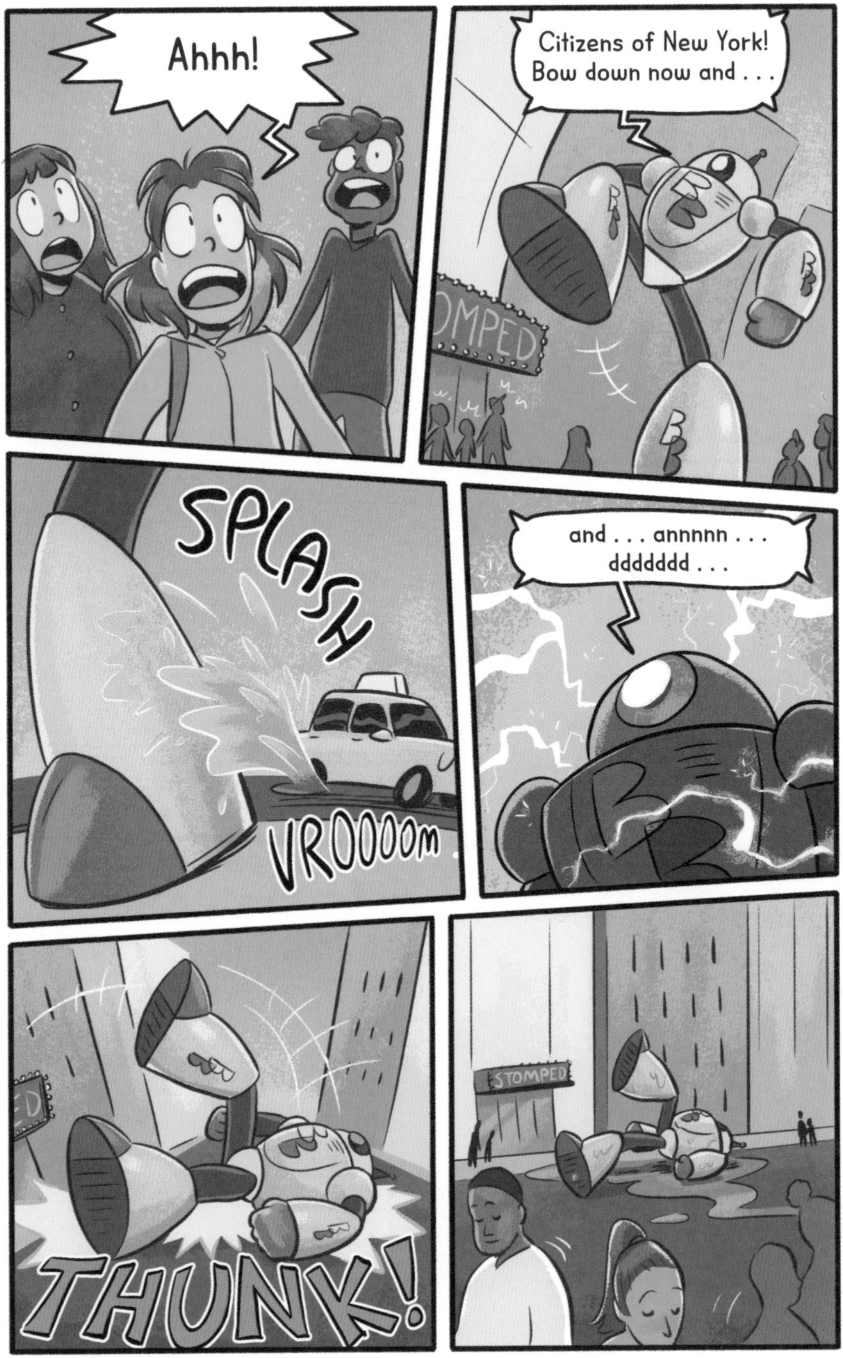
Ahhh!
Citizens of New York! Bow down now and . . .
OMPED
SPLASH
VROOOOm
and . . . annnnn . . . ddddddd . . .
THUNK!
STOMPED

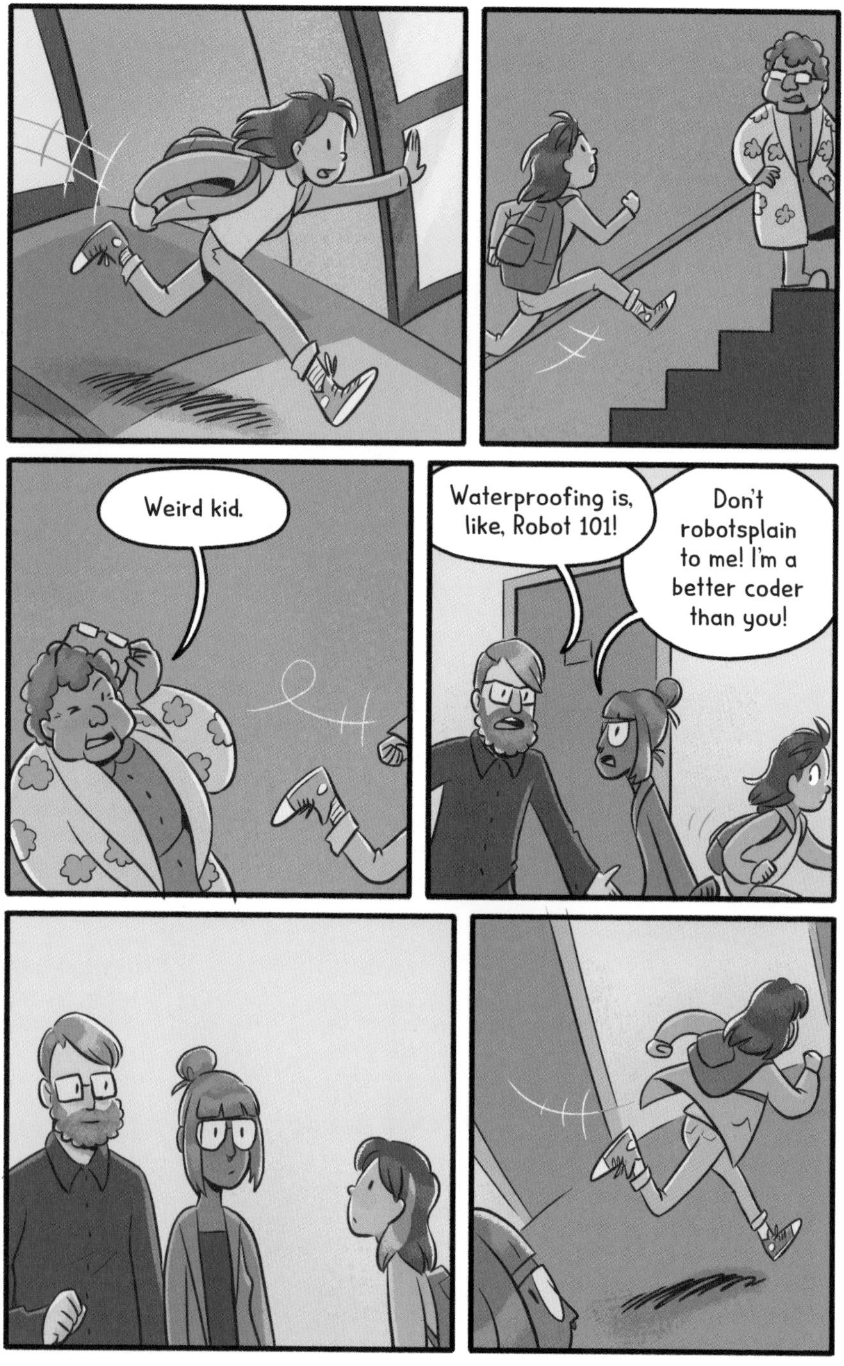
Weird kid.
Waterproofing is, like, Robot 101!
Don't robotsplain to me! I'm a better coder than you!

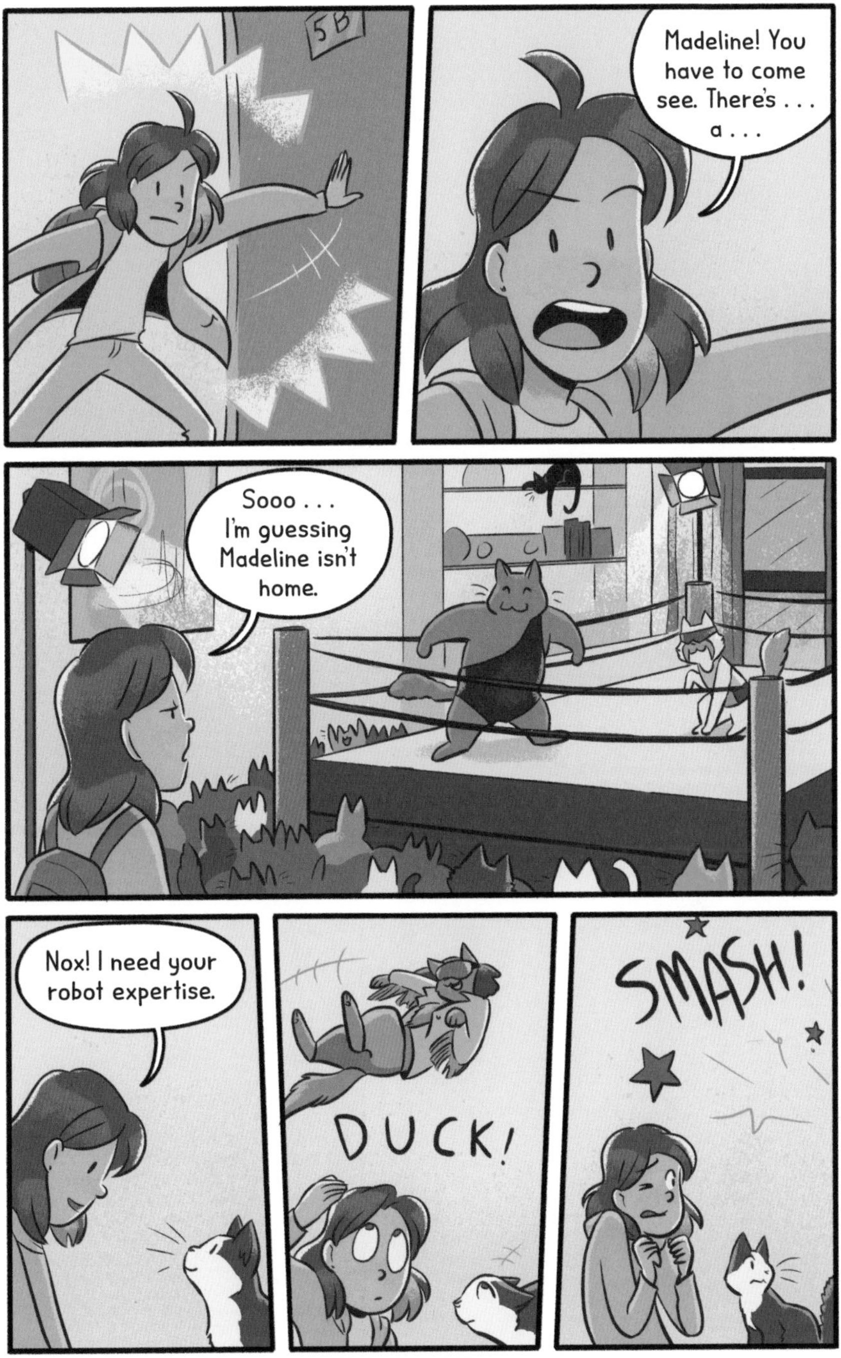

Madeline! You have to come see. There's . . . a . . .
Sooo . . . I'm guessing Madeline isn't home.
Nox! I need your robot expertise.
DUCK!
SMASH!

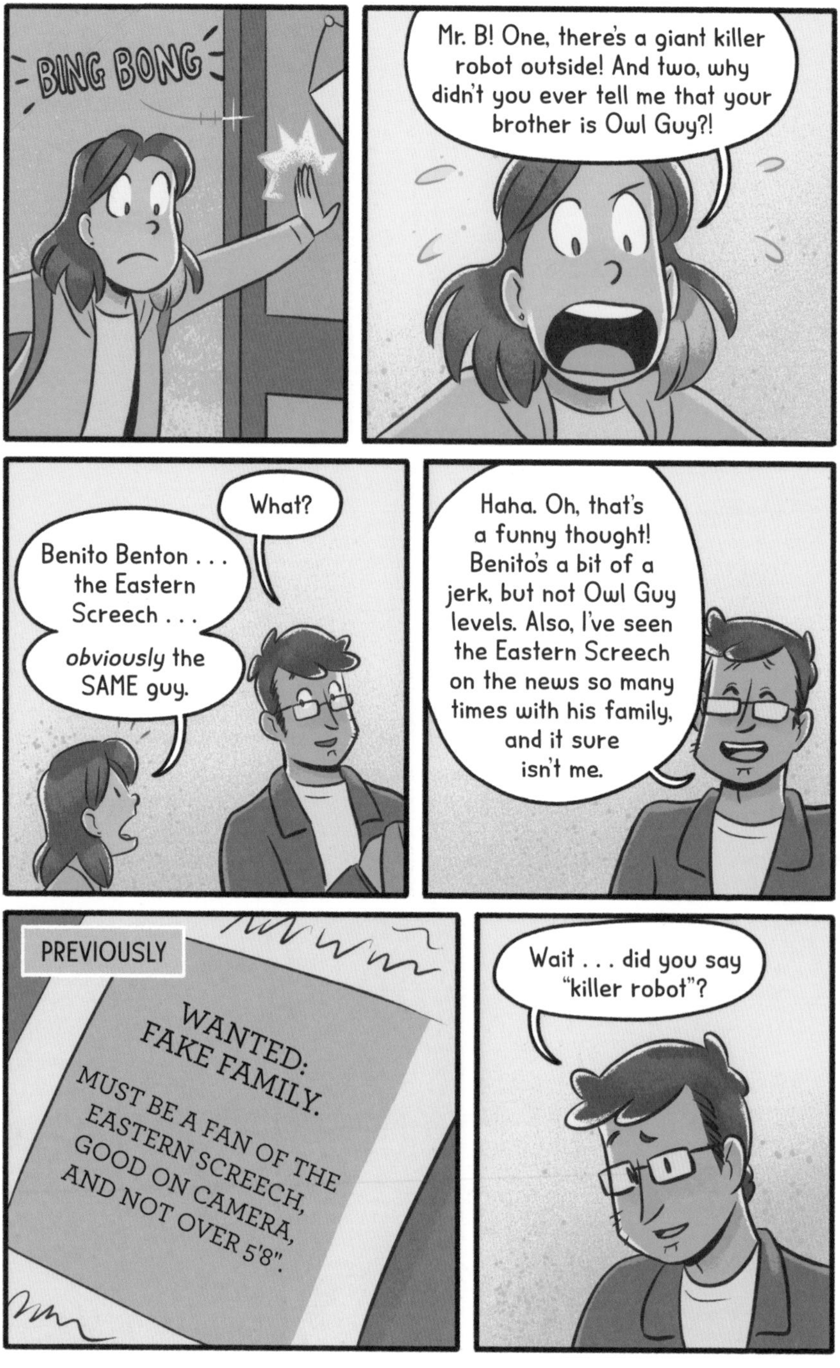
BING BONG
Mr. B! One, there's a giant killer robot outside! And two, why didn't you ever tell me that your brother is Owl Guy?!
What?
Benito Benton . . . the Eastern Screech . . .
obviously the SAME guy.
Haha. Oh, that's a funny thought! Benito's a bit of a jerk, but not Owl Guy levels. Also, I've seen the Eastern Screech on the news so many times with his family, and it sure isn't me.
PREVIOUSLY
WANTED: FAKE FAMILY.
MUST BE A FAN OF THE EASTERN SCREECH, GOOD ON CAMERA, AND NOT OVER 5'8".
Wait . . . did you say "killer robot"?

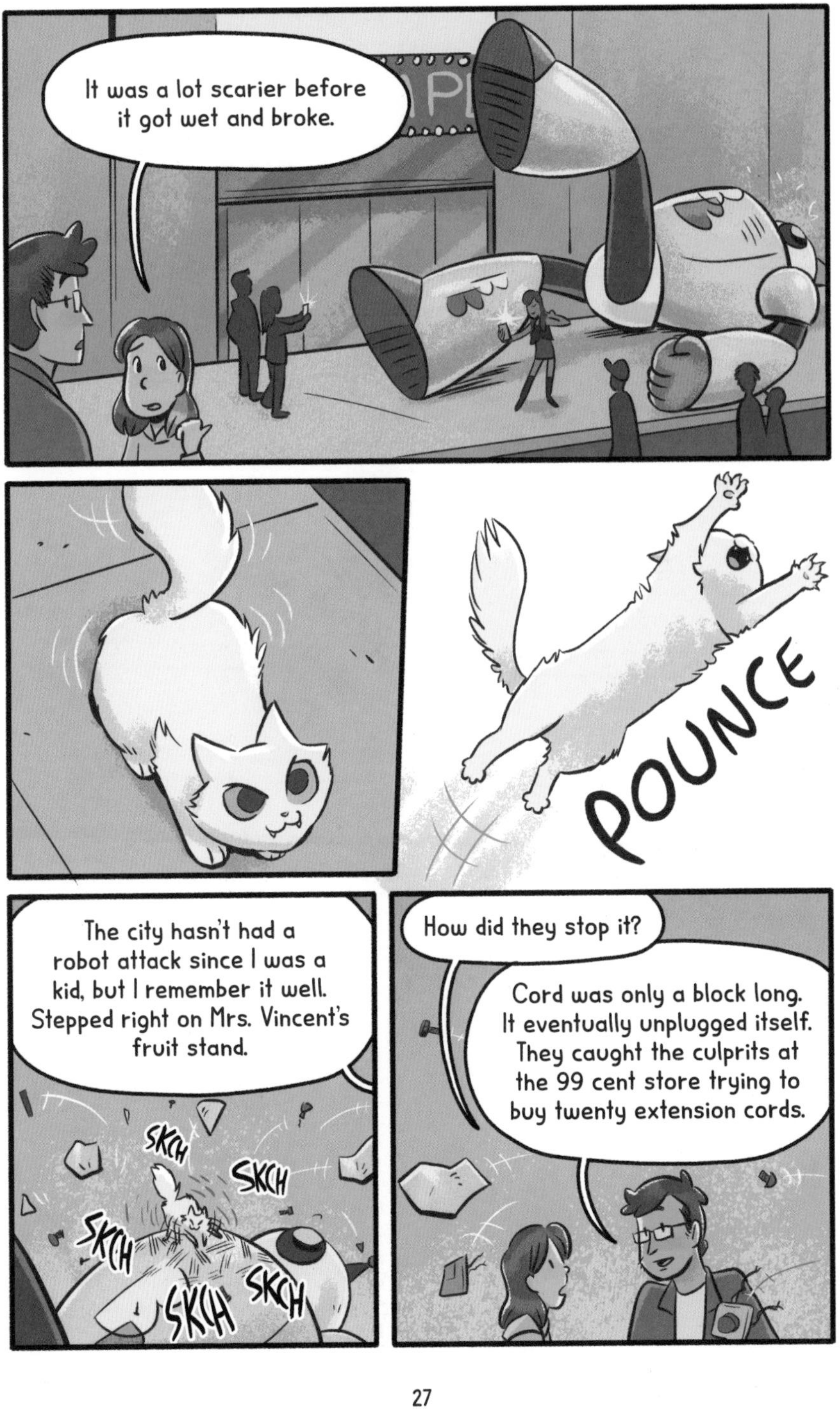
It was a lot scarier before it got wet and broke.
POUNCE
The city hasn't had a robot attack since I was a kid, but I remember it well. Stepped right on Mrs. Vincent's fruit stand.
SKCH
SKCH
SKCH
SKCH
SKCH
How did they stop it?
Cord was only a block long. It eventually unplugged itself. They caught the culprits at the 99 cent store trying to buy twenty extension cords.

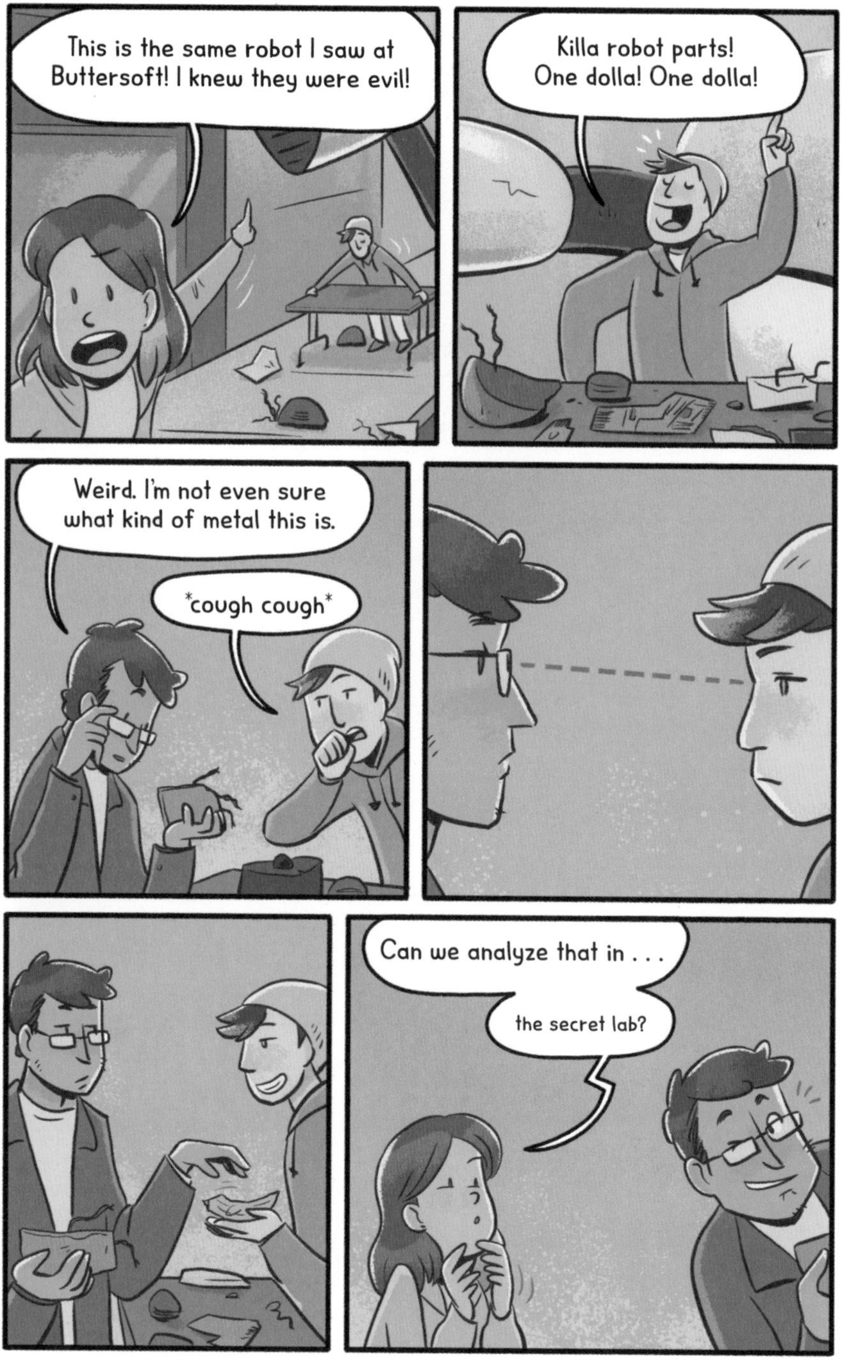
This is the same robot I saw at Buttersoft! I knew they were evil!
Killa robot parts! One dolla! One dolla!
Weird. I'm not even sure what kind of metal this is.
cough cough
Can we analyze that in . . .
the secret lab?

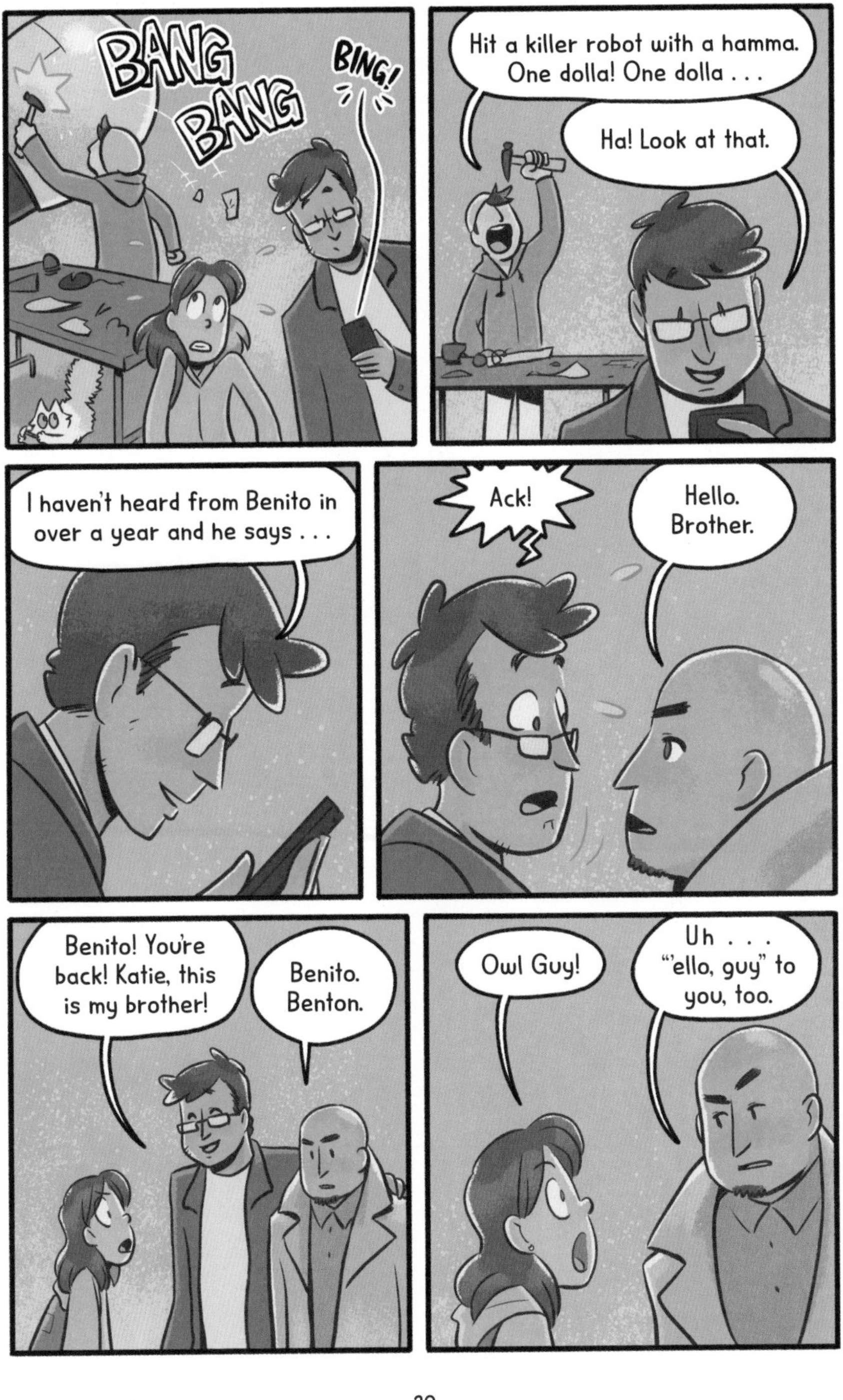
BANG
BANG
BING!
Hit a killer robot with a hamma. One dolla! One dolla . . .
Ha! Look at that.
I haven't heard from Benito in over a year and he says . . .
Ack!
Hello. Brother.
Benito! You're back! Katie, this is my brother!
Benito. Benton.
Owl Guy!
Uh . . . "'ello, guy" to you, too.

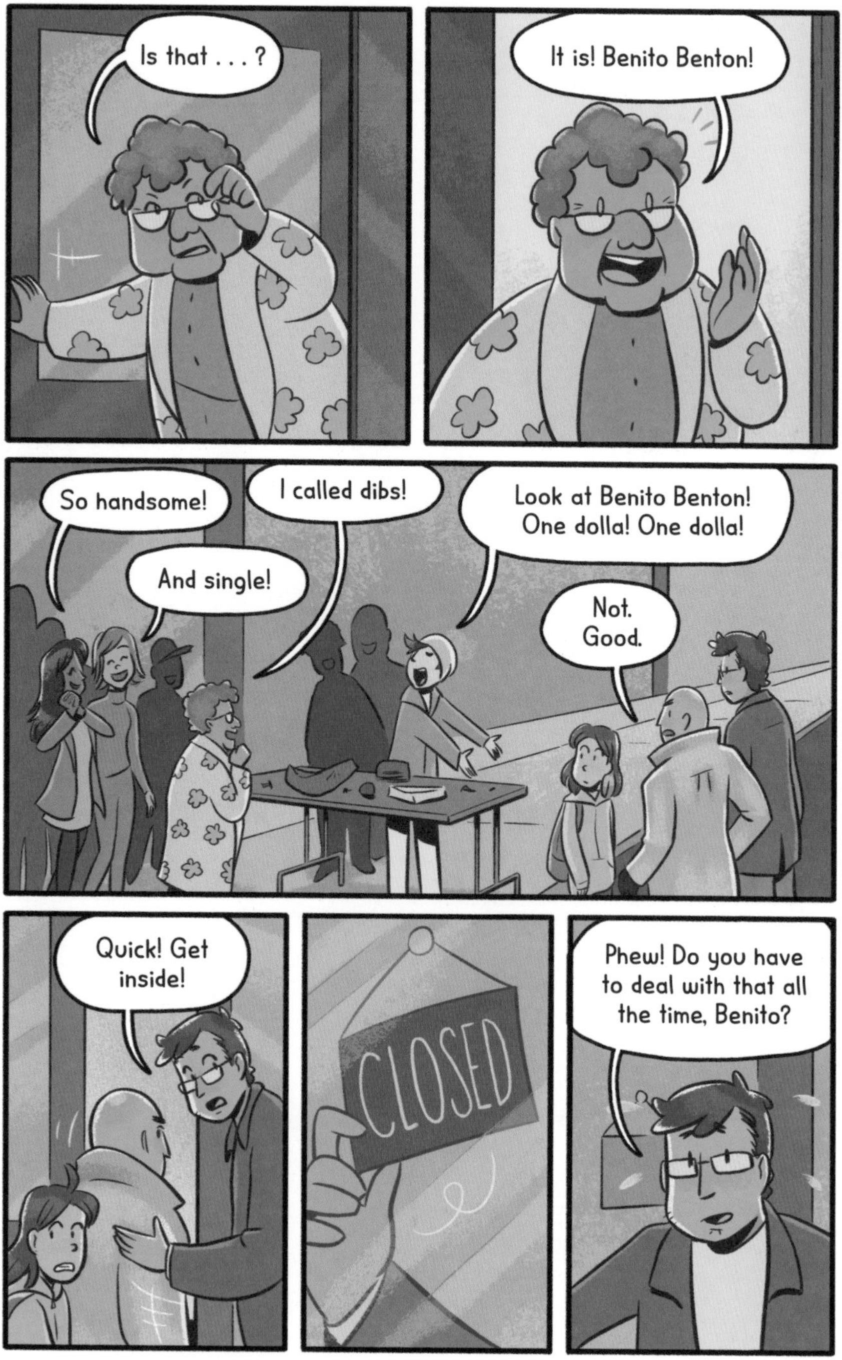
Is that . . . ?
It is! Benito Benton!
So handsome!
I called dibs!
And single!
Look at Benito Benton! One dolla! One dolla!
Not. Good.
Quick! Get inside!
CLOSED
Phew! Do you have to deal with that all the time, Benito?

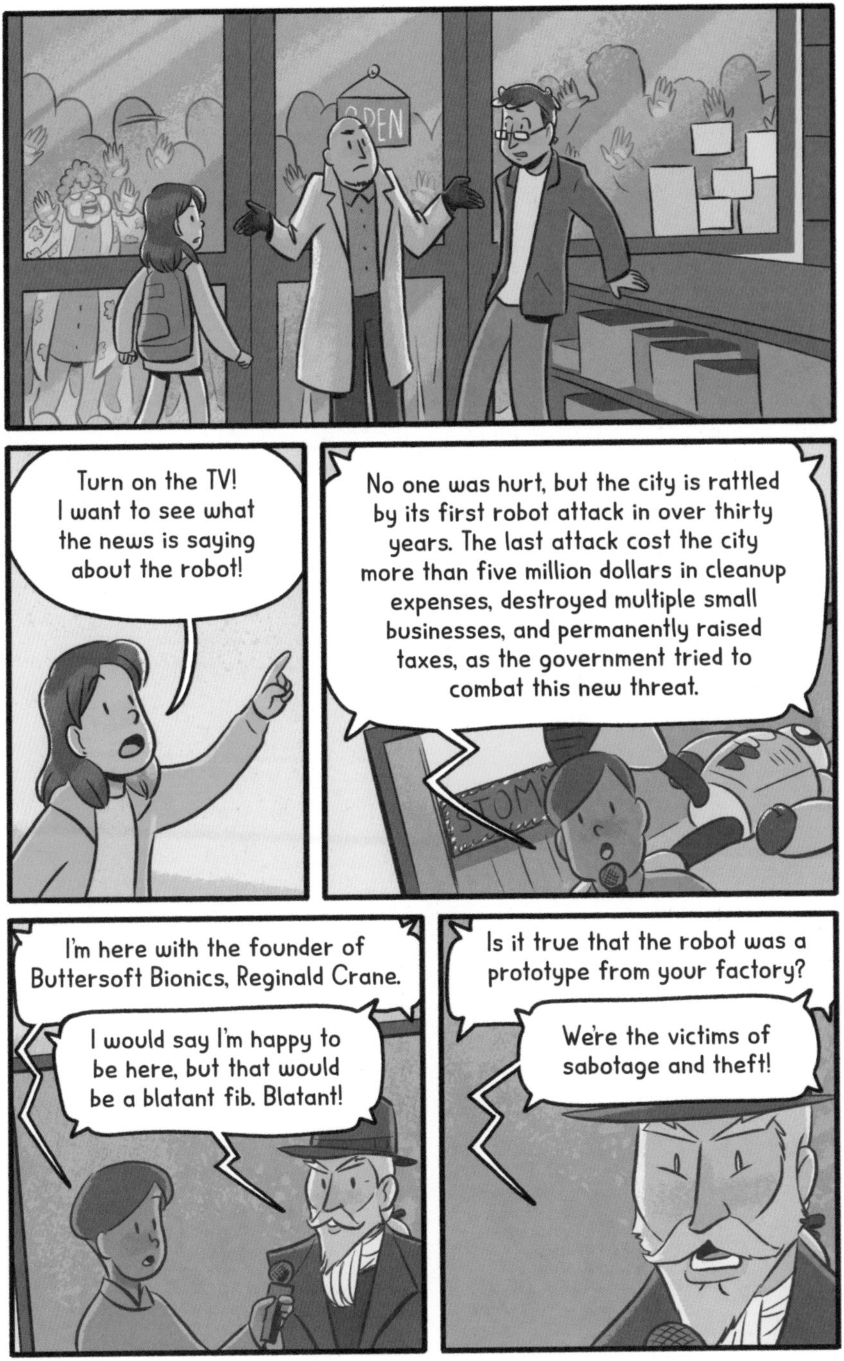
OPEN
Turn on the TV! I want to see what the news is saying about the robot!
No one was hurt, but the city is rattled by its first robot attack in over thirty years. The last attack cost the city more than five million dollars in cleanup expenses, destroyed multiple small businesses, and permanently raised taxes, as the government tried to combat this new threat.
STOMP
I'm here with the founder of Buttersoft Bionics, Reginald Crane.
I would say I'm happy to be here, but that would be a blatant fib. Blatant!
Is it true that the robot was a prototype from your factory?
We're the victims of sabotage and theft!

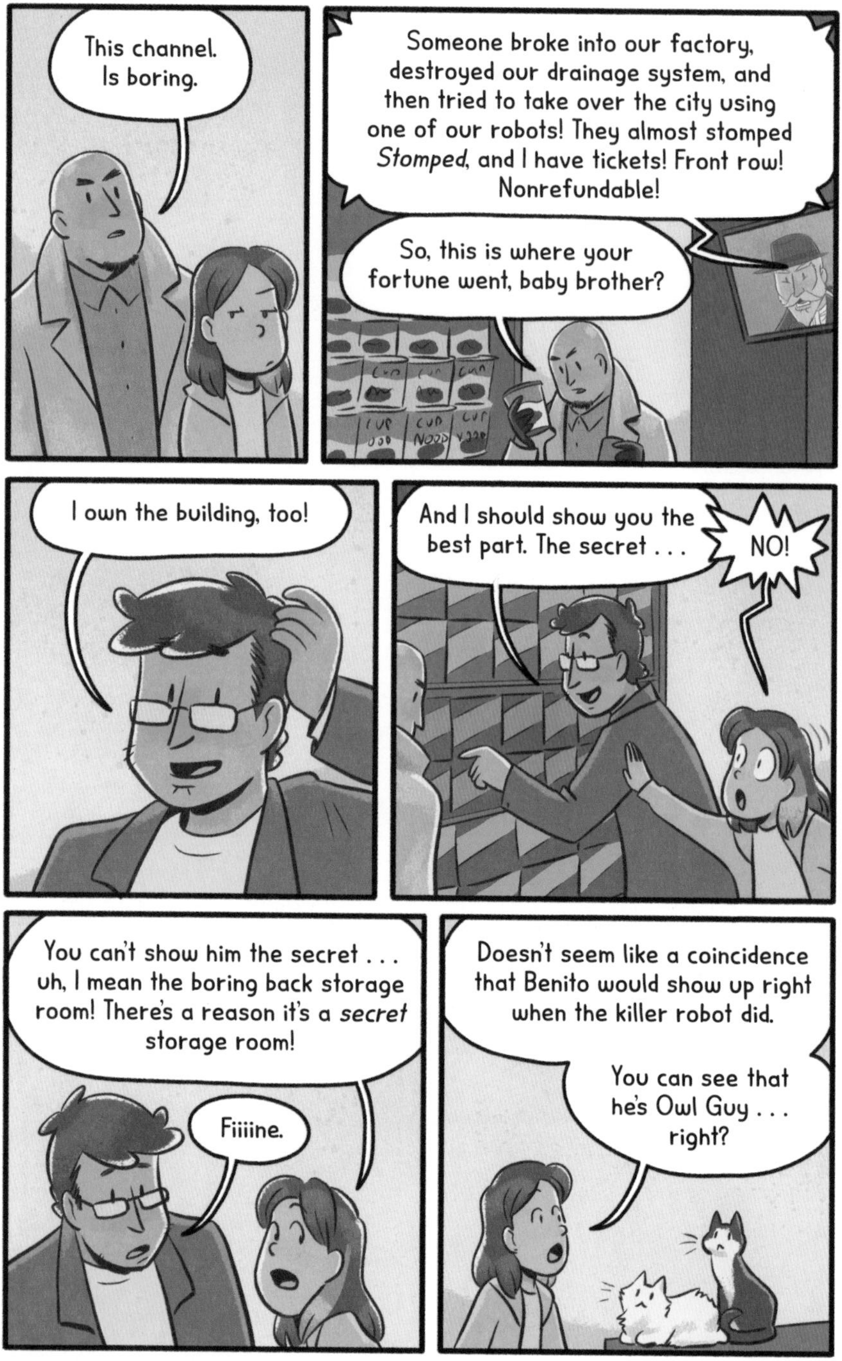

This channel. Is boring.
Someone broke into our factory, destroyed our drainage system, and then tried to take over the city using one of our robots! They almost stomped *Stomped*, and I have tickets! Front row! Nonrefundable!
So, this is where your fortune went, baby brother?
I own the building, too!
And I should show you the best part. The secret . . .
NO!
You can't show him the secret . . . uh, I mean the boring back storage room! There's a reason it's a *secret* storage room!
Fiiiine.
Doesn't seem like a coincidence that Benito would show up right when the killer robot did.
You can see that he's Owl Guy . . . right?

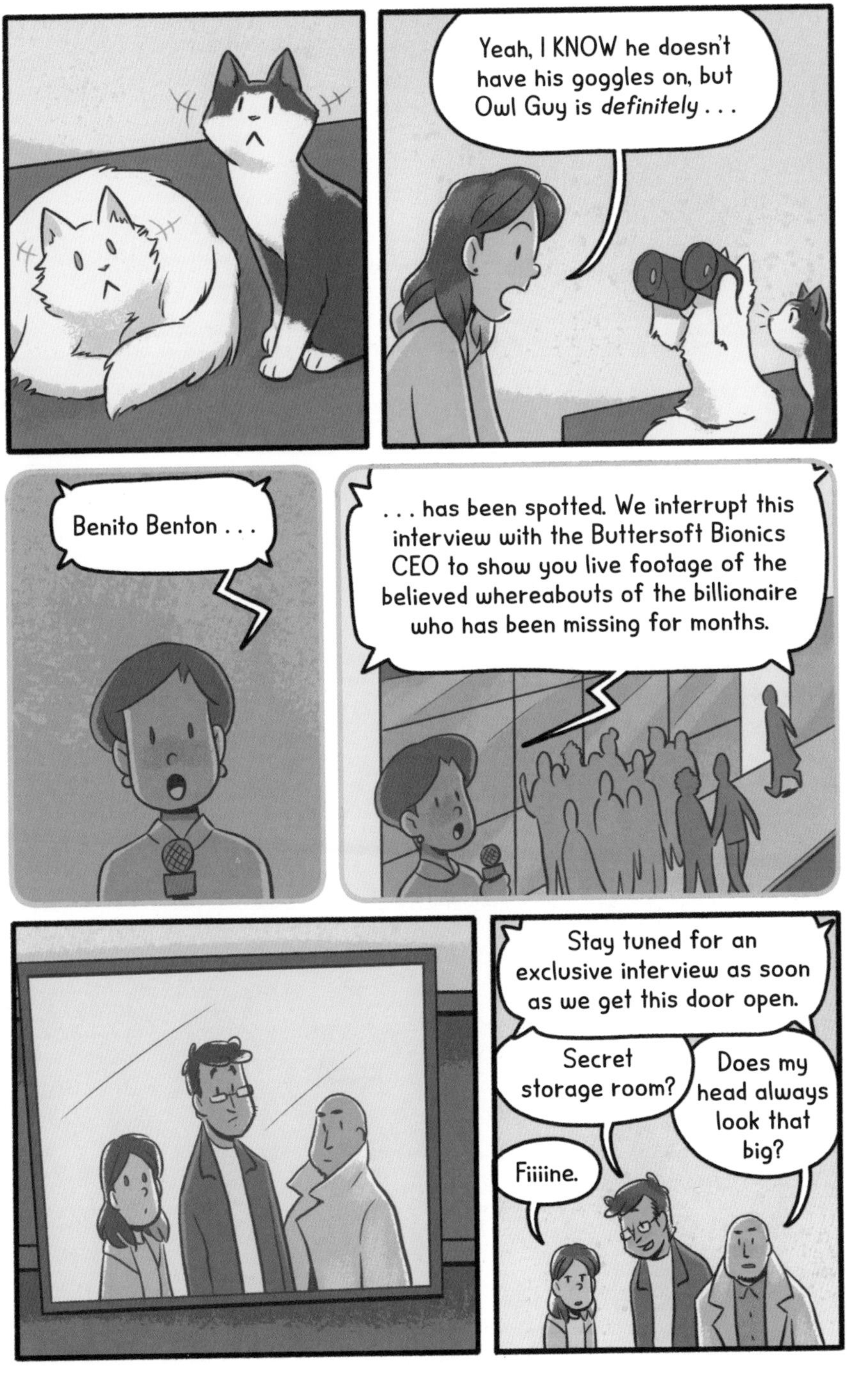

Yeah, I KNOW he doesn't have his goggles on, but Owl Guy is *definitely* . . .
Benito Benton . . .
. . . has been spotted. We interrupt this interview with the Buttersoft Bionics CEO to show you live footage of the believed whereabouts of the billionaire who has been missing for months.
Stay tuned for an exclusive interview as soon as we get this door open.
Secret storage room?
Does my head always look that big?
Fiiiine.

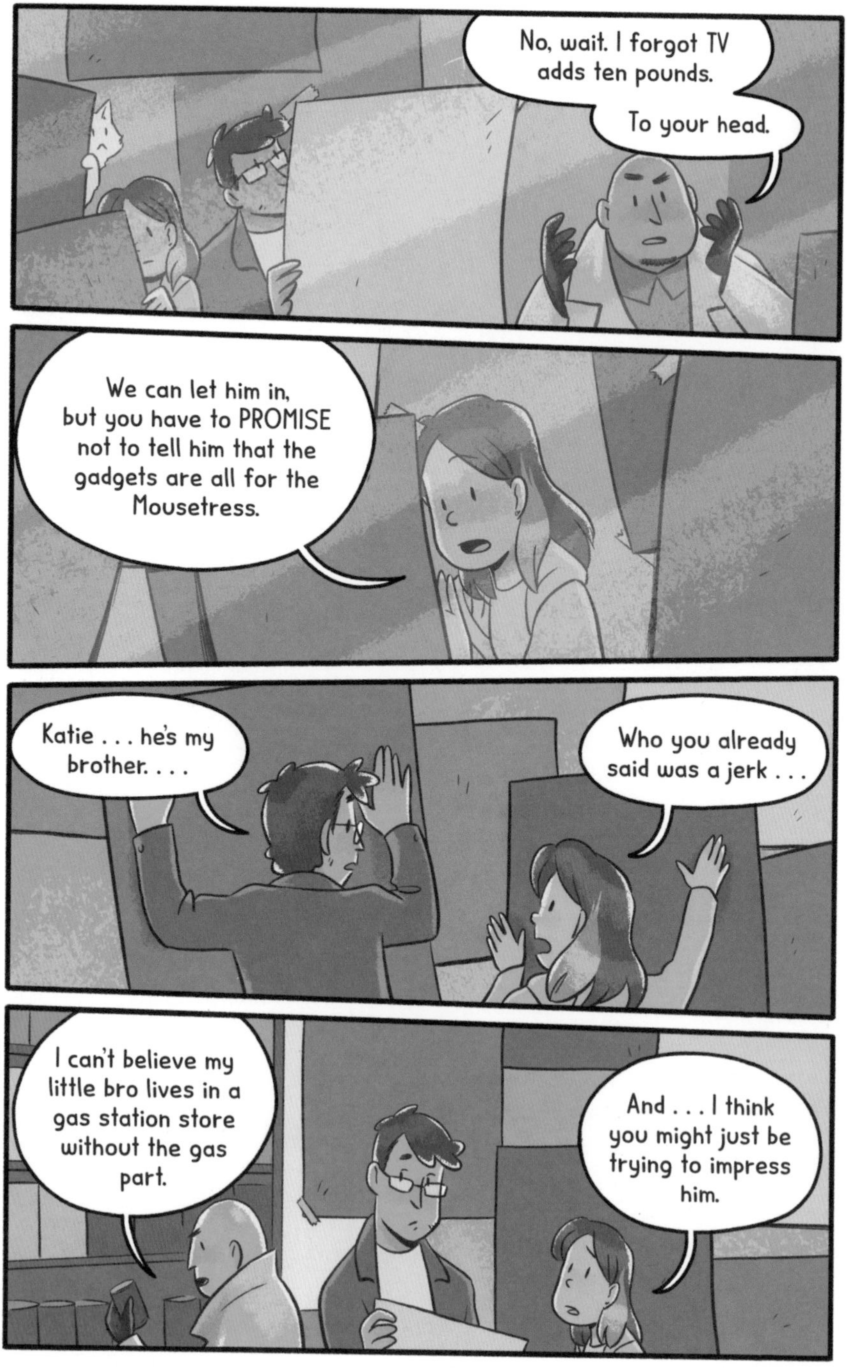
No, wait. I forgot TV adds ten pounds.
To your head.
We can let him in, but you have to PROMISE not to tell him that the gadgets are all for the Mousetress.
Katie . . . he's my brother. . . .
Who you already said was a jerk . . .
I can't believe my little bro lives in a gas station store without the gas part.
And . . . I think you might just be trying to impress him.

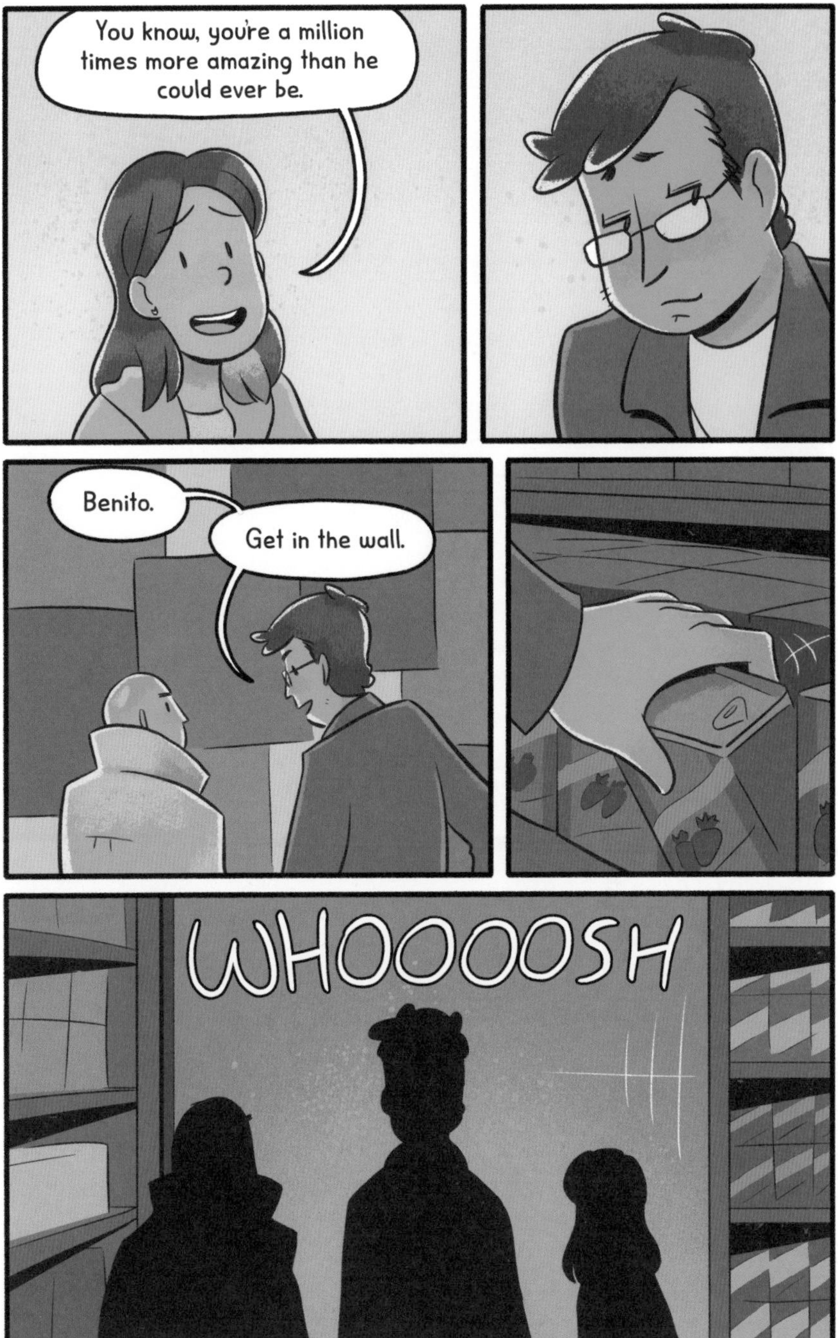
You know, you're a million times more amazing than he could ever be.
Benito.
Get in the wall.
WHOOOOSH

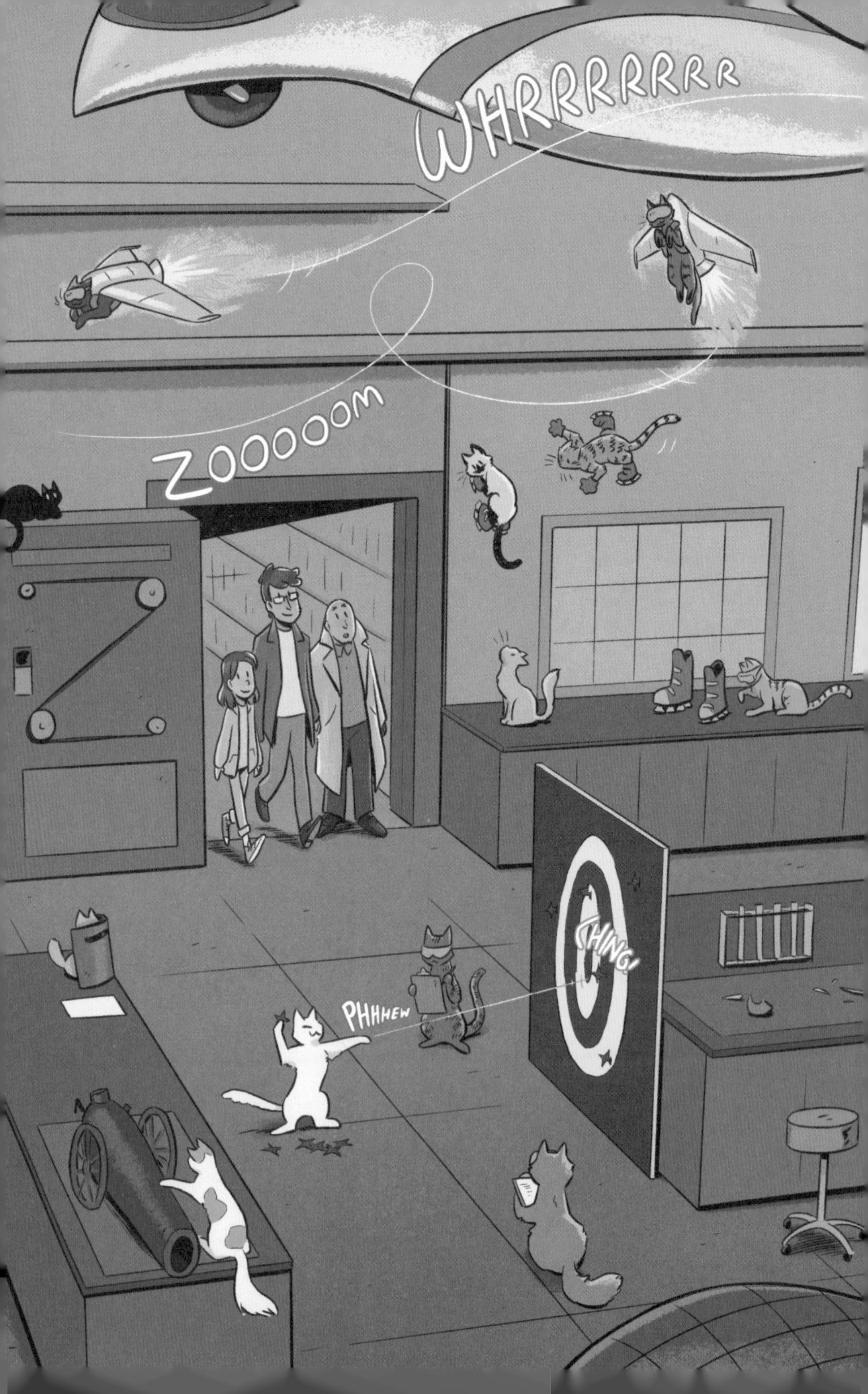
WHRRRRRRR
ZOOOOOM
PHHHEW
CHING!

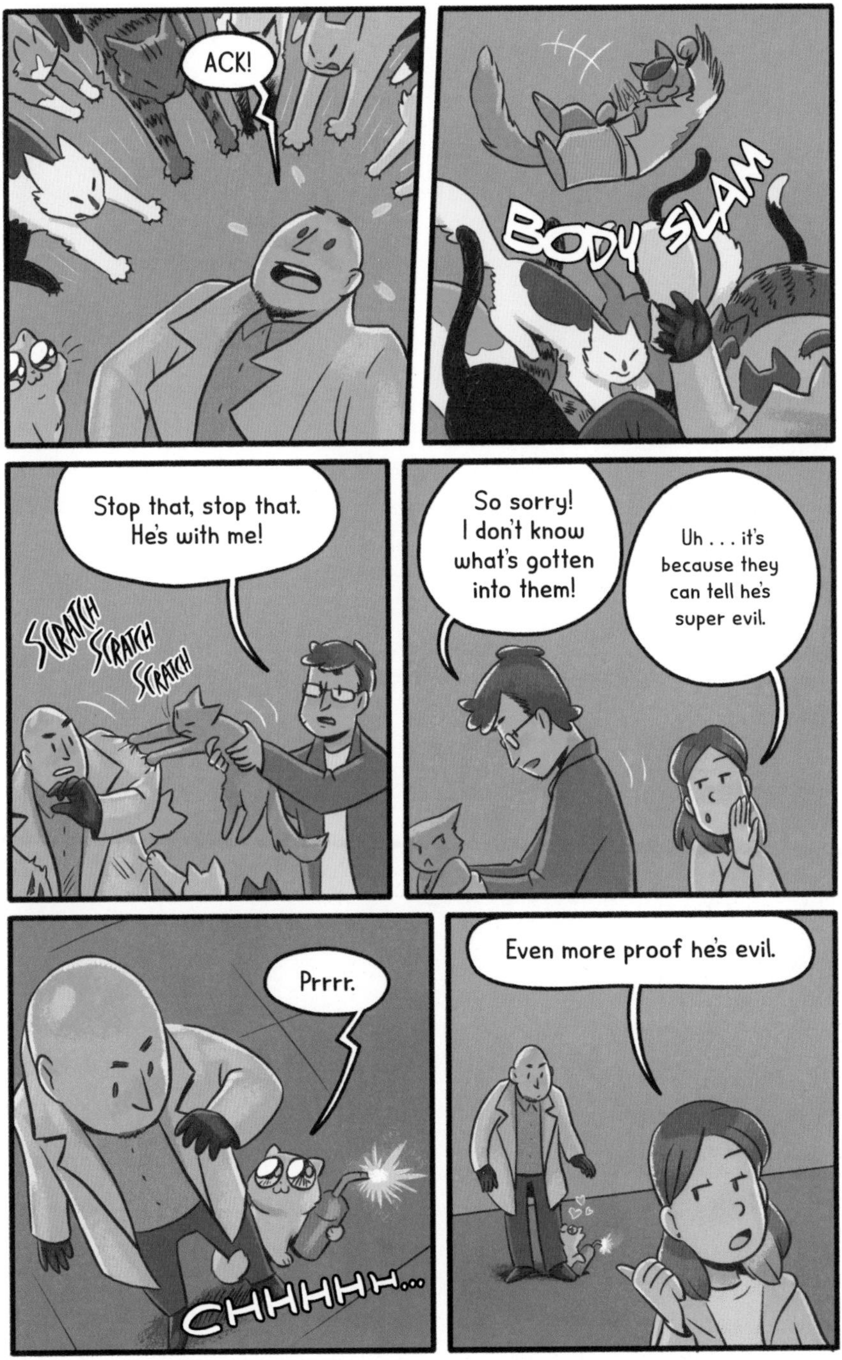
ACK!
BODY SLAM
Stop that, stop that. He's with me!
SCRATCH SCRATCH SCRATCH
So sorry! I don't know what's gotten into them!
Uh . . . it's because they can tell he's super evil.
Prrrr.
CHHHHH...
Even more proof he's evil.

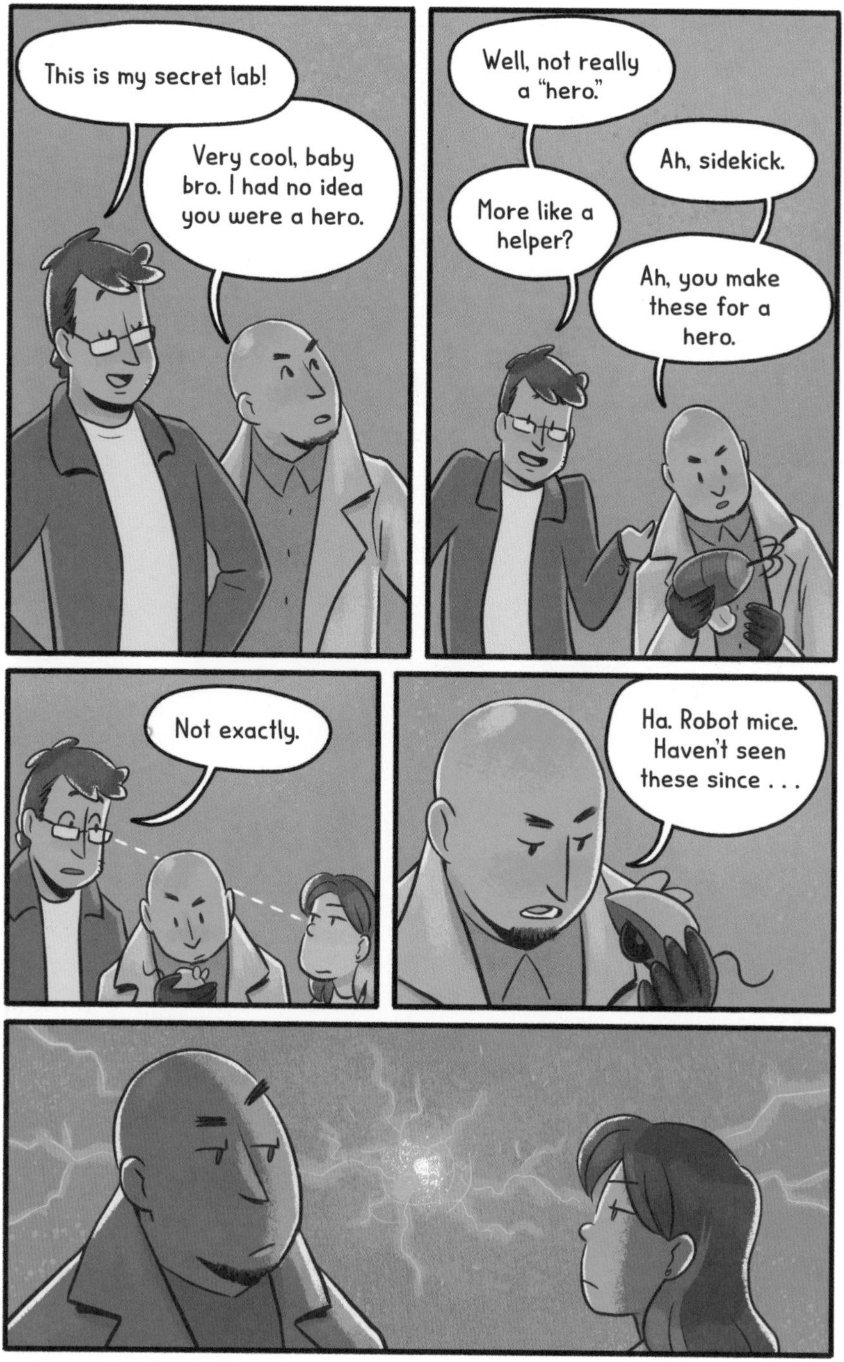
This is my secret lab!
Very cool, baby bro. I had no idea you were a hero.
Well, not really a "hero."
More like a helper?
Ah, sidekick.
Ah, you make these for a hero.
Not exactly.
Ha. Robot mice. Haven't seen these since . . .

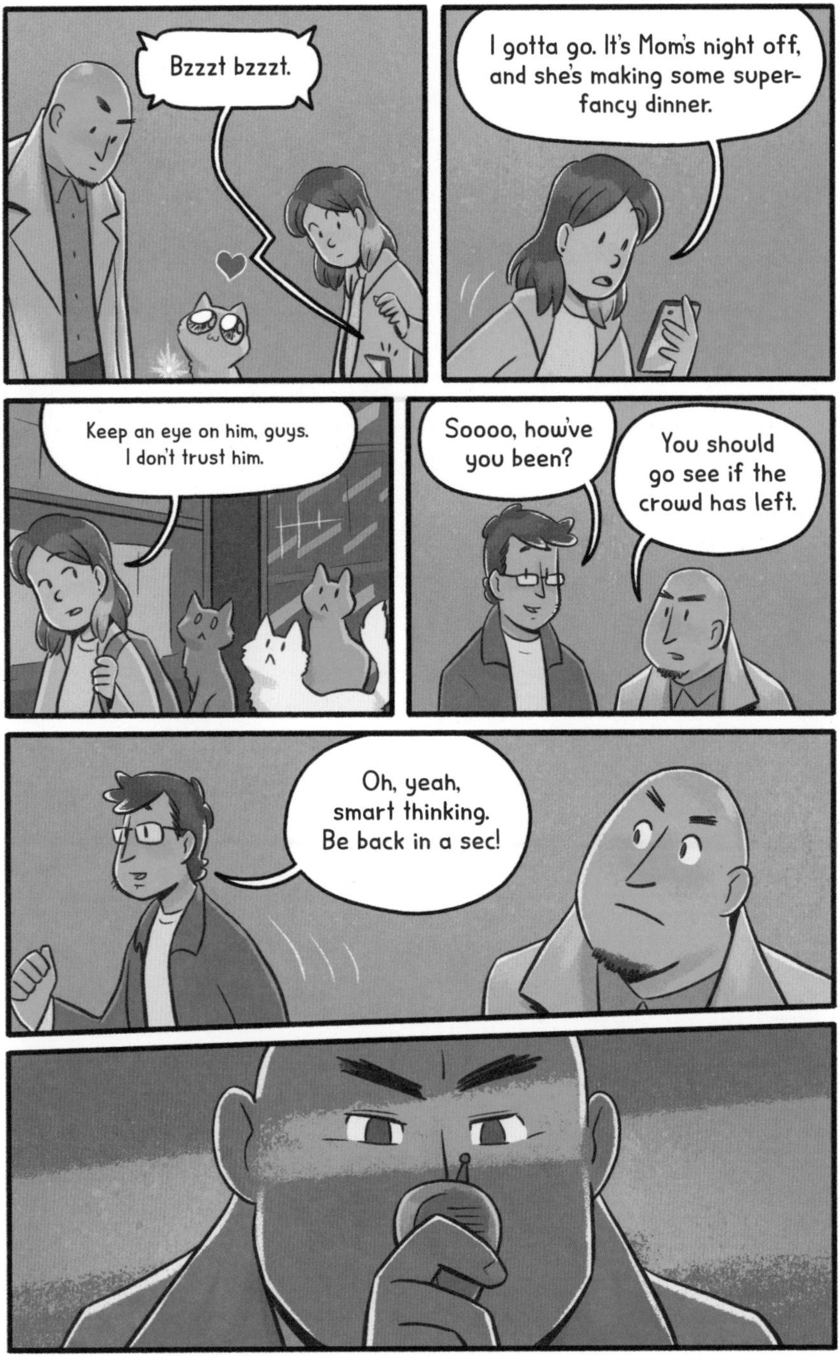
Bzzzt bzzzt.
I gotta go. It's Mom's night off, and she's making some super-fancy dinner.
Keep an eye on him, guys. I don't trust him.
Soooo, how've you been?
You should go see if the crowd has left.
Oh, yeah, smart thinking. Be back in a sec!

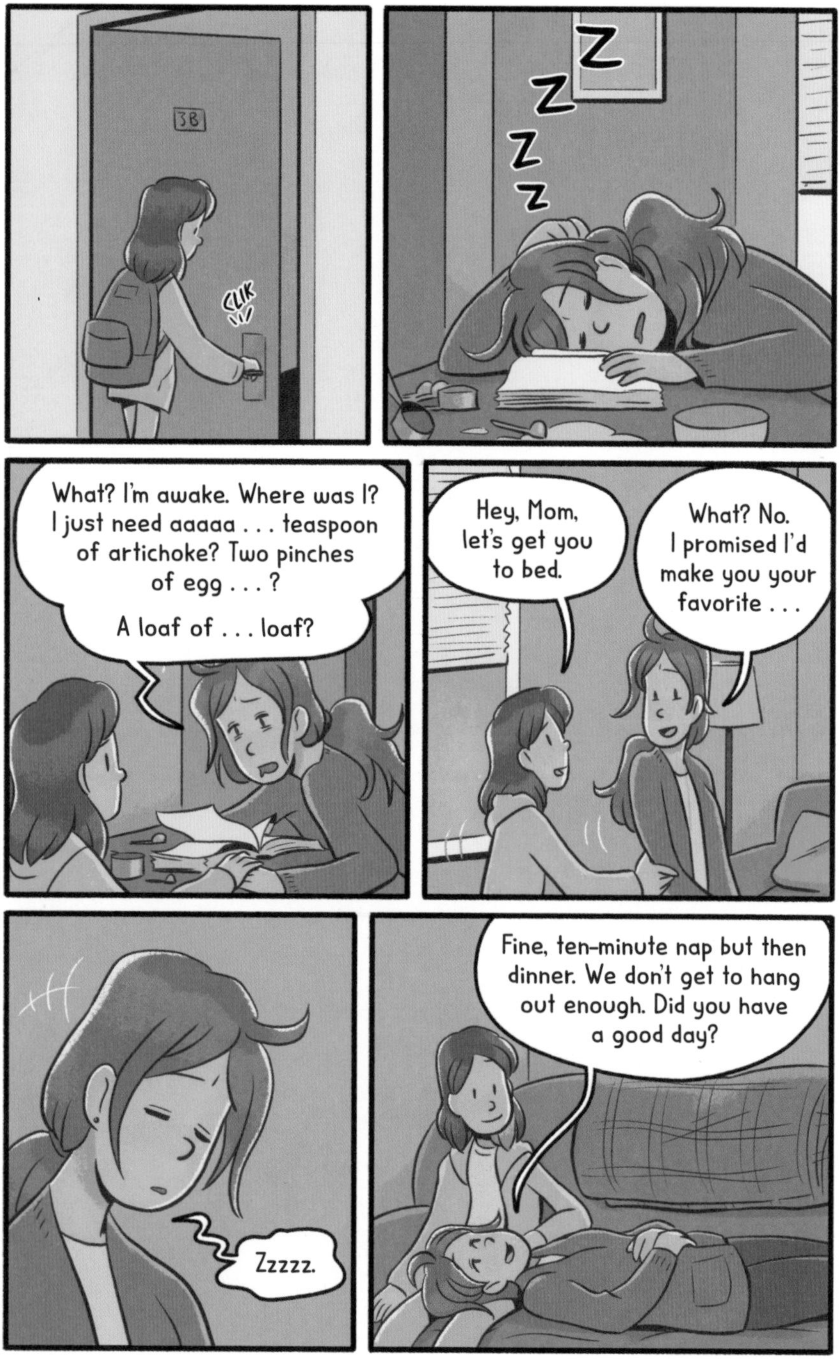
CLIK
Z
Z
Z
Z
What? I'm awake. Where was I? I just need aaaa . . . teaspoon of artichoke? Two pinches of egg . . . ?
A loaf of . . . loaf?
Hey, Mom, let's get you to bed.
What? No. I promised I'd make you your favorite . . .
Zzzzz.
Fine, ten-minute nap but then dinner. We don't get to hang out enough. Did you have a good day?

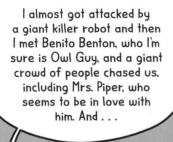

I almost got attacked by a giant killer robot and then I met Benito Benton, who I'm sure is Owl Guy, and a giant crowd of people chased us, including Mrs. Piper, who seems to be in love with him. And . . .

ZZZZZZZ SNOOOORE ZZZZZ ROBOTS ZZZZZZZ

How about I finish dinner?

No! I'm awake. I was listening. I heard the first part. Or first word . . .

Have you ever seen someone and felt in your gut they were evil but no one believes you?

Yes. That guy who sang that "Baby Shark" song you used to love.

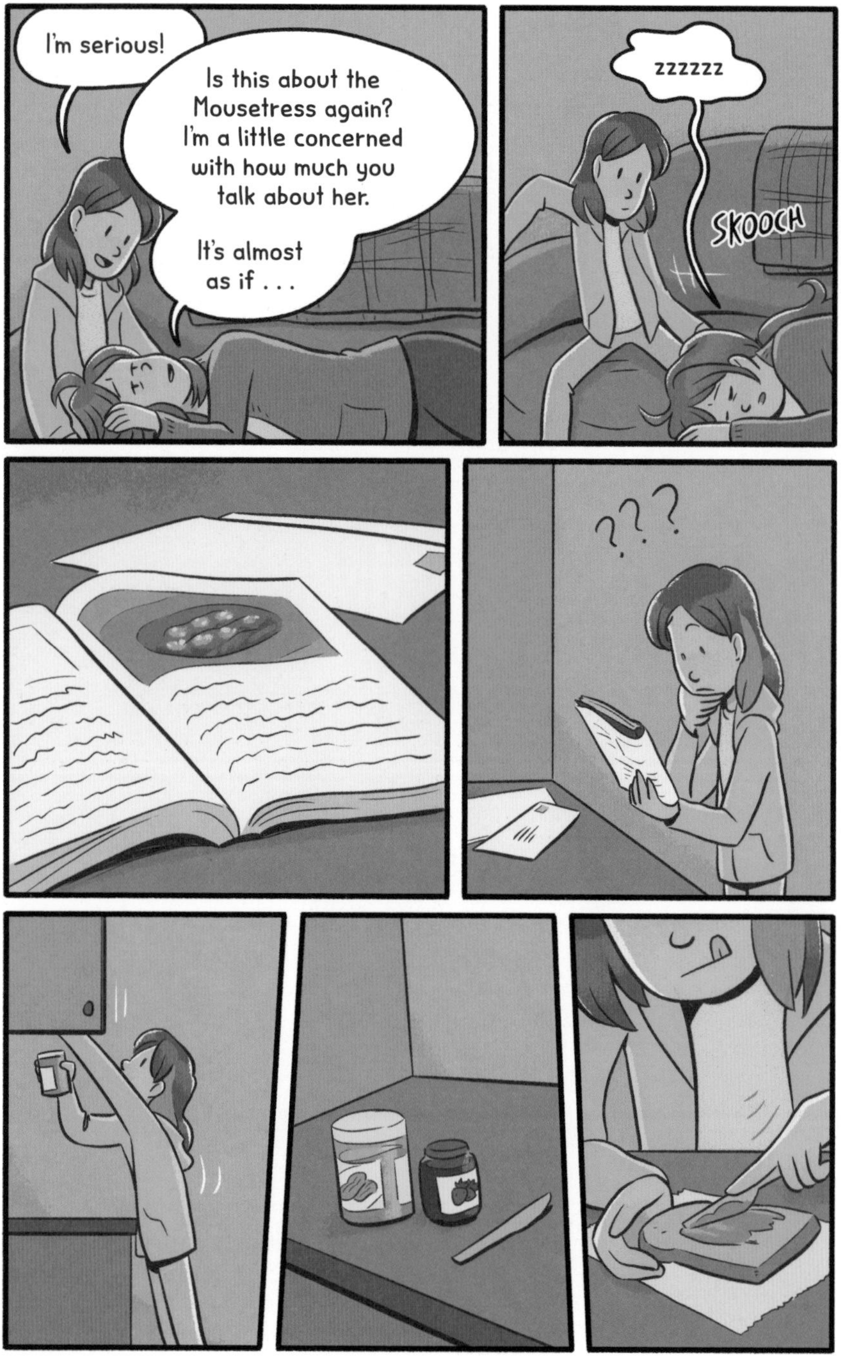
I'm serious!
Is this about the Mousetress again? I'm a little concerned with how much you talk about her.
It's almost as if . . .
zzzzzz
SKOOCH
???

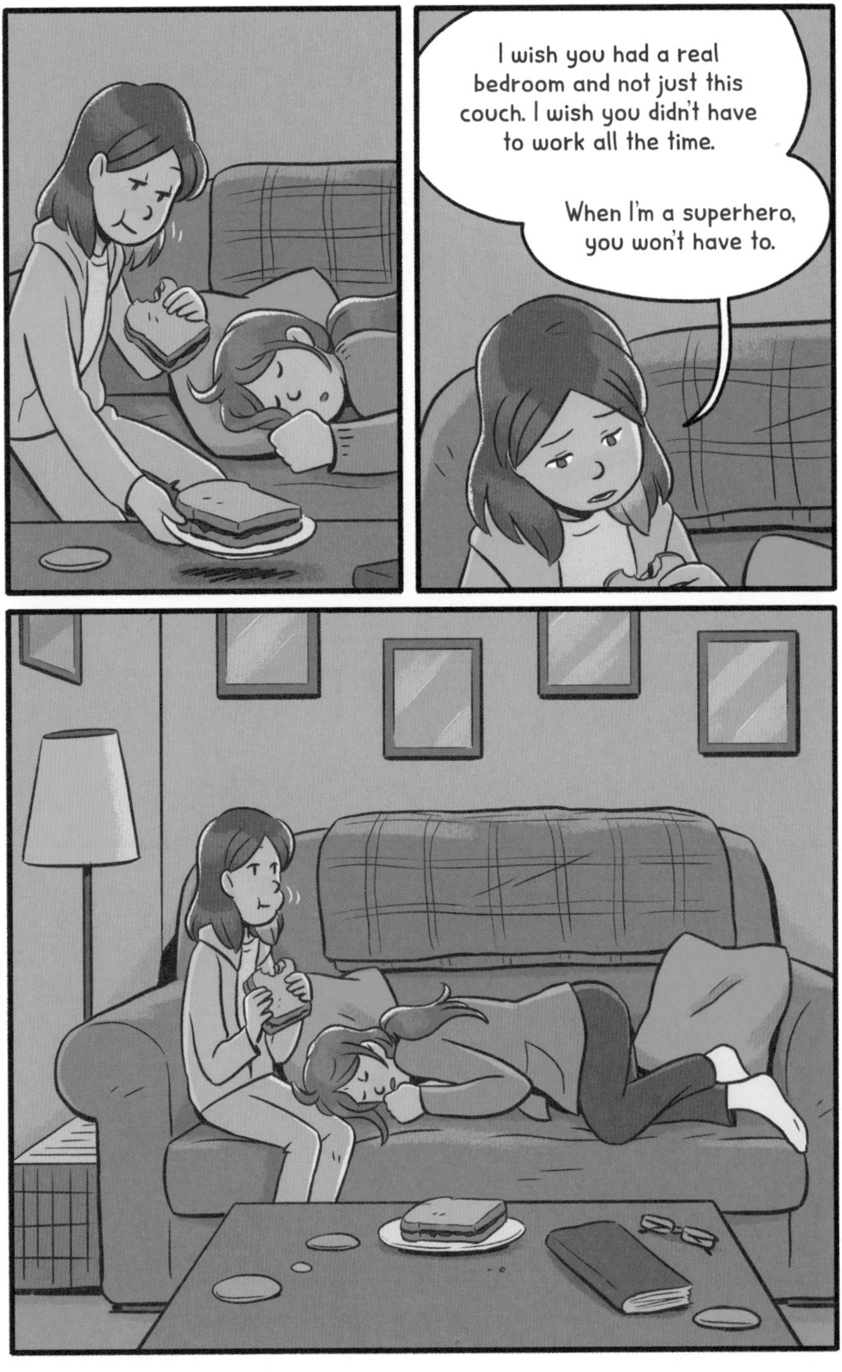
I wish you had a real bedroom and not just this couch. I wish you didn't have to work all the time.
When I'm a superhero, you won't have to.

CHAPTER THREE

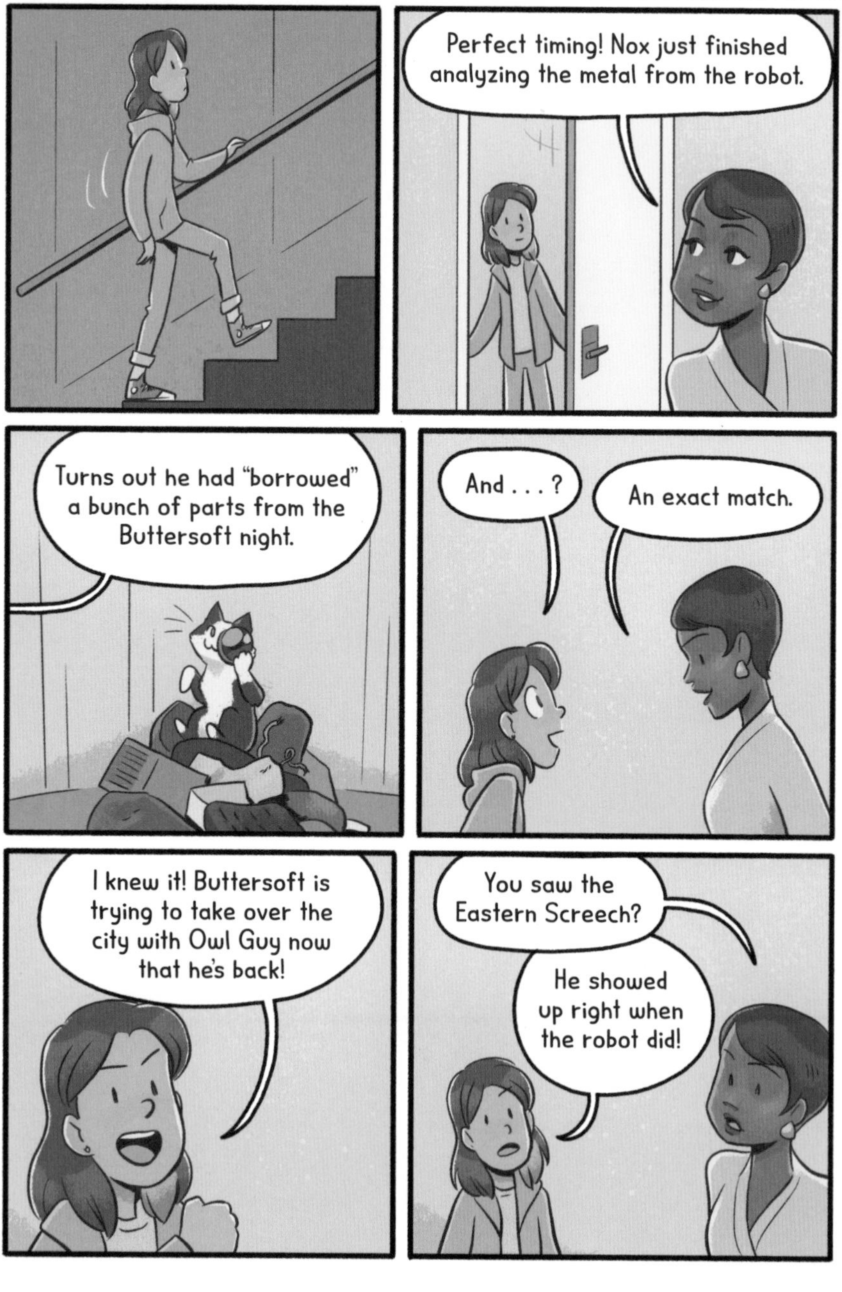

Perfect timing! Nox just finished analyzing the metal from the robot.
Turns out he had "borrowed" a bunch of parts from the Buttersoft night.
And . . . ?
An exact match.
I knew it! Buttersoft is trying to take over the city with Owl Guy now that he's back!
You saw the Eastern Screech?
He showed up right when the robot did!

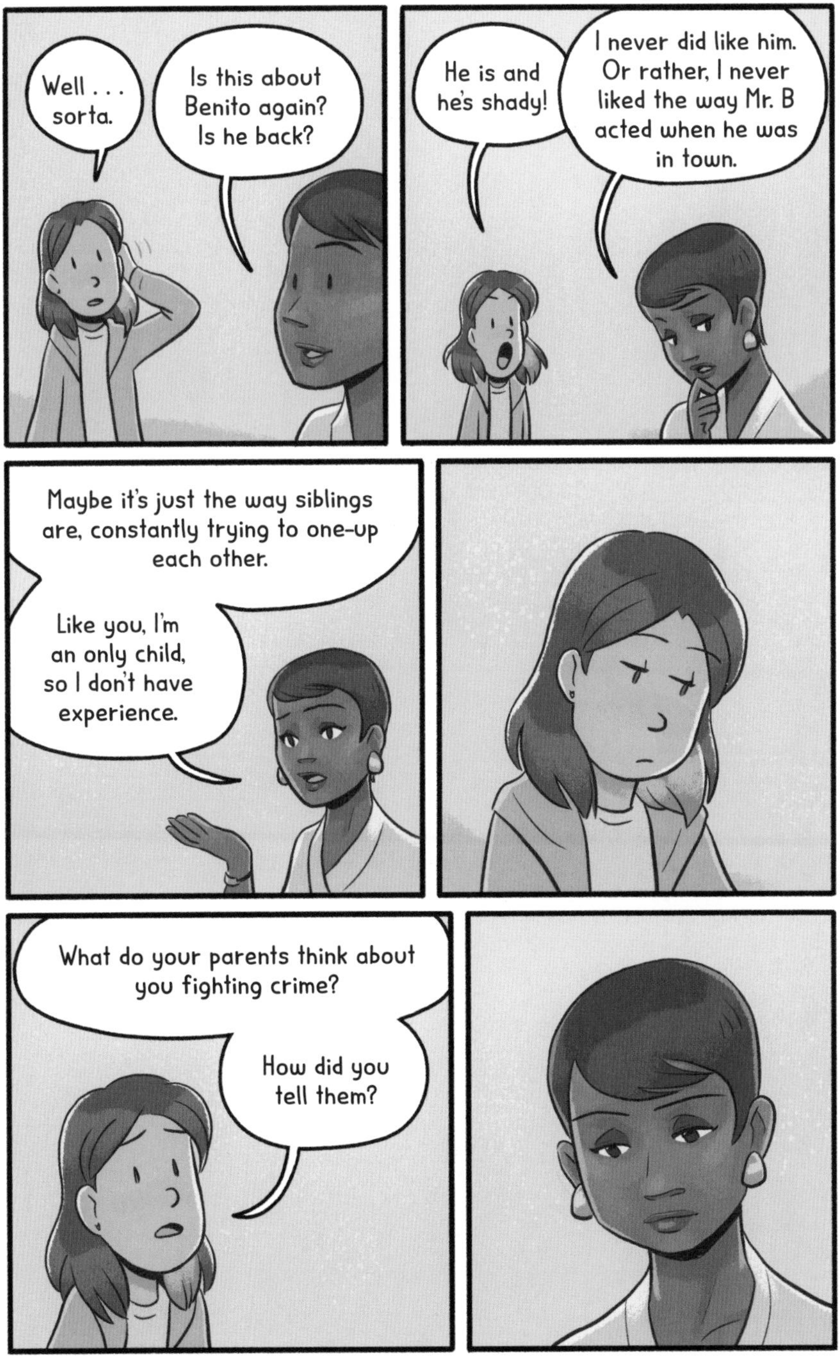
Well . . . sorta.
Is this about Benito again? Is he back?
He is and he's shady!
I never did like him. Or rather, I never liked the way Mr. B acted when he was in town.
Maybe it's just the way siblings are, constantly trying to one-up each other.
Like you, I'm an only child, so I don't have experience.
What do your parents think about you fighting crime?
How did you tell them?

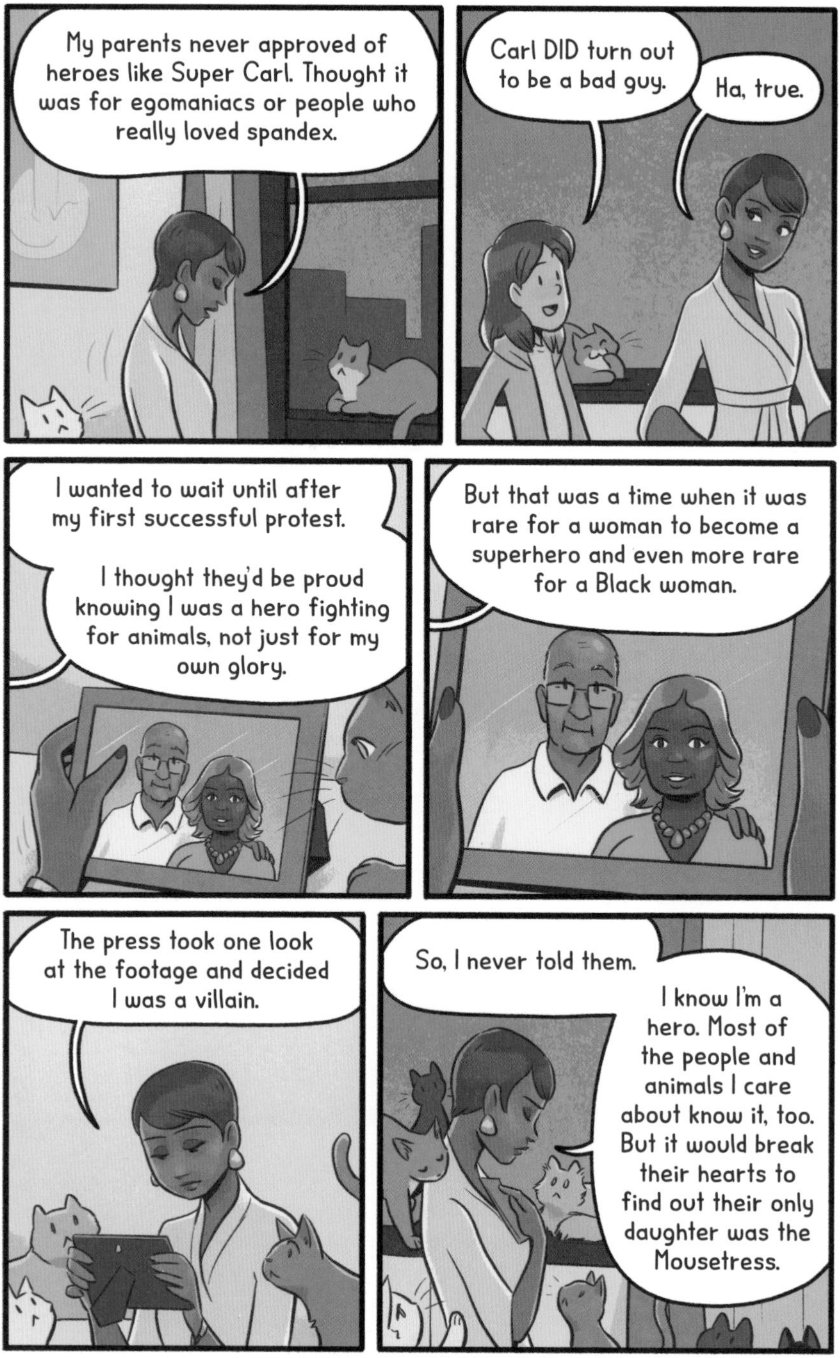

My parents never approved of heroes like Super Carl. Thought it was for egomaniacs or people who really loved spandex.
Carl DID turn out to be a bad guy.
Ha, true.
I wanted to wait until after my first successful protest.
I thought they'd be proud knowing I was a hero fighting for animals, not just for my own glory.
But that was a time when it was rare for a woman to become a superhero and even more rare for a Black woman.
The press took one look at the footage and decided I was a villain.
So, I never told them.
I know I'm a hero. Most of the people and animals I care about know it, too. But it would break their hearts to find out their only daughter was the Mousetress.

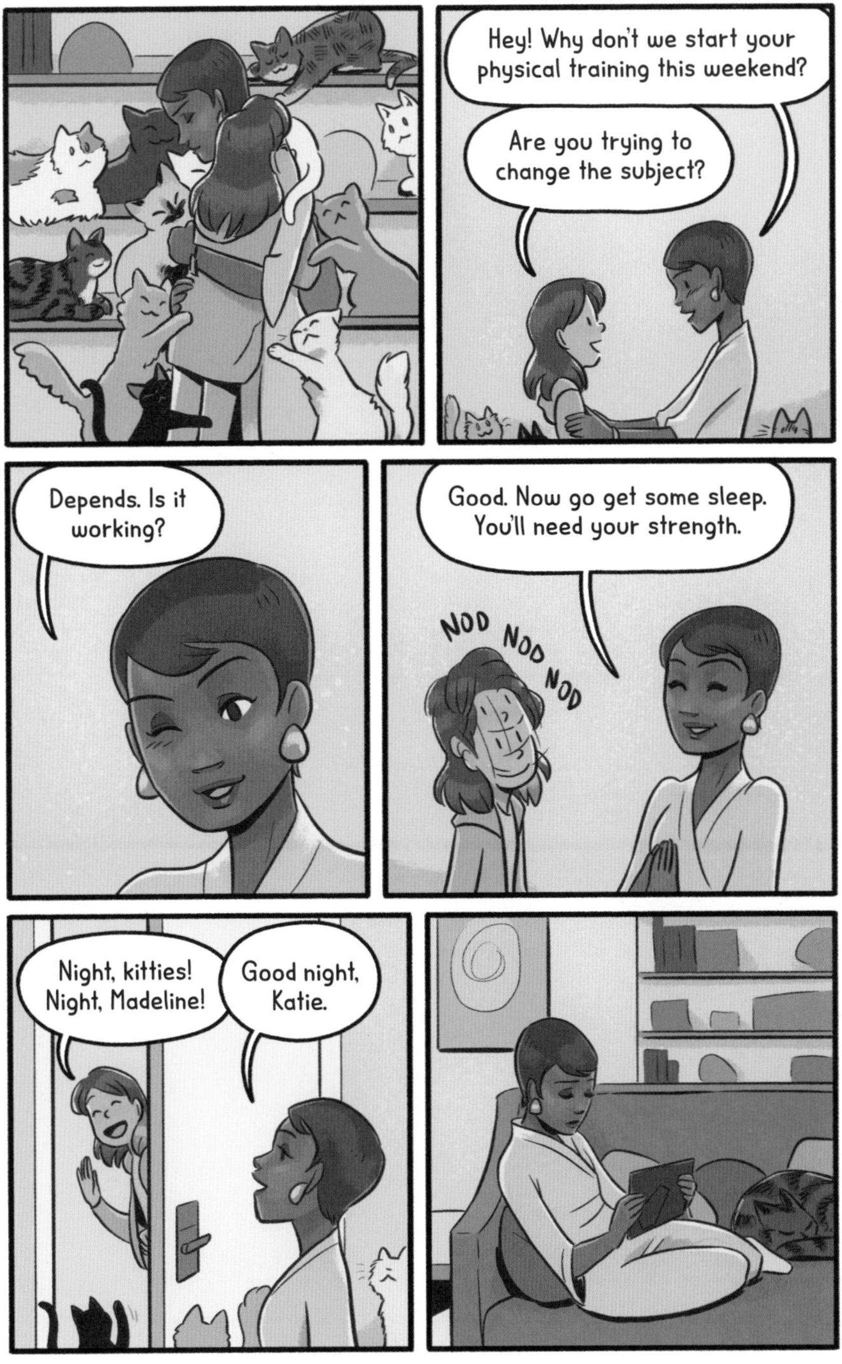

Hey! Why don't we start your physical training this weekend?
Are you trying to change the subject?
Depends. Is it working?
Good. Now go get some sleep. You'll need your strength.
NOD NOD NOD
Night, kitties! Night, Madeline!
Good night, Katie.

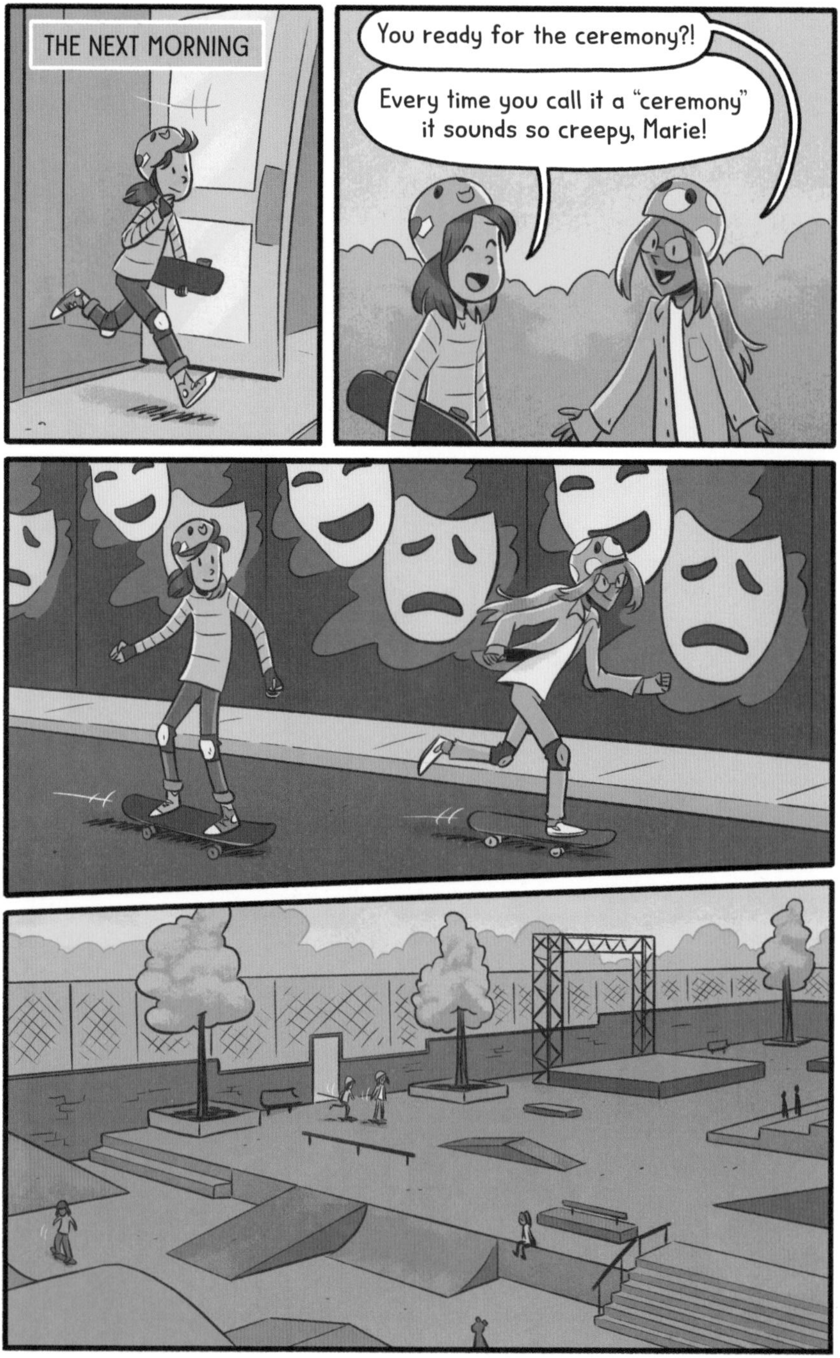
THE NEXT MORNING
You ready for the ceremony?!
Every time you call it a "ceremony" it sounds so creepy, Marie!

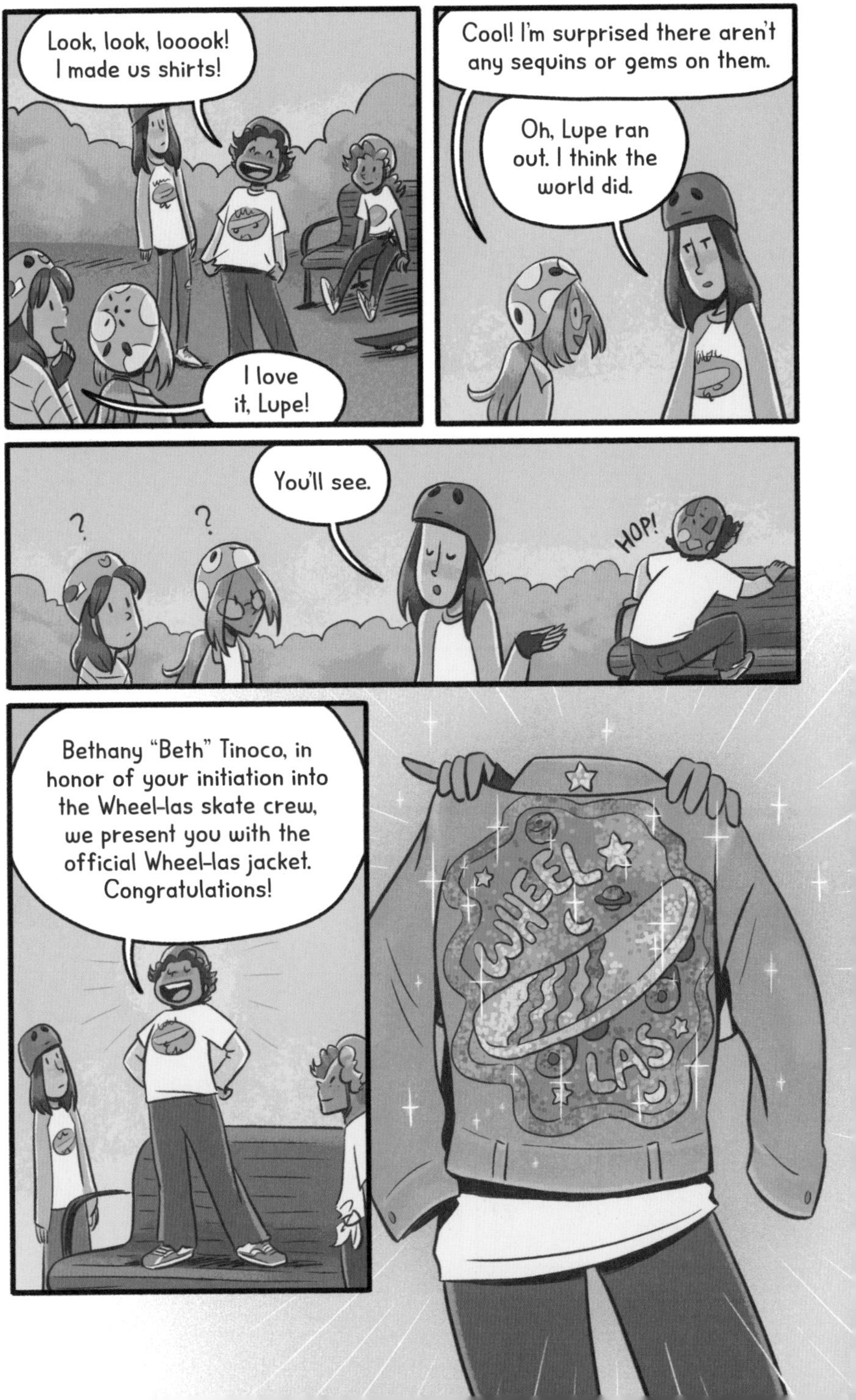
Look, look, looook! I made us shirts!
I love it, Lupe!
Cool! I'm surprised there aren't any sequins or gems on them.
Oh, Lupe ran out. I think the world did.
?
?
You'll see.
HOP!
Bethany "Beth" Tinoco, in honor of your initiation into the Wheel-las skate crew, we present you with the official Wheel-las jacket. Congratulations!
WHEEL LAS

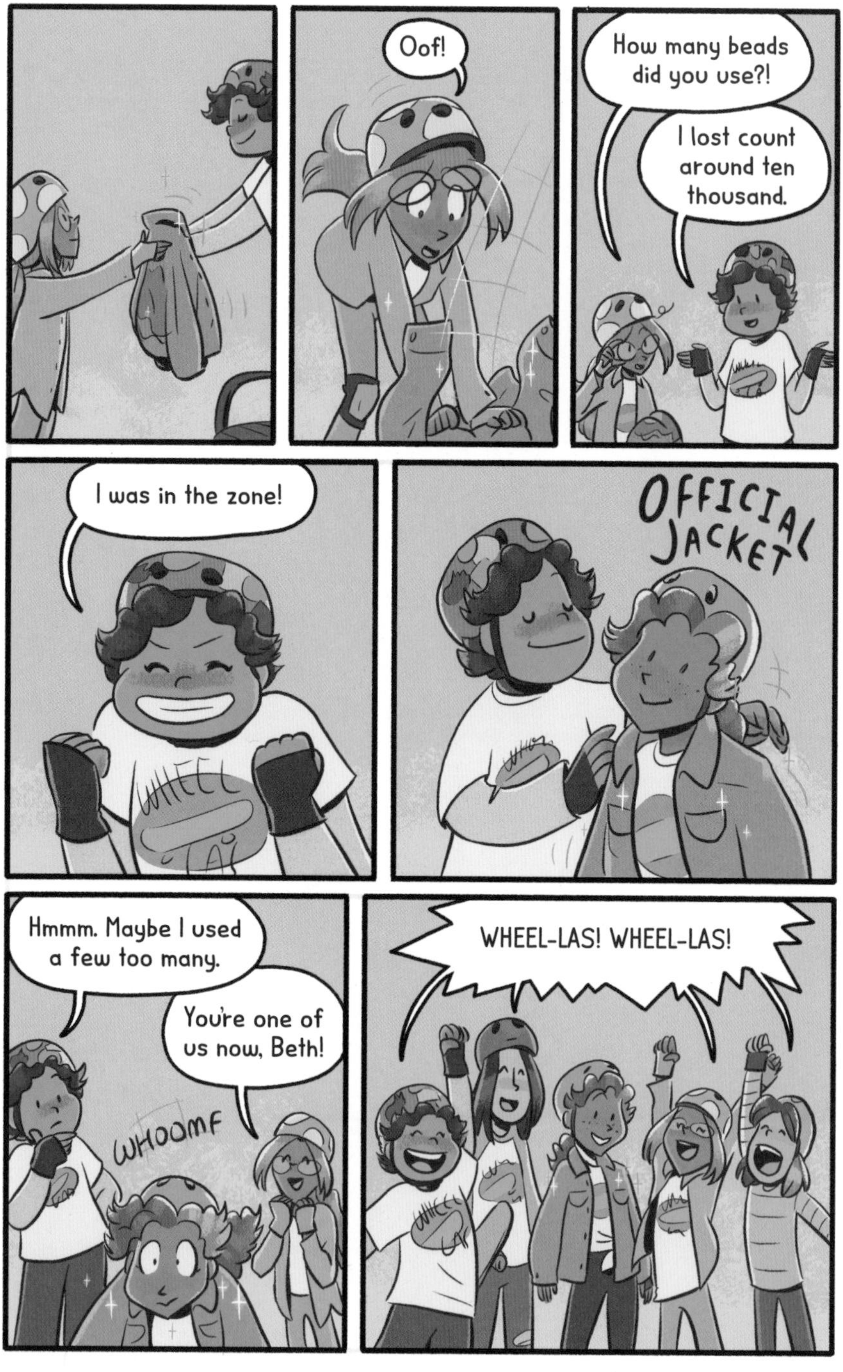
Oof!
How many beads did you use?!
I lost count around ten thousand.
I was in the zone!
OFFICIAL JACKET
Hmmm. Maybe I used a few too many.
You're one of us now, Beth!
WHOOMF
WHEEL-LAS! WHEEL-LAS!

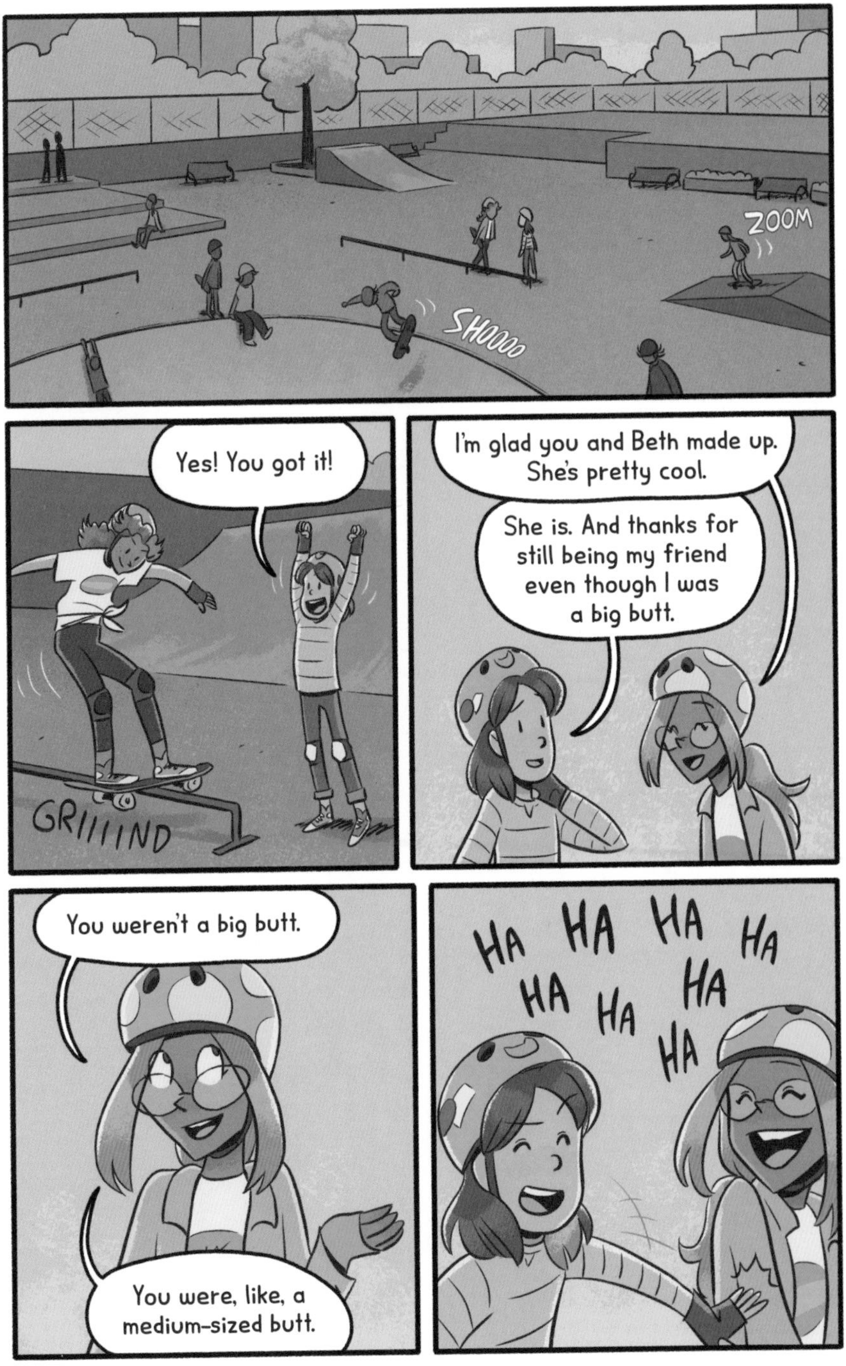
ZOOM
SHOOOO
Yes! You got it!
GRIIIIND
I'm glad you and Beth made up. She's pretty cool.
She is. And thanks for still being my friend even though I was a big butt.
You weren't a big butt.
You were, like, a medium-sized butt.
HA HA HA HA HA HA HA HA

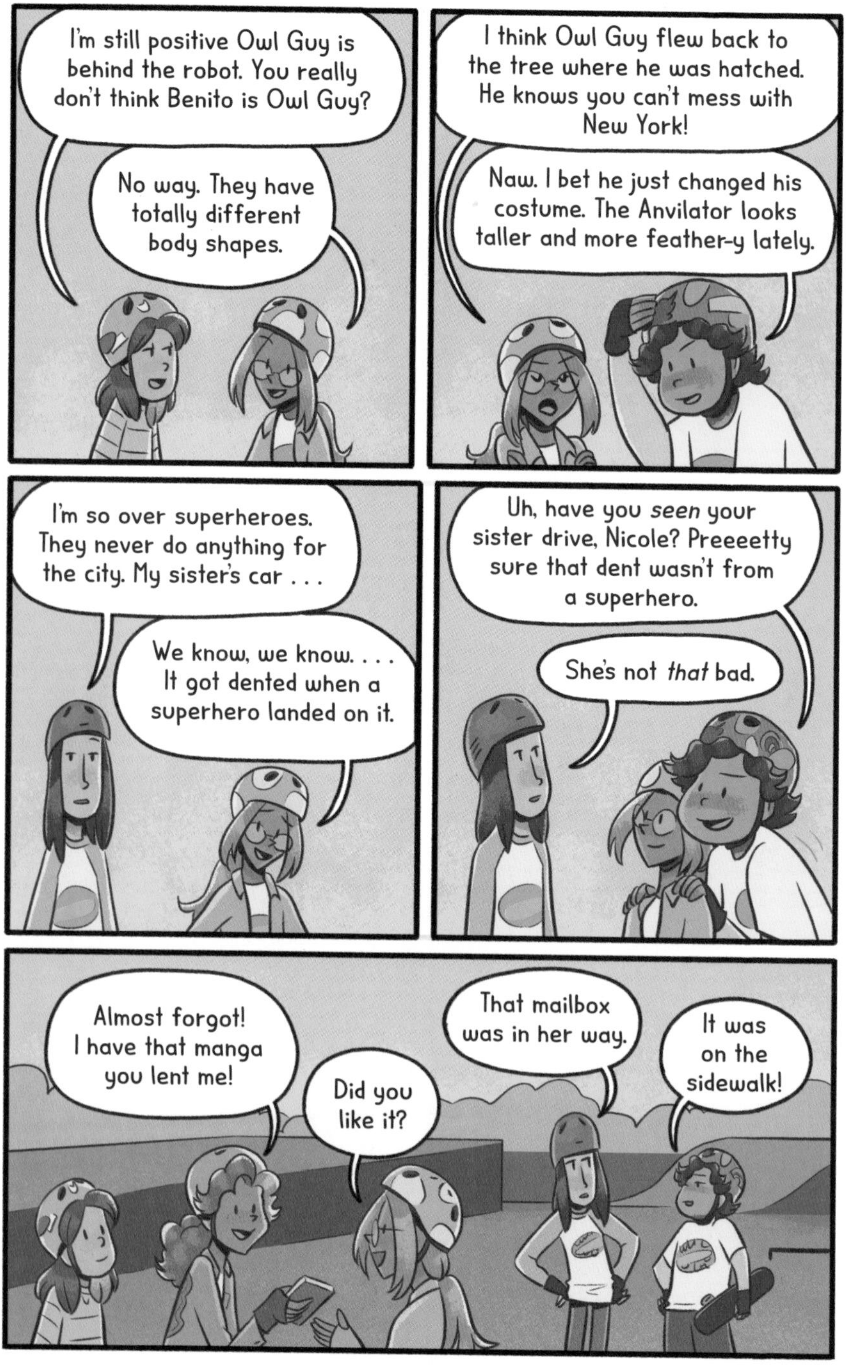
I'm still positive Owl Guy is behind the robot. You really don't think Benito is Owl Guy?
No way. They have totally different body shapes.
I think Owl Guy flew back to the tree where he was hatched. He knows you can't mess with New York!
Naw. I bet he just changed his costume. The Anvilator looks taller and more feather-y lately.
I'm so over superheroes. They never do anything for the city. My sister's car . . .
We know, we know. . . . It got dented when a superhero landed on it.
Uh, have you *seen* your sister drive, Nicole? Preeeetty sure that dent wasn't from a superhero.
She's not *that* bad.
Almost forgot! I have that manga you lent me!
Did you like it?
That mailbox was in her way.
It was on the sidewalk!

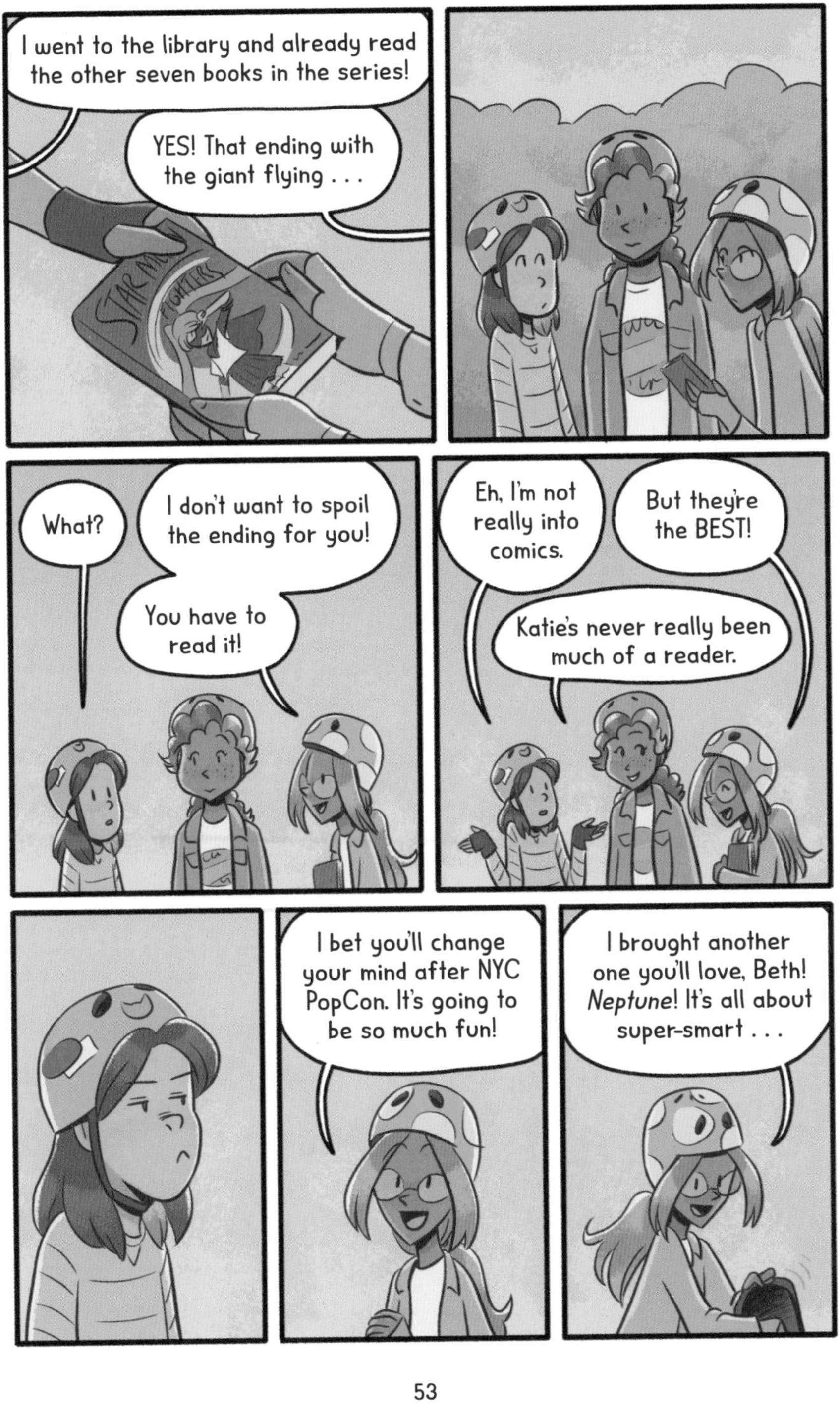

I went to the library and already read the other seven books in the series!
YES! That ending with the giant flying . . .
STAR MEN FIGHTERS
What?
I don't want to spoil the ending for you!
You have to read it!
Eh, I'm not really into comics.
But they're the BEST!
Katie's never really been much of a reader.
I bet you'll change your mind after NYC PopCon. It's going to be so much fun!
I brought another one you'll love, Beth! *Neptune*! It's all about super-smart . . .

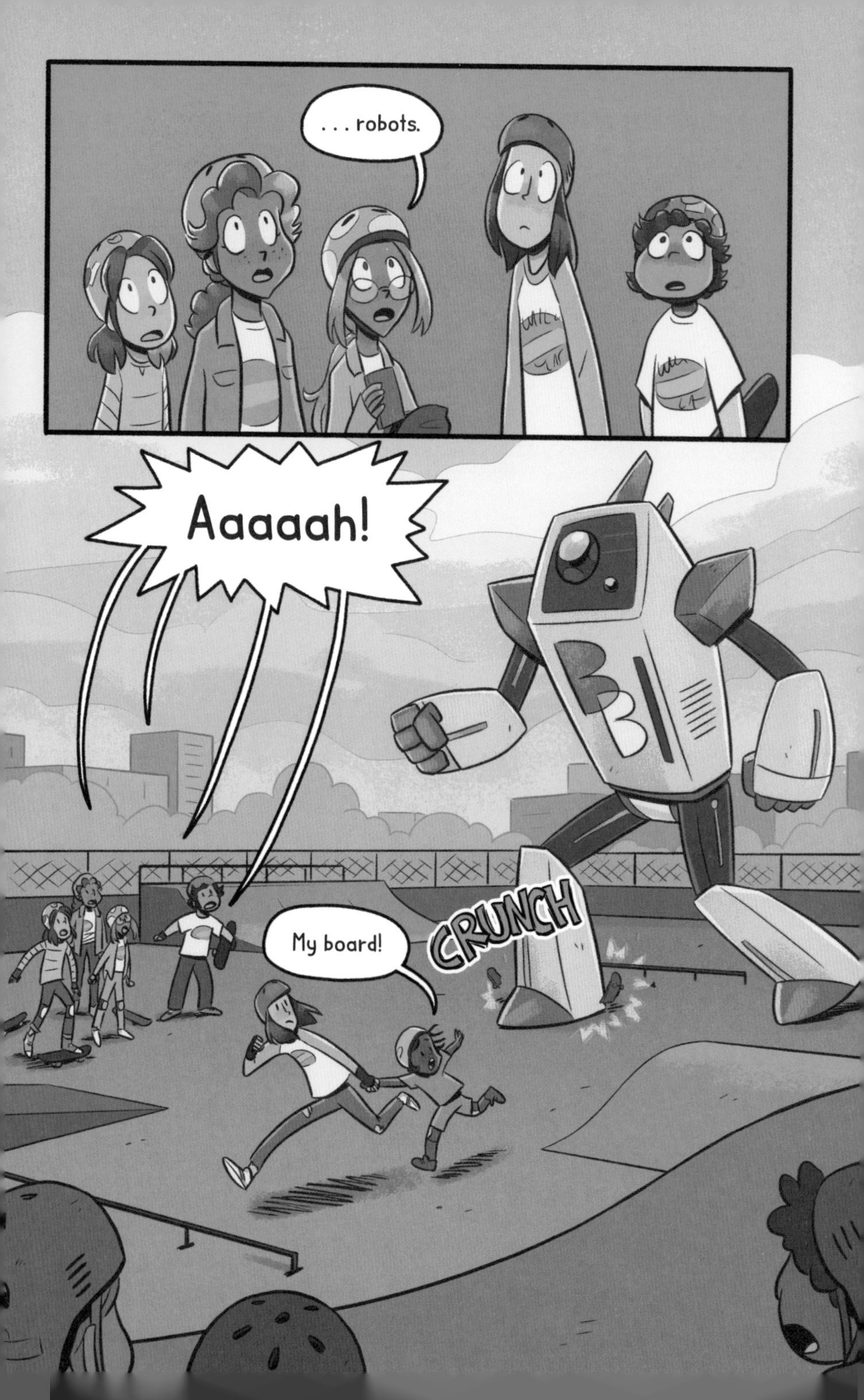
. . . robots.
Aaaaah!
My board!
CRUNCH

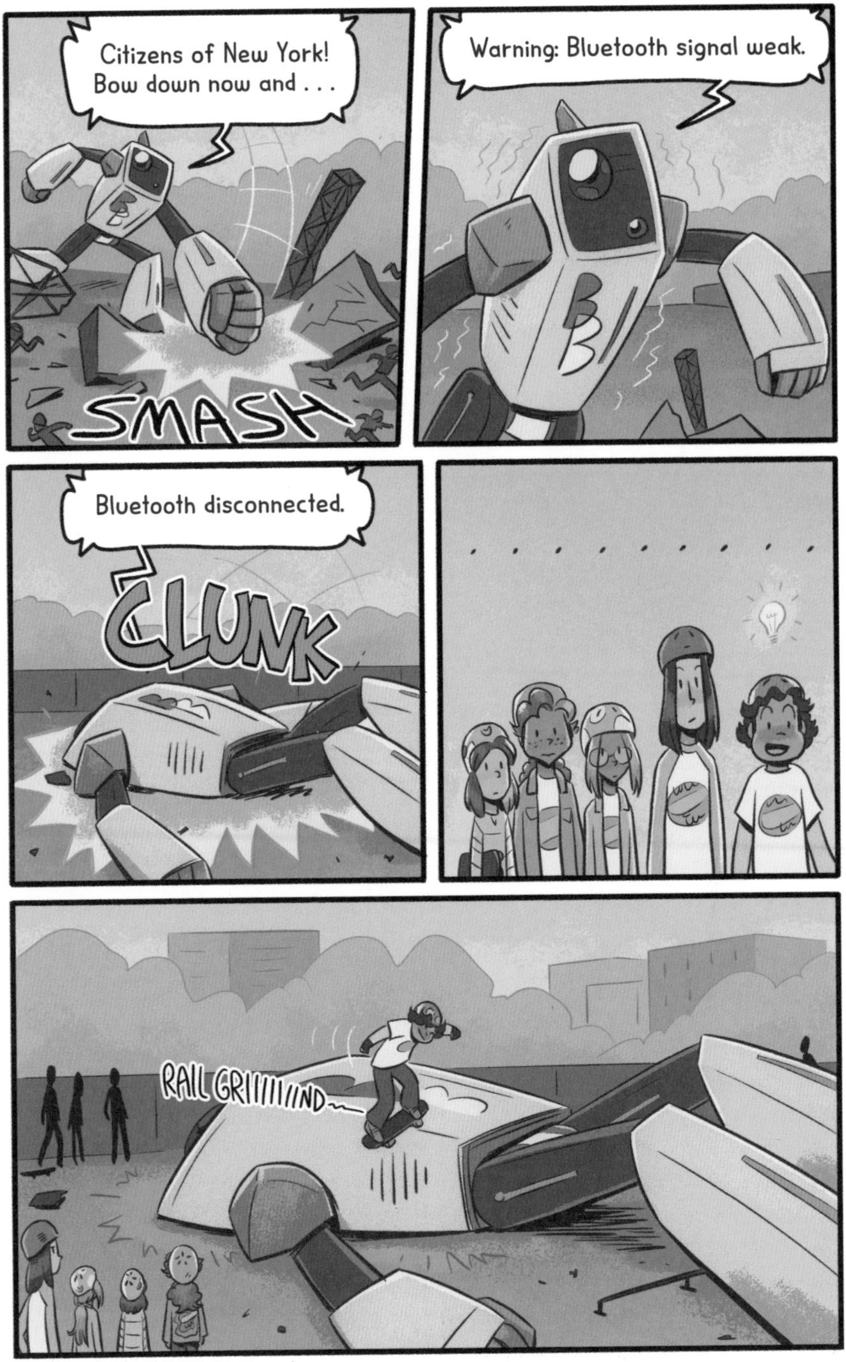
Citizens of New York! Bow down now and . . .
SMASH
Warning: Bluetooth signal weak.
Bluetooth disconnected.
CLUNK
. . . .
RAIL GRIIIIIIIND

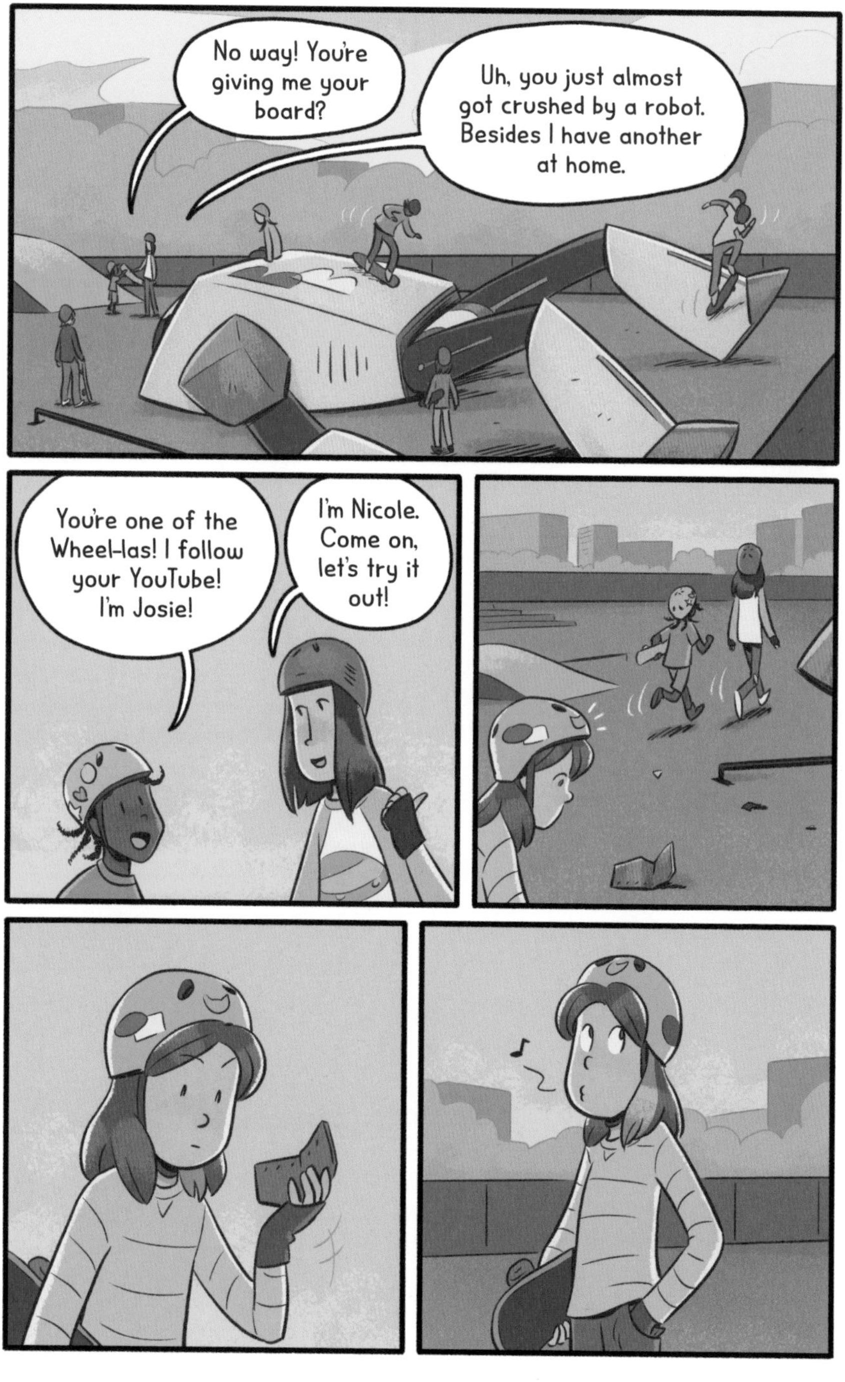
No way! You're giving me your board?
Uh, you just almost got crushed by a robot. Besides I have another at home.
You're one of the Wheel-las! I follow your YouTube! I'm Josie!
I'm Nicole. Come on, let's try it out!

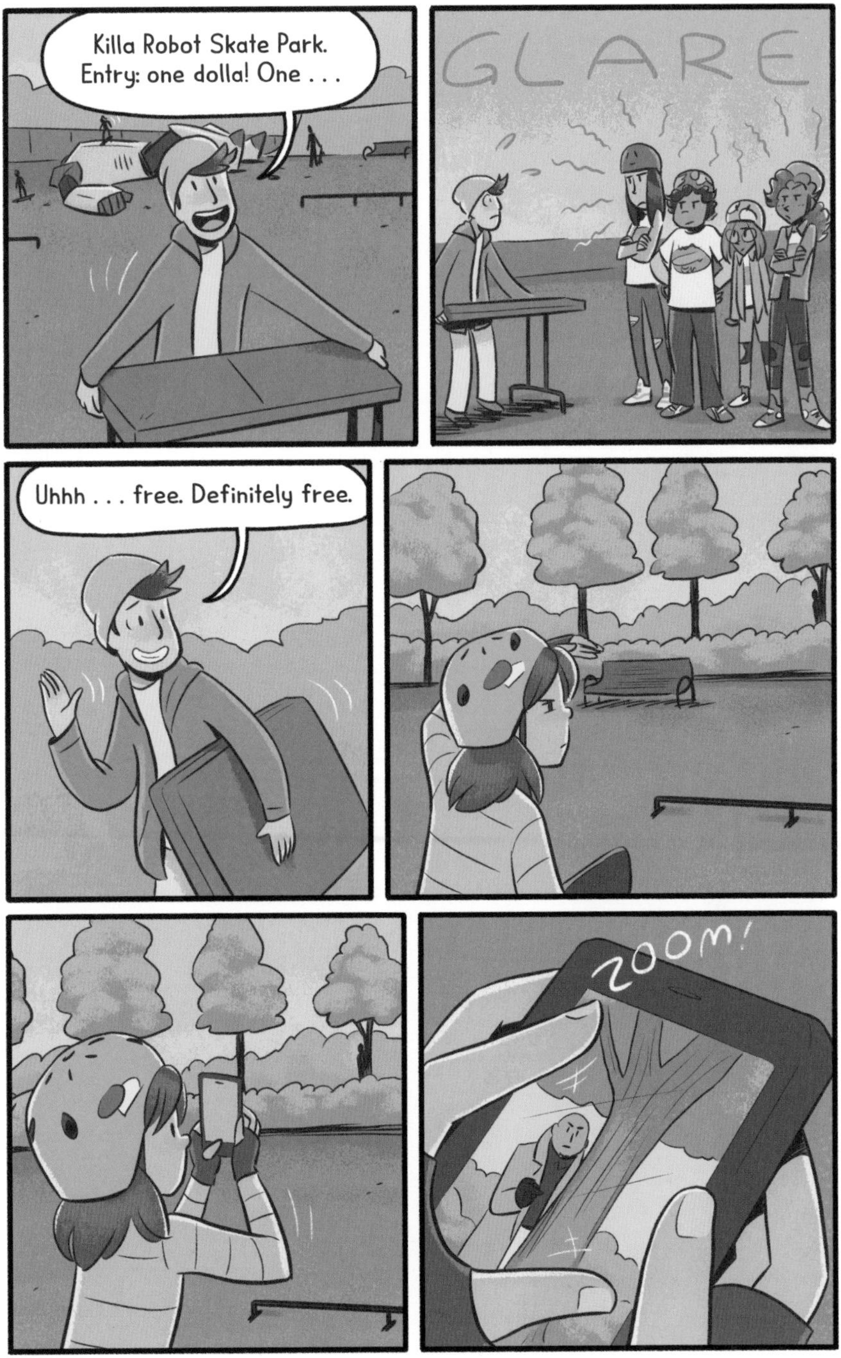
Killa Robot Skate Park. Entry: one dolla! One . . .
GLARE
Uhhh . . . free. Definitely free.
ZOOM!

There was another robot! It almost stepped on this girl, Josie!

What?! Is everyone okay?

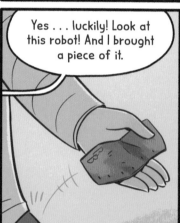

Yes . . . luckily! Look at this robot! And I brought a piece of it.

I don't understand why they would make their logo even bigger.

Uh, I think you're holding that pan upside down.

I know. For some reason the muffins won't come out.

CLUNK

Scroll to the next pic.

Is that . . . ?

Benito.

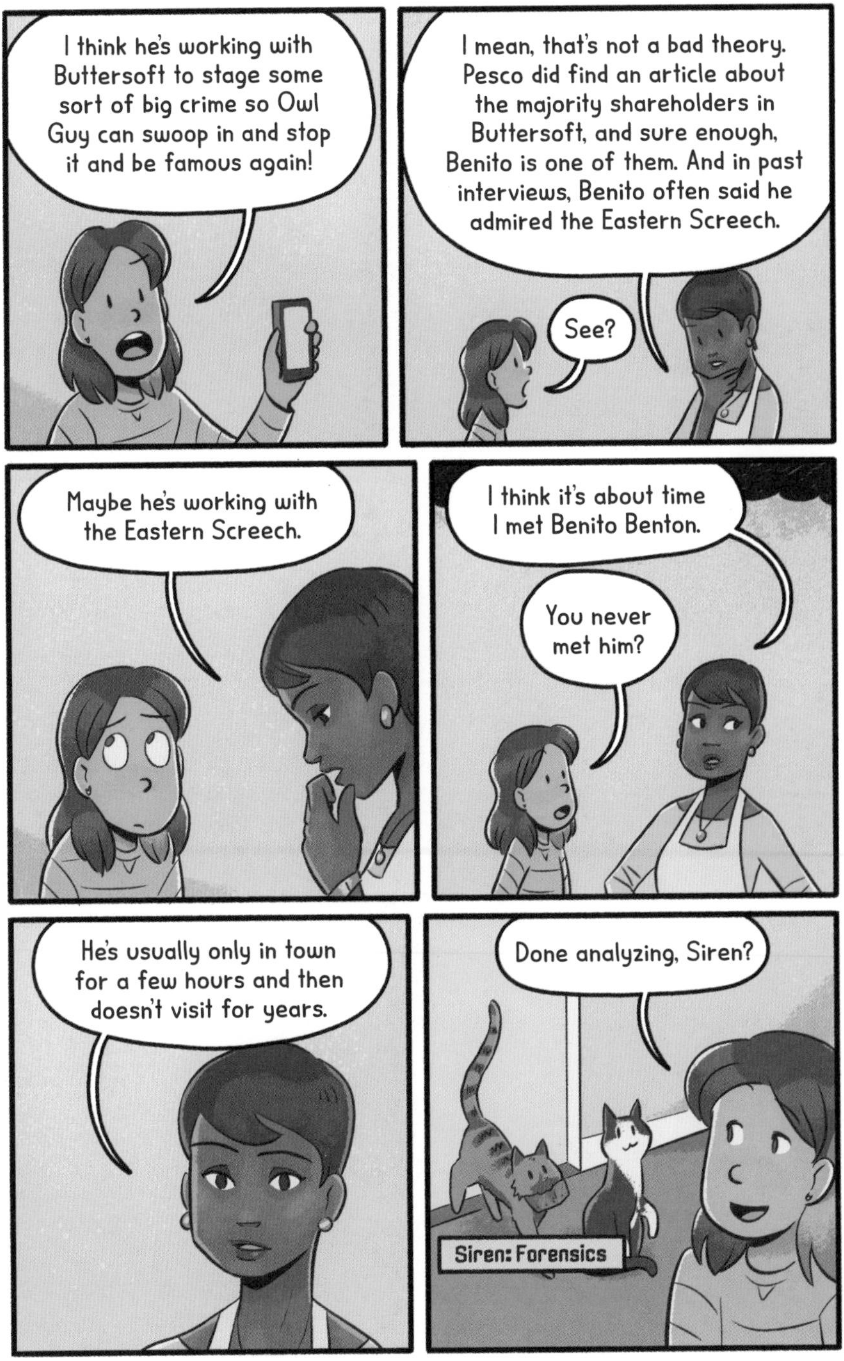
I think he's working with Buttersoft to stage some sort of big crime so Owl Guy can swoop in and stop it and be famous again!
I mean, that's not a bad theory. Pesco did find an article about the majority shareholders in Buttersoft, and sure enough, Benito is one of them. And in past interviews, Benito often said he admired the Eastern Screech.
See?
Maybe he's working with the Eastern Screech.
I think it's about time I met Benito Benton.
You never met him?
He's usually only in town for a few hours and then doesn't visit for years.
Done analyzing, Siren?
Siren: Forensics

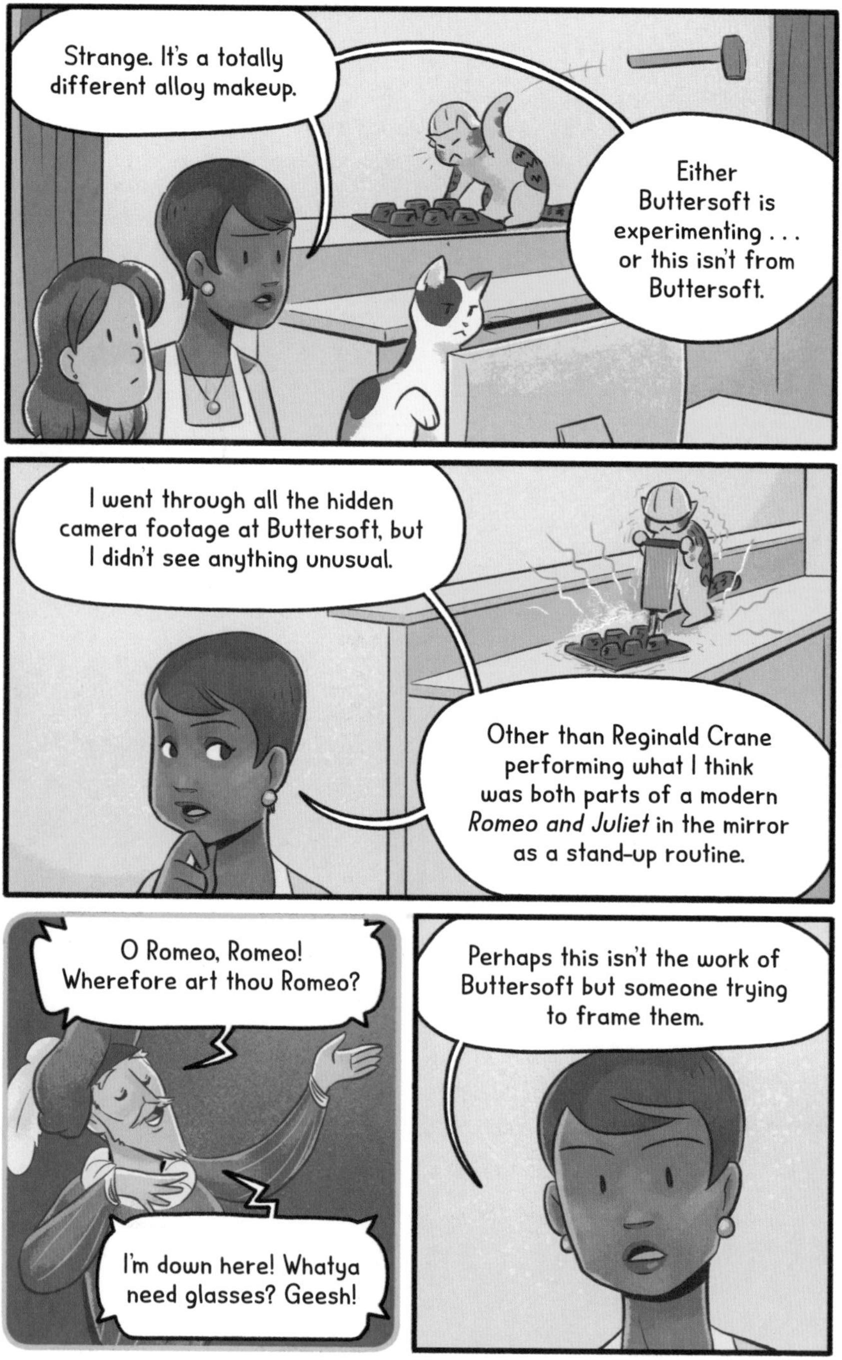
Strange. It's a totally different alloy makeup.
Either Buttersoft is experimenting . . . or this isn't from Buttersoft.
I went through all the hidden camera footage at Buttersoft, but I didn't see anything unusual.
Other than Reginald Crane performing what I think was both parts of a modern *Romeo and Juliet* in the mirror as a stand-up routine.
O Romeo, Romeo! Wherefore art thou Romeo?
I'm down here! Whatya need glasses? Geesh!
Perhaps this isn't the work of Buttersoft but someone trying to frame them.

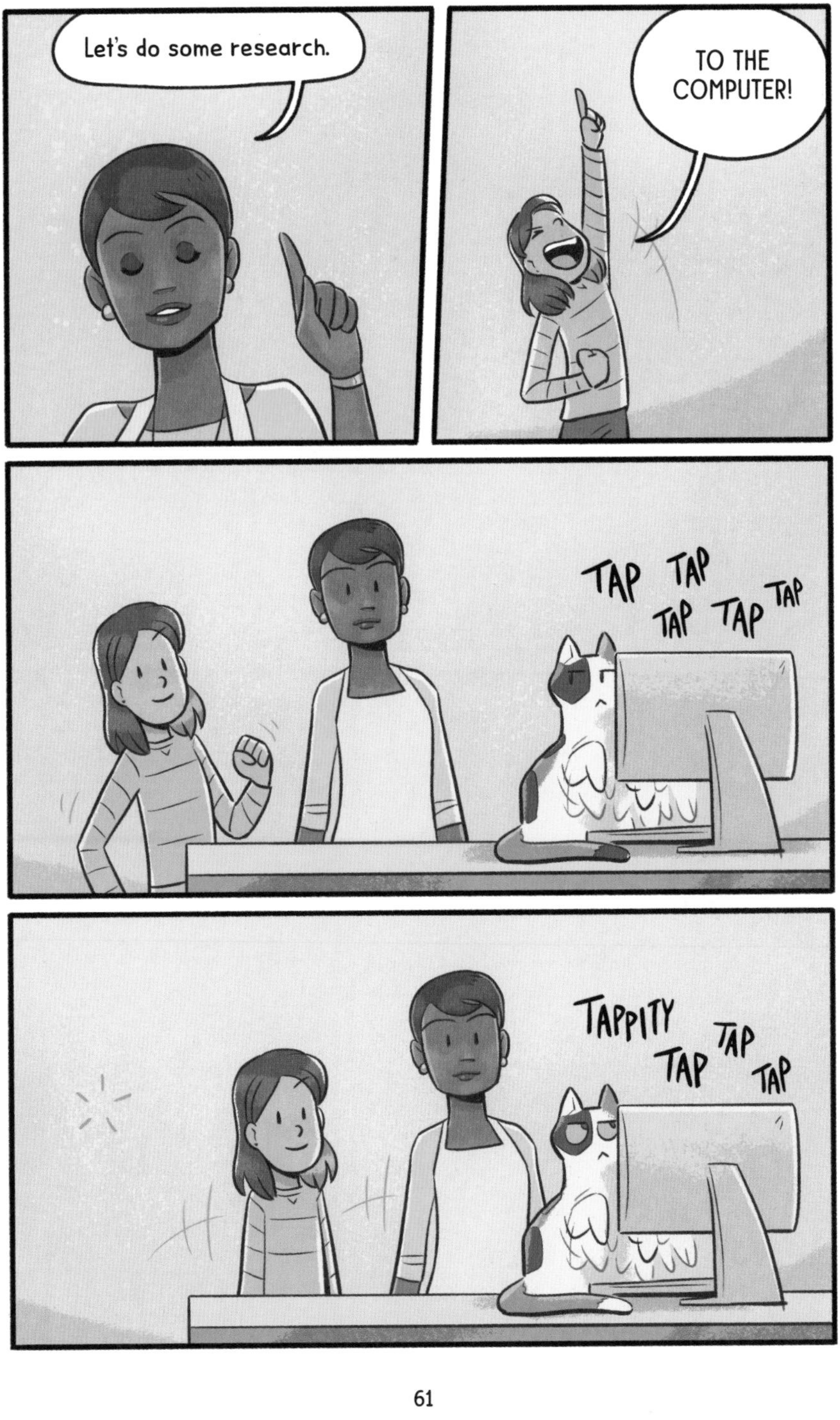
Let's do some research.
TO THE COMPUTER!
TAP TAP
TAP TAP TAP
TAPPITY
TAP TAP
TAP

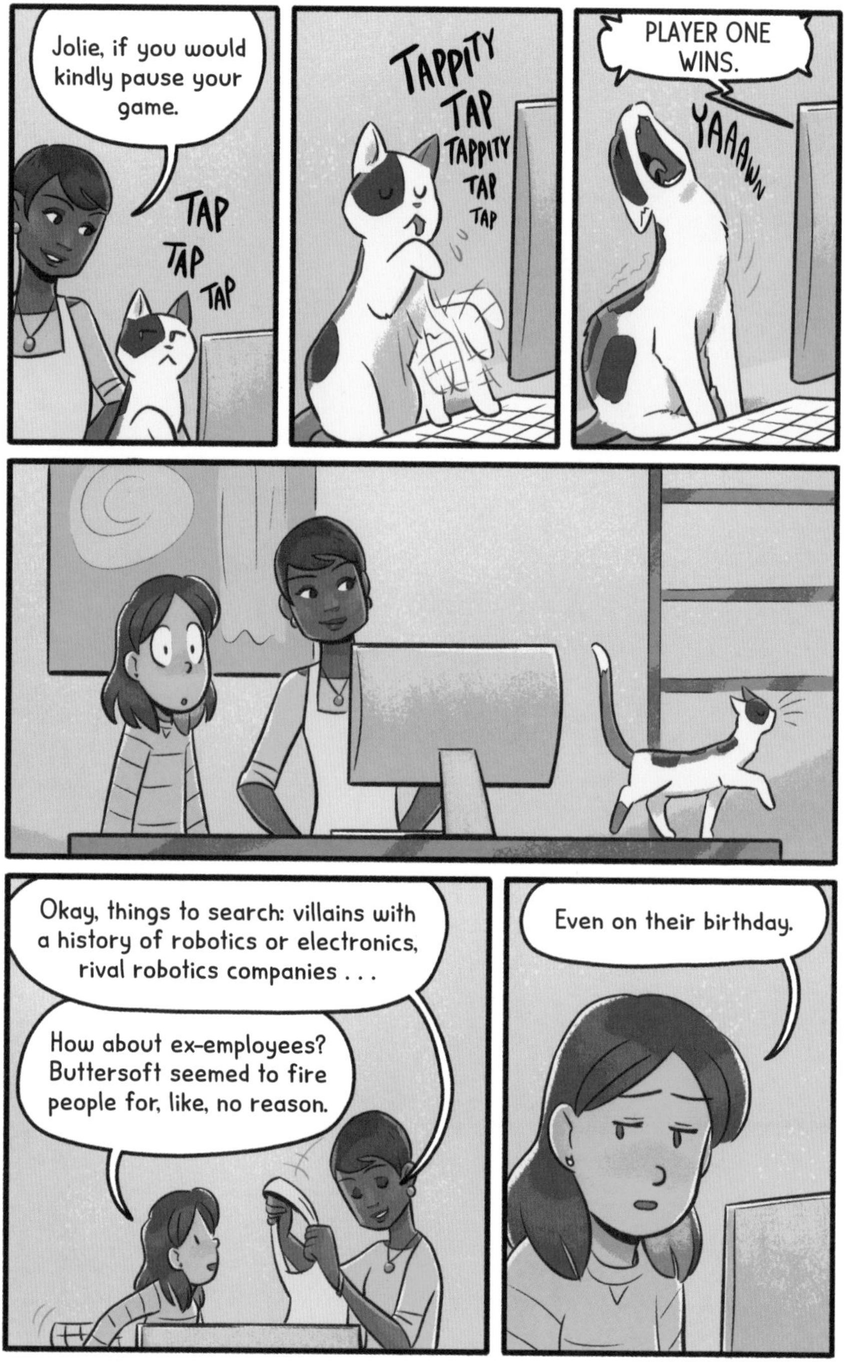
Jolie, if you would kindly pause your game.
TAP
TAP
TAP
TAPPITY
TAP
TAPPITY
TAP
TAP
PLAYER ONE WINS.
YAAAWN
Okay, things to search: villains with a history of robotics or electronics, rival robotics companies . . .
How about ex-employees? Buttersoft seemed to fire people for, like, no reason.
Even on their birthday.

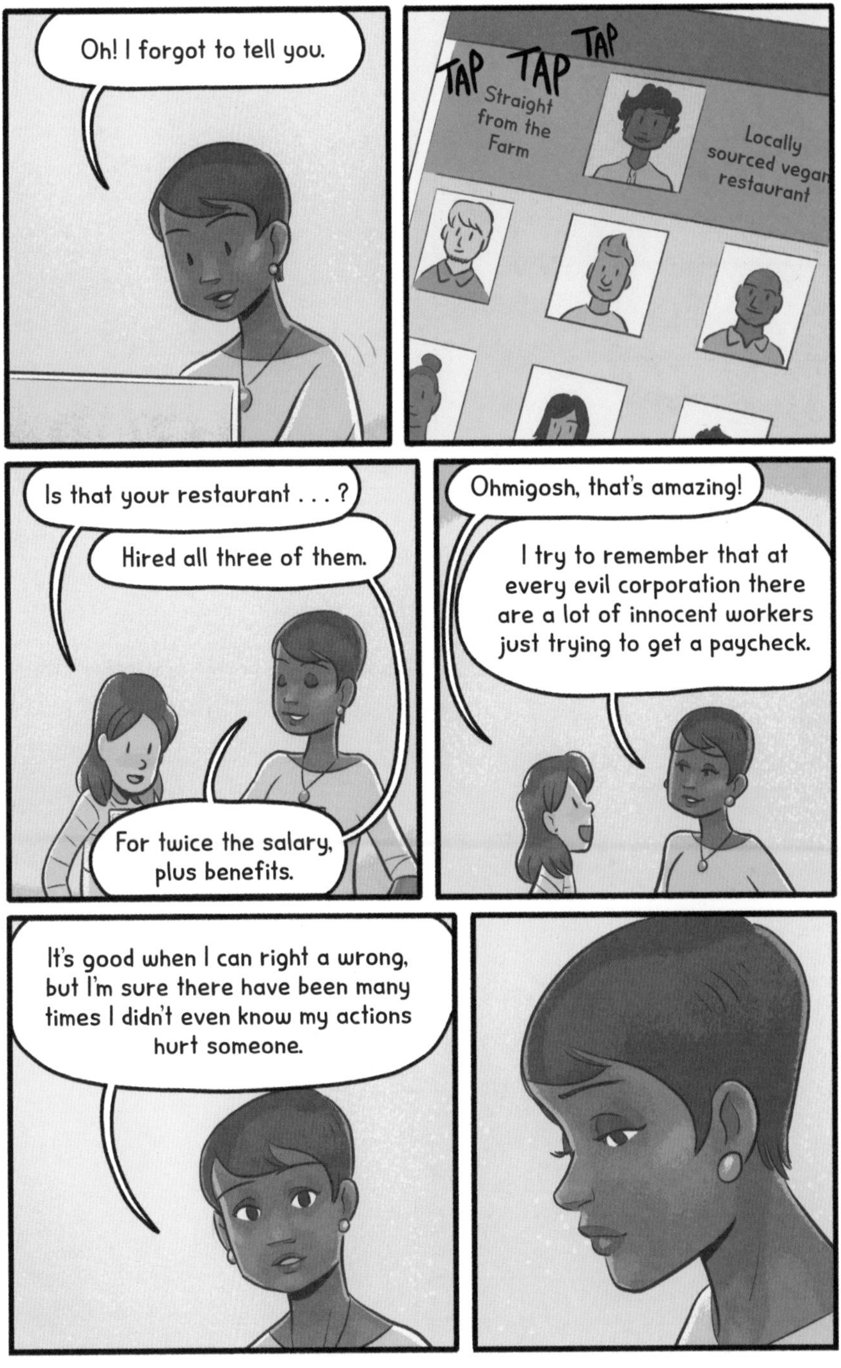
Oh! I forgot to tell you.
TAP TAP TAP
Straight from the Farm
Locally sourced vegan restaurant
Is that your restaurant . . . ?
Hired all three of them.
For twice the salary, plus benefits.
Ohmigosh, that's amazing!
I try to remember that at every evil corporation there are a lot of innocent workers just trying to get a paycheck.
It's good when I can right a wrong, but I'm sure there have been many times I didn't even know my actions hurt someone.

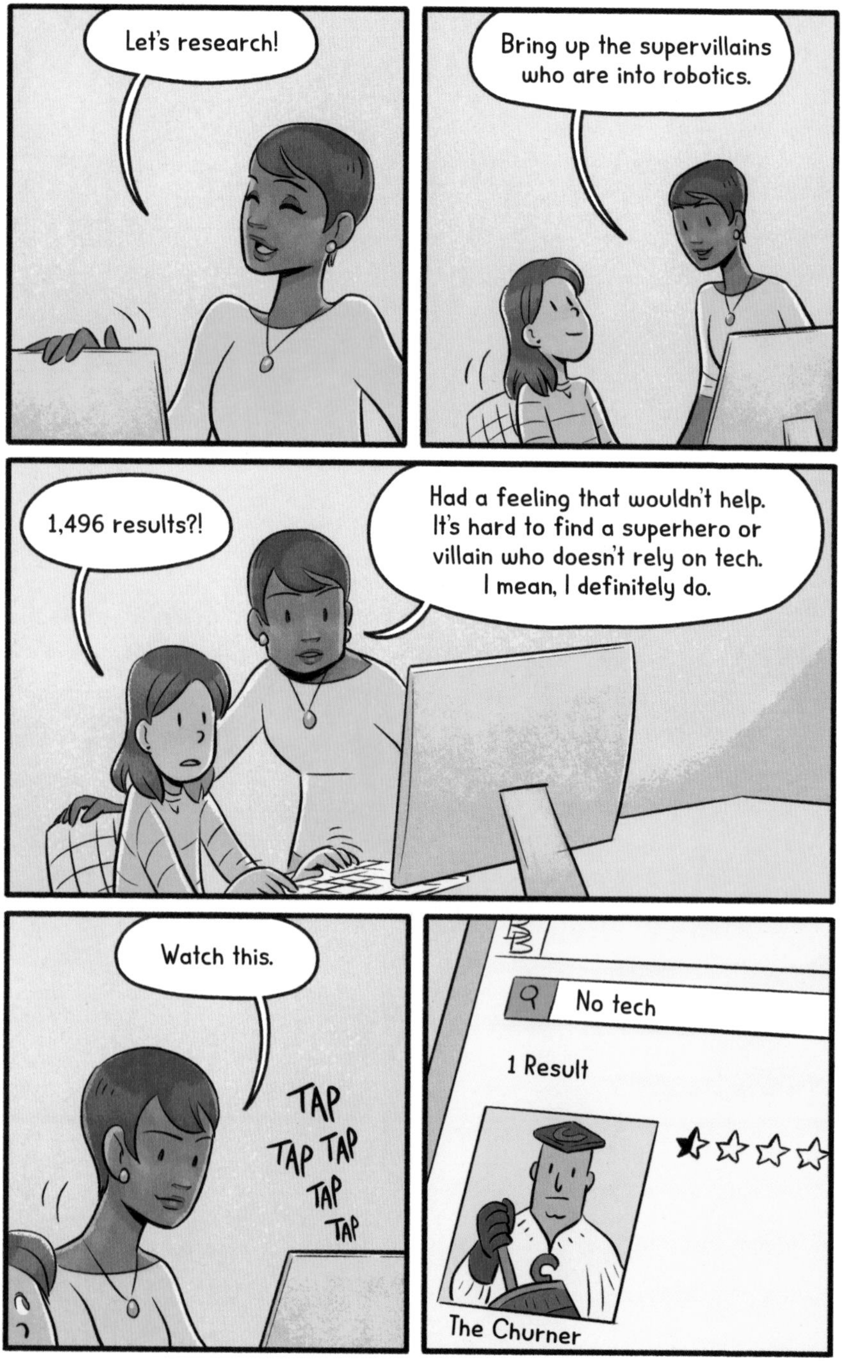

Let's research!
Bring up the supervillains who are into robotics.
1,496 results?!
Had a feeling that wouldn't help. It's hard to find a superhero or villain who doesn't rely on tech. I mean, I definitely do.
Watch this.
TAP TAP TAP TAP TAP
No tech
1 Result
The Churner

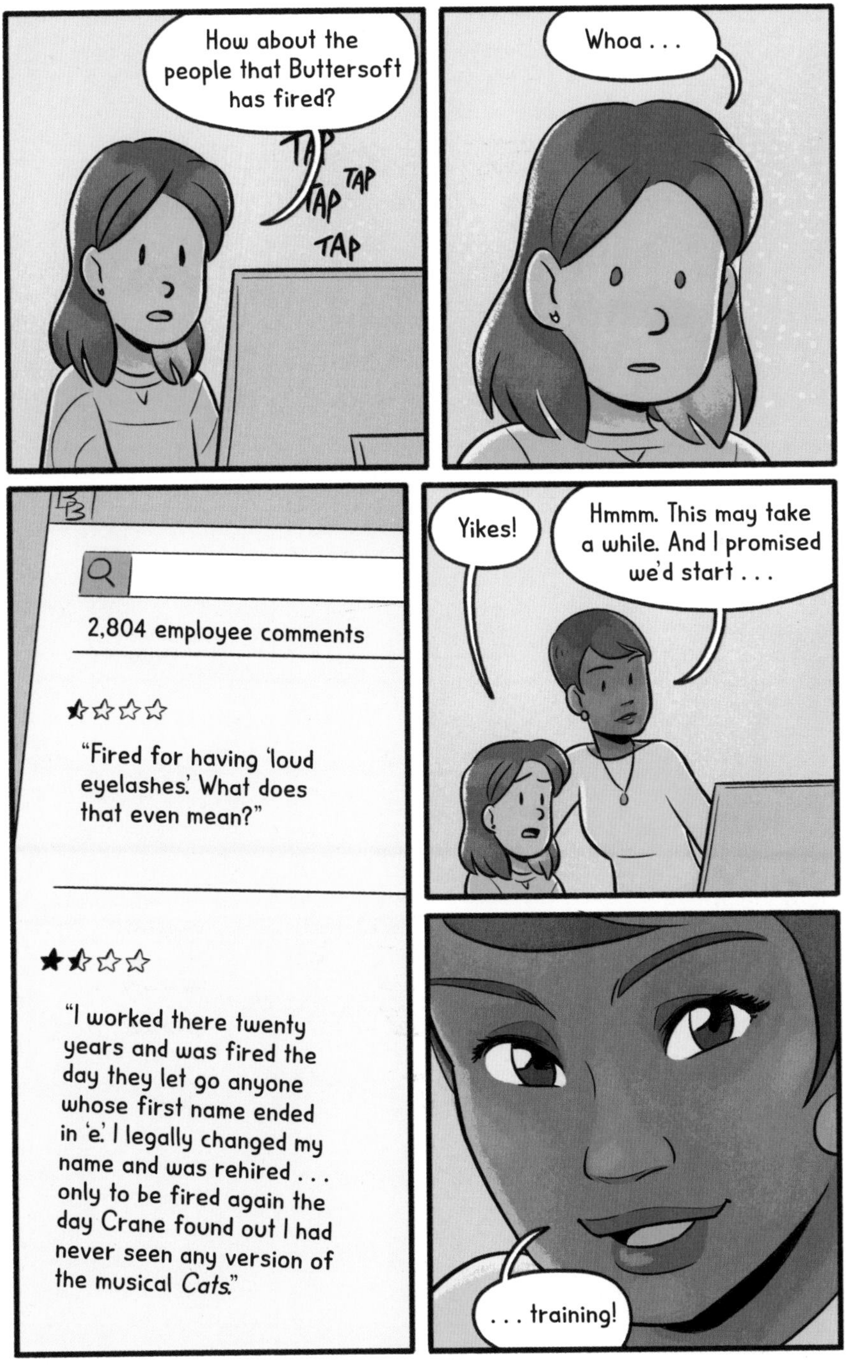
How about the people that Buttersoft has fired?
TAP
TAP
TAP
TAP
Whoa . . .
2,804 employee comments
"Fired for having 'loud eyelashes.' What does that even mean?"
"I worked there twenty years and was fired the day they let go anyone whose first name ended in 'e.' I legally changed my name and was rehired . . . only to be fired again the day Crane found out I had never seen any version of the musical *Cats*."
Yikes!
Hmmm. This may take a while. And I promised we'd start . . .
. . . training!

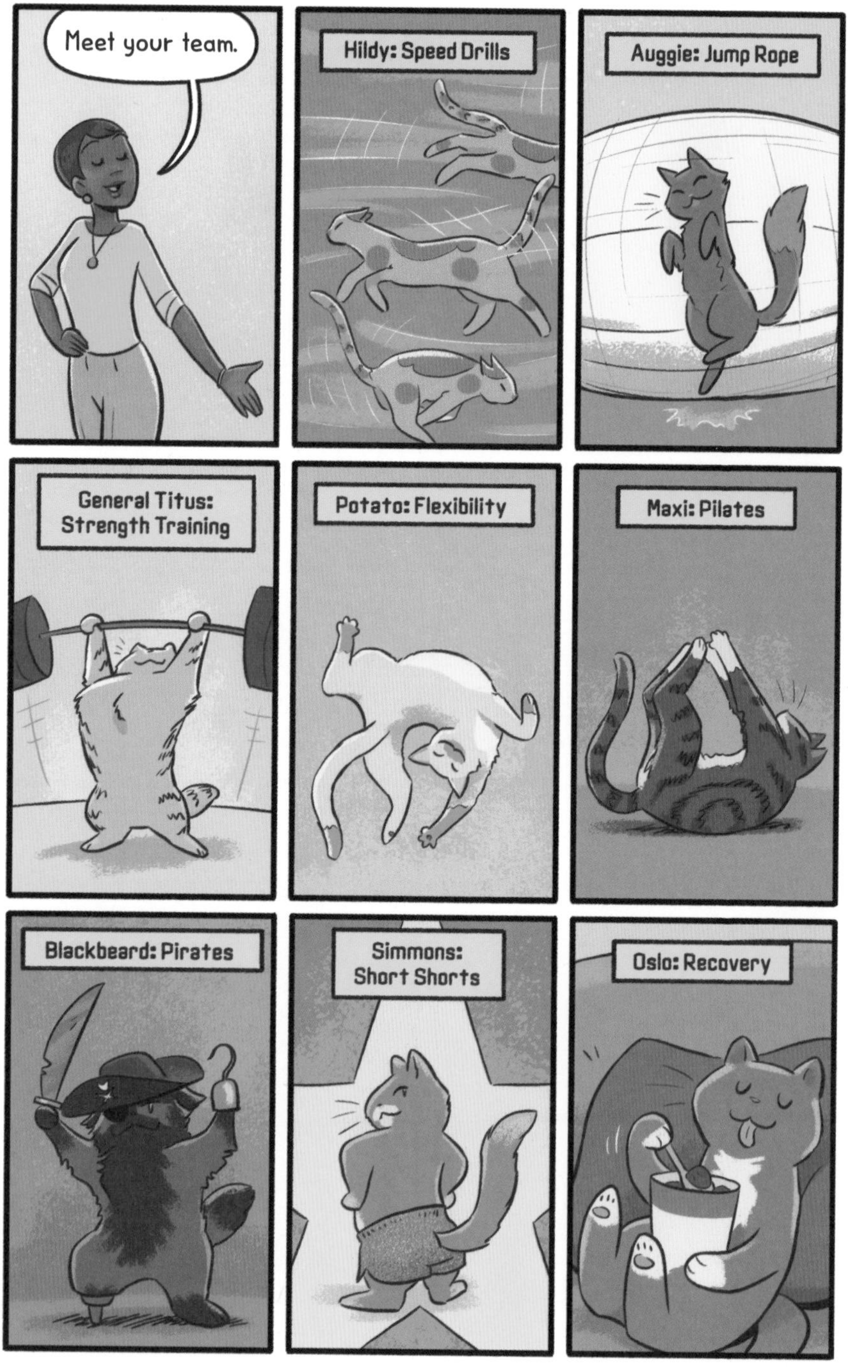
Meet your team.
Hildy: Speed Drills
Auggie: Jump Rope
General Titus: Strength Training
Potato: Flexibility
Maxi: Pilates
Blackbeard: Pirates
Simmons: Short Shorts
Oslo: Recovery

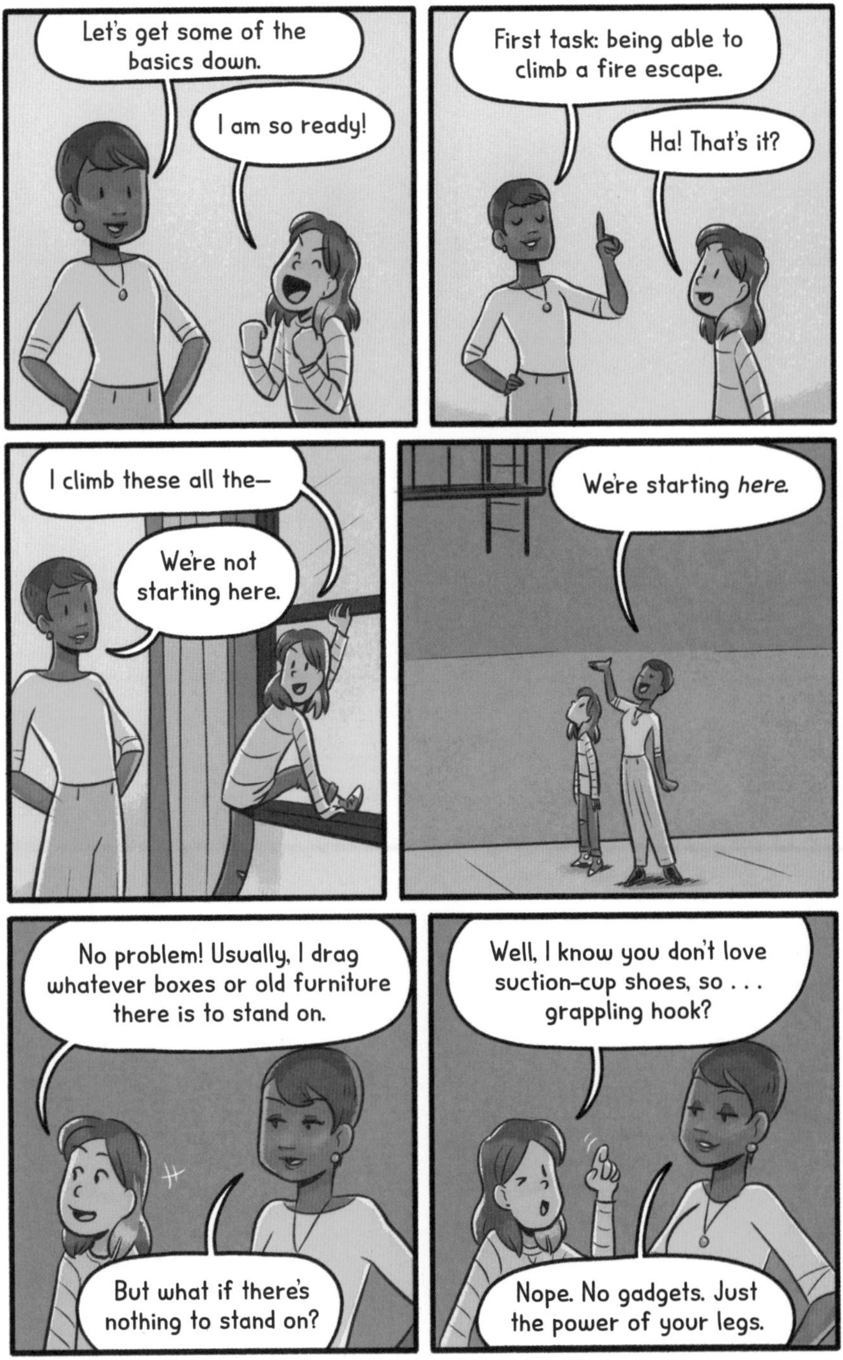
Let's get some of the basics down.
I am so ready!
First task: being able to climb a fire escape.
Ha! That's it?
I climb these all the—
We're not starting here.
We're starting *here*.
No problem! Usually, I drag whatever boxes or old furniture there is to stand on.
But what if there's nothing to stand on?
Well, I know you don't love suction-cup shoes, so . . . grappling hook?
Nope. No gadgets. Just the power of your legs.

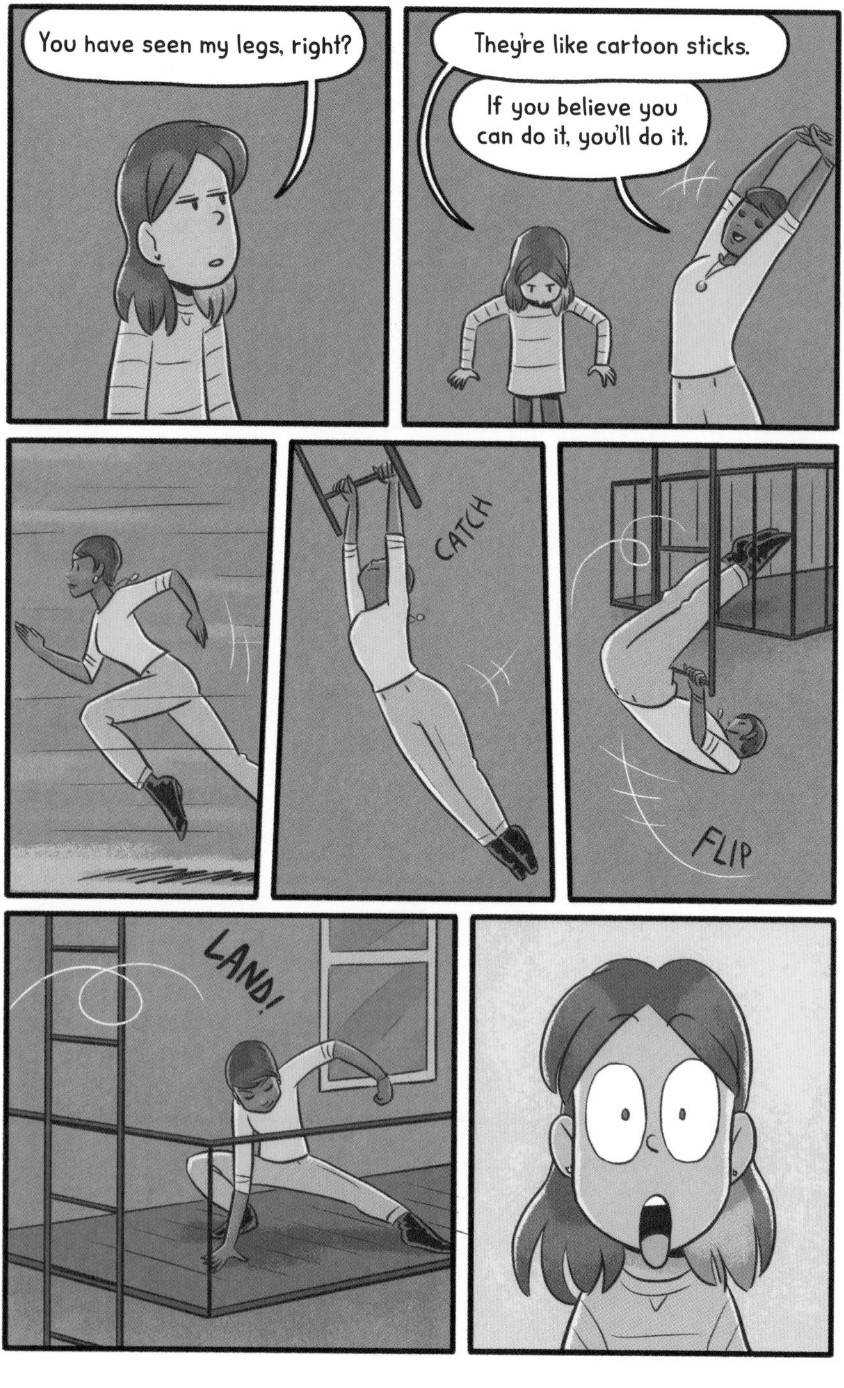
You have seen my legs, right?
They're like cartoon sticks.
If you believe you can do it, you'll do it.
CATCH
FLIP
LAND!

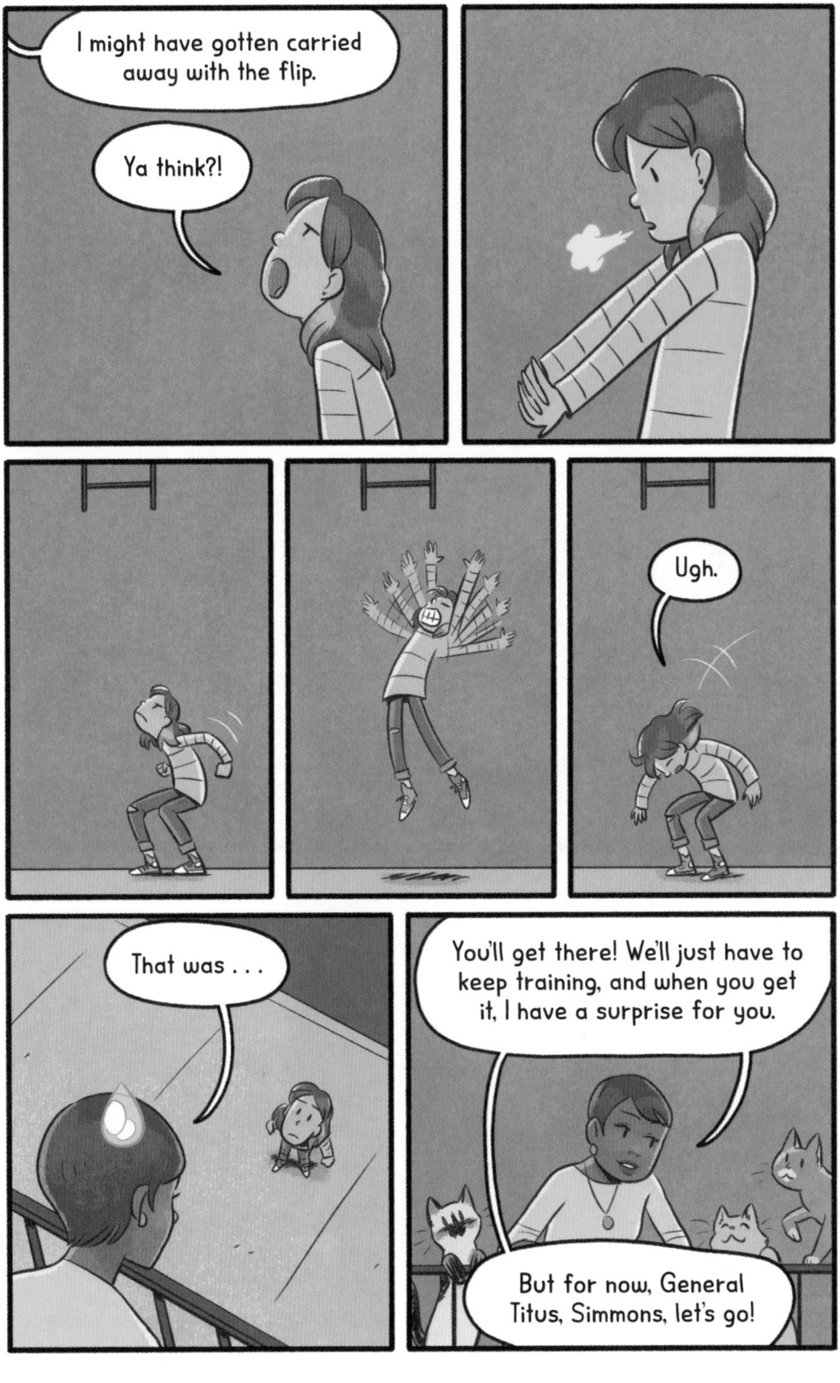
I might have gotten carried away with the flip.
Ya think?!
Ugh.
That was . . .
You'll get there! We'll just have to keep training, and when you get it, I have a surprise for you.
But for now, General Titus, Simmons, let's go!

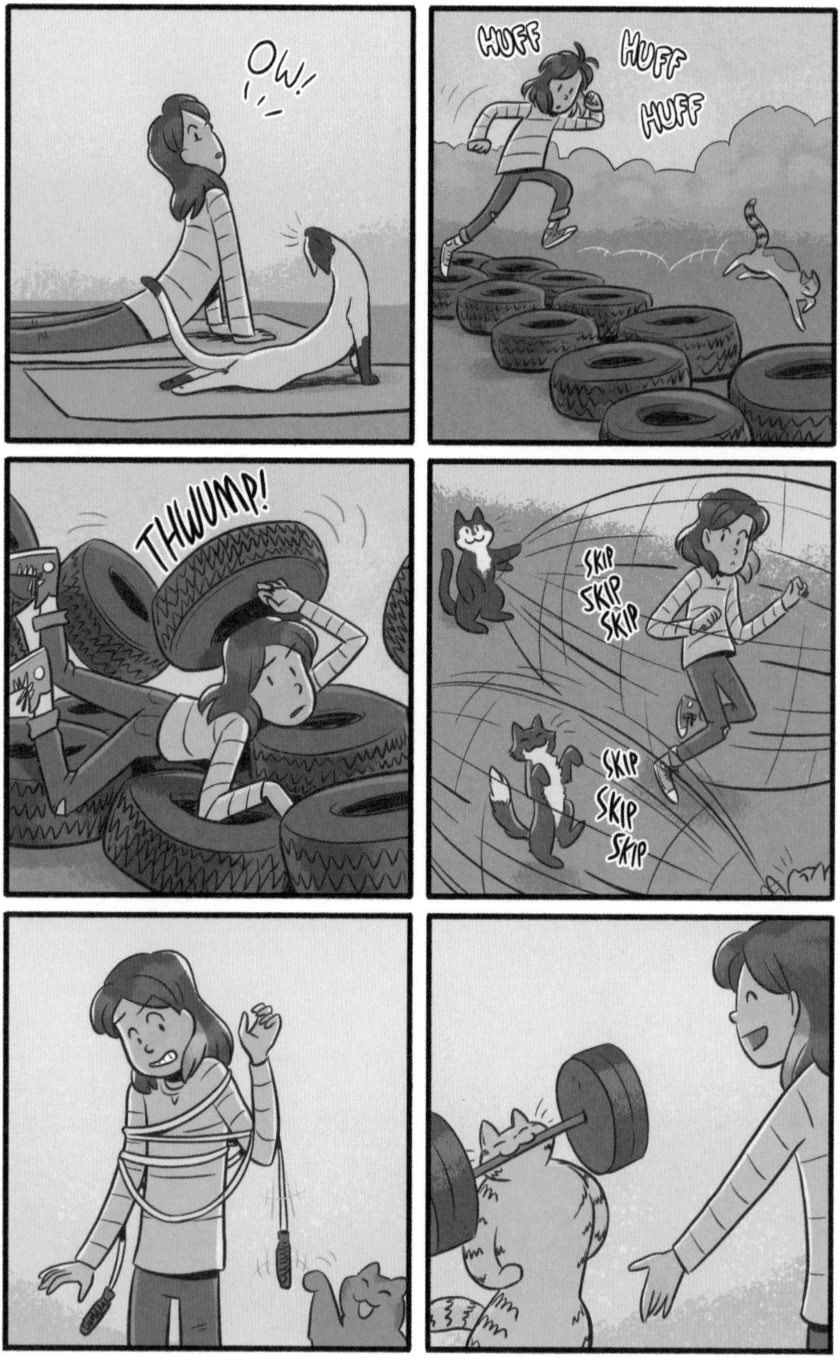
OW!
HUFF
HUFF
HUFF
THWUMP!
SKIP
SKIP
SKIP
SKIP
SKIP
SKIP

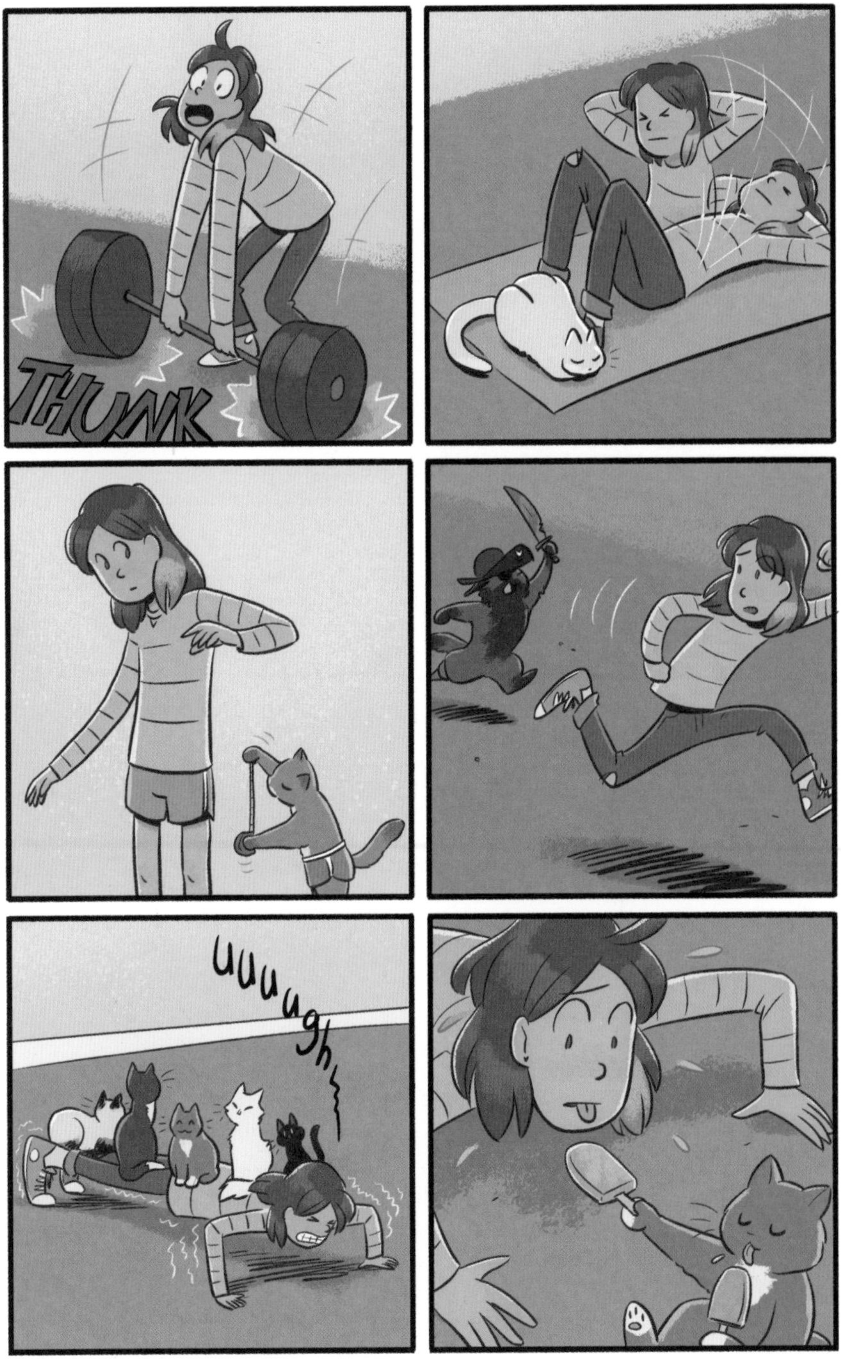
THUNK
uuuugh

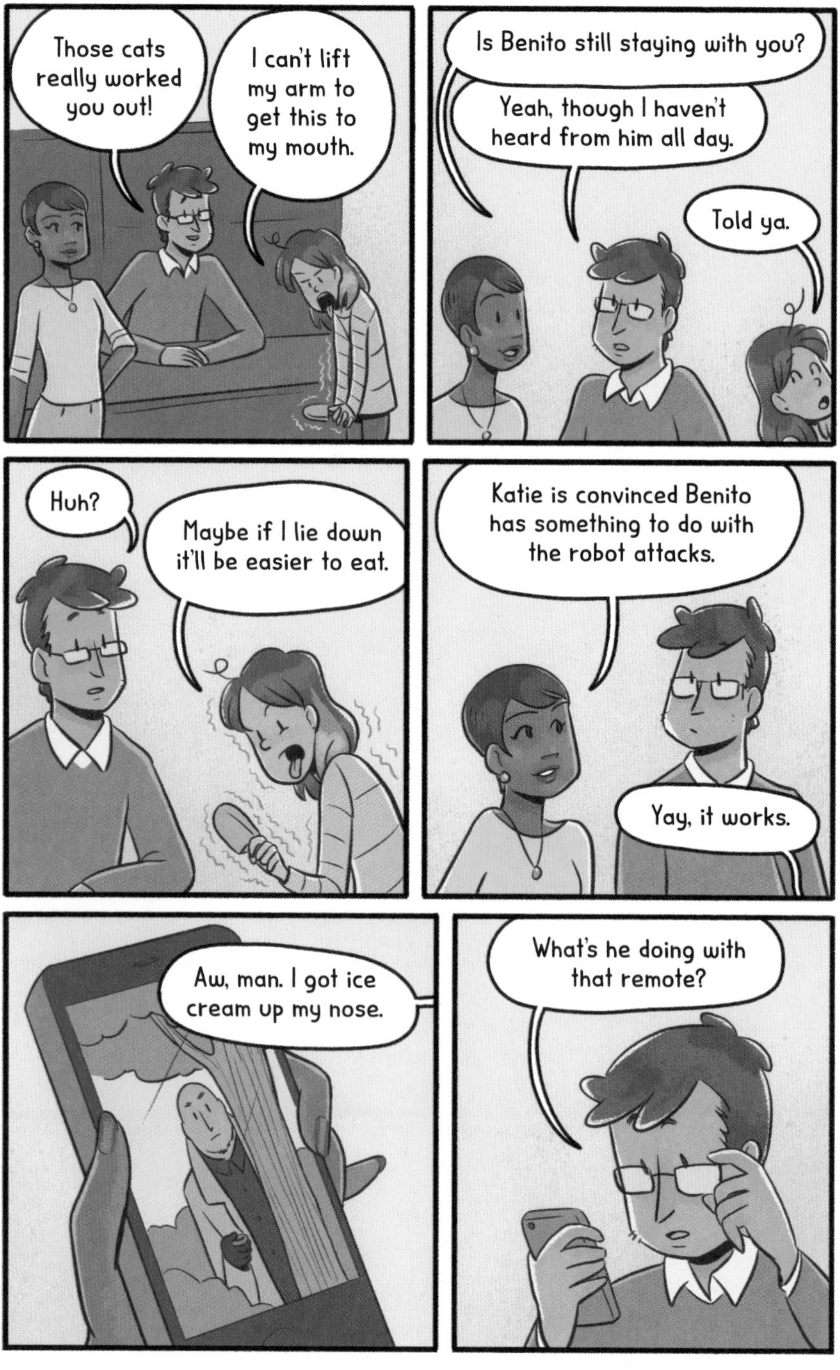
Those cats really worked you out!
I can't lift my arm to get this to my mouth.
Is Benito still staying with you?
Yeah, though I haven't heard from him all day.
Told ya.
Huh?
Maybe if I lie down it'll be easier to eat.
Katie is convinced Benito has something to do with the robot attacks.
Yay, it works.
Aw, man. I got ice cream up my nose.
What's he doing with that remote?

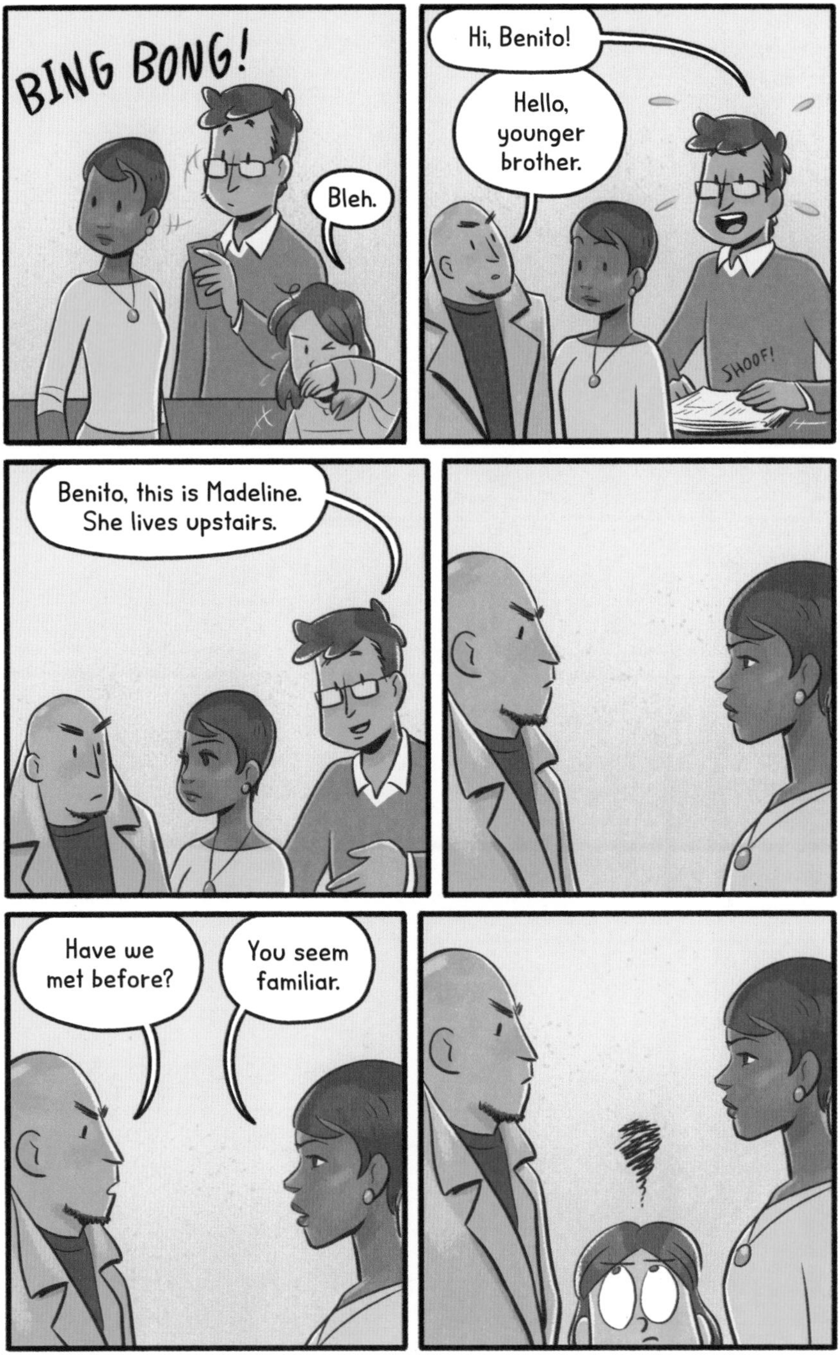
BING BONG!
Bleh.
Hi, Benito!
Hello, younger brother.
SHOOF!
Benito, this is Madeline. She lives upstairs.
Have we met before?
You seem familiar.

CHAPTER FOUR

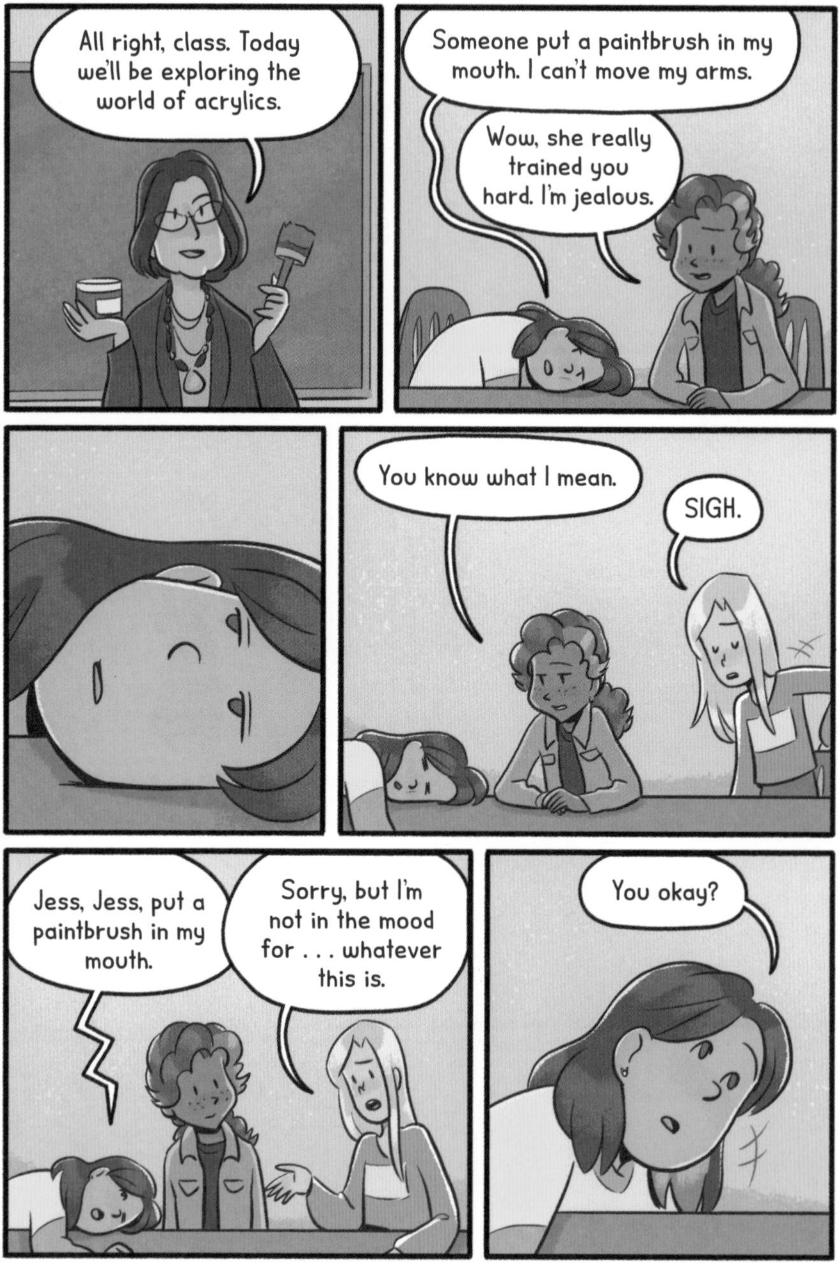
All right, class. Today we'll be exploring the world of acrylics.
Someone put a paintbrush in my mouth. I can't move my arms.
Wow, she really trained you hard. I'm jealous.
You know what I mean.
SIGH.
Jess, Jess, put a paintbrush in my mouth.
Sorry, but I'm not in the mood for . . . whatever this is.
You okay?

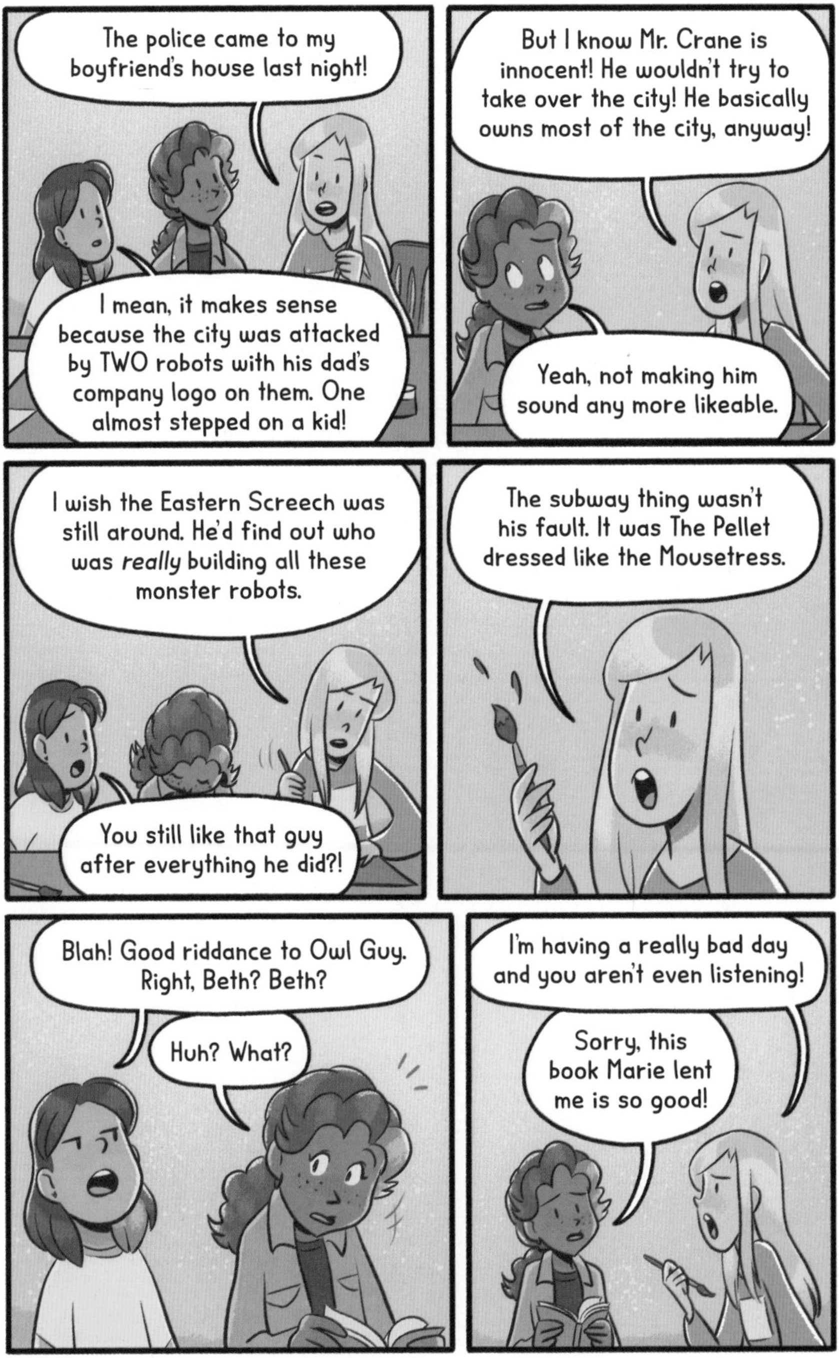
The police came to my boyfriend's house last night!
I mean, it makes sense because the city was attacked by TWO robots with his dad's company logo on them. One almost stepped on a kid!
But I know Mr. Crane is innocent! He wouldn't try to take over the city! He basically owns most of the city, anyway!
Yeah, not making him sound any more likeable.
I wish the Eastern Screech was still around. He'd find out who was *really* building all these monster robots.
You still like that guy after everything he did?!
The subway thing wasn't his fault. It was The Pellet dressed like the Mousetress.
Blah! Good riddance to Owl Guy. Right, Beth? Beth?
Huh? What?
I'm having a really bad day and you aren't even listening!
Sorry, this book Marie lent me is so good!

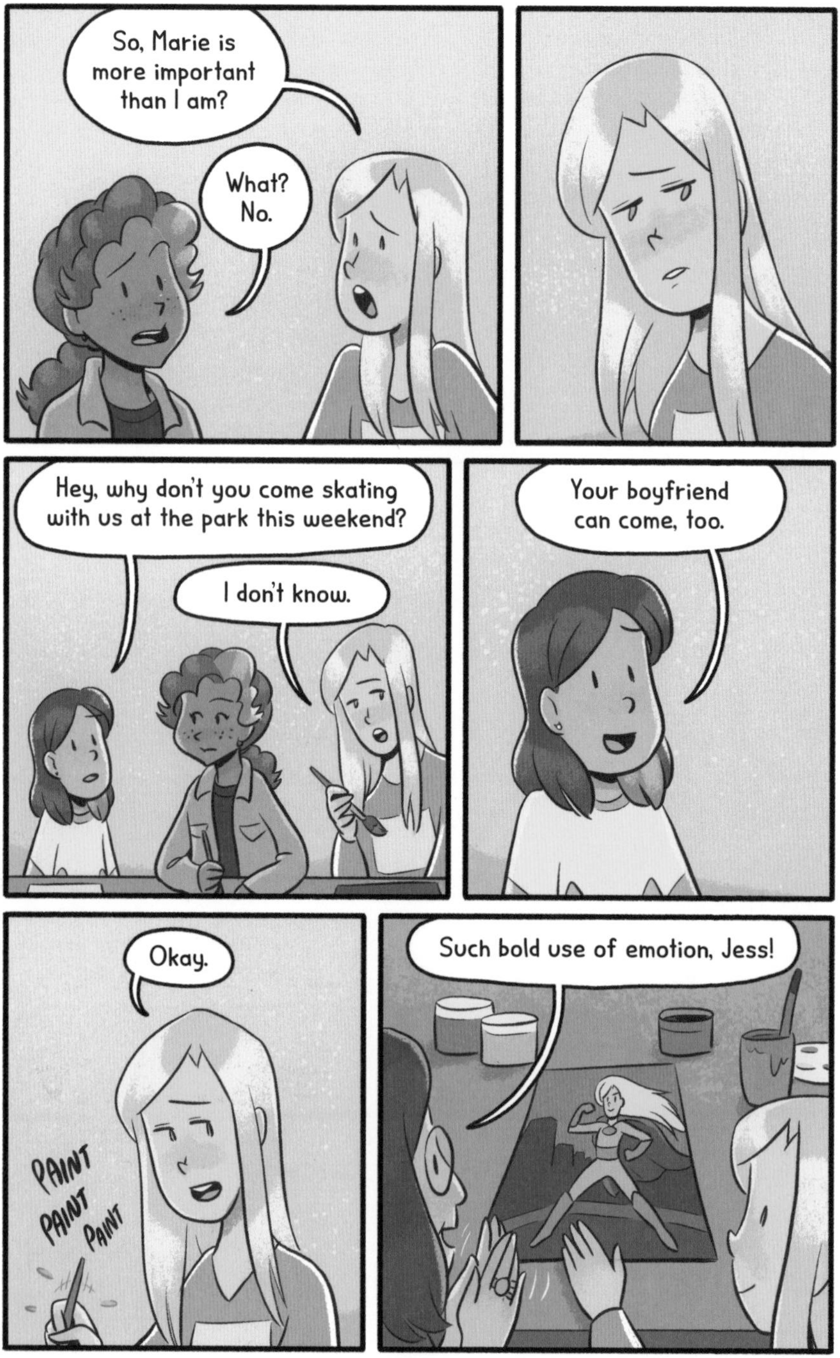
So, Marie is more important than I am?
What? No.
Hey, why don't you come skating with us at the park this weekend?
I don't know.
Your boyfriend can come, too.
Okay.
PAINT
PAINT
PAINT
Such bold use of emotion, Jess!

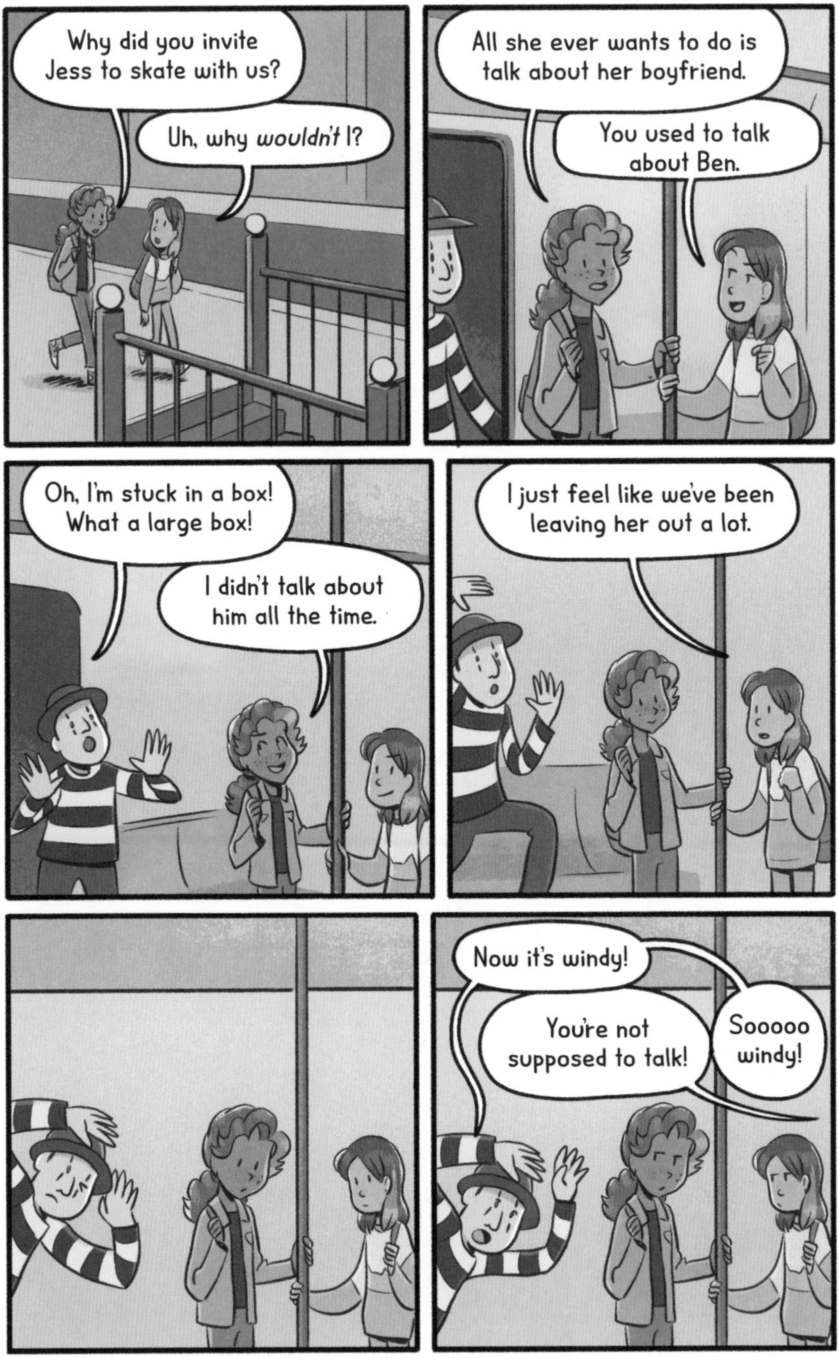
Why did you invite Jess to skate with us?
Uh, why *wouldn't* I?
All she ever wants to do is talk about her boyfriend.
You used to talk about Ben.
Oh, I'm stuck in a box! What a large box!
I didn't talk about him all the time.
I just feel like we've been leaving her out a lot.
Now it's windy!
You're not supposed to talk!
Sooooo windy!

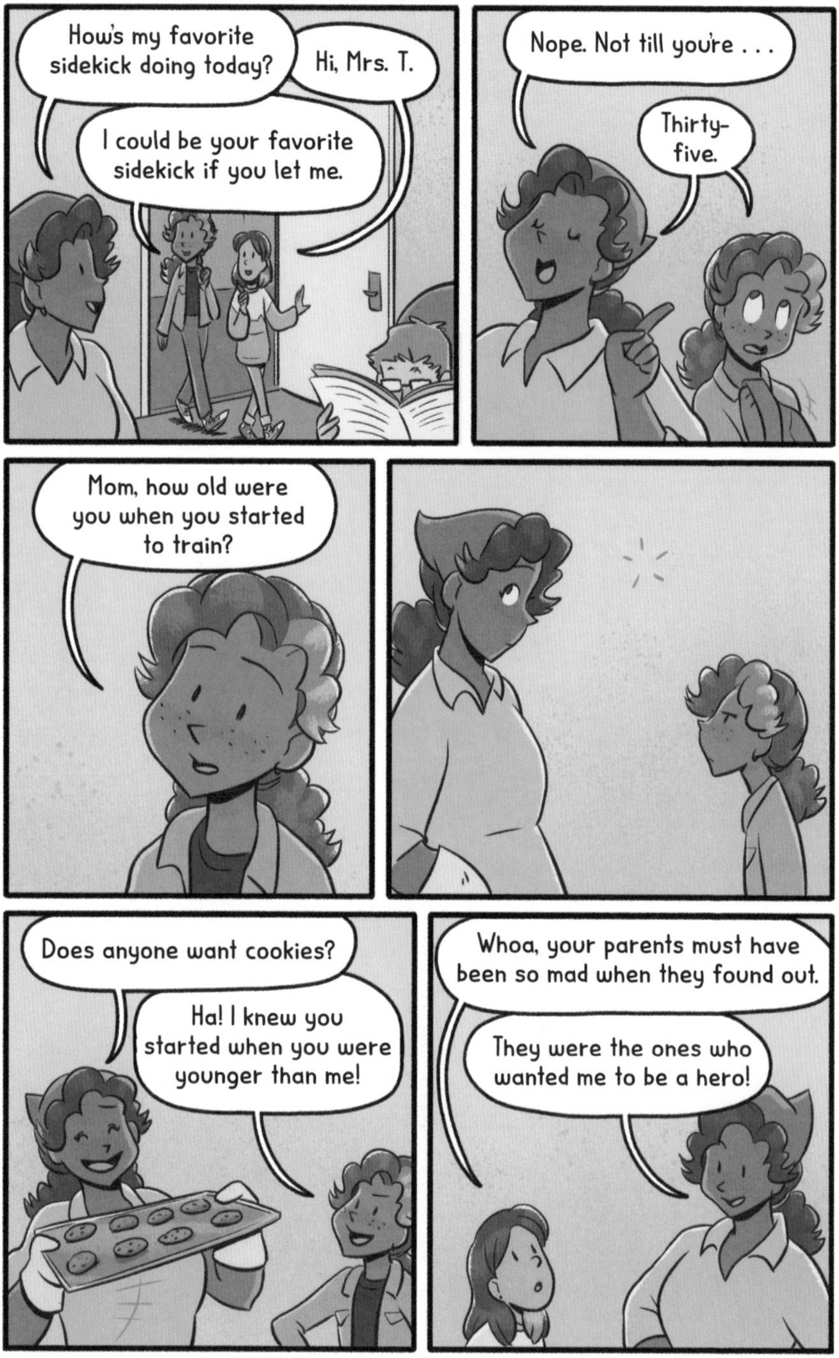
How's my favorite sidekick doing today?
Hi, Mrs. T.
I could be your favorite sidekick if you let me.
Nope. Not till you're . . .
Thirty-five.
Mom, how old were you when you started to train?
Does anyone want cookies?
Ha! I knew you started when you were younger than me!
Whoa, your parents must have been so mad when they found out.
They were the ones who wanted me to be a hero!

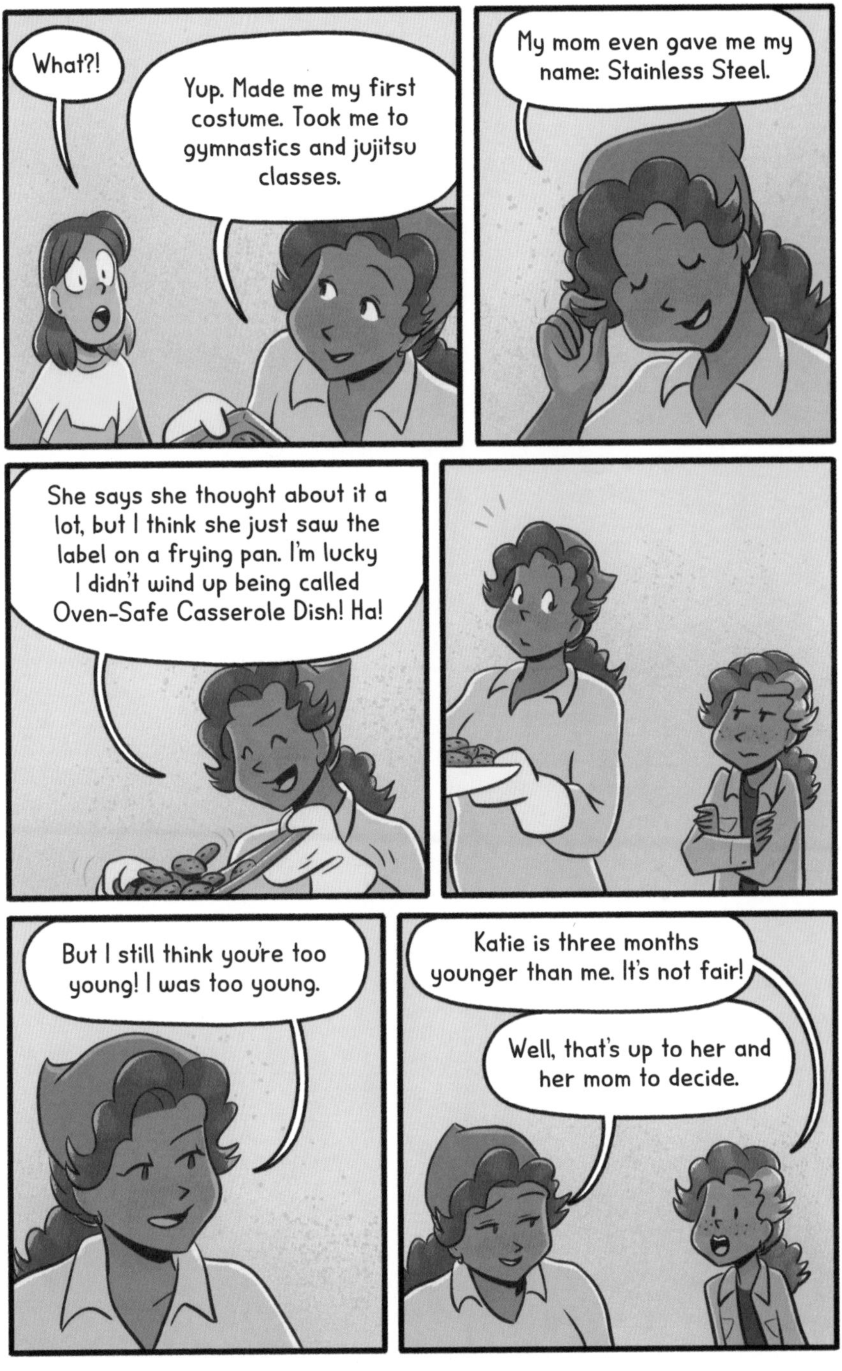
What?!
Yup. Made me my first costume. Took me to gymnastics and jujitsu classes.
My mom even gave me my name: Stainless Steel.
She says she thought about it a lot, but I think she just saw the label on a frying pan. I'm lucky I didn't wind up being called Oven-Safe Casserole Dish! Ha!
But I still think you're too young! I was too young.
Katie is three months younger than me. It's not fair!
Well, that's up to her and her mom to decide.

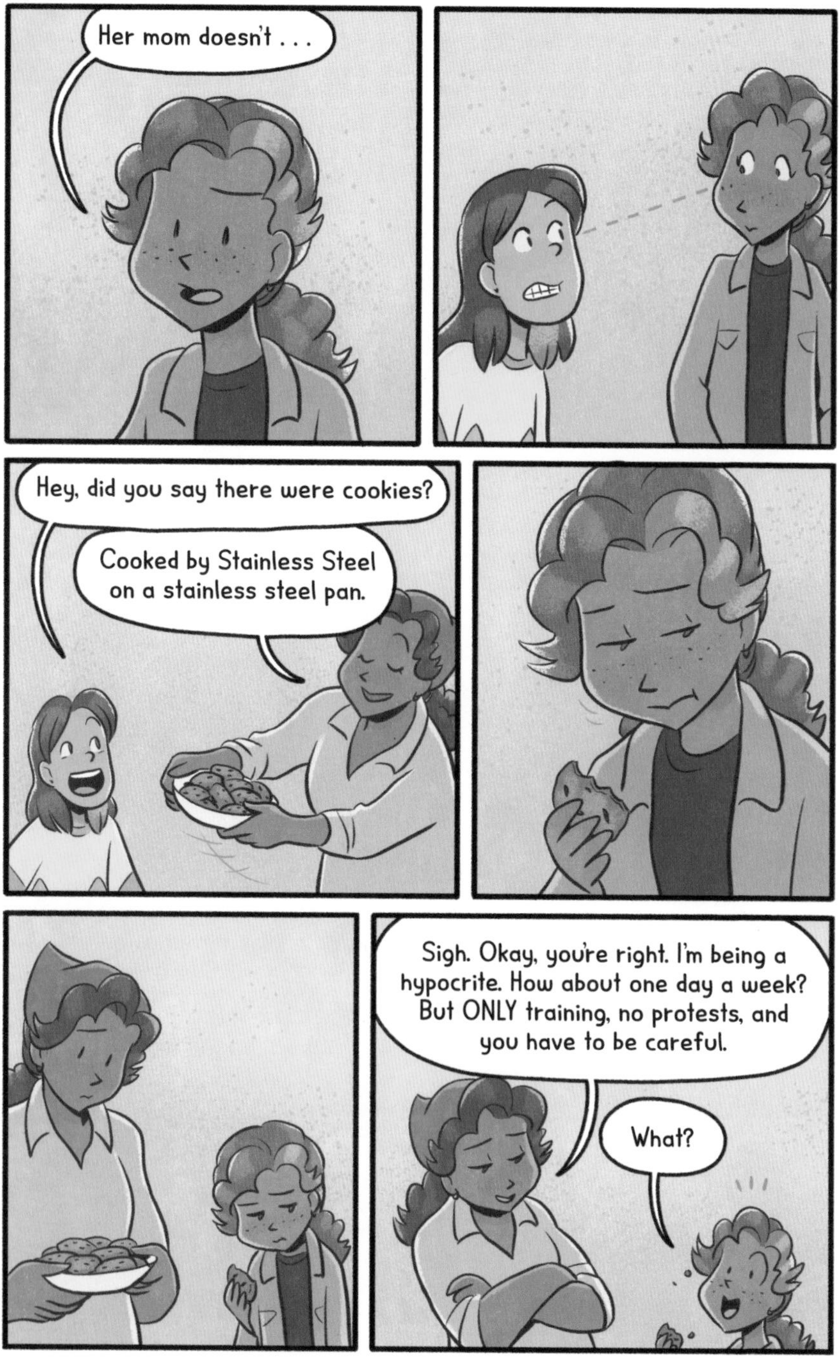
Her mom doesn't . . .
Hey, did you say there were cookies?
Cooked by Stainless Steel on a stainless steel pan.
Sigh. Okay, you're right. I'm being a hypocrite. How about one day a week? But ONLY training, no protests, and you have to be careful.
What?

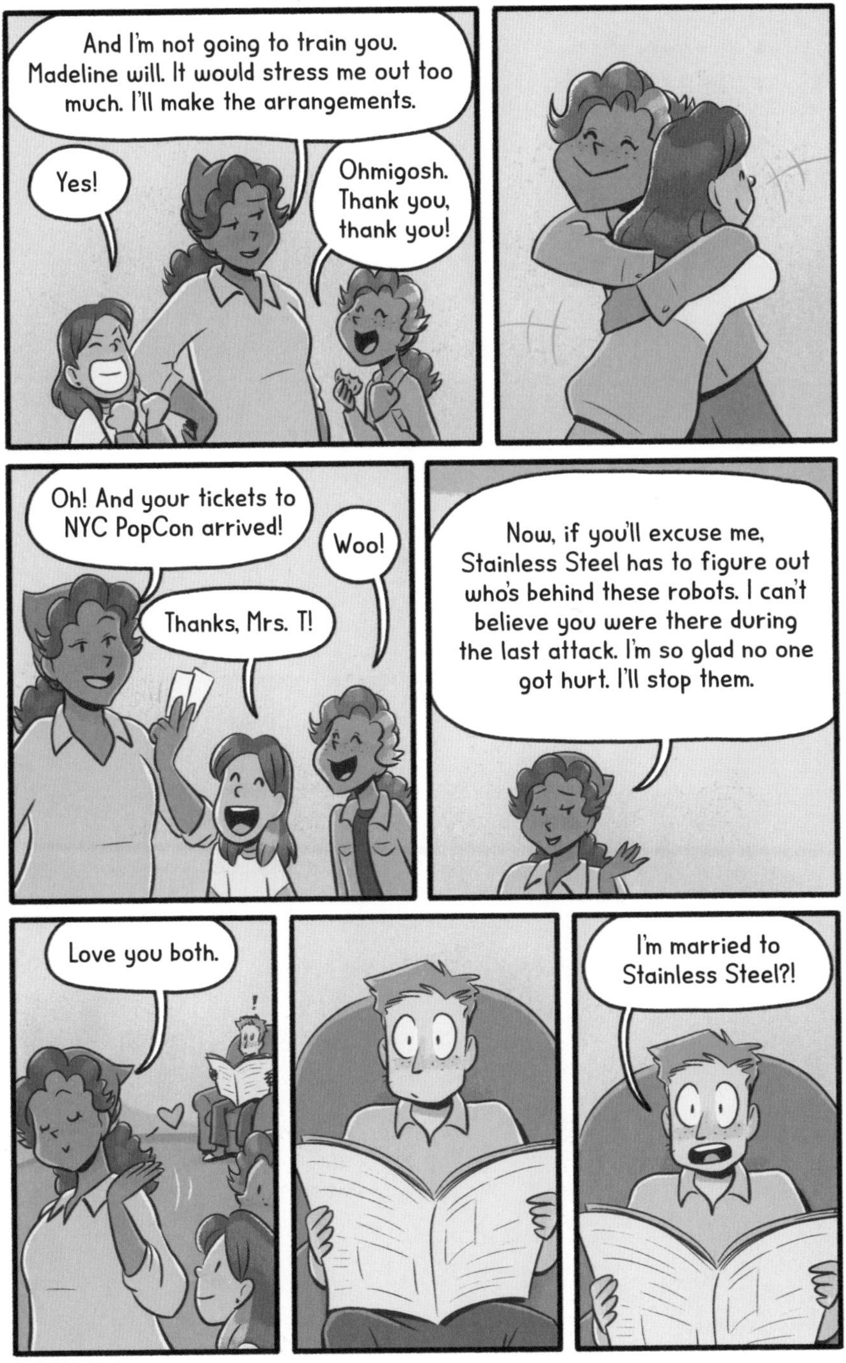
And I'm not going to train you. Madeline will. It would stress me out too much. I'll make the arrangements.
Yes!
Ohmigosh. Thank you, thank you!
Oh! And your tickets to NYC PopCon arrived!
Woo!
Thanks, Mrs. T!
Now, if you'll excuse me, Stainless Steel has to figure out who's behind these robots. I can't believe you were there during the last attack. I'm so glad no one got hurt. I'll stop them.
Love you both.
!
I'm married to Stainless Steel?!

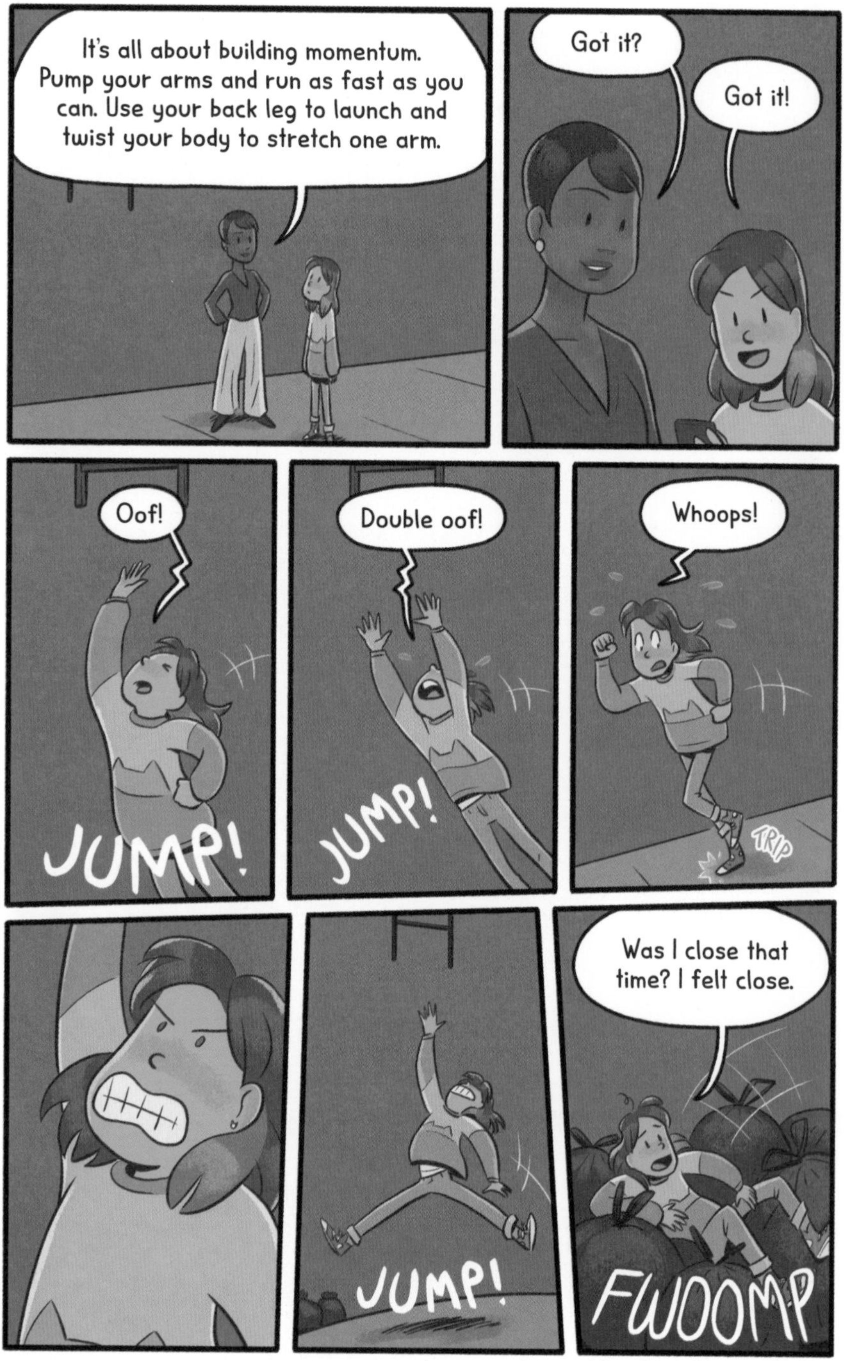
It's all about building momentum. Pump your arms and run as fast as you can. Use your back leg to launch and twist your body to stretch one arm.
Got it?
Got it!
Oof!
JUMP!
Double oof!
JUMP!
Whoops!
TRIP
JUMP!
Was I close that time? I felt close.
FWOOMP

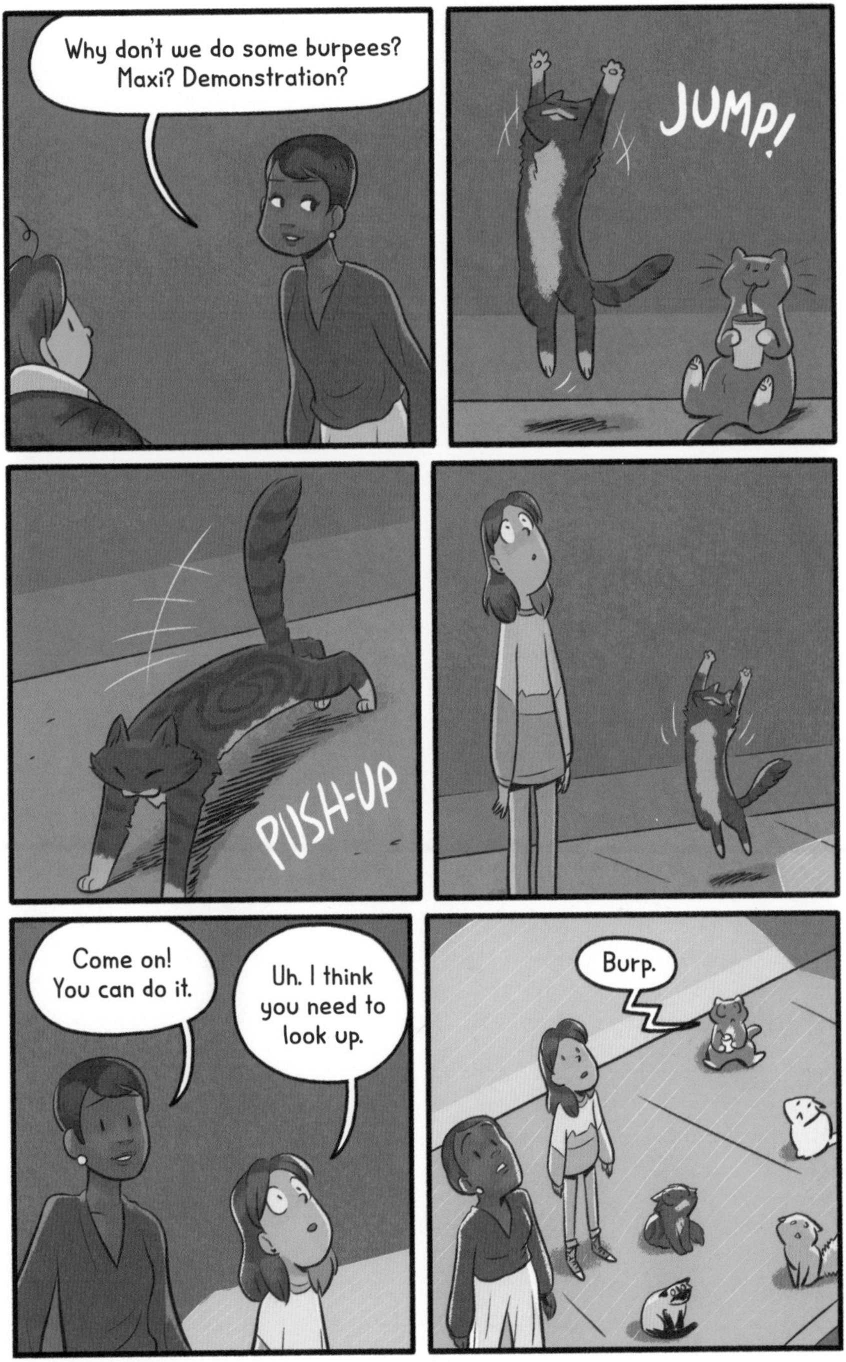
Why don't we do some burpees? Maxi? Demonstration?
JUMP!
PUSH-UP
Come on! You can do it.
Uh. I think you need to look up.
Burp.

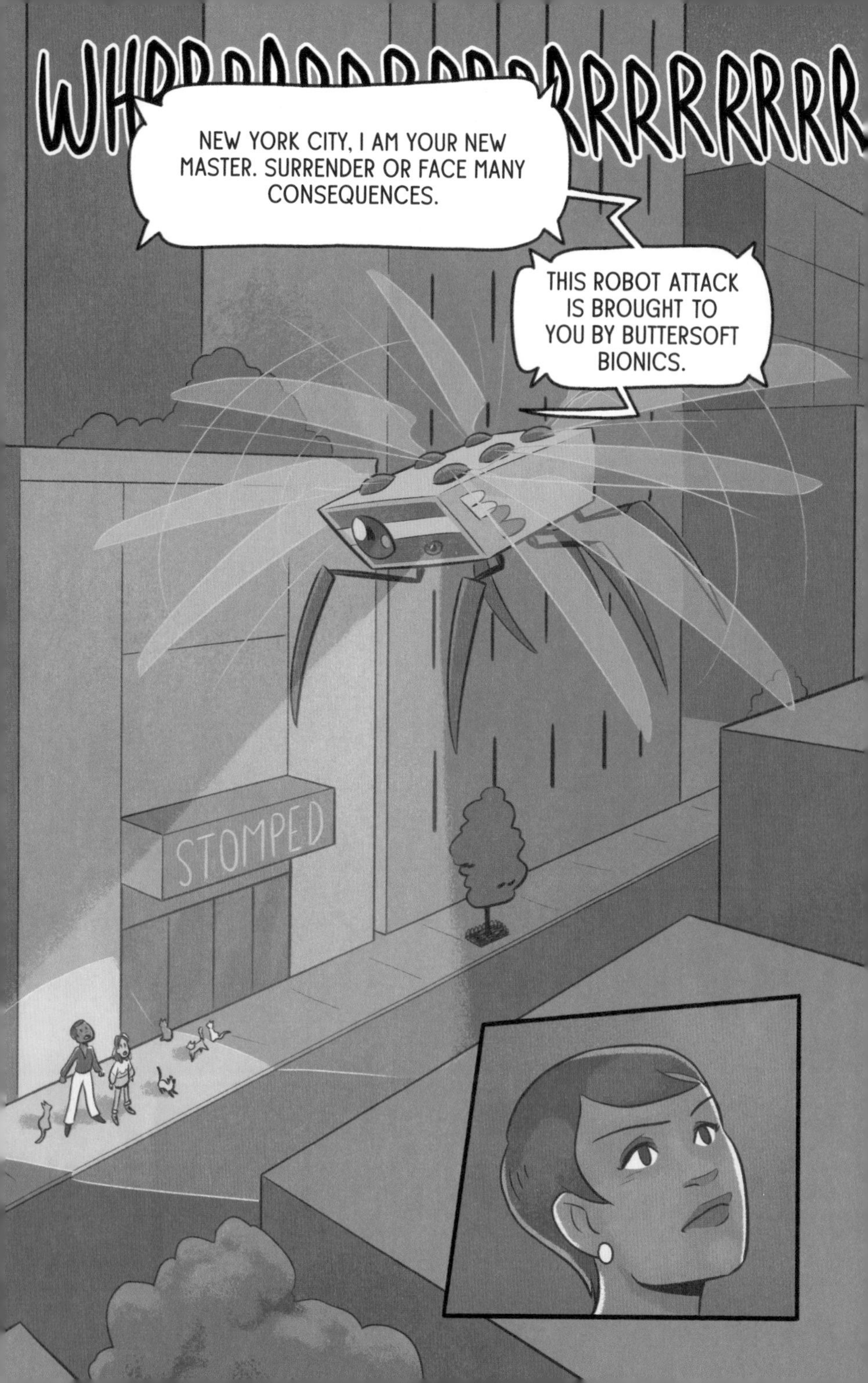
WHRRRRRRRRRRRRRRRRRR
NEW YORK CITY, I AM YOUR NEW MASTER. SURRENDER OR FACE MANY CONSEQUENCES.
THIS ROBOT ATTACK IS BROUGHT TO YOU BY BUTTERSOFT BIONICS.
STOMPED

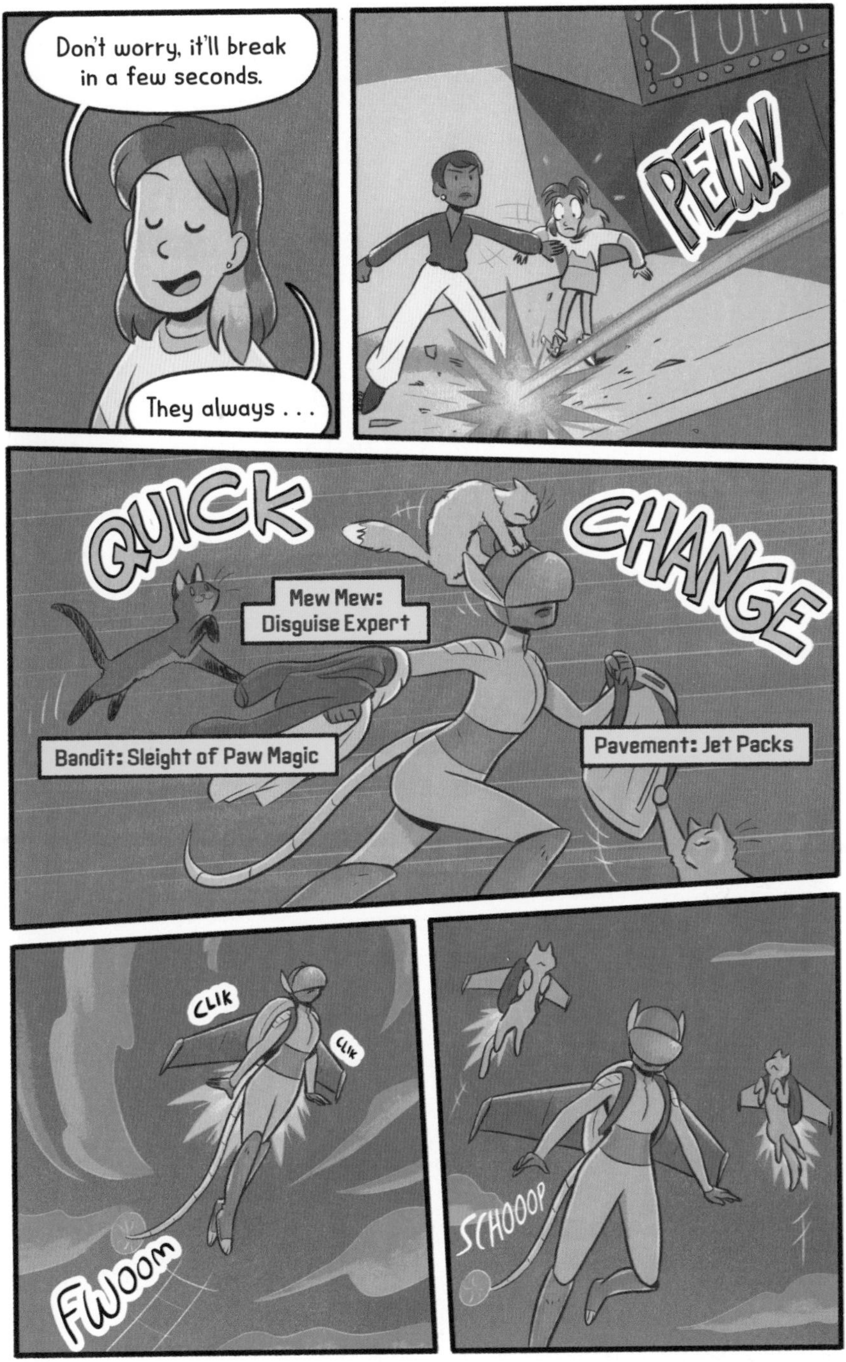
Don't worry, it'll break in a few seconds.
They always . . .
STUM
PEW!
QUICK
CHANGE
Mew Mew: Disguise Expert
Bandit: Sleight of Paw Magic
Pavement: Jet Packs
CLIK
CLIK
FWOOM
SCHOOOP

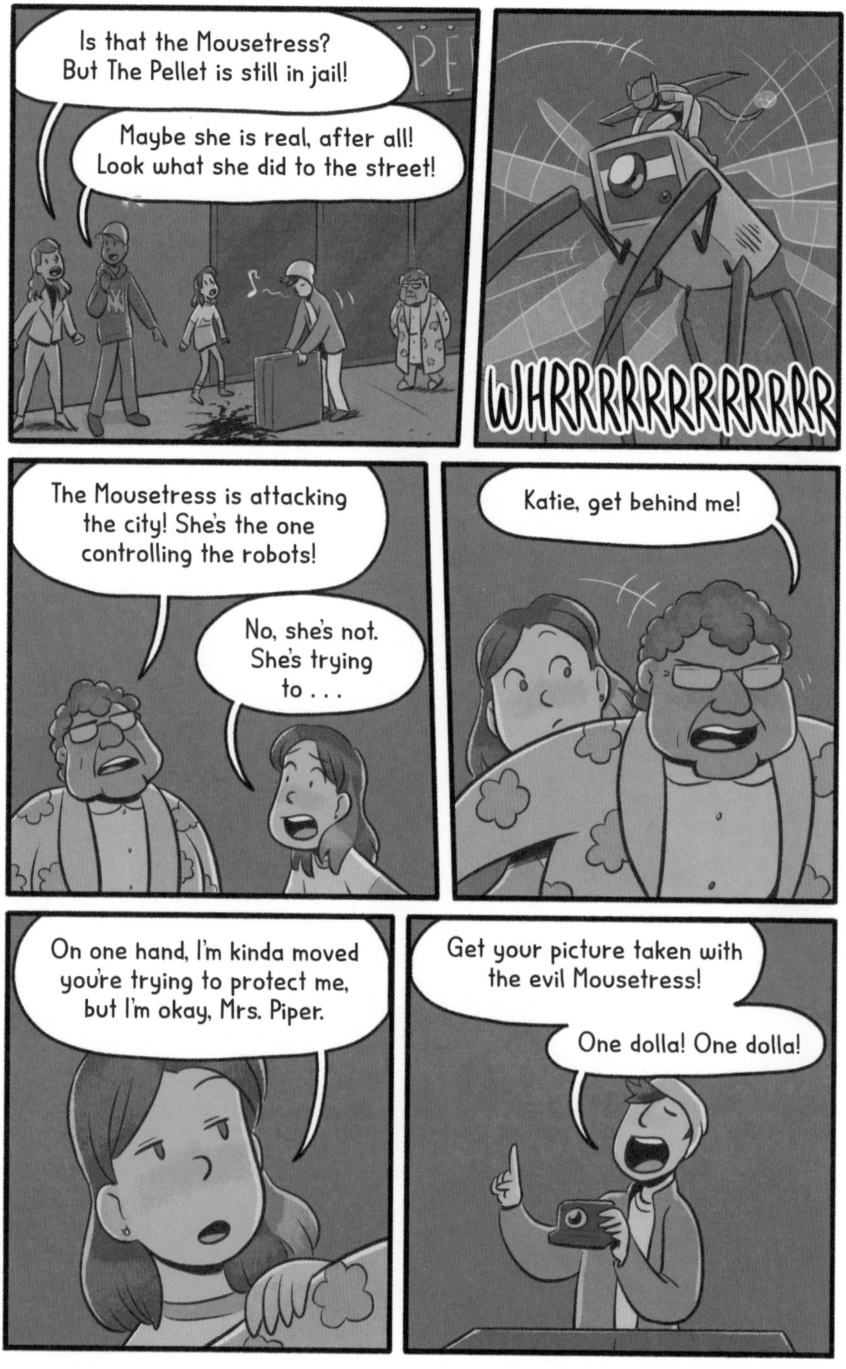
Is that the Mousetress? But The Pellet is still in jail!
Maybe she is real, after all! Look what she did to the street!
WHRRRRRRRRRRR
The Mousetress is attacking the city! She's the one controlling the robots!
No, she's not. She's trying to . . .
Katie, get behind me!
On one hand, I'm kinda moved you're trying to protect me, but I'm okay, Mrs. Piper.
Get your picture taken with the evil Mousetress!
One dolla! One dolla!

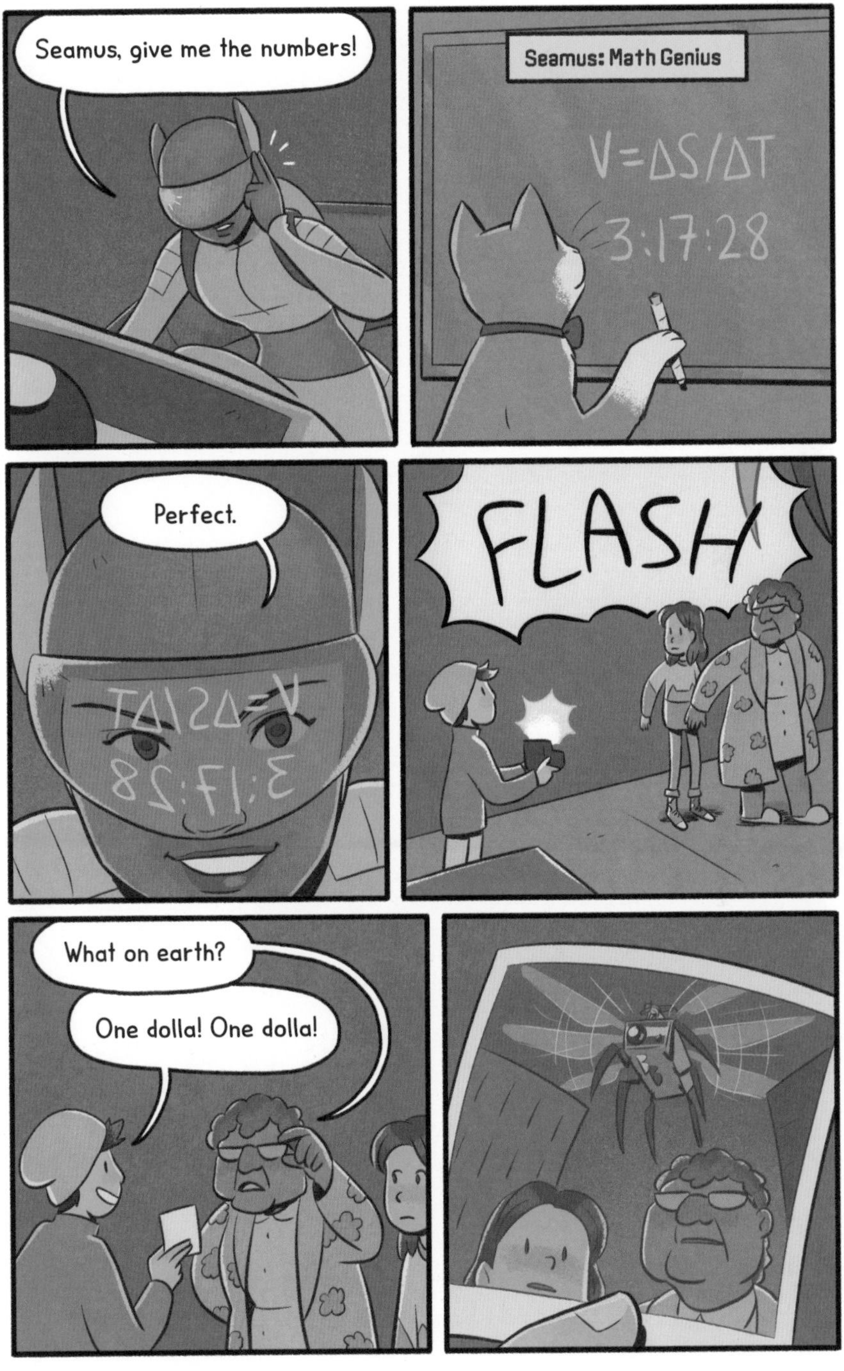
Seamus, give me the numbers!
Seamus: Math Genius
V=ΔS/ΔT
3:17:28
Perfect.
FLASH
What on earth?
One dolla! One dolla!

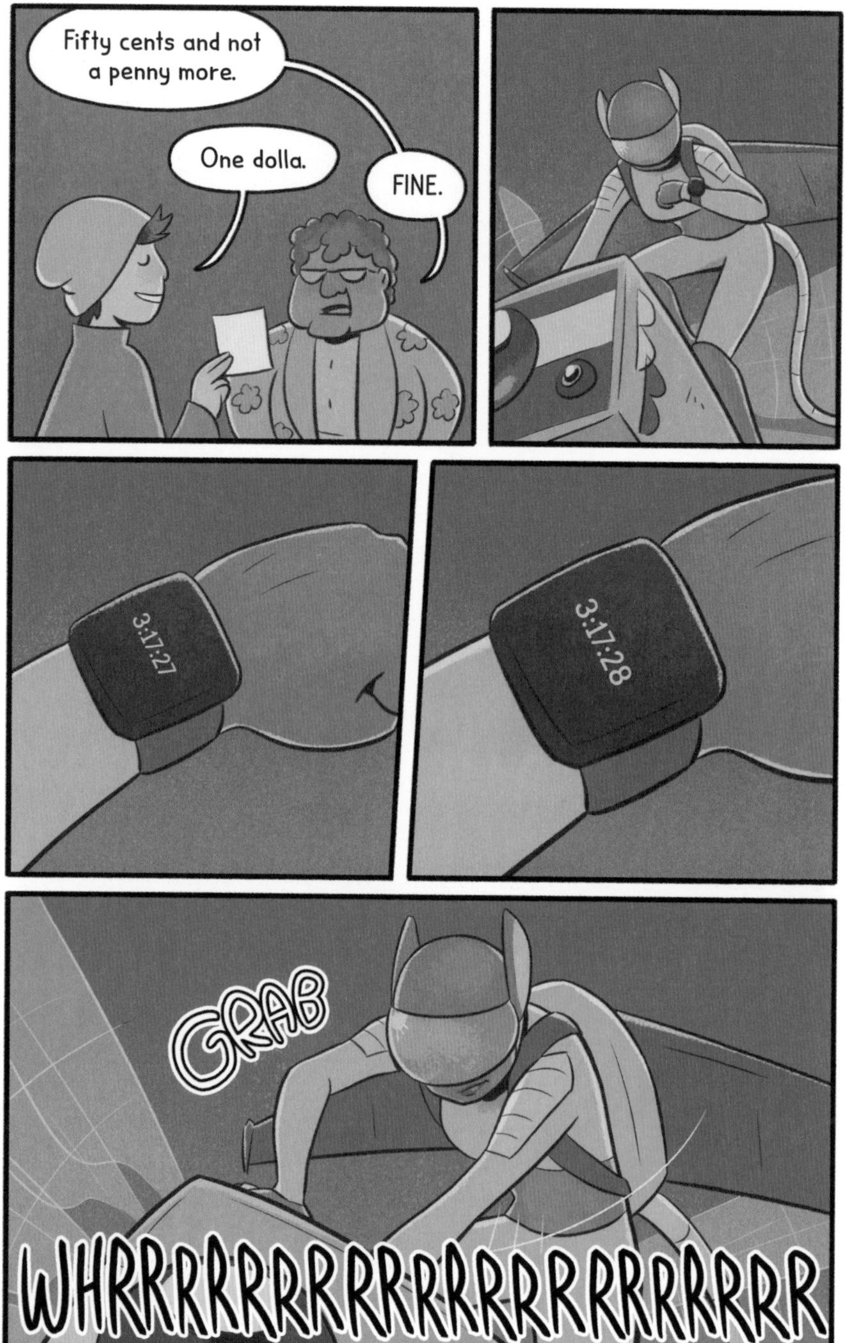
Fifty cents and not a penny more.
One dolla.
FINE.
3:17:27
3:17:28
GRAB
WHRRRRRRRRRRRRRRRRRRRRR

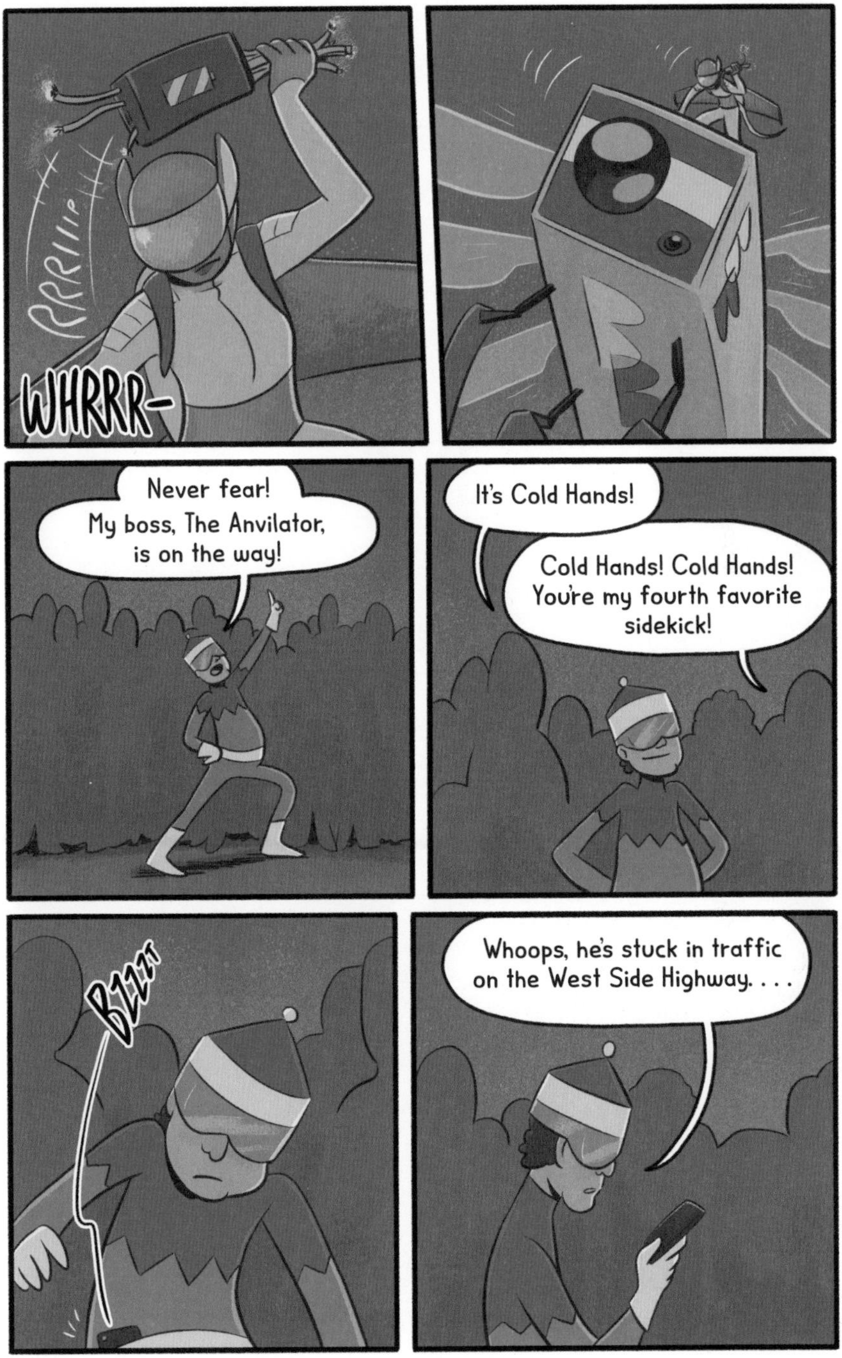
PRRIIIP
WHRRR-
Never fear! My boss, The Anvilator, is on the way!
It's Cold Hands!
Cold Hands! Cold Hands! You're my fourth favorite sidekick!
BZZZT
Whoops, he's stuck in traffic on the West Side Highway. . . .

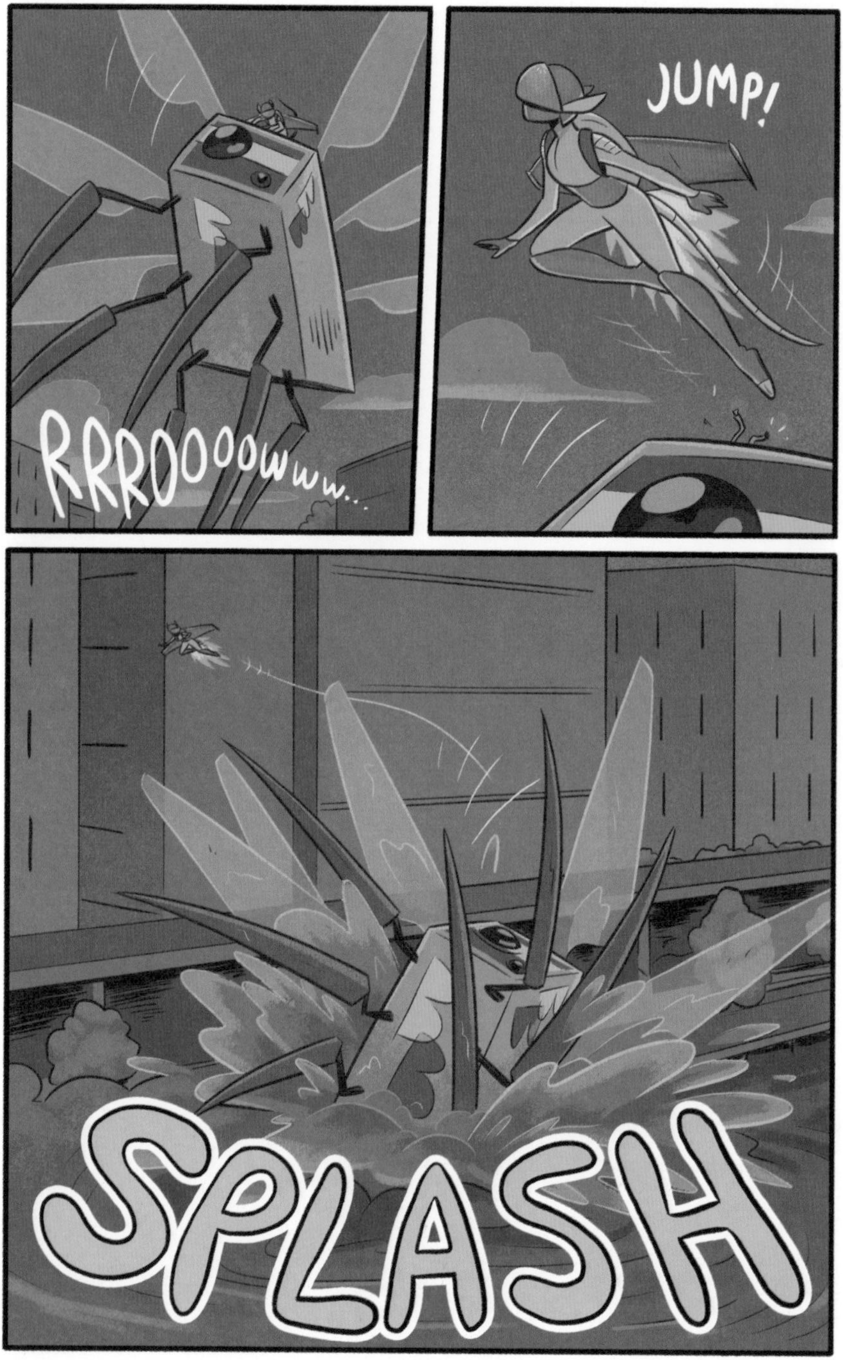
RRROOOOwwww...
JUMP!
SPLASH

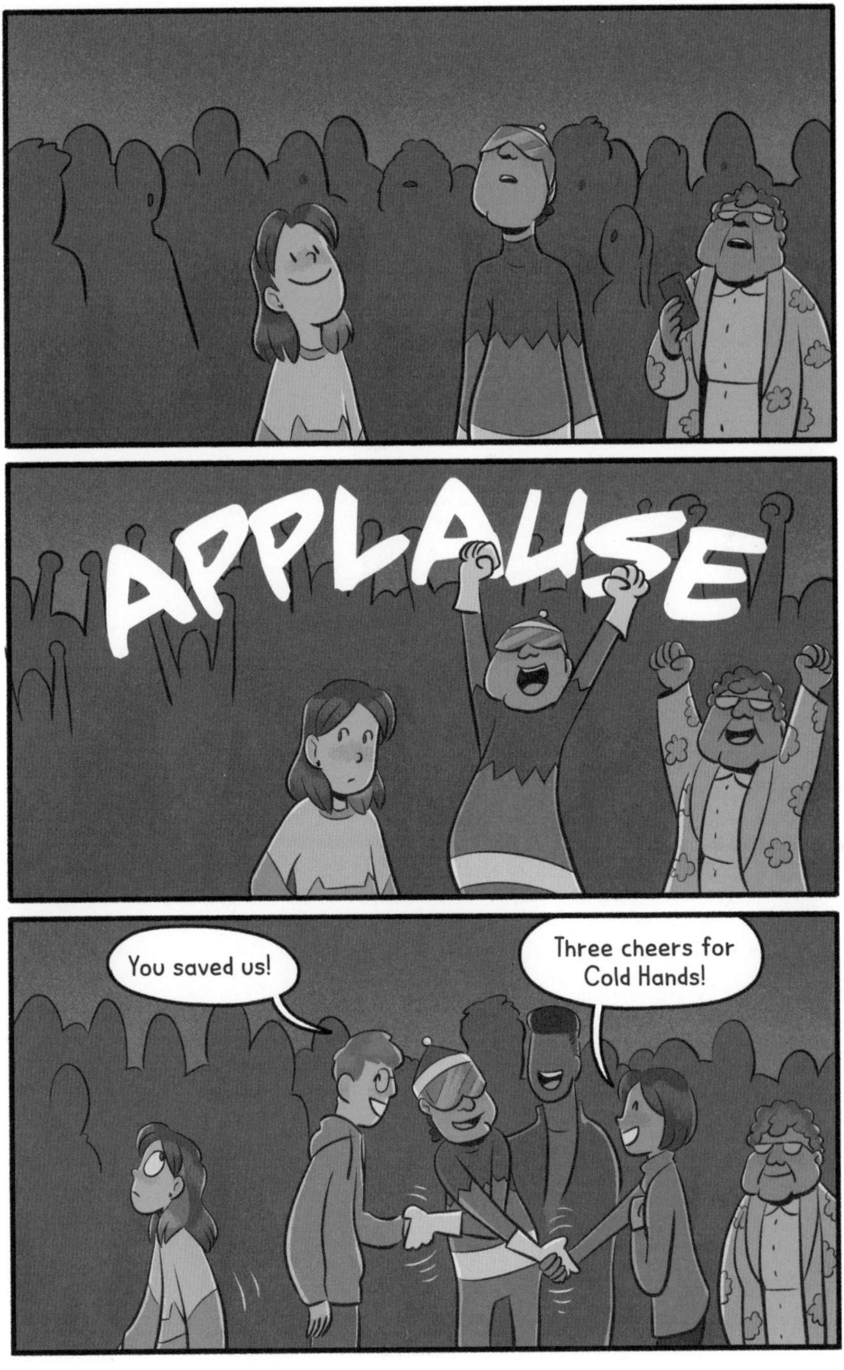
APPLAUSE
You saved us!
Three cheers for Cold Hands!

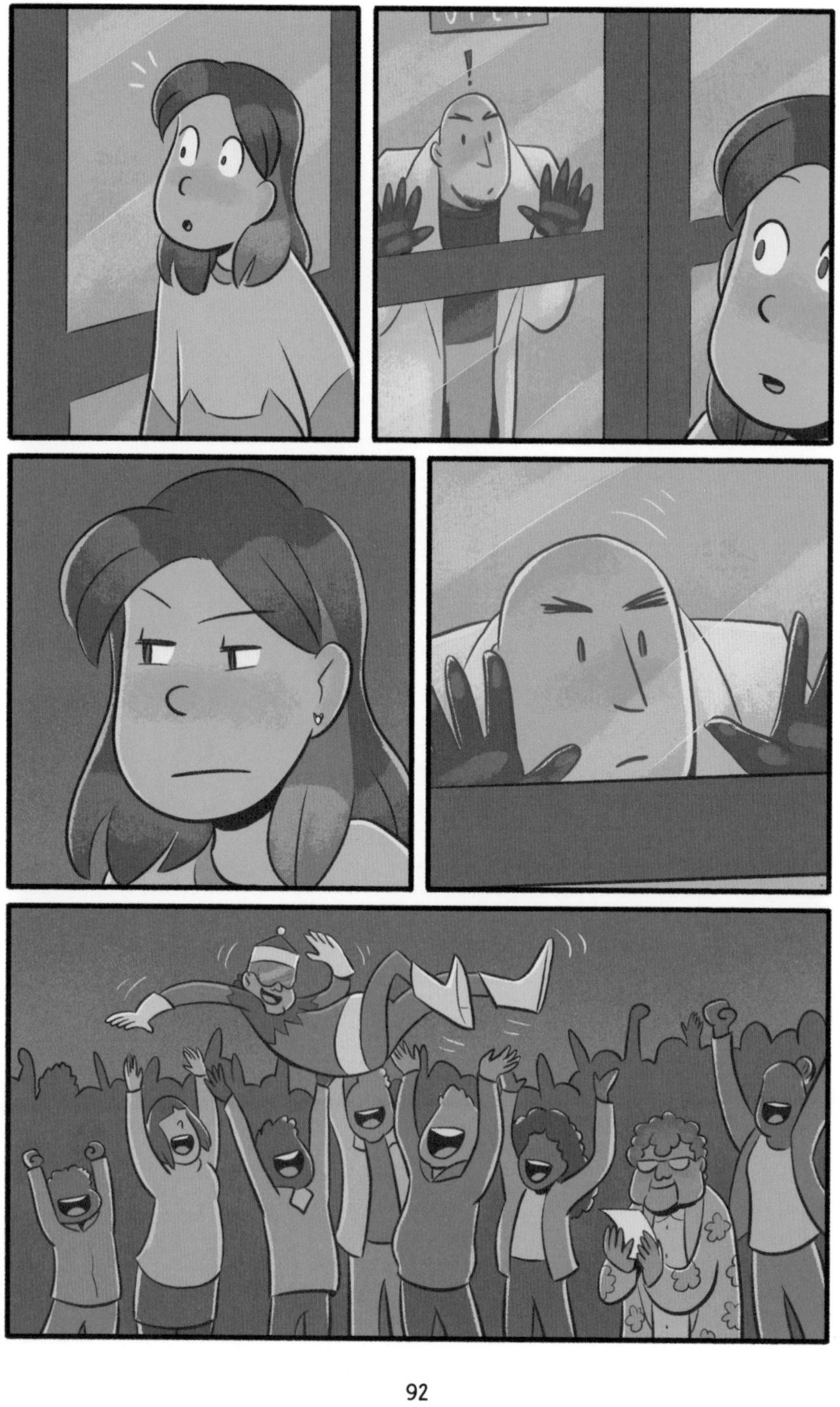

CHAPTER FIVE

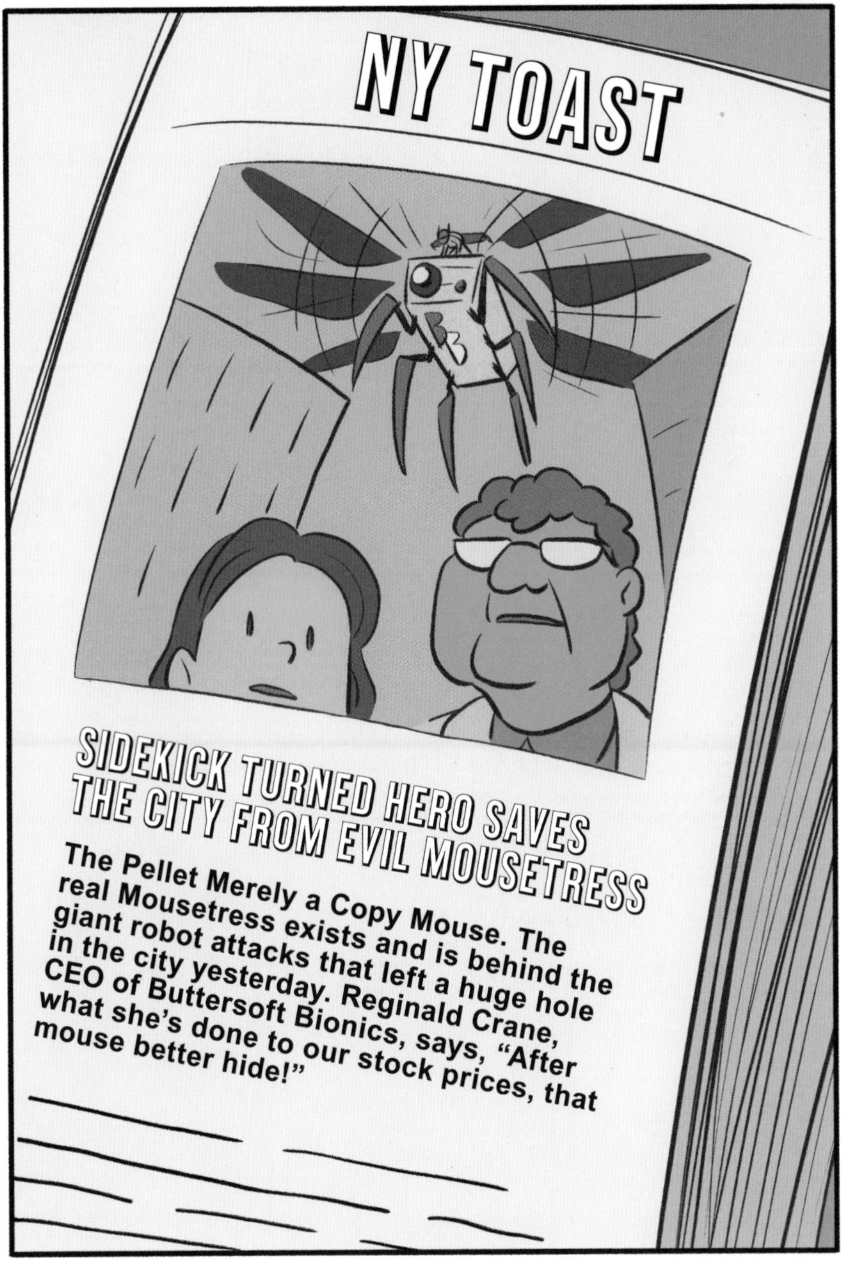
NY TOAST
SIDEKICK TURNED HERO SAVES THE CITY FROM EVIL MOUSETRESS
The Pellet Merely a Copy Mouse. The real Mousetress exists and is behind the giant robot attacks that left a huge hole in the city yesterday. Reginald Crane, CEO of Buttersoft Bionics, says, "After what she's done to our stock prices, that mouse better hide!"

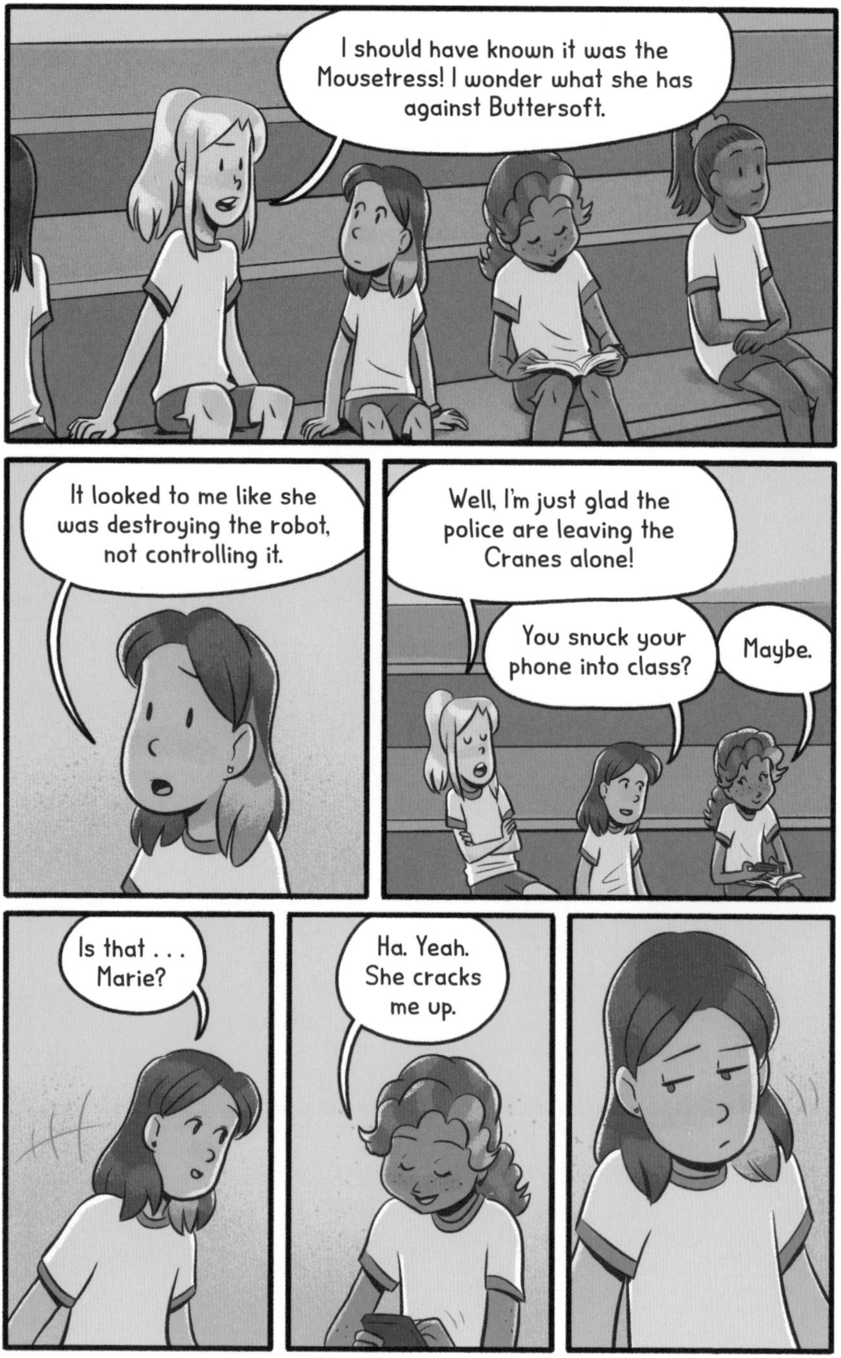
I should have known it was the Mousetress! I wonder what she has against Buttersoft.
It looked to me like she was destroying the robot, not controlling it.
Well, I'm just glad the police are leaving the Cranes alone!
You snuck your phone into class?
Maybe.
Is that . . . Marie?
Ha. Yeah. She cracks me up.

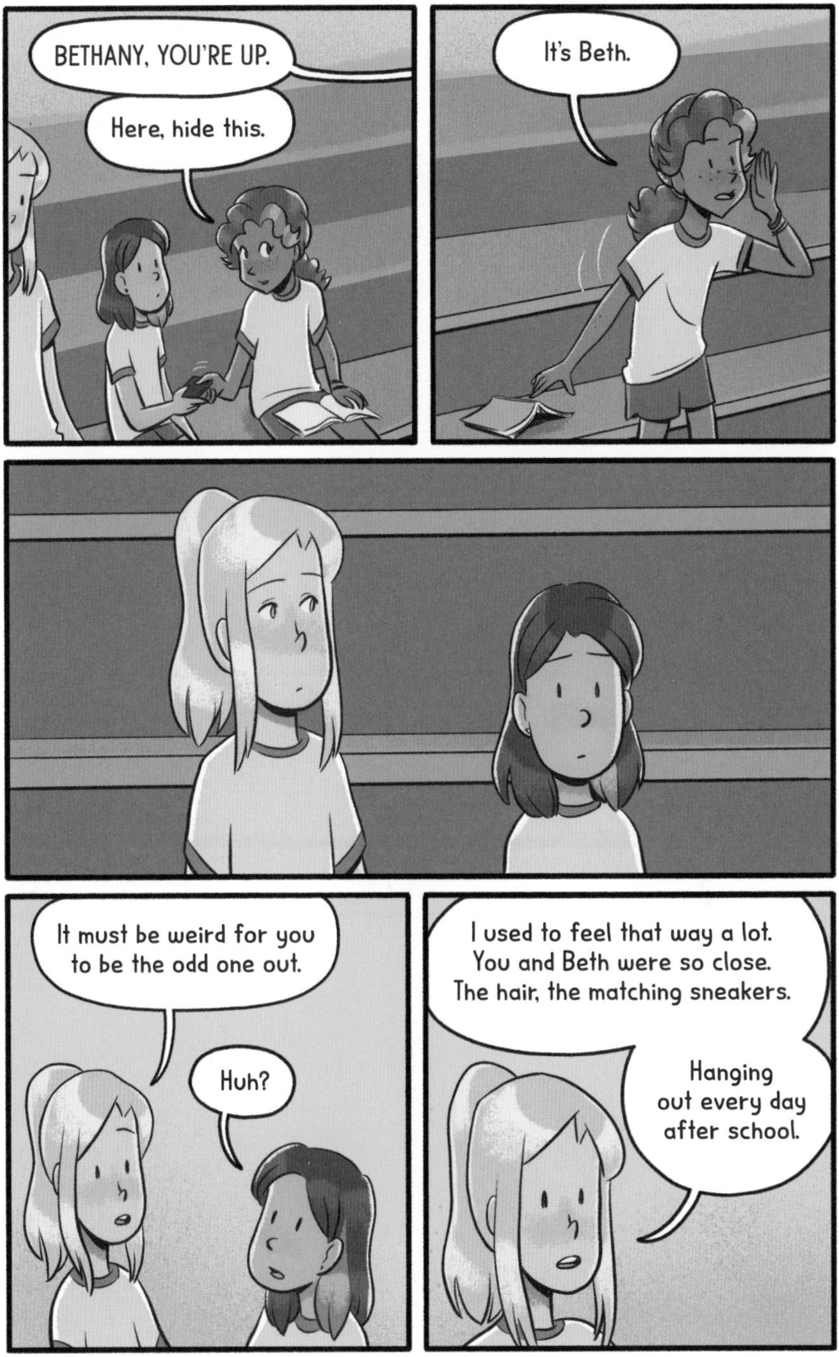
BETHANY, YOU'RE UP.
Here, hide this.
It's Beth.
It must be weird for you to be the odd one out.
Huh?
I used to feel that way a lot. You and Beth were so close. The hair, the matching sneakers.
Hanging out every day after school.

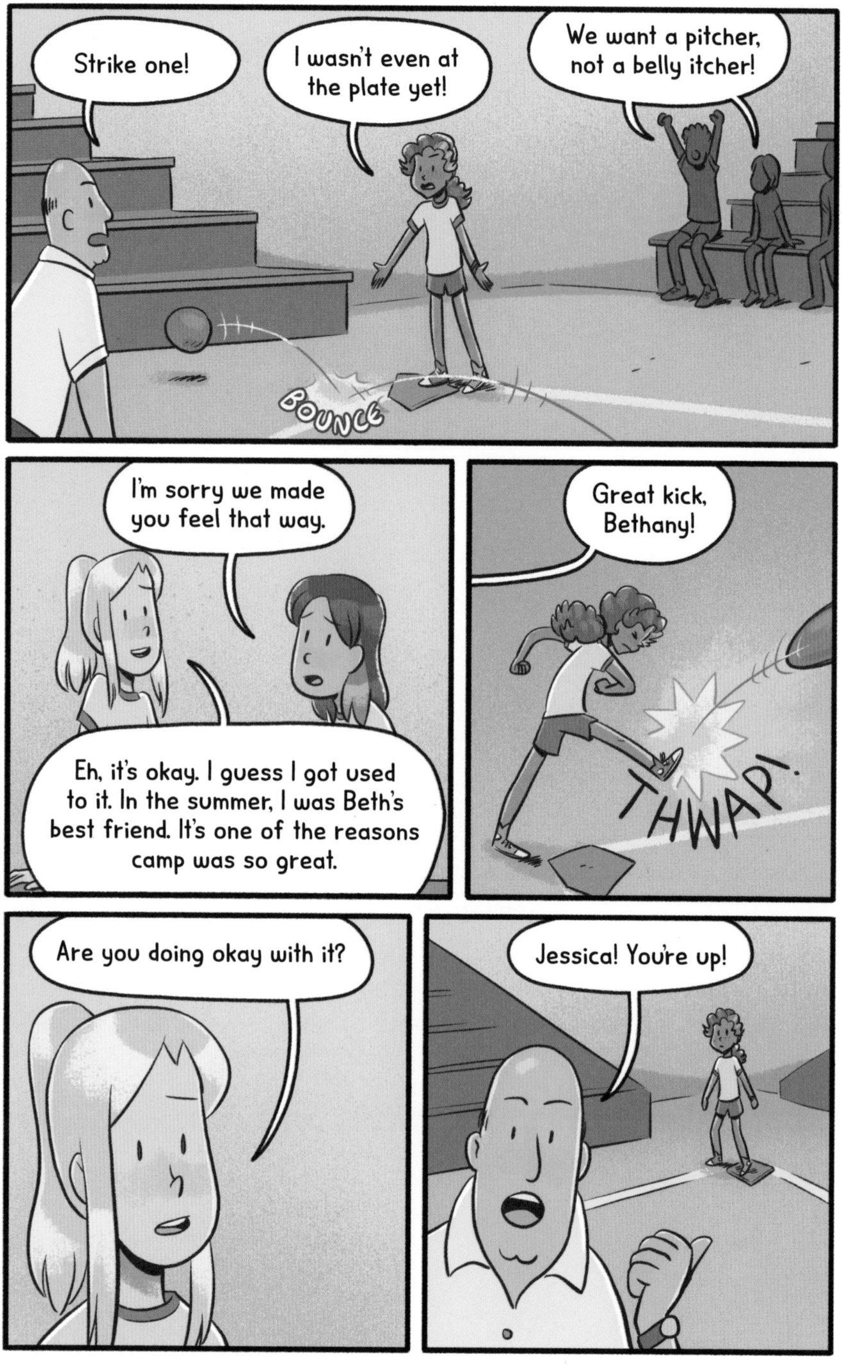
Strike one!
I wasn't even at the plate yet!
We want a pitcher, not a belly itcher!
BOUNCE
I'm sorry we made you feel that way.
Eh, it's okay. I guess I got used to it. In the summer, I was Beth's best friend. It's one of the reasons camp was so great.
Great kick, Bethany!
THWAP!
Are you doing okay with it?
Jessica! You're up!

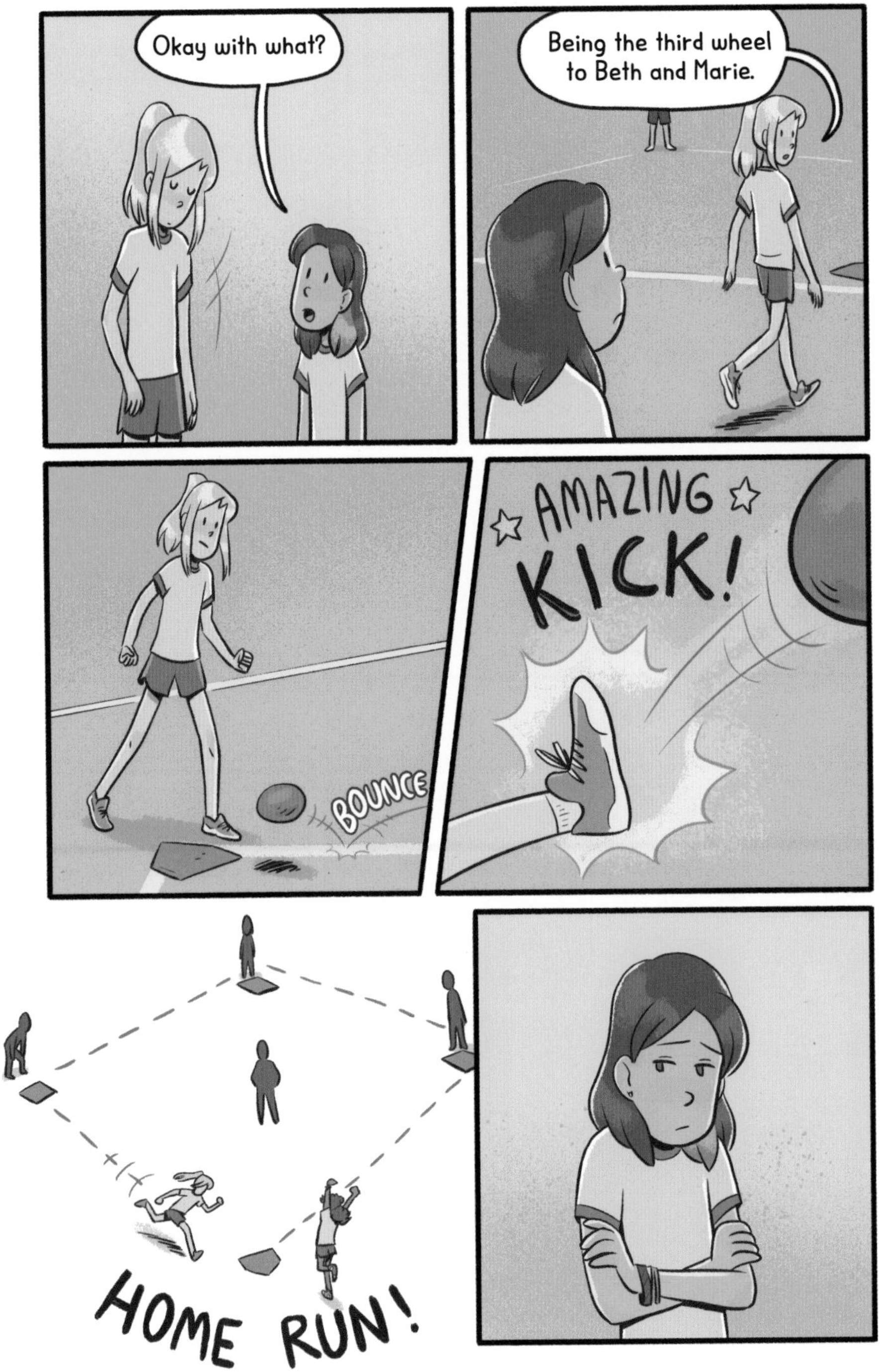
Okay with what?
Being the third wheel to Beth and Marie.
BOUNCE
AMAZING KICK!
HOME RUN!

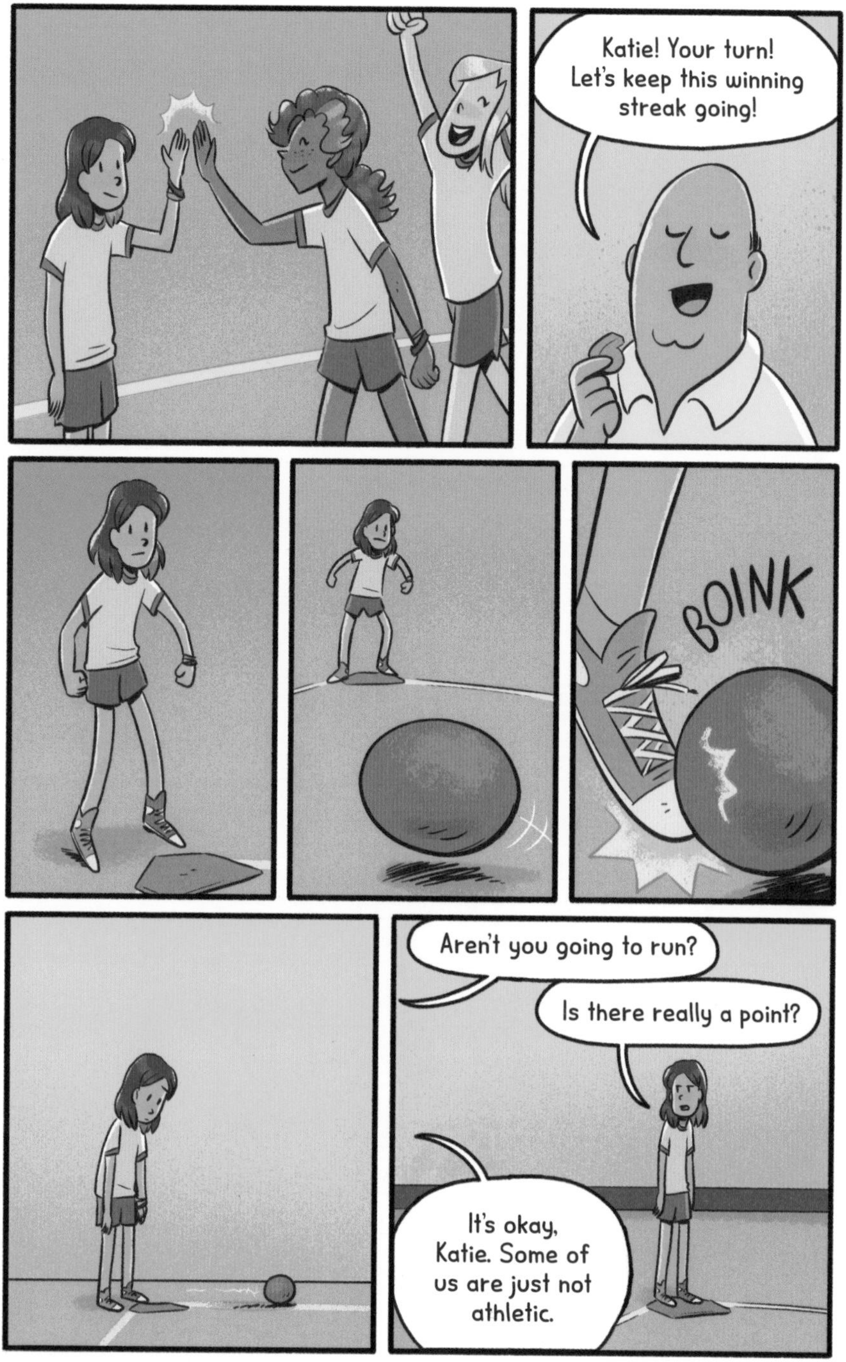
Katie! Your turn! Let's keep this winning streak going!
BOINK
Aren't you going to run?
Is there really a point?
It's okay, Katie. Some of us are just not athletic.

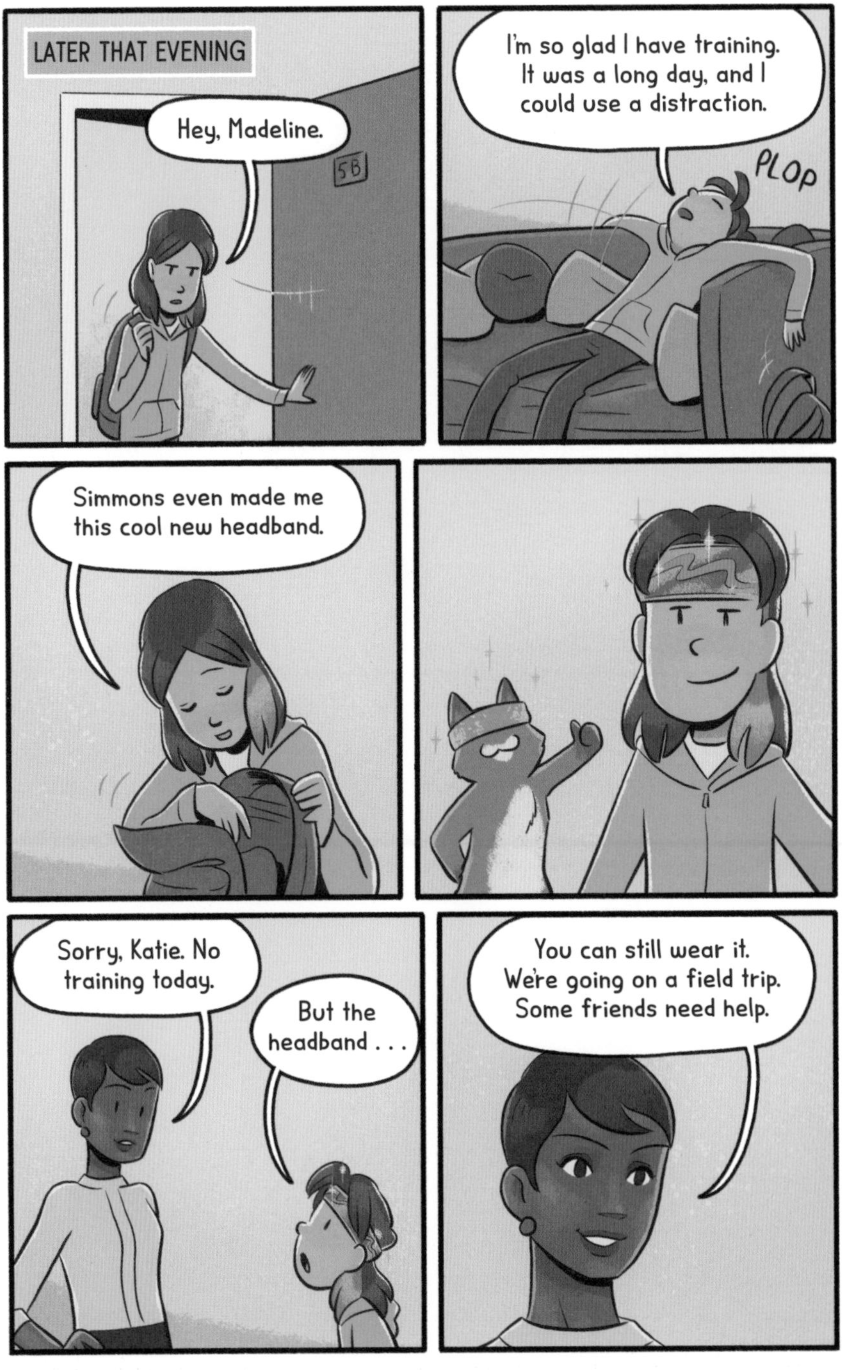
LATER THAT EVENING
Hey, Madeline.
5B
I'm so glad I have training. It was a long day, and I could use a distraction.
PLOP
Simmons even made me this cool new headband.
Sorry, Katie. No training today.
But the headband . . .
You can still wear it. We're going on a field trip. Some friends need help.

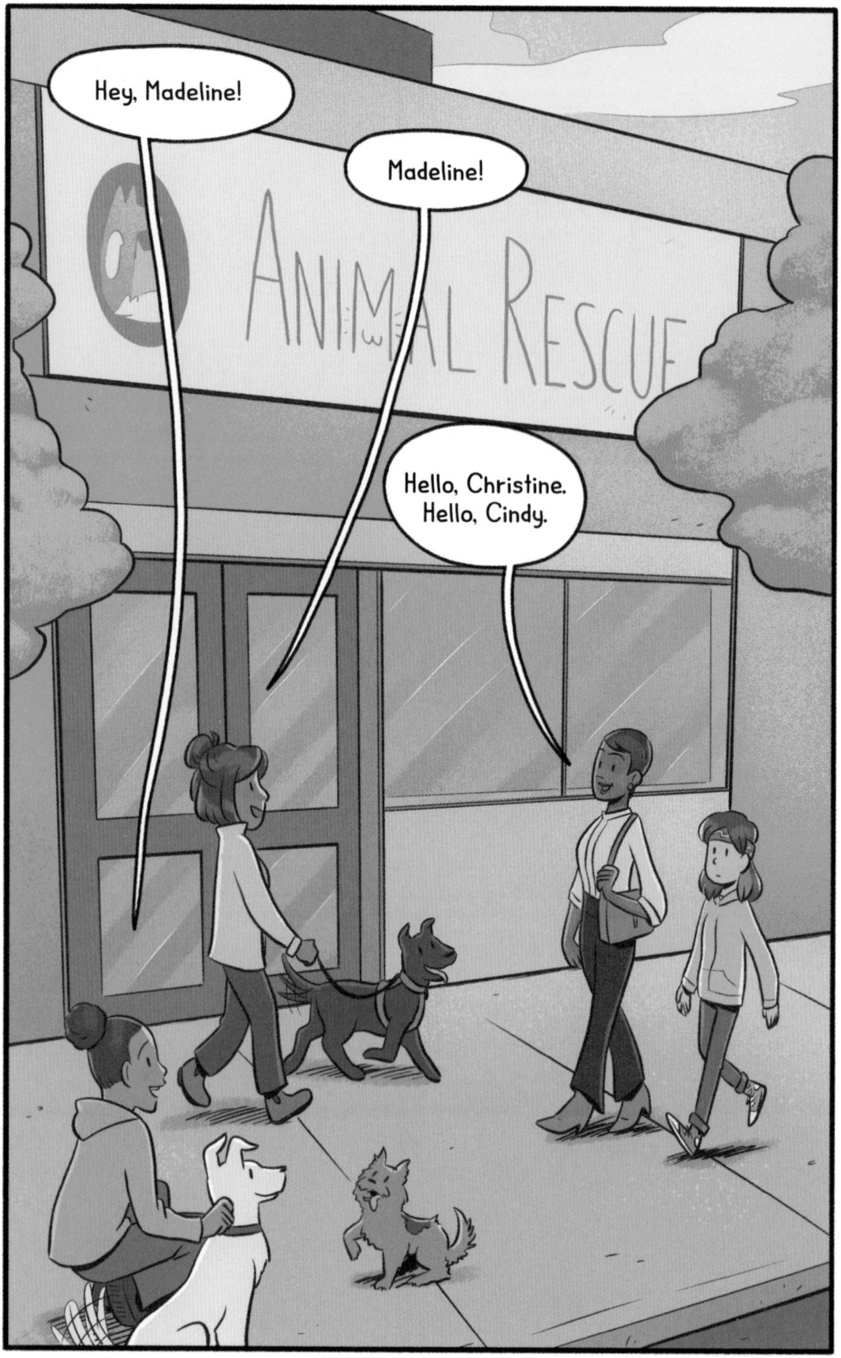
Animal Rescue
Hey, Madeline!
Madeline!
Hello, Christine.
Hello, Cindy.

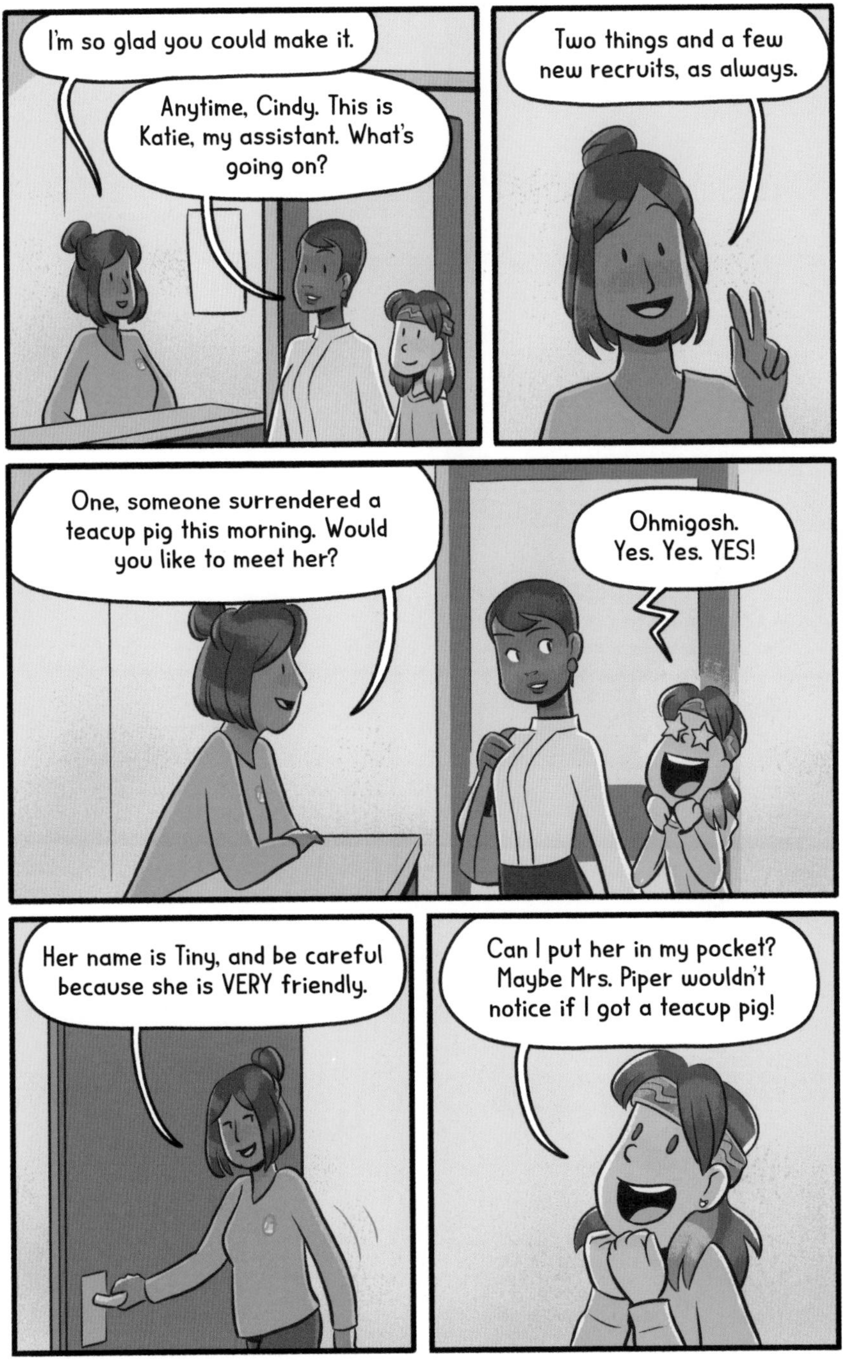
I'm so glad you could make it.
Anytime, Cindy. This is Katie, my assistant. What's going on?
Two things and a few new recruits, as always.
One, someone surrendered a teacup pig this morning. Would you like to meet her?
Ohmigosh. Yes. Yes. YES!
Her name is Tiny, and be careful because she is VERY friendly.
Can I put her in my pocket? Maybe Mrs. Piper wouldn't notice if I got a teacup pig!

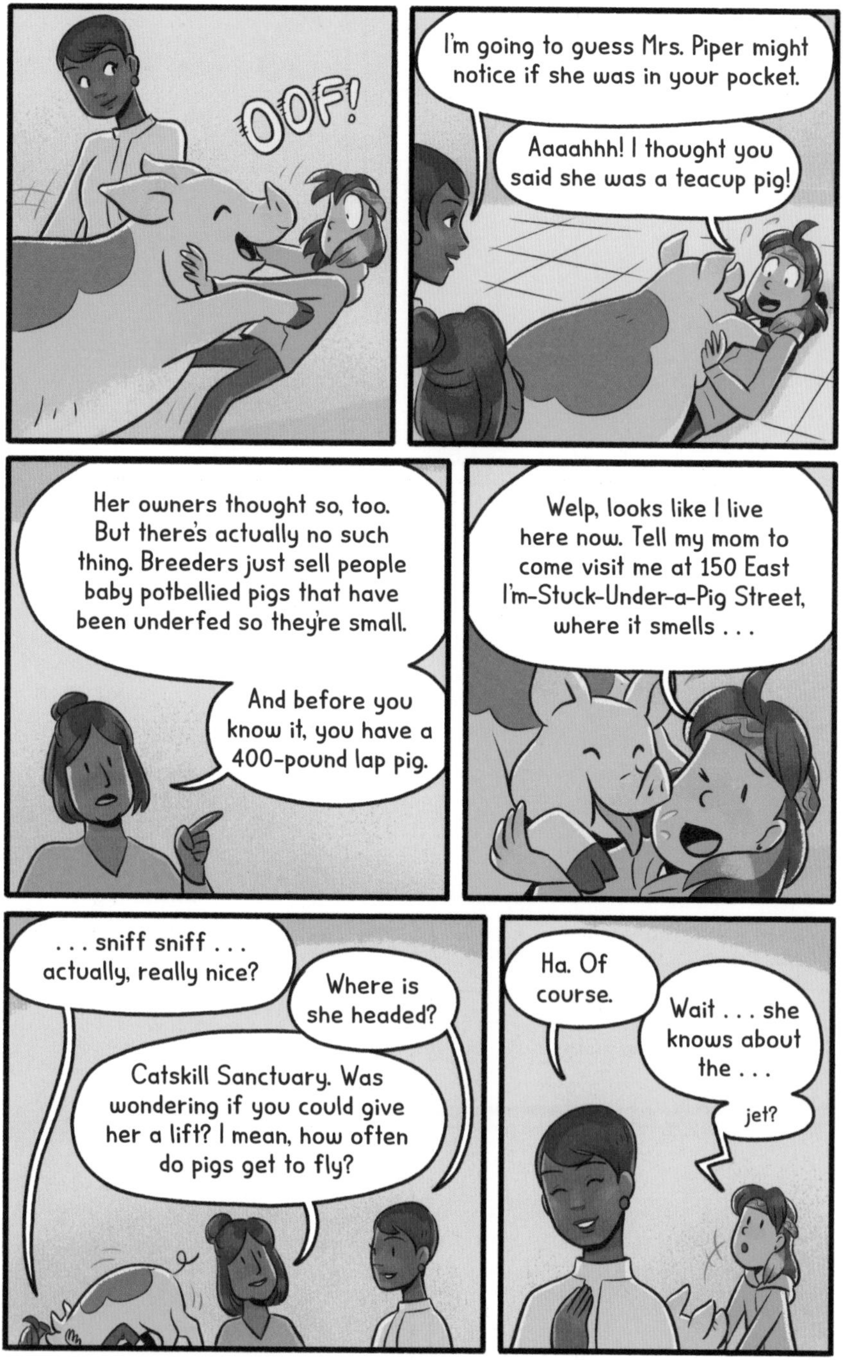
OOF!
I'm going to guess Mrs. Piper might notice if she was in your pocket.
Aaaahhh! I thought you said she was a teacup pig!
Her owners thought so, too. But there's actually no such thing. Breeders just sell people baby potbellied pigs that have been underfed so they're small.
And before you know it, you have a 400-pound lap pig.
Welp, looks like I live here now. Tell my mom to come visit me at 150 East I'm-Stuck-Under-a-Pig Street, where it smells . . .
. . . sniff sniff . . . actually, really nice?
Where is she headed?
Catskill Sanctuary. Was wondering if you could give her a lift? I mean, how often do pigs get to fly?
Ha. Of course.
Wait . . . she knows about the . . .
jet?

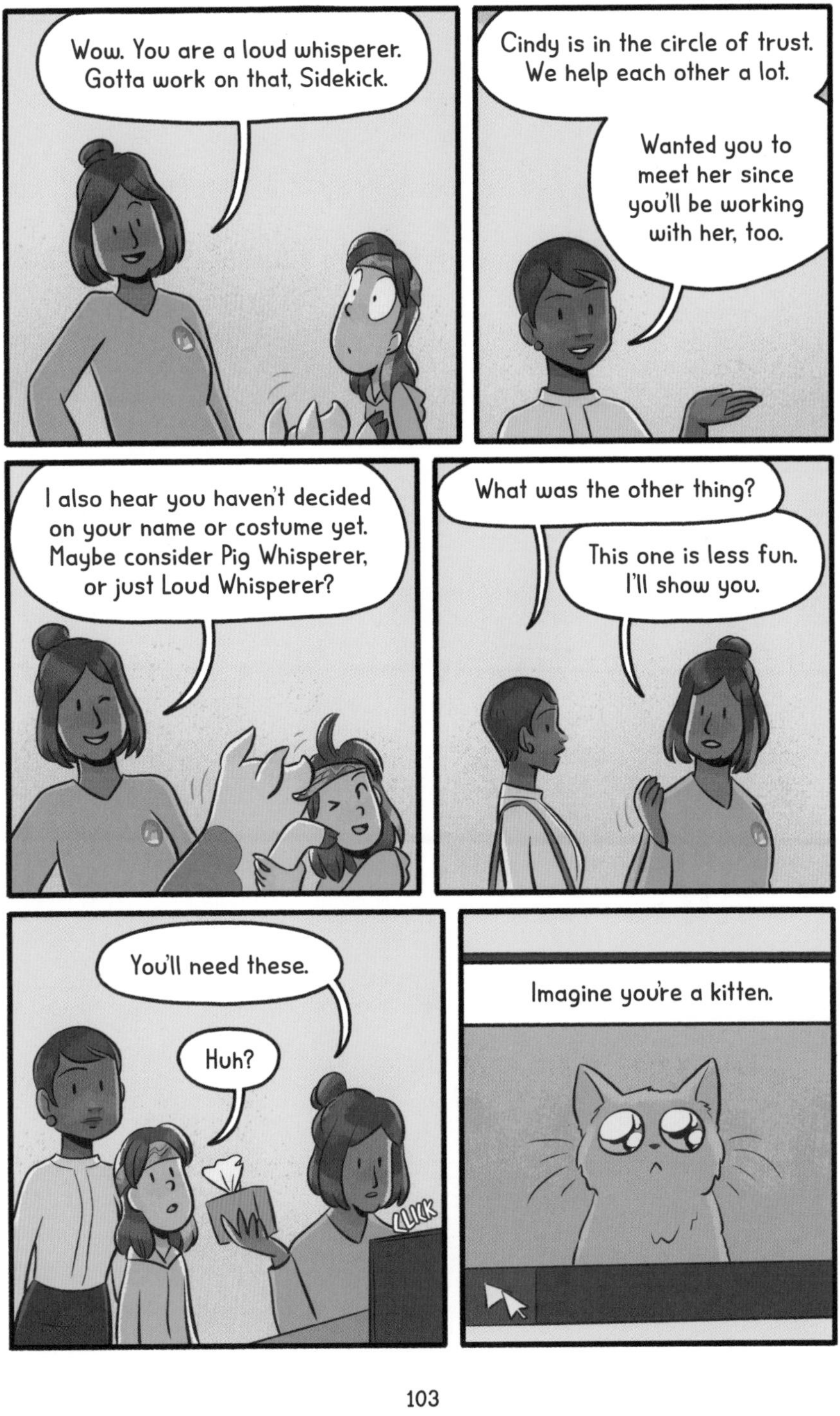
Wow. You are a loud whisperer. Gotta work on that, Sidekick.
Cindy is in the circle of trust. We help each other a lot.
Wanted you to meet her since you'll be working with her, too.
I also hear you haven't decided on your name or costume yet. Maybe consider Pig Whisperer, or just Loud Whisperer?
What was the other thing?
This one is less fun. I'll show you.
You'll need these.
Huh?
CLICK
Imagine you're a kitten.

Cold. Alone. Abandoned.

Super-sad music playing

The wind howls. Your fur isn't thick enough.

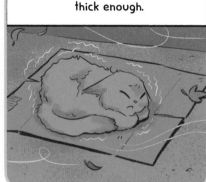

They sent your mother to the sad, dark shelter. But you . . . you don't make it.

Unless . . .

Imagine a place where all the kittens are saved. Where they can play and climb and live until they find their perfect owner.

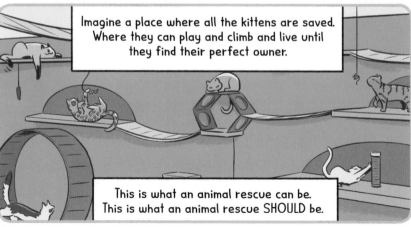

This is what an animal rescue can be. This is what an animal rescue SHOULD be.

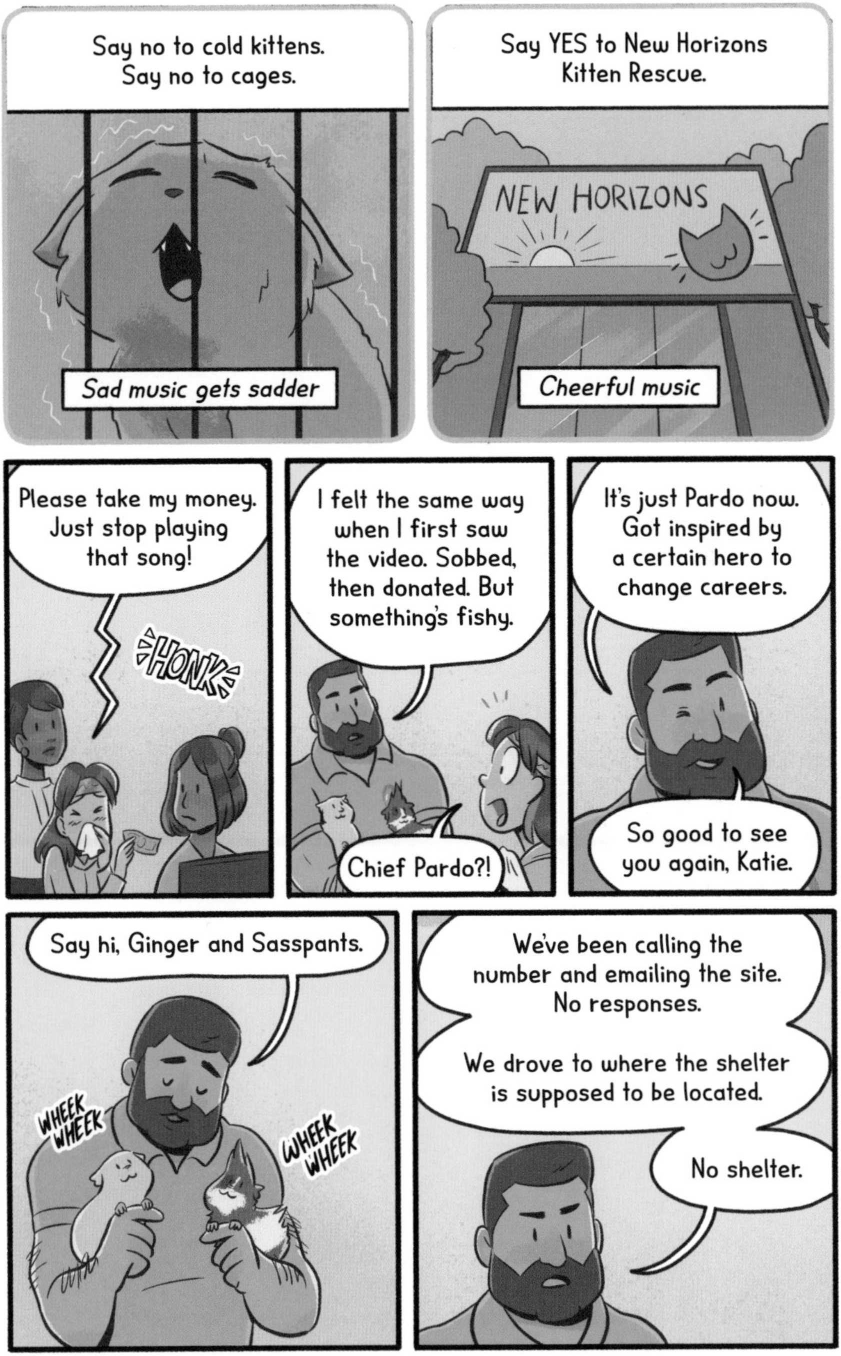
Say no to cold kittens.
Say no to cages.
Sad music gets sadder
Say YES to New Horizons Kitten Rescue.
NEW HORIZONS
Cheerful music
Please take my money. Just stop playing that song!
HONK
I felt the same way when I first saw the video. Sobbed, then donated. But something's fishy.
Chief Pardo?!
It's just Pardo now. Got inspired by a certain hero to change careers.
So good to see you again, Katie.
Say hi, Ginger and Sasspants.
WHEEK WHEEK
WHEEK WHEEK
We've been calling the number and emailing the site. No responses.
We drove to where the shelter is supposed to be located.
No shelter.

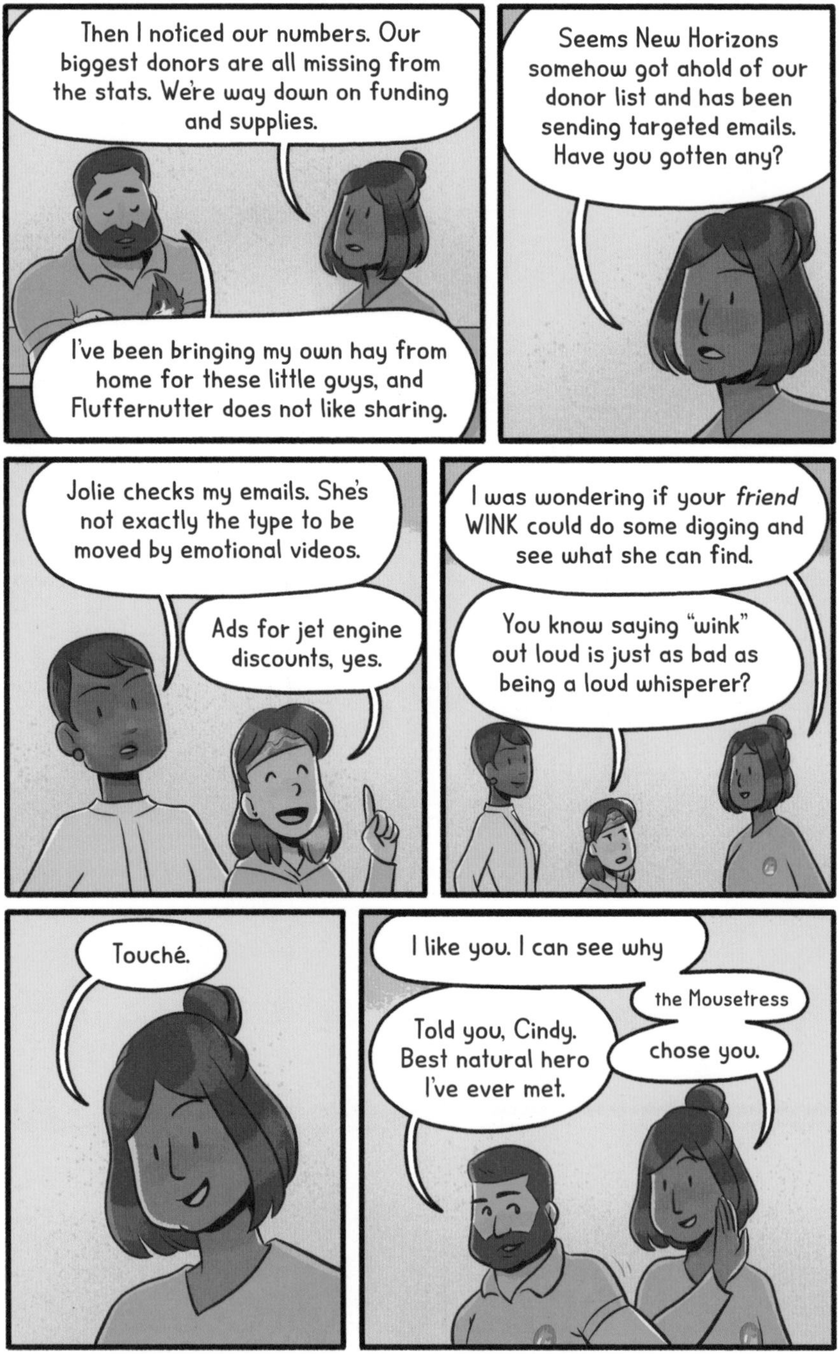
Then I noticed our numbers. Our biggest donors are all missing from the stats. We're way down on funding and supplies.
I've been bringing my own hay from home for these little guys, and Fluffernutter does not like sharing.
Seems New Horizons somehow got ahold of our donor list and has been sending targeted emails. Have you gotten any?
Jolie checks my emails. She's not exactly the type to be moved by emotional videos.
Ads for jet engine discounts, yes.
I was wondering if your *friend* WINK could do some digging and see what she can find.
You know saying "wink" out loud is just as bad as being a loud whisperer?
Touché.
I like you. I can see why
the Mousetress
chose you.
Told you, Cindy. Best natural hero I've ever met.

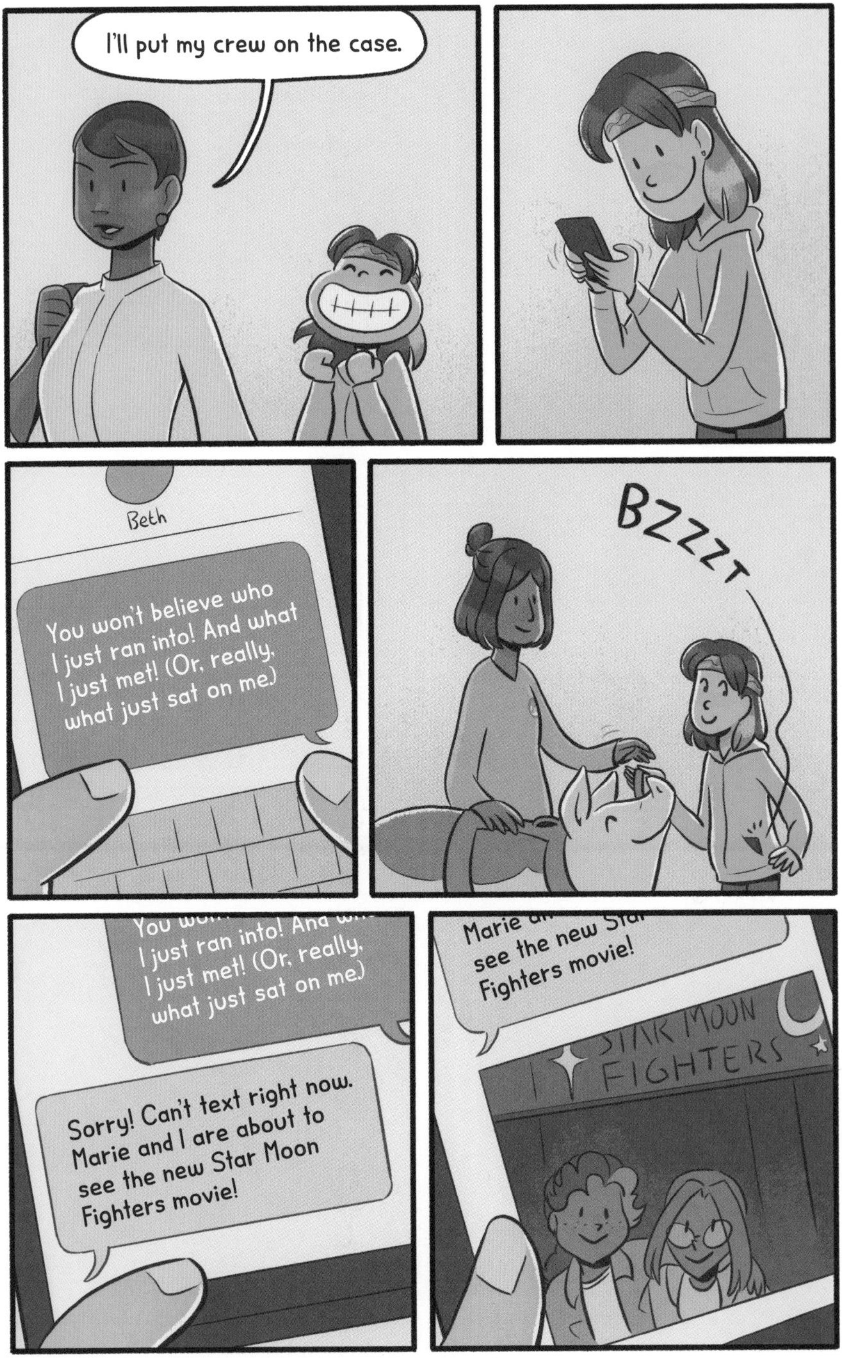
I'll put my crew on the case.
Beth
You won't believe who I just ran into! And what I just met! (Or, really, what just sat on me.)
BZZZZT
I just ran into! And wh I just met! (Or, really, what just sat on me.)
Sorry! Can't text right now. Marie and I are about to see the new Star Moon Fighters movie!
see the new Star Fighters movie!
STAR MOON FIGHTERS

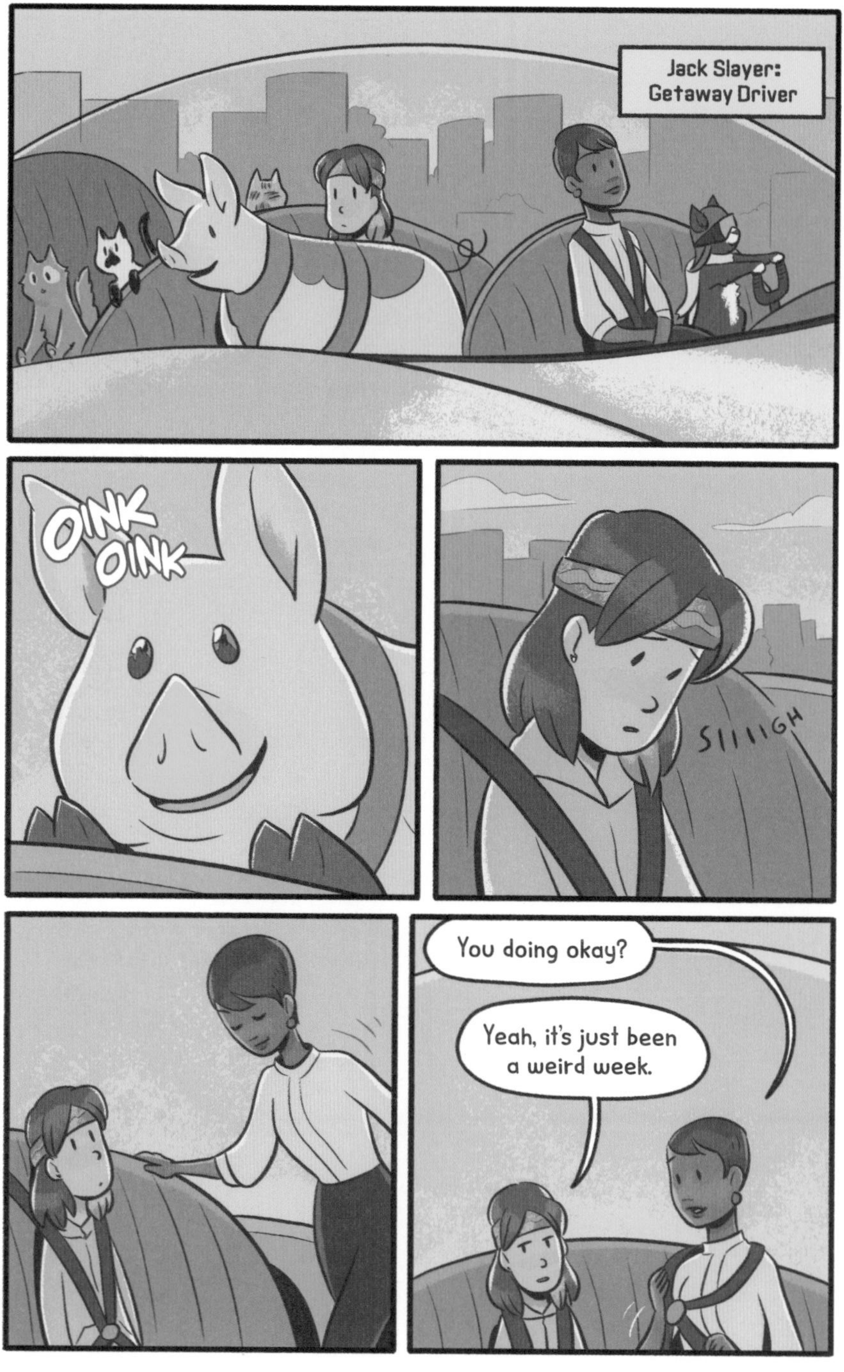
Jack Slayer:
Getaway Driver
OINK OINK
SIIIIGH
You doing okay?
Yeah, it's just been a weird week.

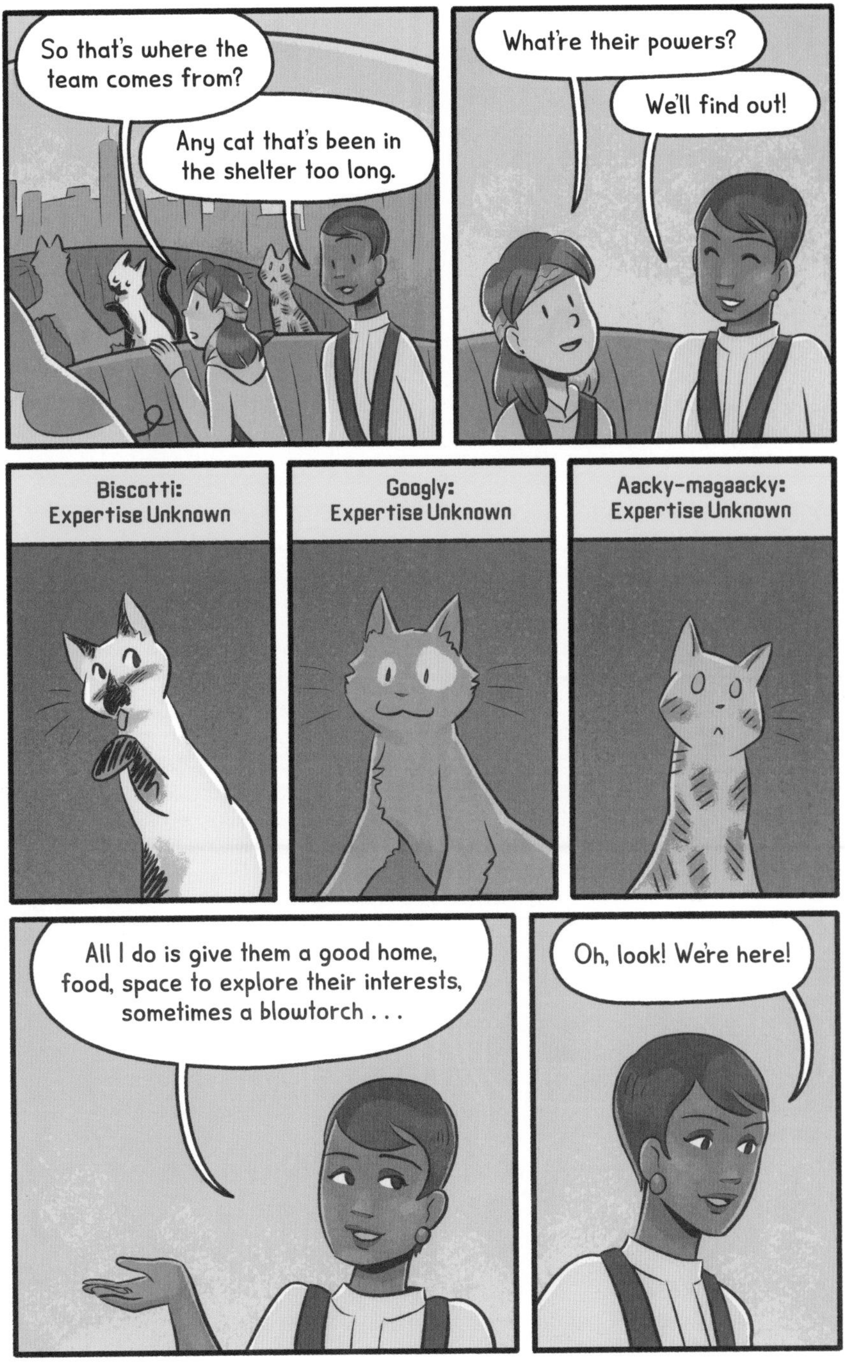
So that's where the team comes from?
Any cat that's been in the shelter too long.
What're their powers?
We'll find out!
Biscotti: Expertise Unknown
Googly: Expertise Unknown
Aacky-magaacky: Expertise Unknown
All I do is give them a good home, food, space to explore their interests, sometimes a blowtorch . . .
Oh, look! We're here!

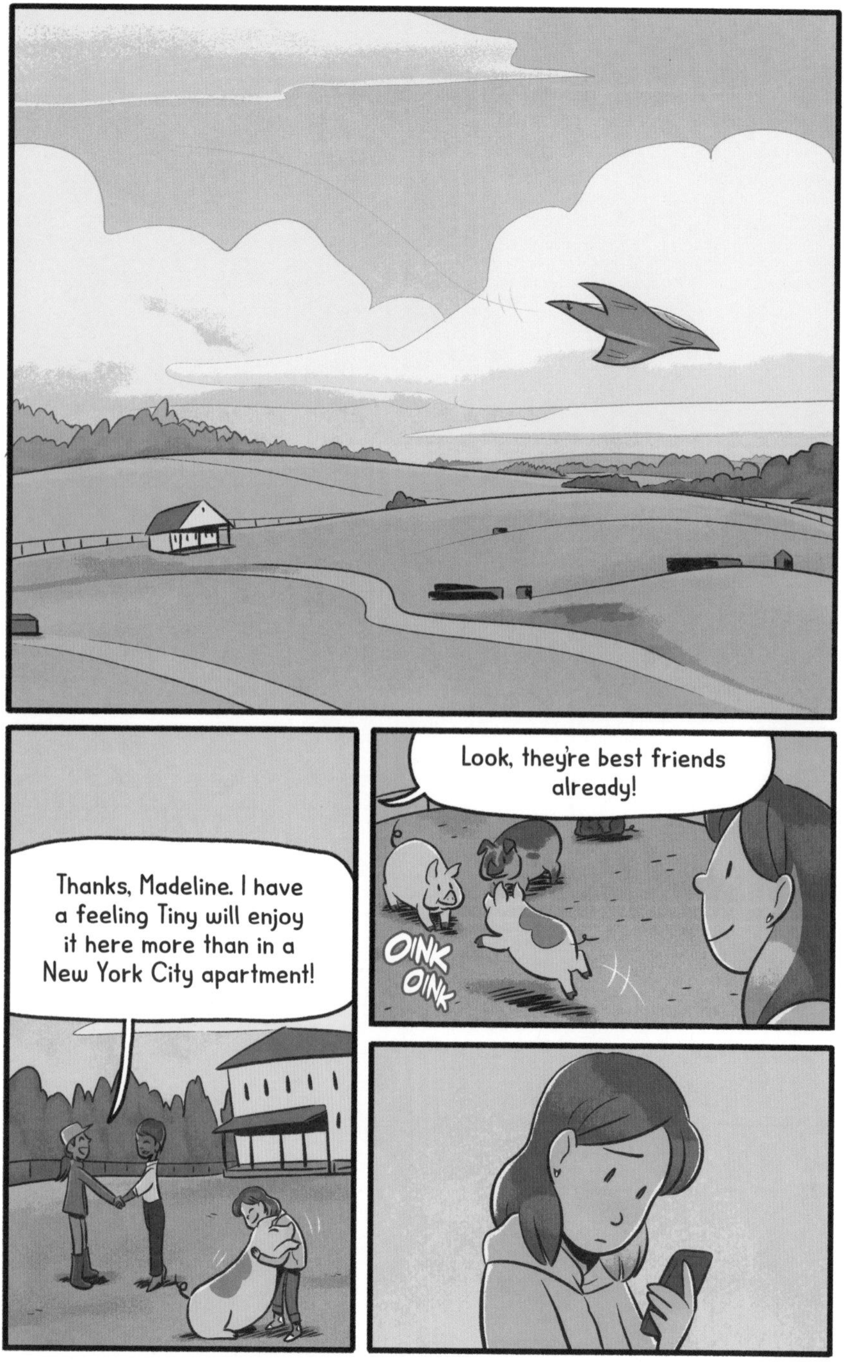
Thanks, Madeline. I have a feeling Tiny will enjoy it here more than in a New York City apartment!
Look, they're best friends already!
OINK OINK

CHAPTER SIX

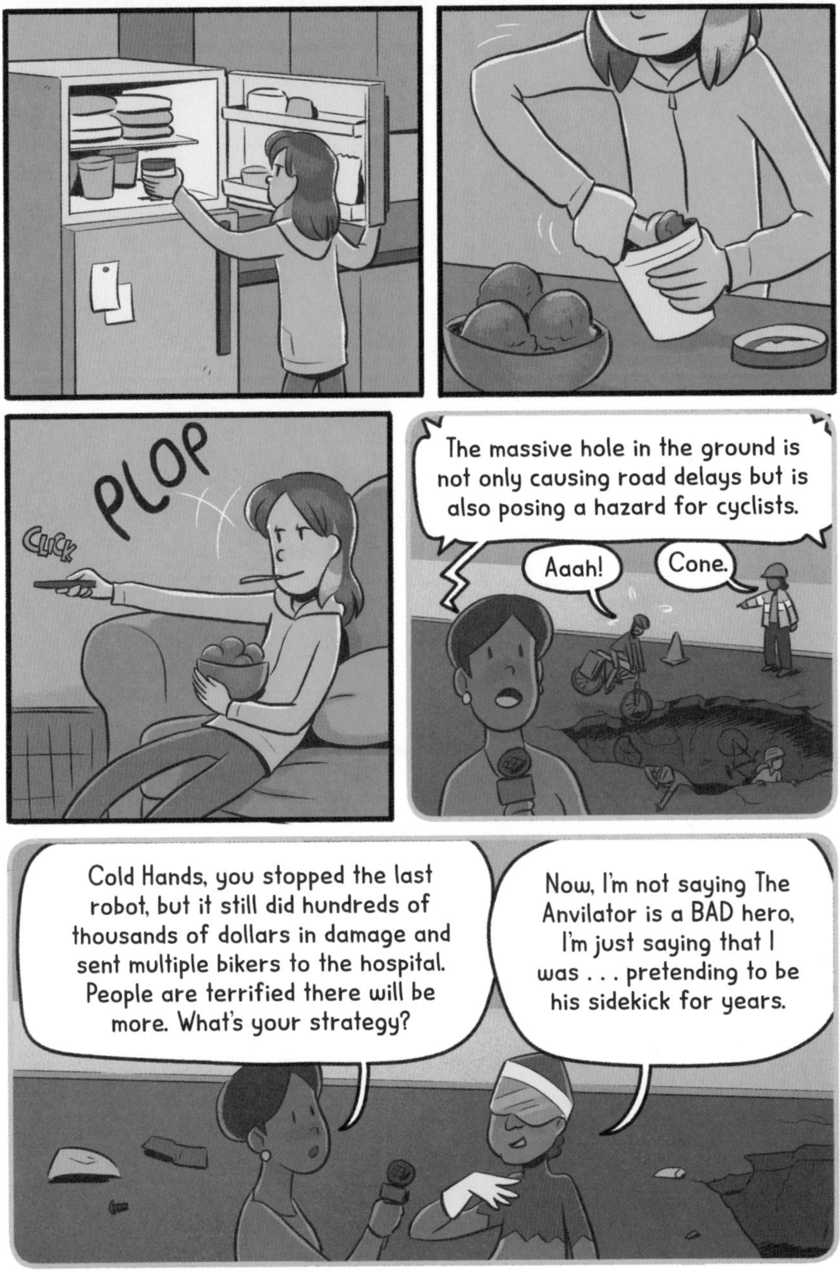
PLOP
CLICK
The massive hole in the ground is not only causing road delays but is also posing a hazard for cyclists.
Aaah!
Cone.
Cold Hands, you stopped the last robot, but it still did hundreds of thousands of dollars in damage and sent multiple bikers to the hospital. People are terrified there will be more. What's your strategy?
Now, I'm not saying The Anvilator is a BAD hero, I'm just saying that I was . . . pretending to be his sidekick for years.

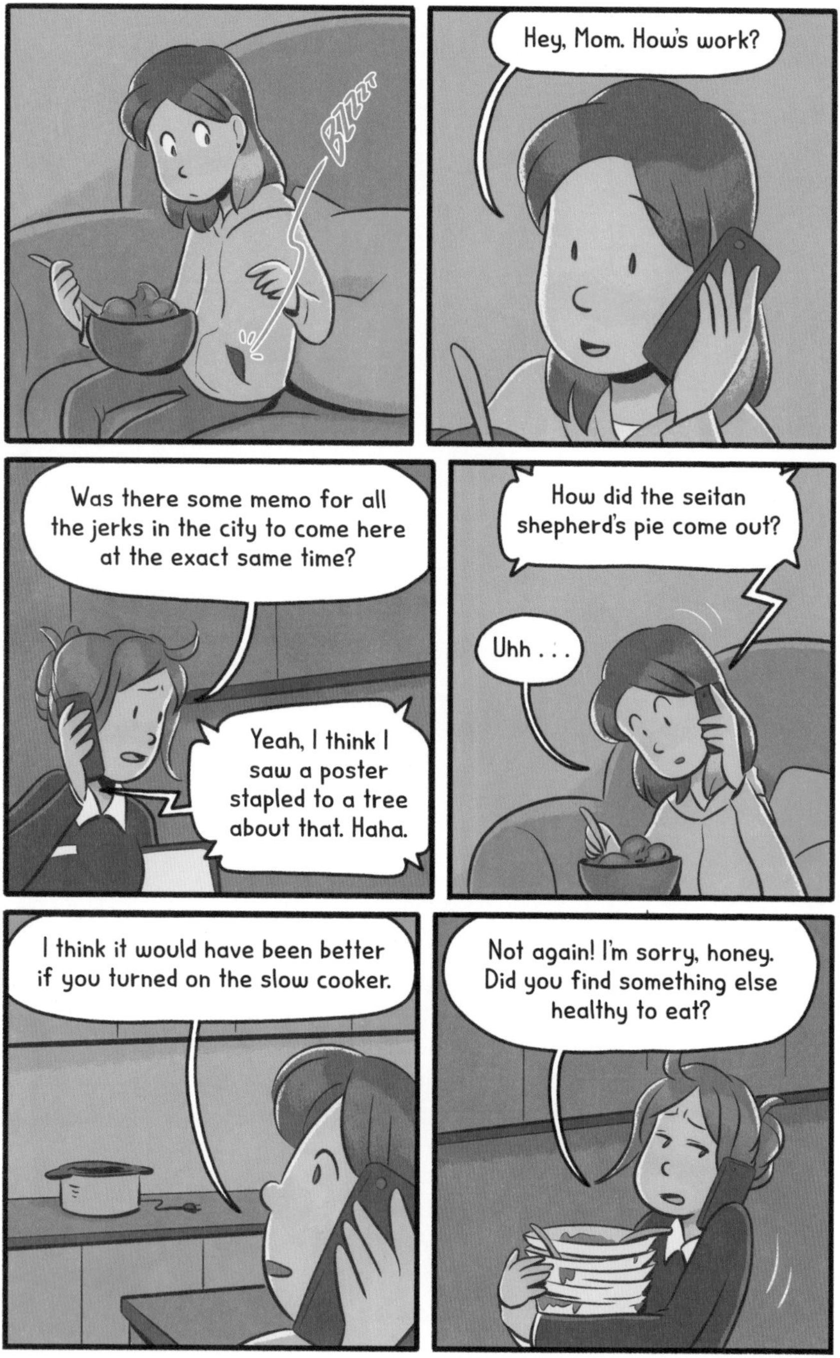
BZZZzT
Hey, Mom. How's work?
Was there some memo for all the jerks in the city to come here at the exact same time?
Yeah, I think I saw a poster stapled to a tree about that. Haha.
How did the seitan shepherd's pie come out?
Uhh . . .
I think it would have been better if you turned on the slow cooker.
Not again! I'm sorry, honey. Did you find something else healthy to eat?

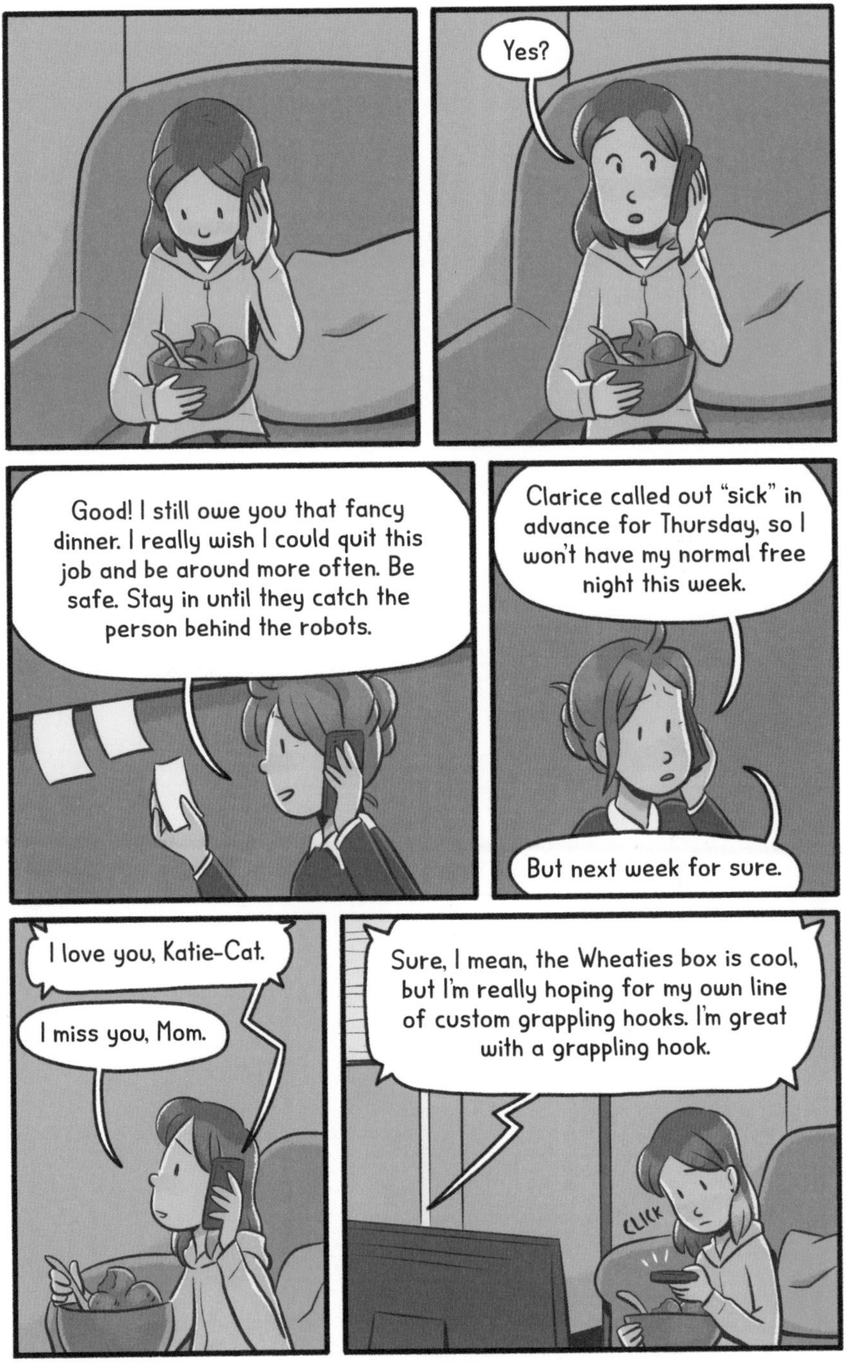
Yes?
Good! I still owe you that fancy dinner. I really wish I could quit this job and be around more often. Be safe. Stay in until they catch the person behind the robots.
Clarice called out "sick" in advance for Thursday, so I won't have my normal free night this week.
But next week for sure.
I love you, Katie-Cat.
I miss you, Mom.
Sure, I mean, the Wheaties box is cool, but I'm really hoping for my own line of custom grappling hooks. I'm great with a grappling hook.
CLICK

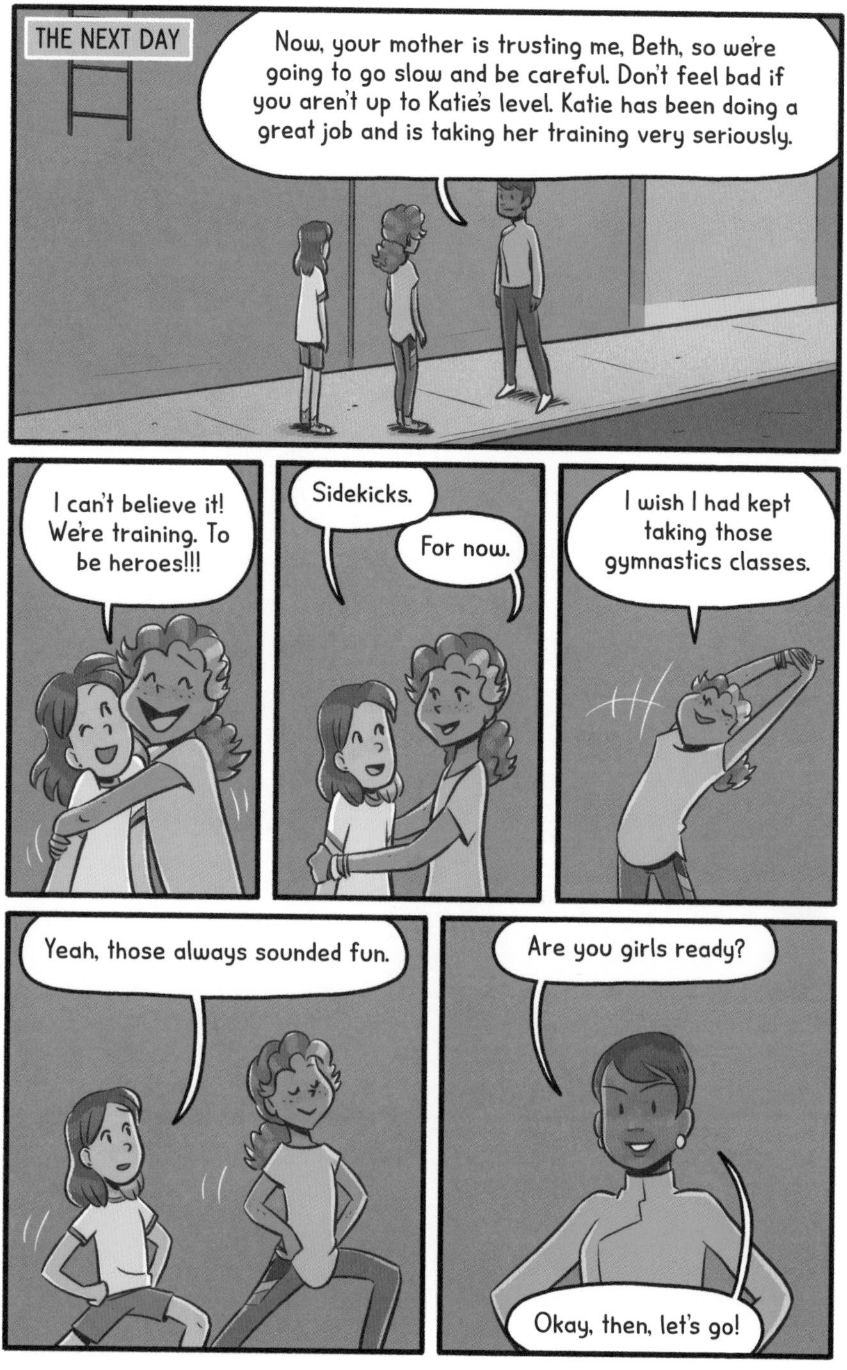
THE NEXT DAY
Now, your mother is trusting me, Beth, so we're going to go slow and be careful. Don't feel bad if you aren't up to Katie's level. Katie has been doing a great job and is taking her training very seriously.
I can't believe it! We're training. To be heroes!!!
Sidekicks.
For now.
I wish I had kept taking those gymnastics classes.
Yeah, those always sounded fun.
Are you girls ready?
Okay, then, let's go!

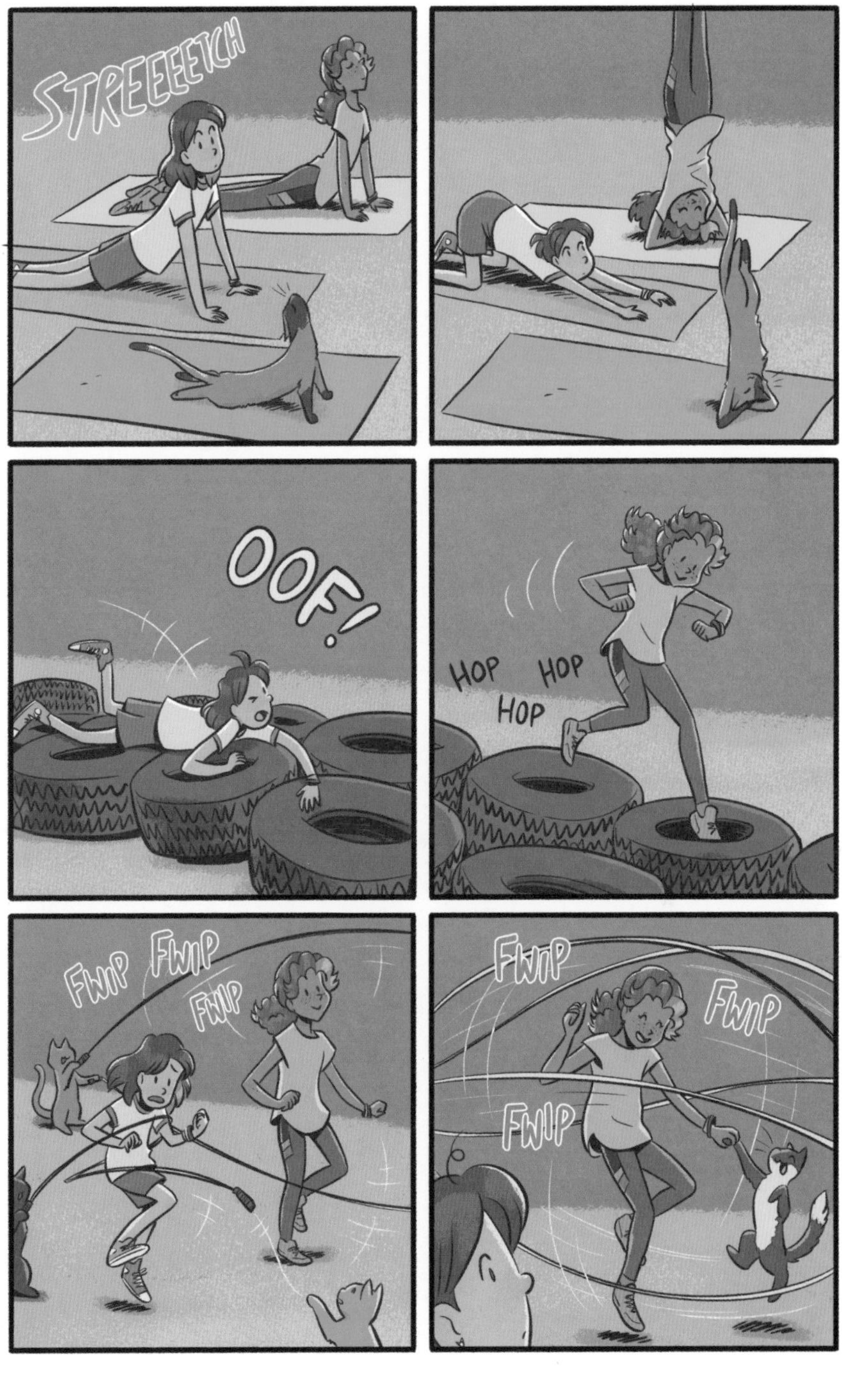
STREEEEETCH
OOF!
HOP HOP
HOP
FWIP FWIP
FWIP
FWIP
FWIP
FWIP

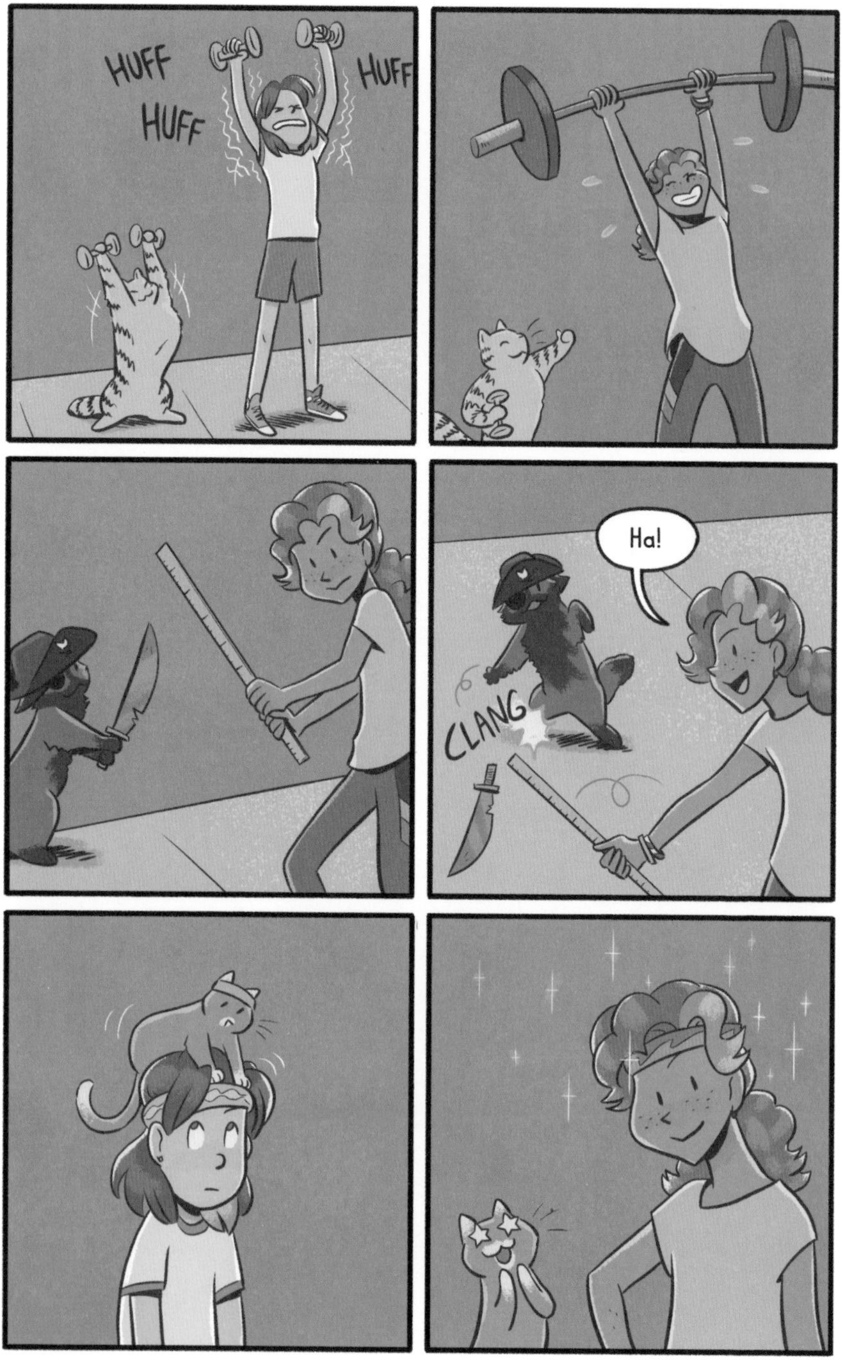
HUFF
HUFF
HUFF
Ha!
CLANG

I'm impressed, Beth. Why don't we try—

The fire escape thing? Katie told me about it. Let's go!

LAUNCH!

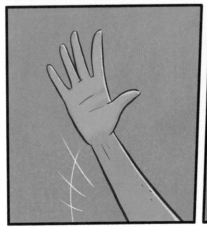

GRAB!

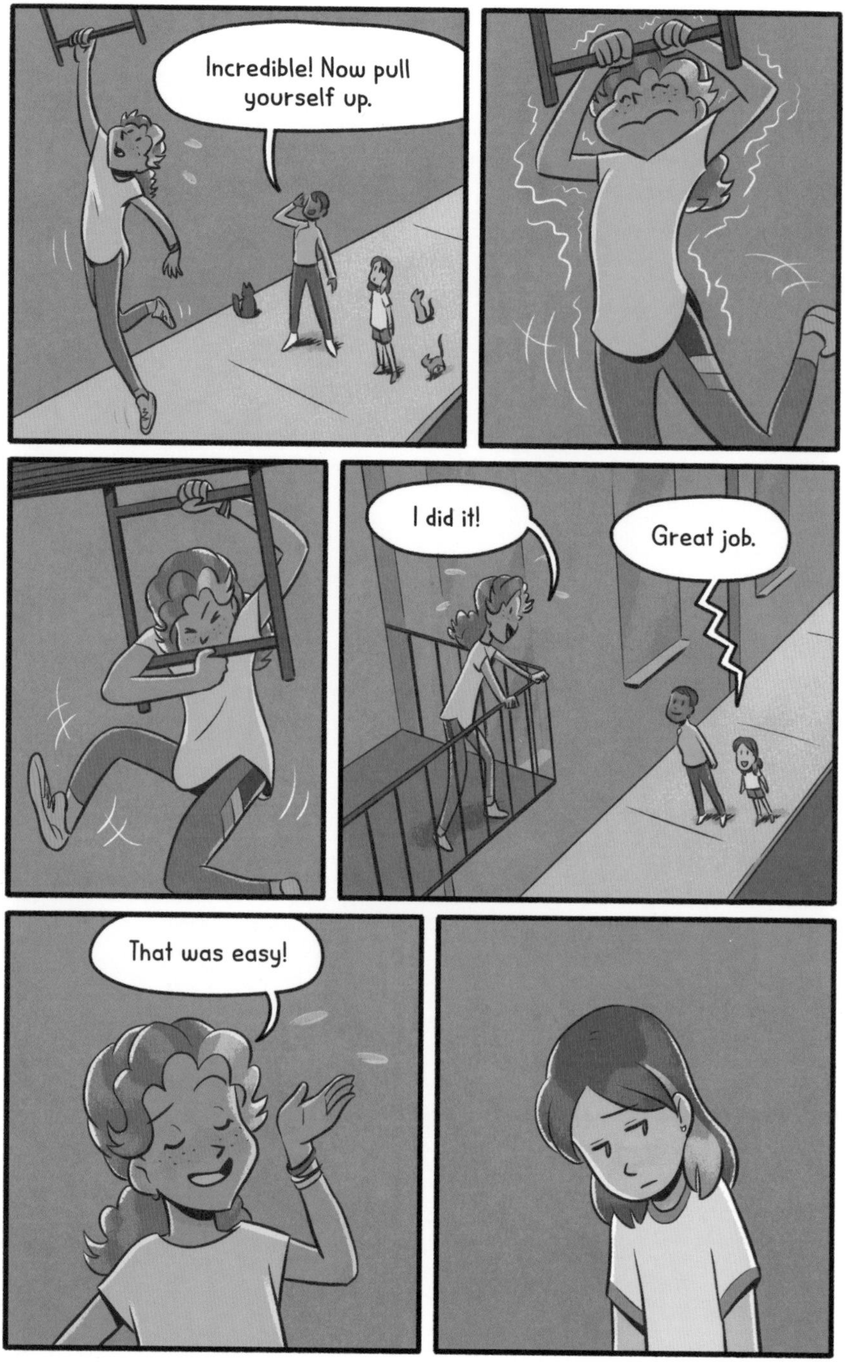
Incredible! Now pull yourself up.
I did it!
Great job.
That was easy!

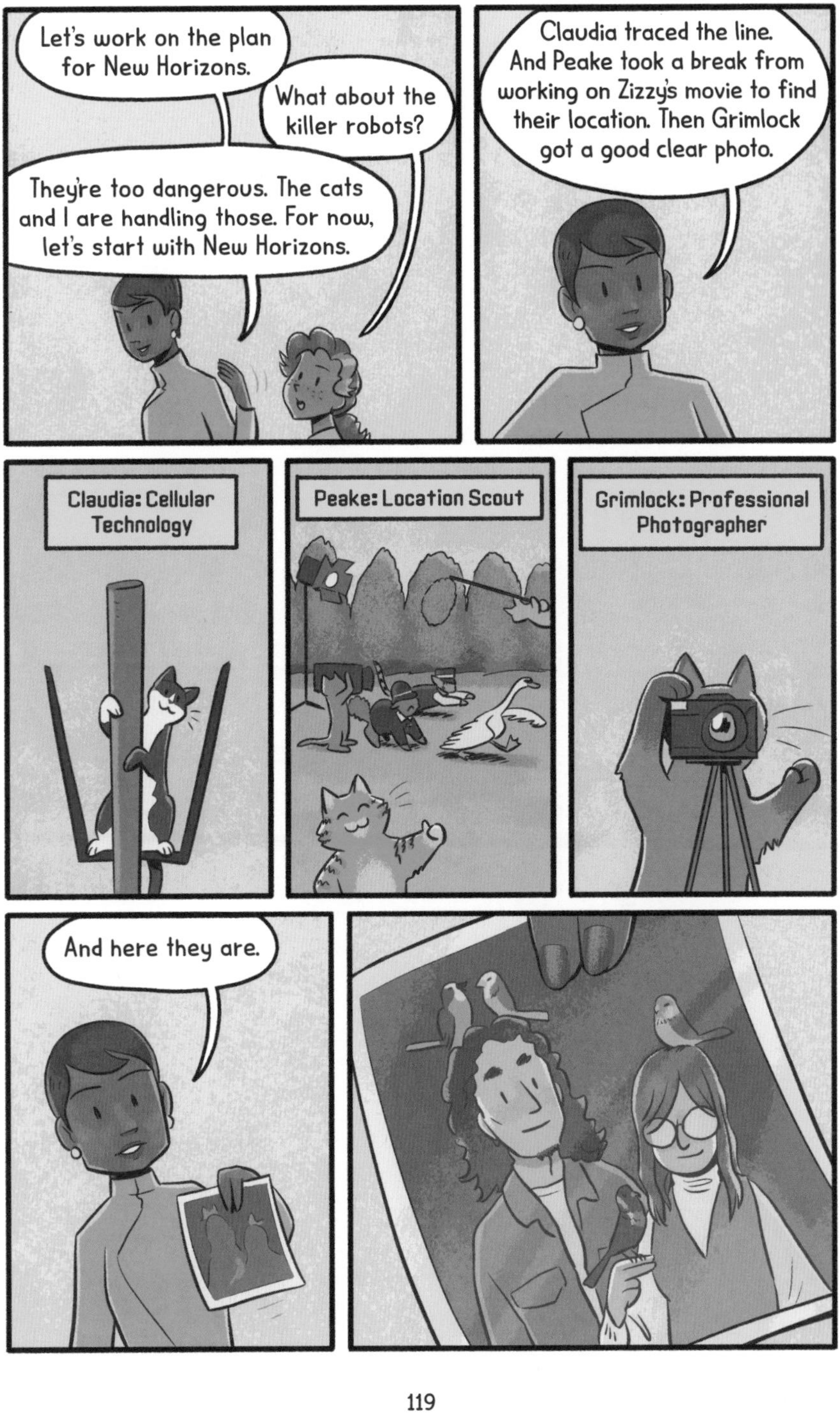
Let's work on the plan for New Horizons.
What about the killer robots?
They're too dangerous. The cats and I are handling those. For now, let's start with New Horizons.
Claudia traced the line. And Peake took a break from working on Zizzy's movie to find their location. Then Grimlock got a good clear photo.
Claudia: Cellular Technology
Peake: Location Scout
Grimlock: Professional Photographer
And here they are.

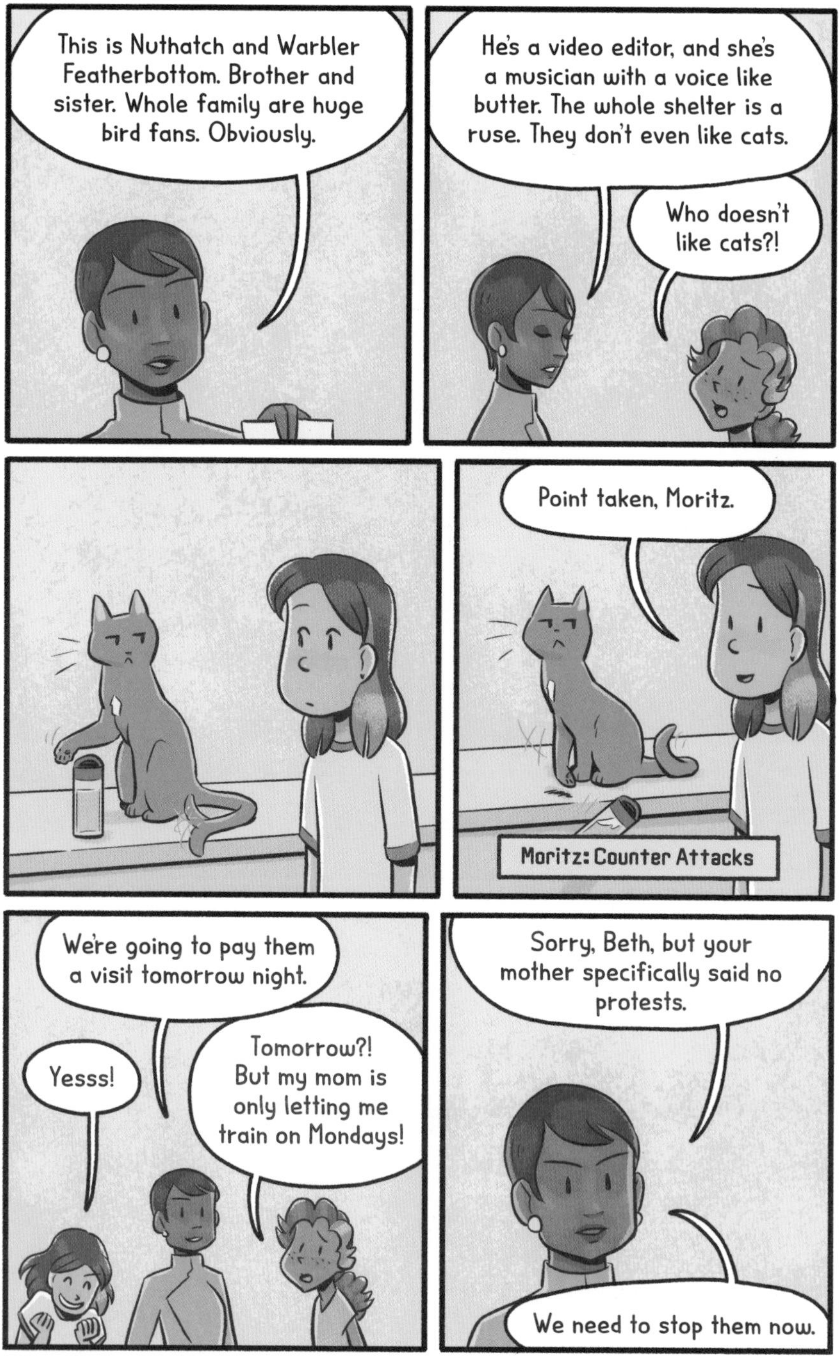
This is Nuthatch and Warbler Featherbottom. Brother and sister. Whole family are huge bird fans. Obviously.
He's a video editor, and she's a musician with a voice like butter. The whole shelter is a ruse. They don't even like cats.
Who doesn't like cats?!
Point taken, Moritz.
Moritz: Counter Attacks
We're going to pay them a visit tomorrow night.
Yesss!
Tomorrow?! But my mom is only letting me train on Mondays!
Sorry, Beth, but your mother specifically said no protests.
We need to stop them now.

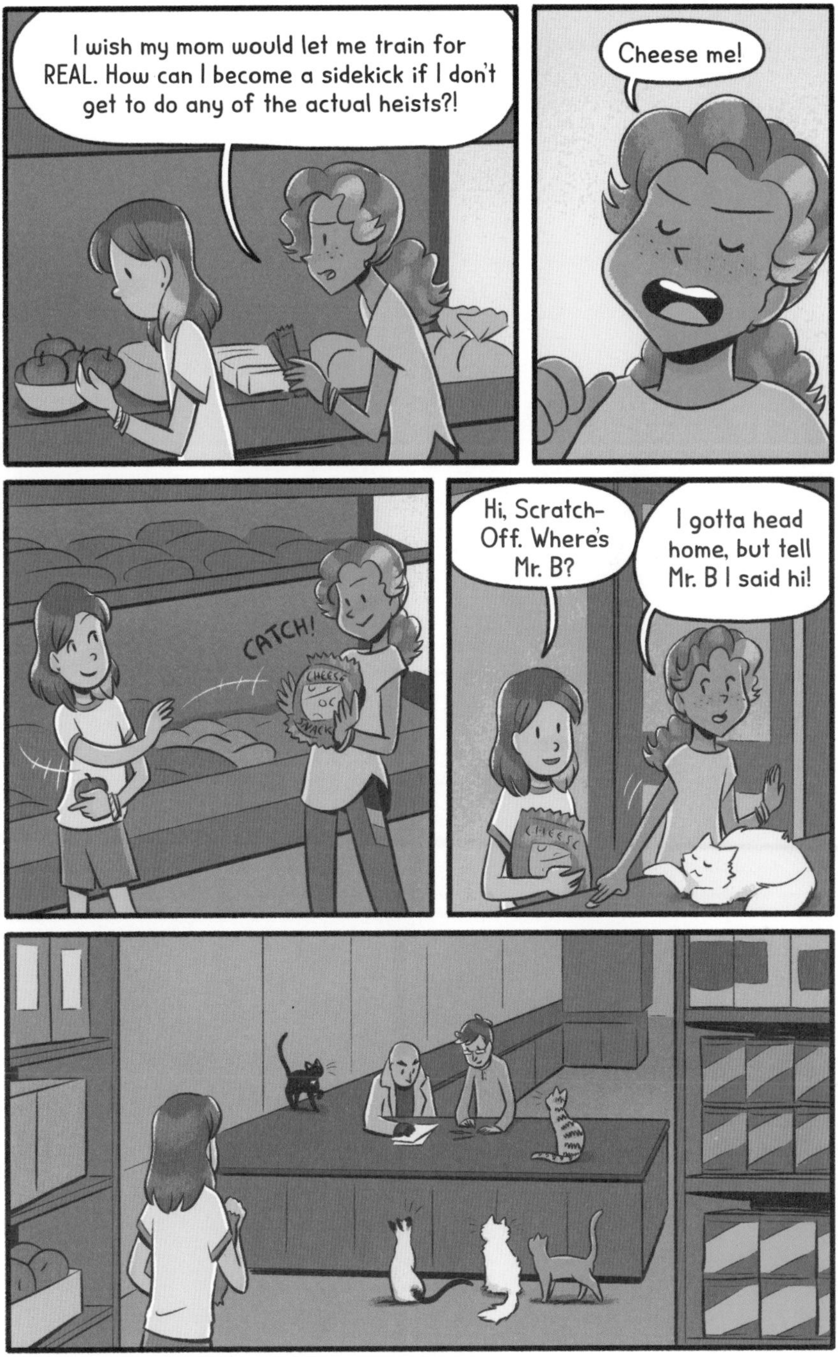
I wish my mom would let me train for REAL. How can I become a sidekick if I don't get to do any of the actual heists?!
Cheese me!
CATCH!
CHEESE SNACK
Hi, Scratch-Off. Where's Mr. B?
I gotta head home, but tell Mr. B I said hi!

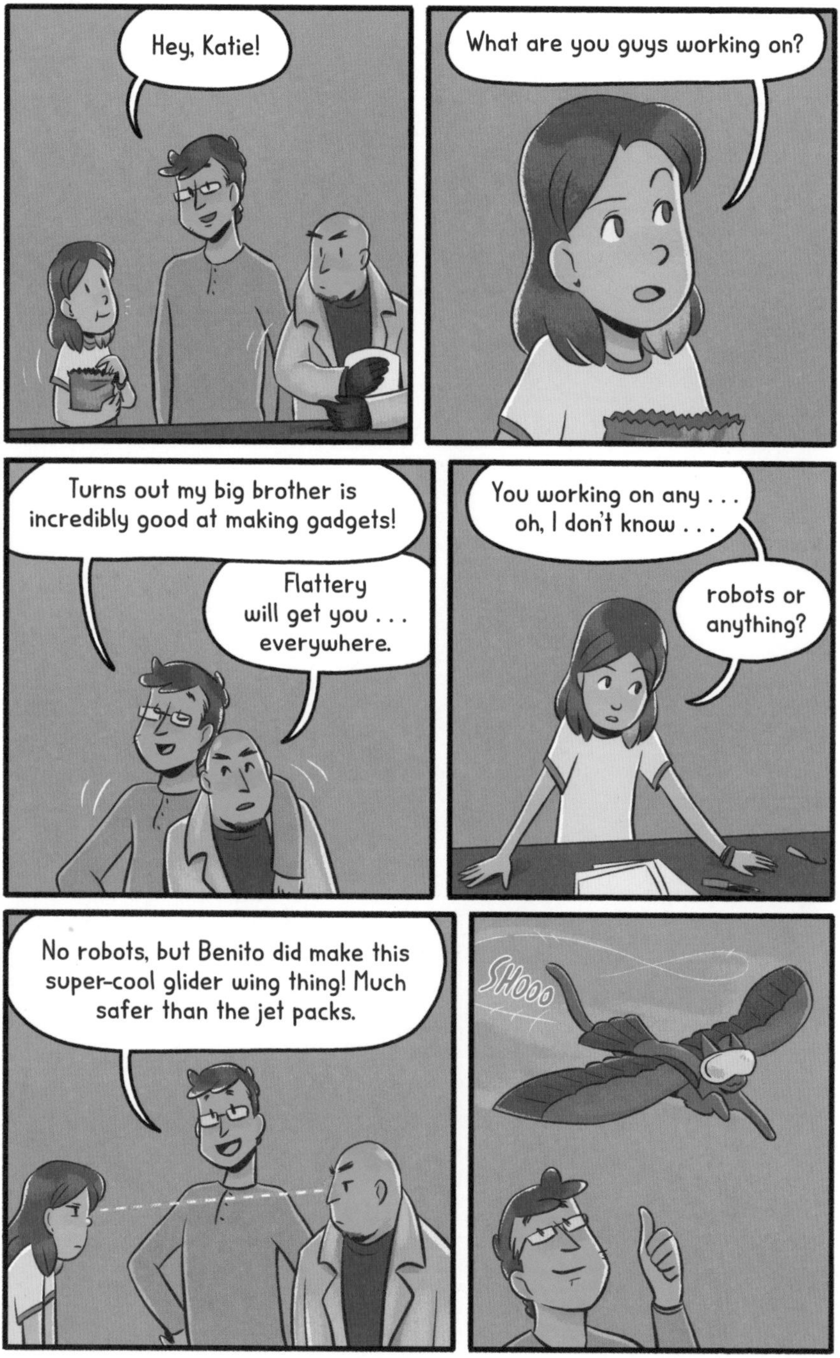
Hey, Katie!
What are you guys working on?
Turns out my big brother is incredibly good at making gadgets!
Flattery will get you . . . everywhere.
You working on any . . . oh, I don't know . . .
robots or anything?
No robots, but Benito did make this super-cool glider wing thing! Much safer than the jet packs.
SHOOO

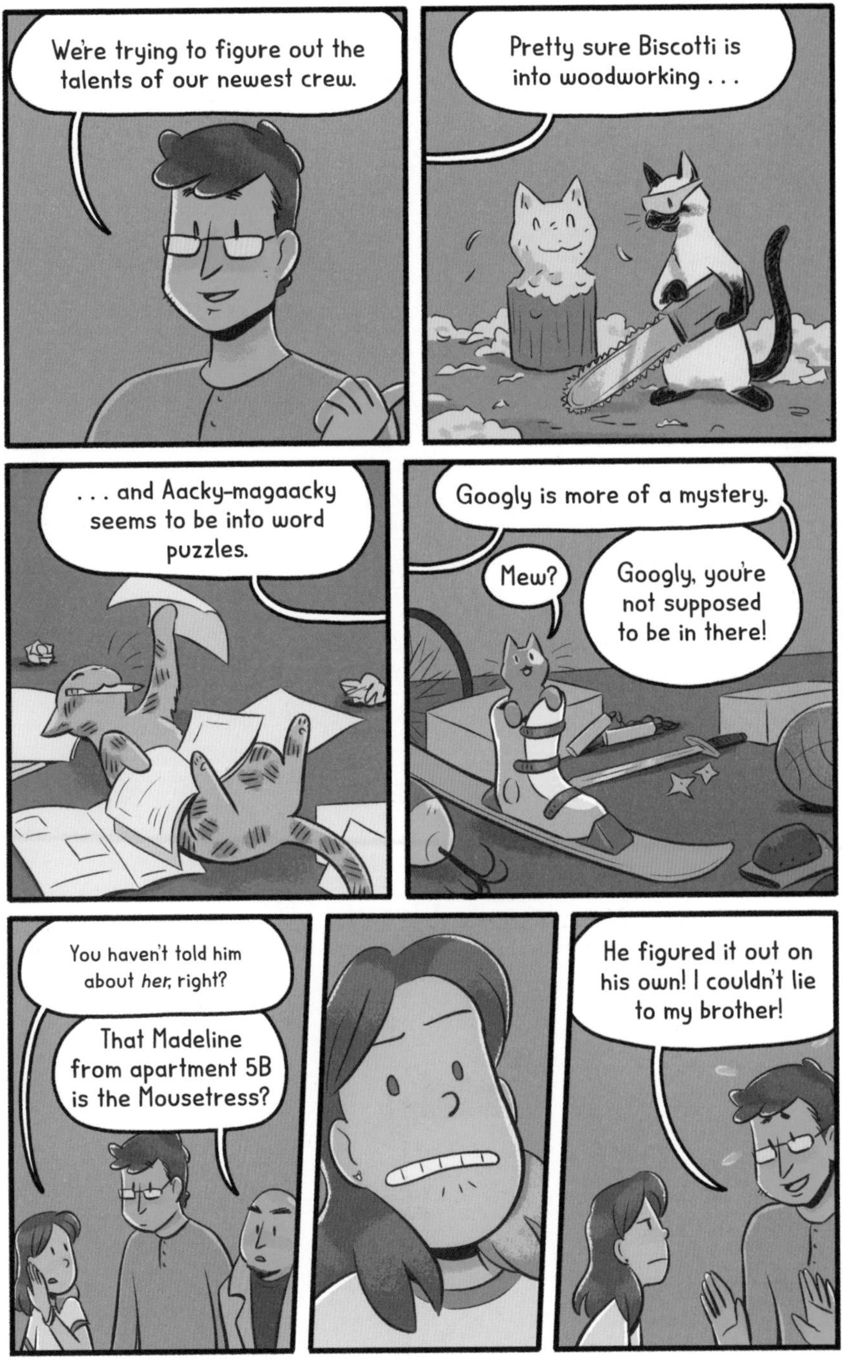
We're trying to figure out the talents of our newest crew.
Pretty sure Biscotti is into woodworking . . .
. . . and Aacky-magaacky seems to be into word puzzles.
Googly is more of a mystery.
Mew?
Googly, you're not supposed to be in there!
You haven't told him about *her*, right?
That Madeline from apartment 5B is the Mousetress?
He figured it out on his own! I couldn't lie to my brother!

CHAPTER SEVEN

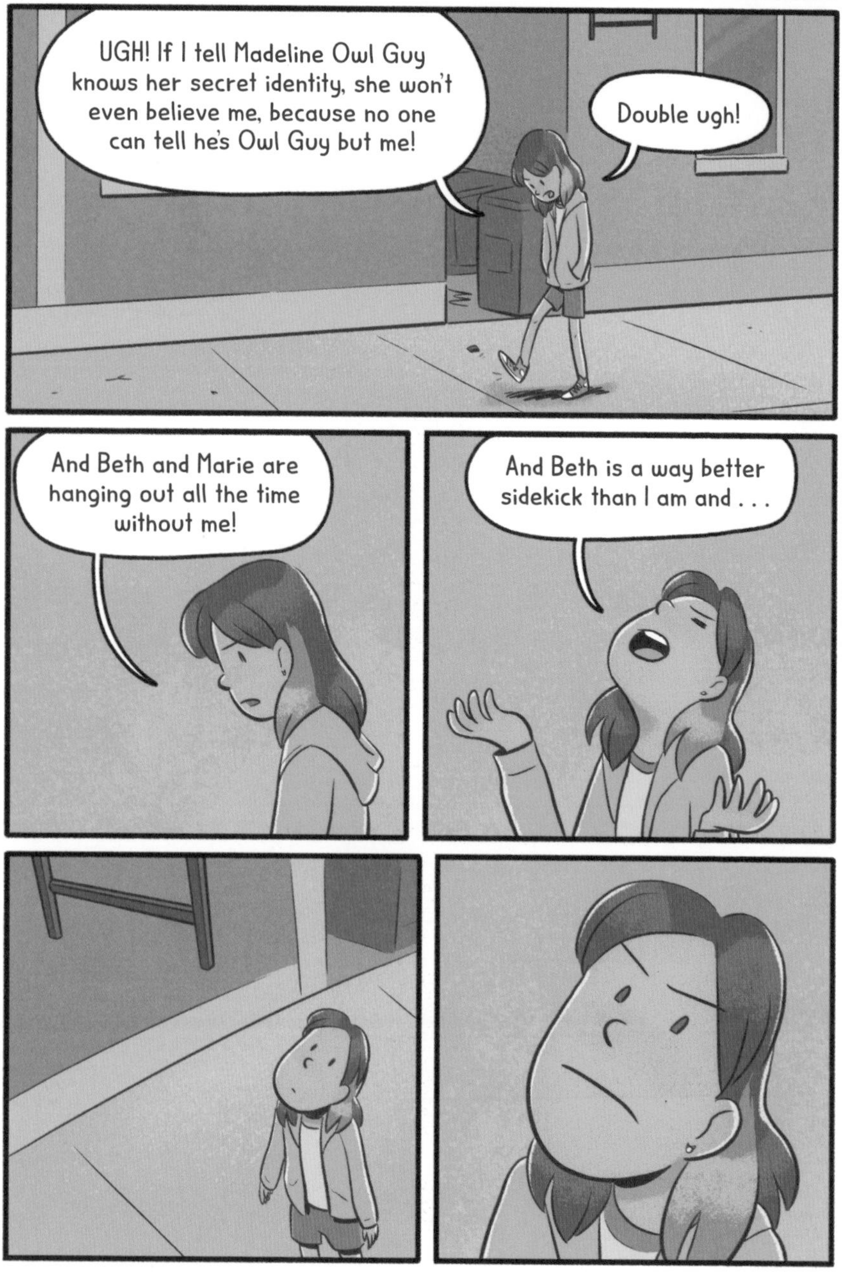

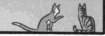

UGH! If I tell Madeline Owl Guy knows her secret identity, she won't even believe me, because no one can tell he's Owl Guy but me!
Double ugh!
And Beth and Marie are hanging out all the time without me!
And Beth is a way better sidekick than I am and . . .

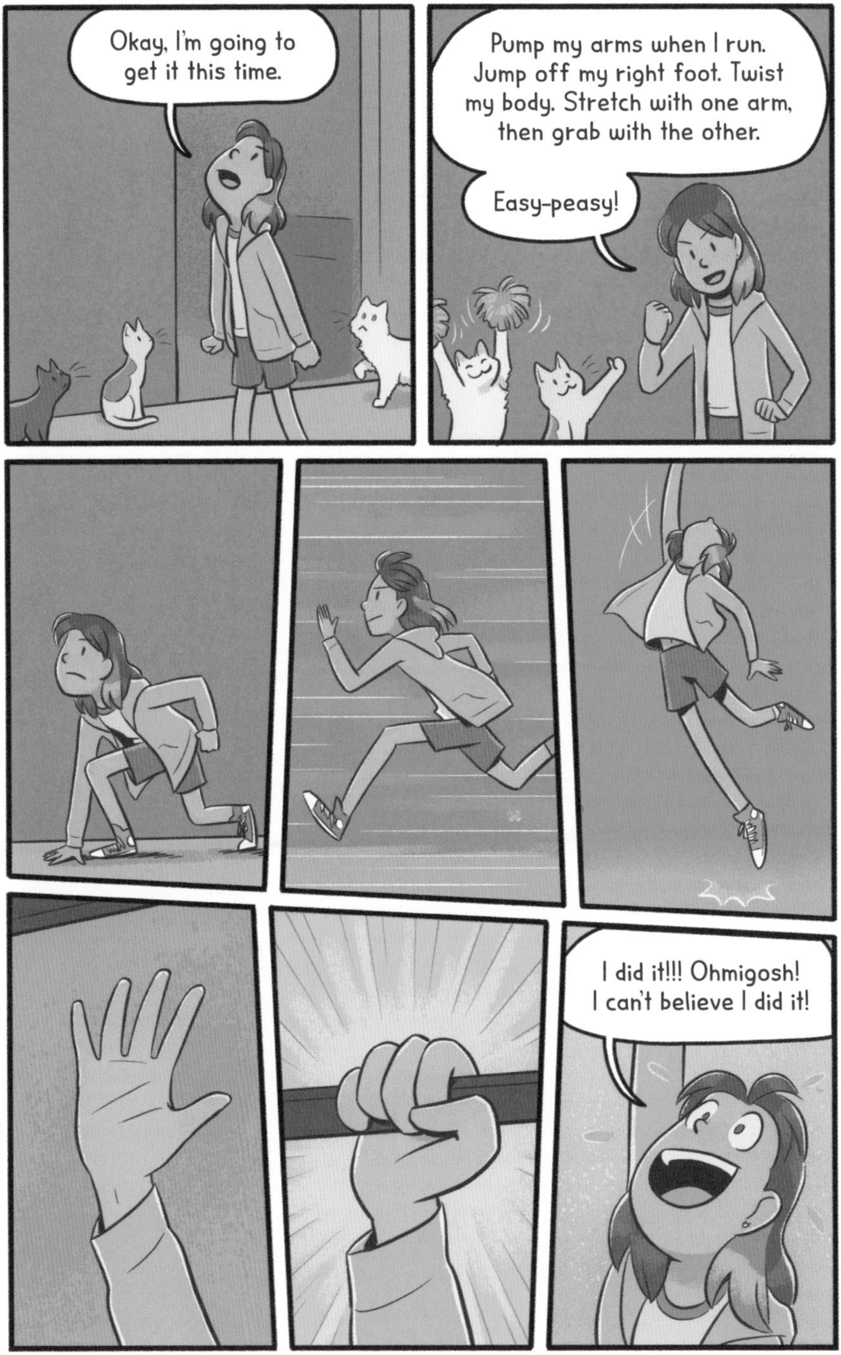
Okay, I'm going to get it this time.
Pump my arms when I run. Jump off my right foot. Twist my body. Stretch with one arm, then grab with the other.
Easy-peasy!
I did it!!! Ohmigosh! I can't believe I did it!

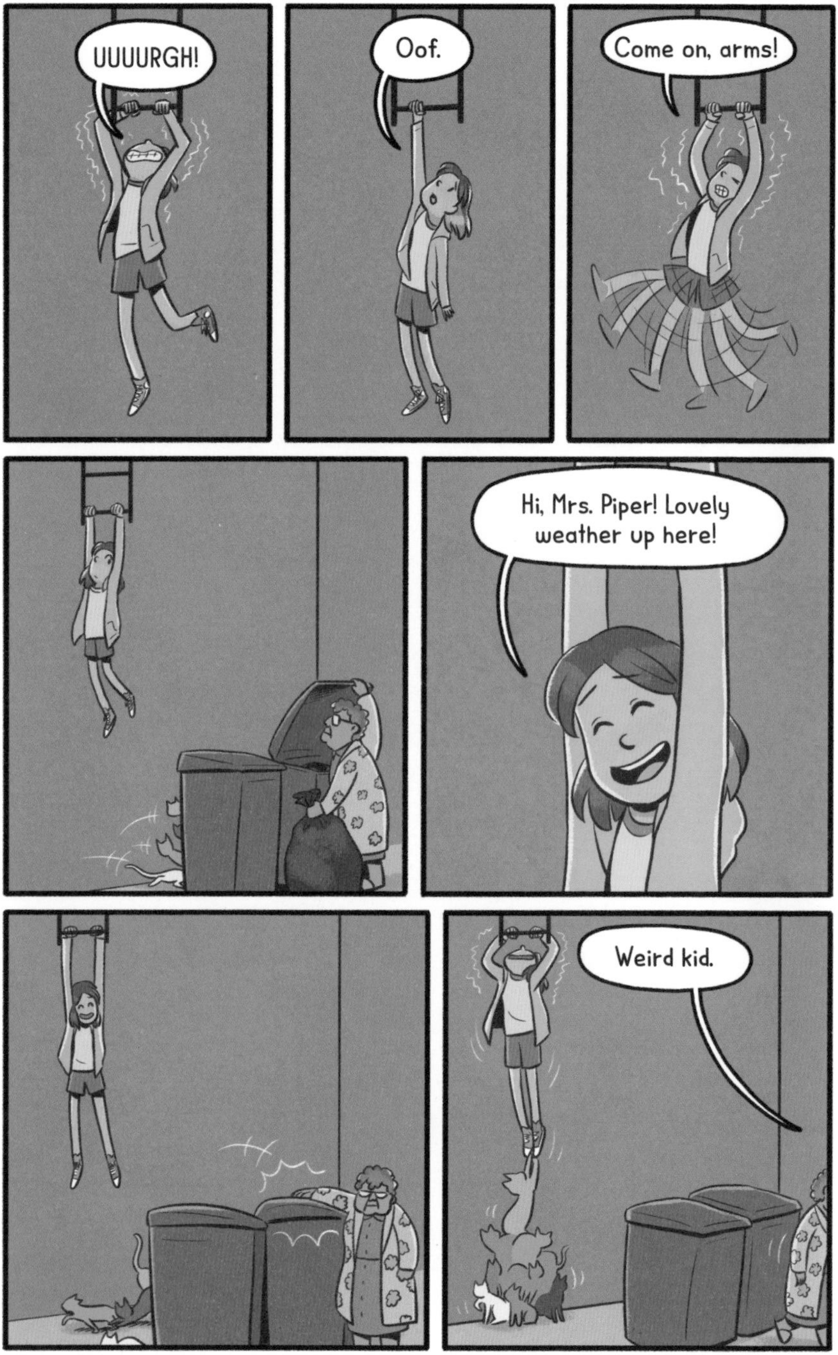
UUUURGH!
Oof.
Come on, arms!
Hi, Mrs. Piper! Lovely weather up here!
Weird kid.

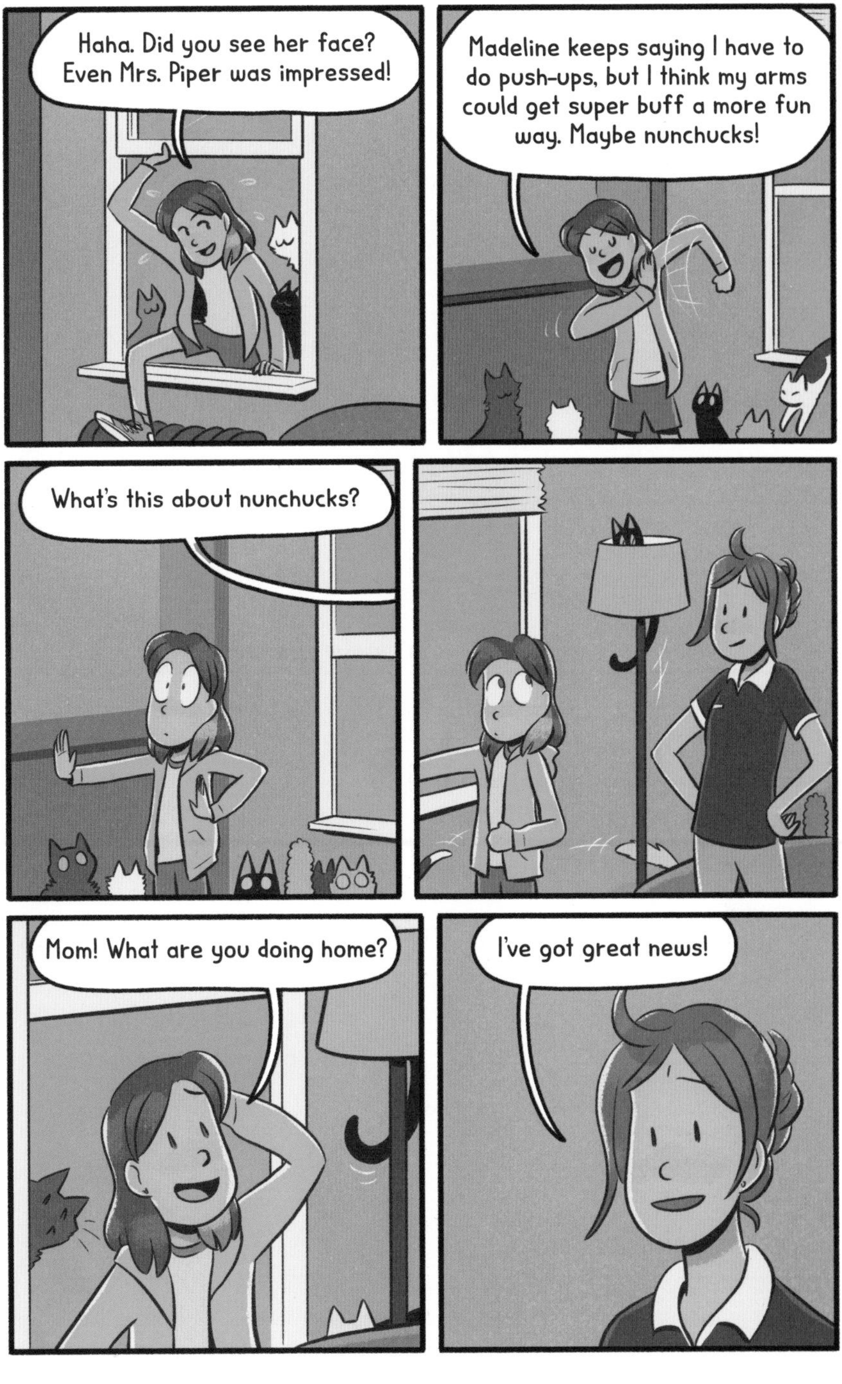
Haha. Did you see her face? Even Mrs. Piper was impressed!
Madeline keeps saying I have to do push-ups, but I think my arms could get super buff a more fun way. Maybe nunchucks!
What's this about nunchucks?
Mom! What are you doing home?
I've got great news!

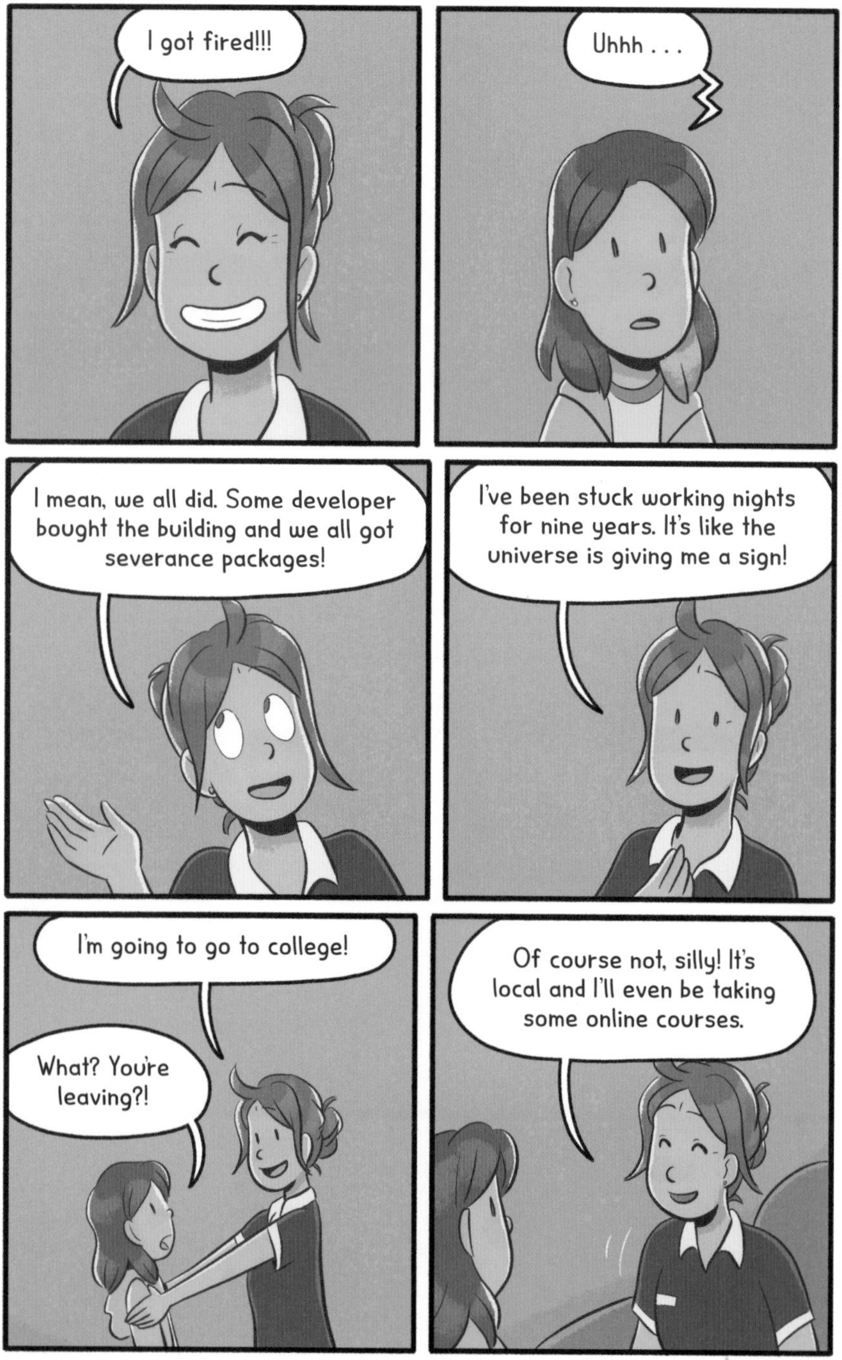
I got fired!!!
Uhhh . . .
I mean, we all did. Some developer bought the building and we all got severance packages!
I've been stuck working nights for nine years. It's like the universe is giving me a sign!
I'm going to go to college!
What? You're leaving?!
Of course not, silly! It's local and I'll even be taking some online courses.

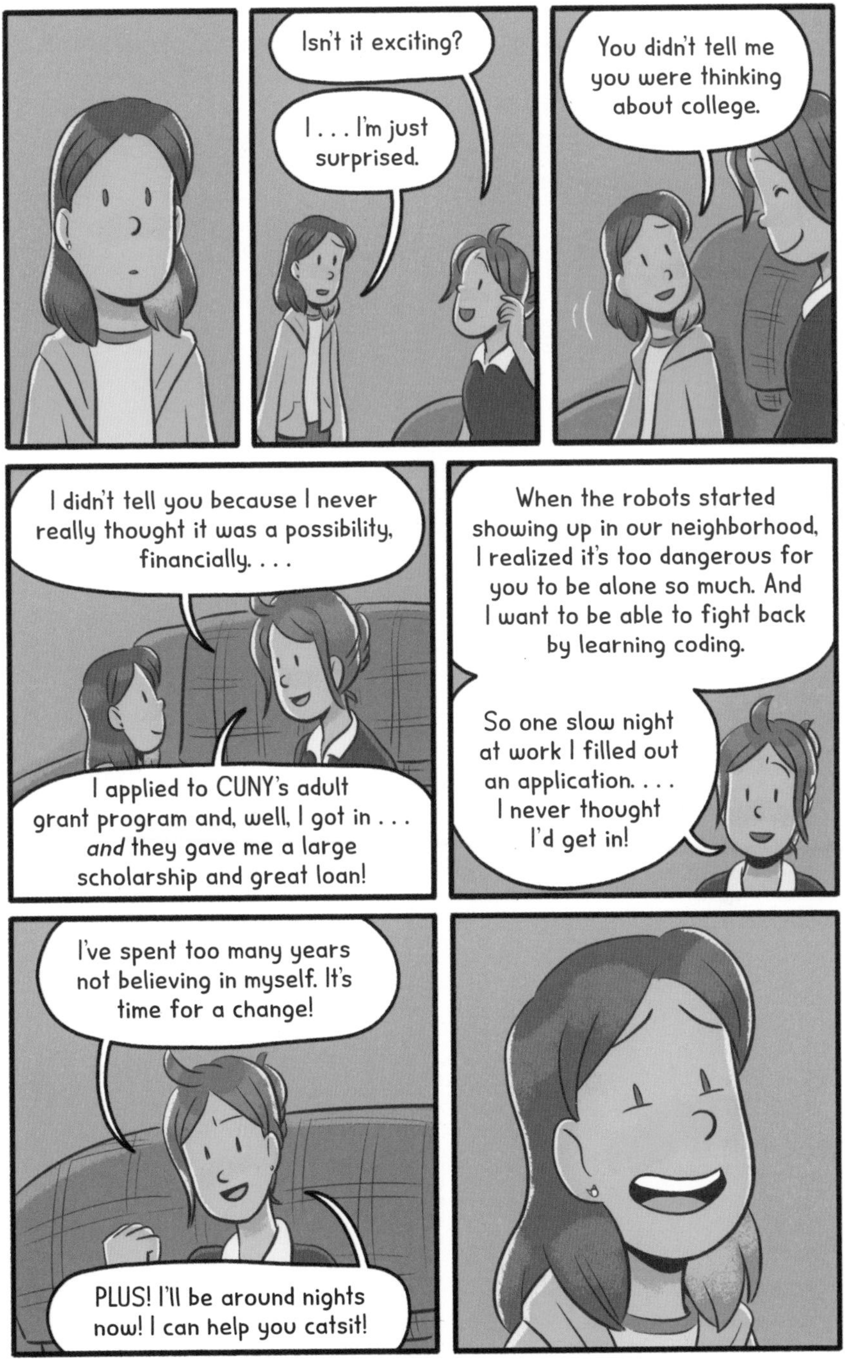
Isn't it exciting?
I . . . I'm just surprised.
You didn't tell me you were thinking about college.
I didn't tell you because I never really thought it was a possibility, financially. . . .
I applied to CUNY's adult grant program and, well, I got in . . . *and* they gave me a large scholarship and great loan!
When the robots started showing up in our neighborhood, I realized it's too dangerous for you to be alone so much. And I want to be able to fight back by learning coding.
So one slow night at work I filled out an application. . . . I never thought I'd get in!
I've spent too many years not believing in myself. It's time for a change!
PLUS! I'll be around nights now! I can help you catsit!

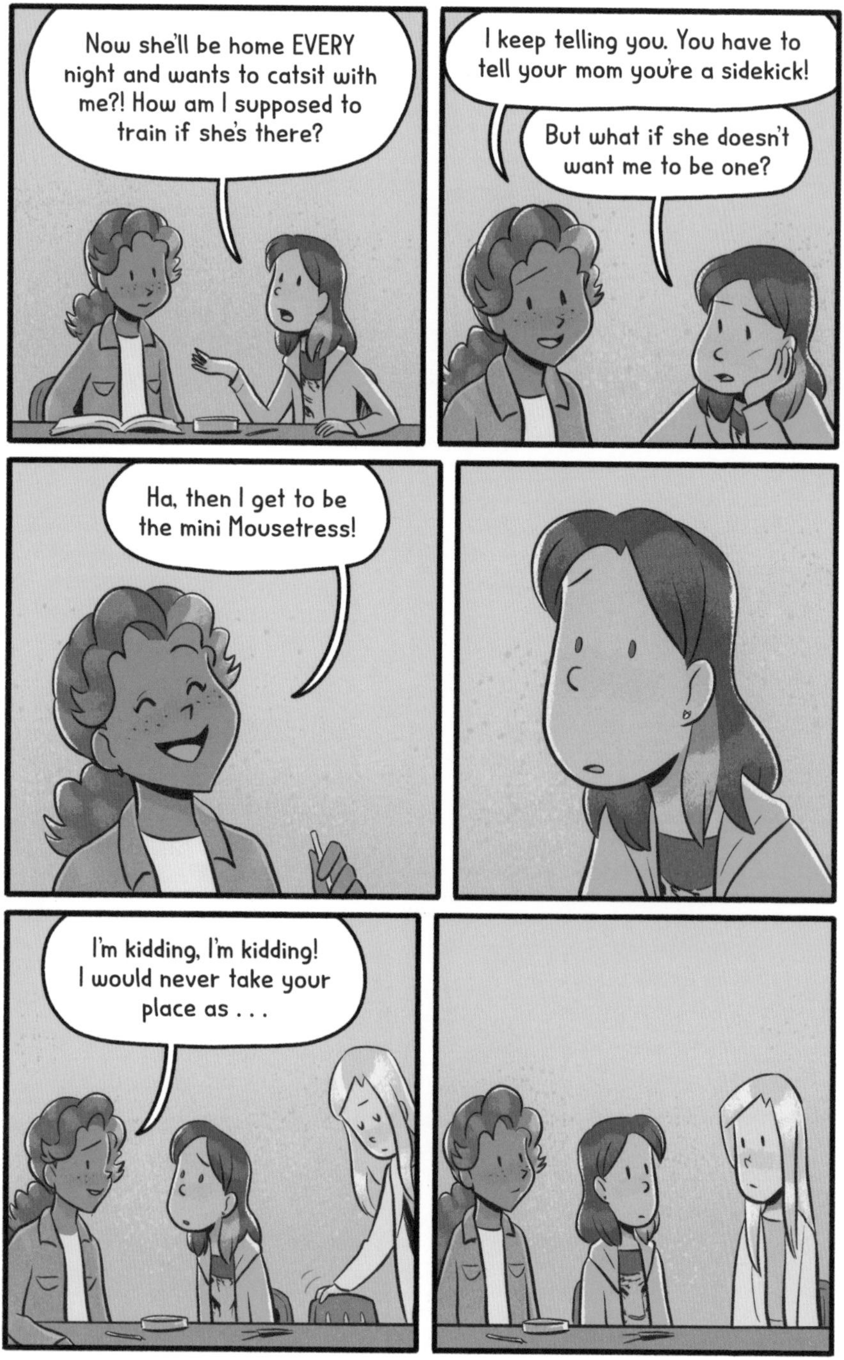
Now she'll be home EVERY night and wants to catsit with me?! How am I supposed to train if she's there?
I keep telling you. You have to tell your mom you're a sidekick!
But what if she doesn't want me to be one?
Ha, then I get to be the mini Mousetress!
I'm kidding, I'm kidding! I would never take your place as . . .

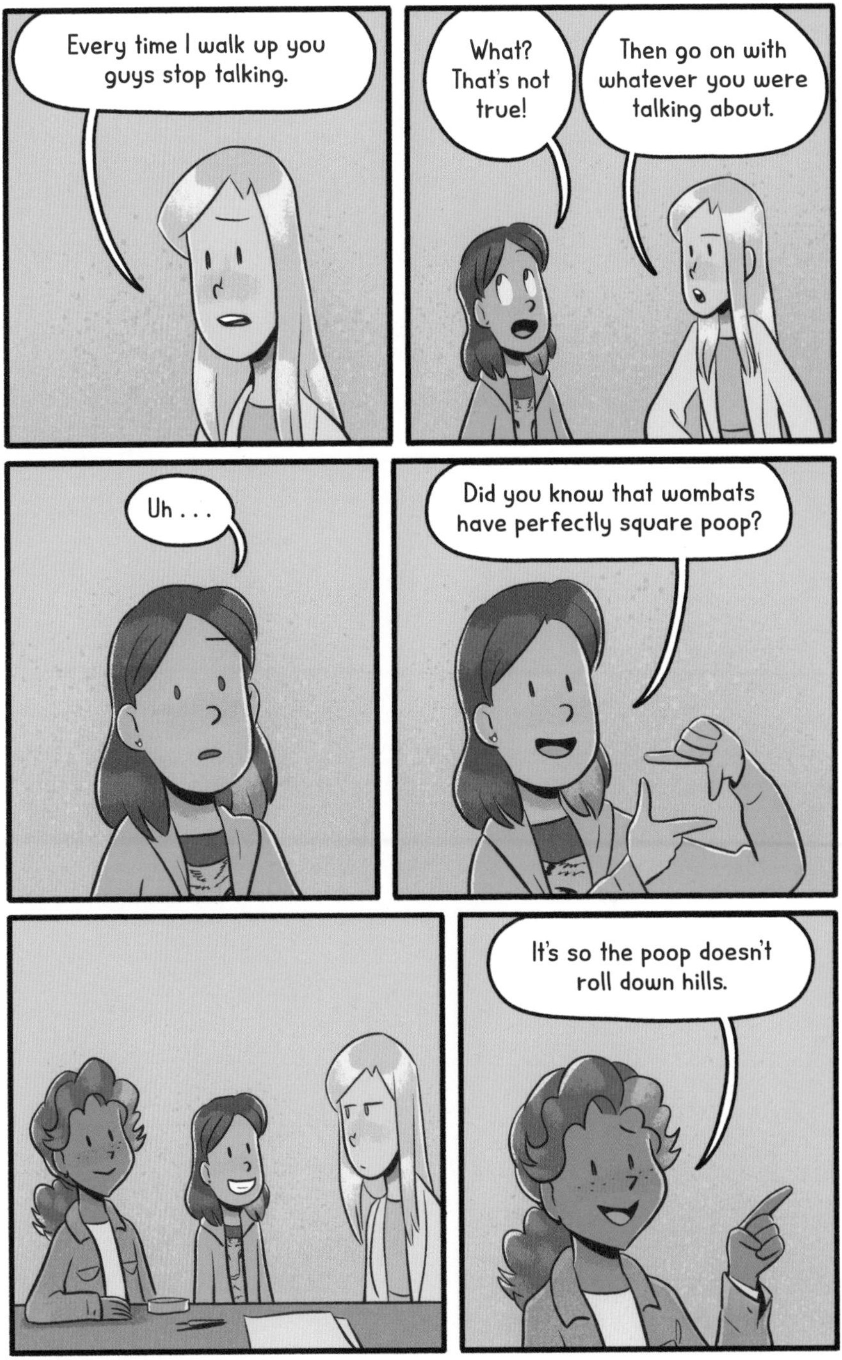
Every time I walk up you guys stop talking.
What? That's not true!
Then go on with whatever you were talking about.
Uh . . .
Did you know that wombats have perfectly square poop?
It's so the poop doesn't roll down hills.

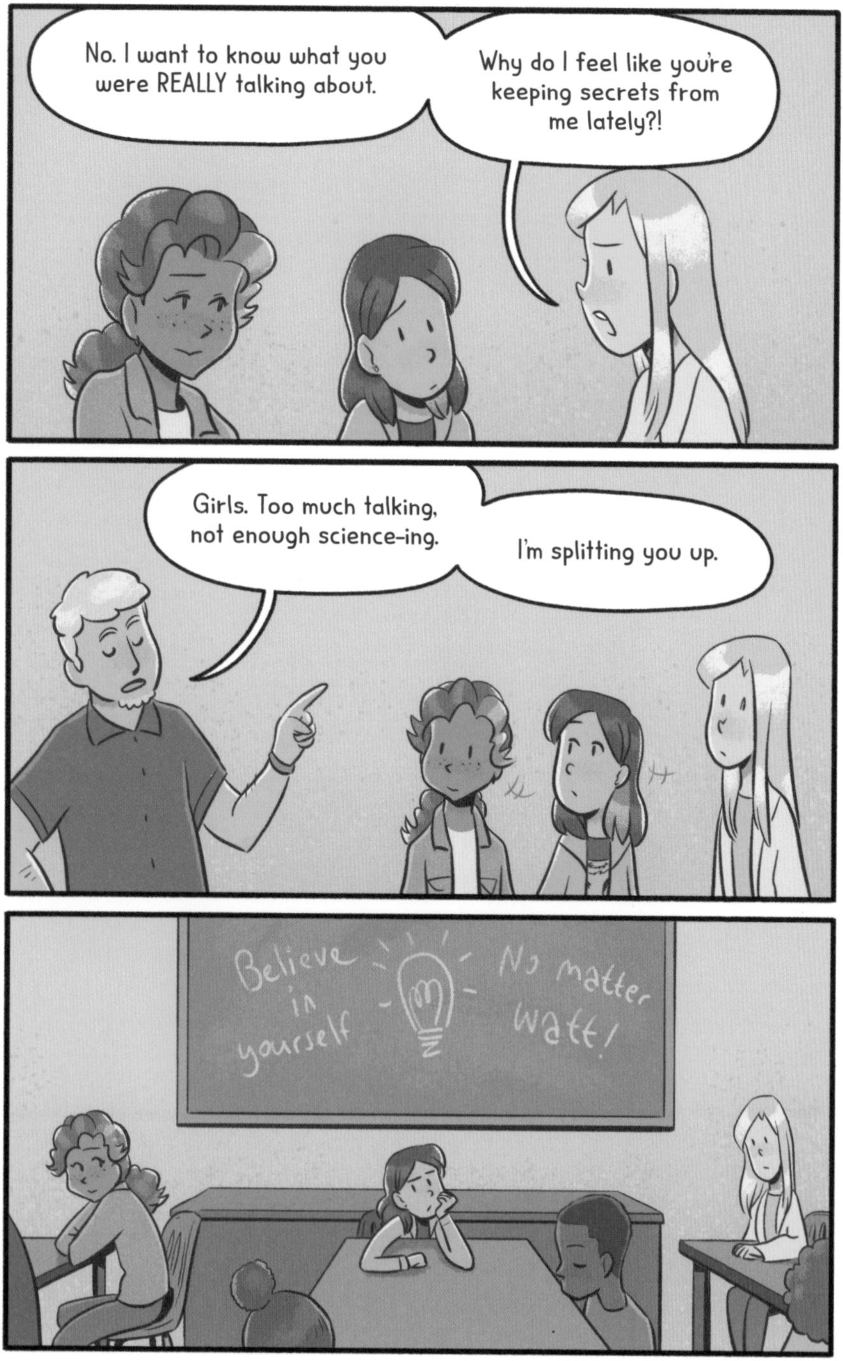
No. I want to know what you were REALLY talking about.
Why do I feel like you're keeping secrets from me lately?!
Girls. Too much talking, not enough science-ing.
I'm splitting you up.
Believe in yourself
No matter watt!

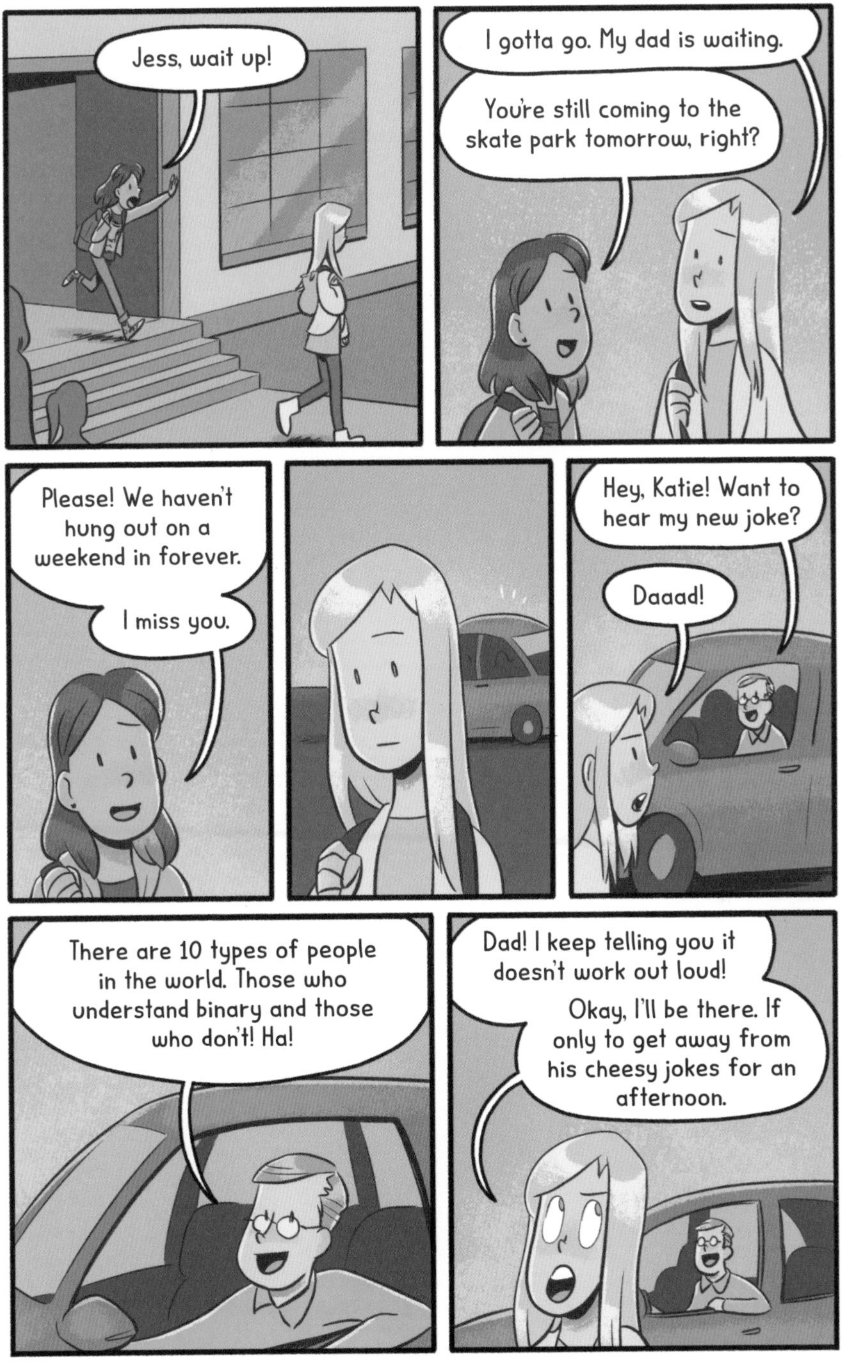
Jess, wait up!
I gotta go. My dad is waiting.
You're still coming to the skate park tomorrow, right?
Please! We haven't hung out on a weekend in forever.
I miss you.
Hey, Katie! Want to hear my new joke?
Daaad!
There are 10 types of people in the world. Those who understand binary and those who don't! Ha!
Dad! I keep telling you it doesn't work out loud!
Okay, I'll be there. If only to get away from his cheesy jokes for an afternoon.

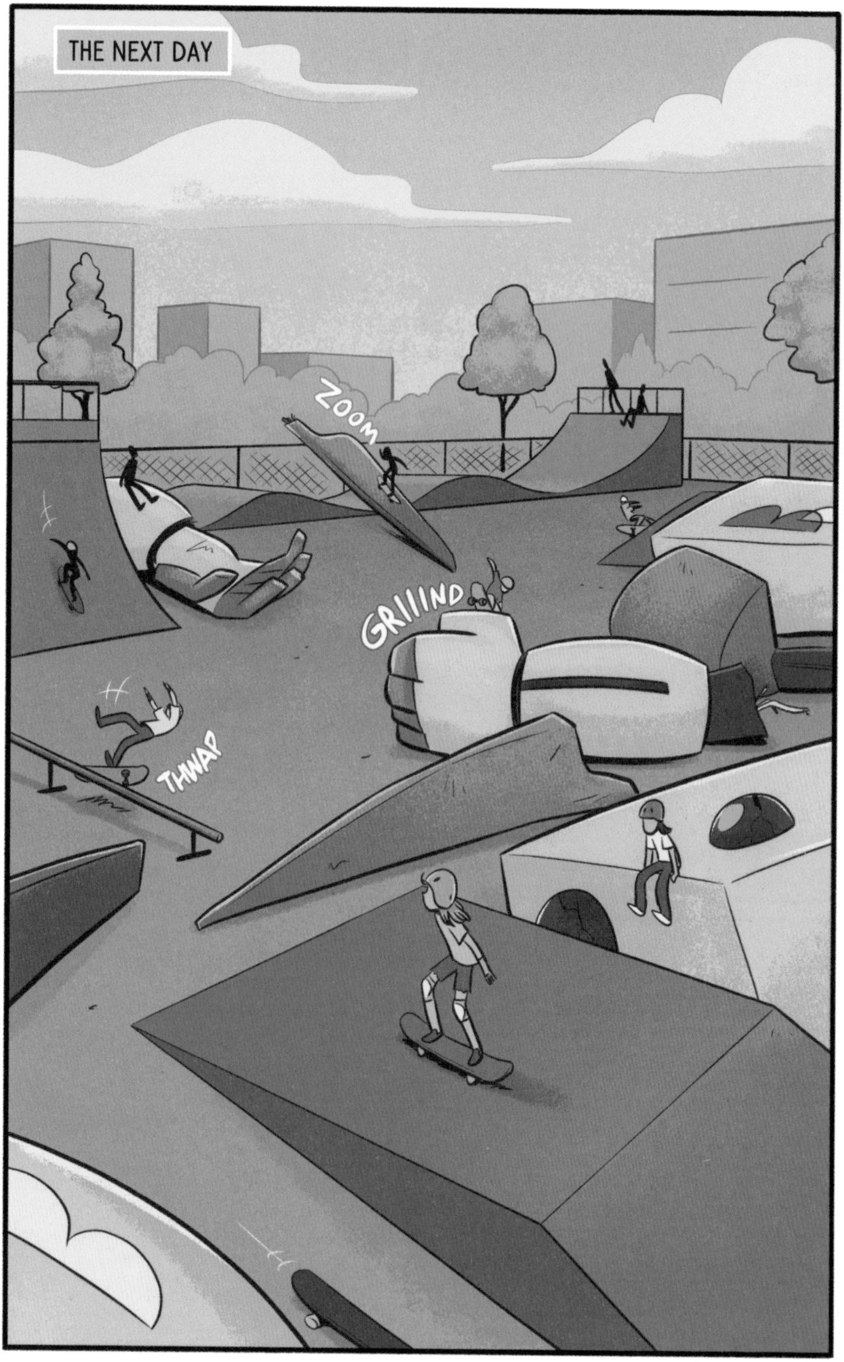
THE NEXT DAY
ZOOM
GRIIIND
THWAP

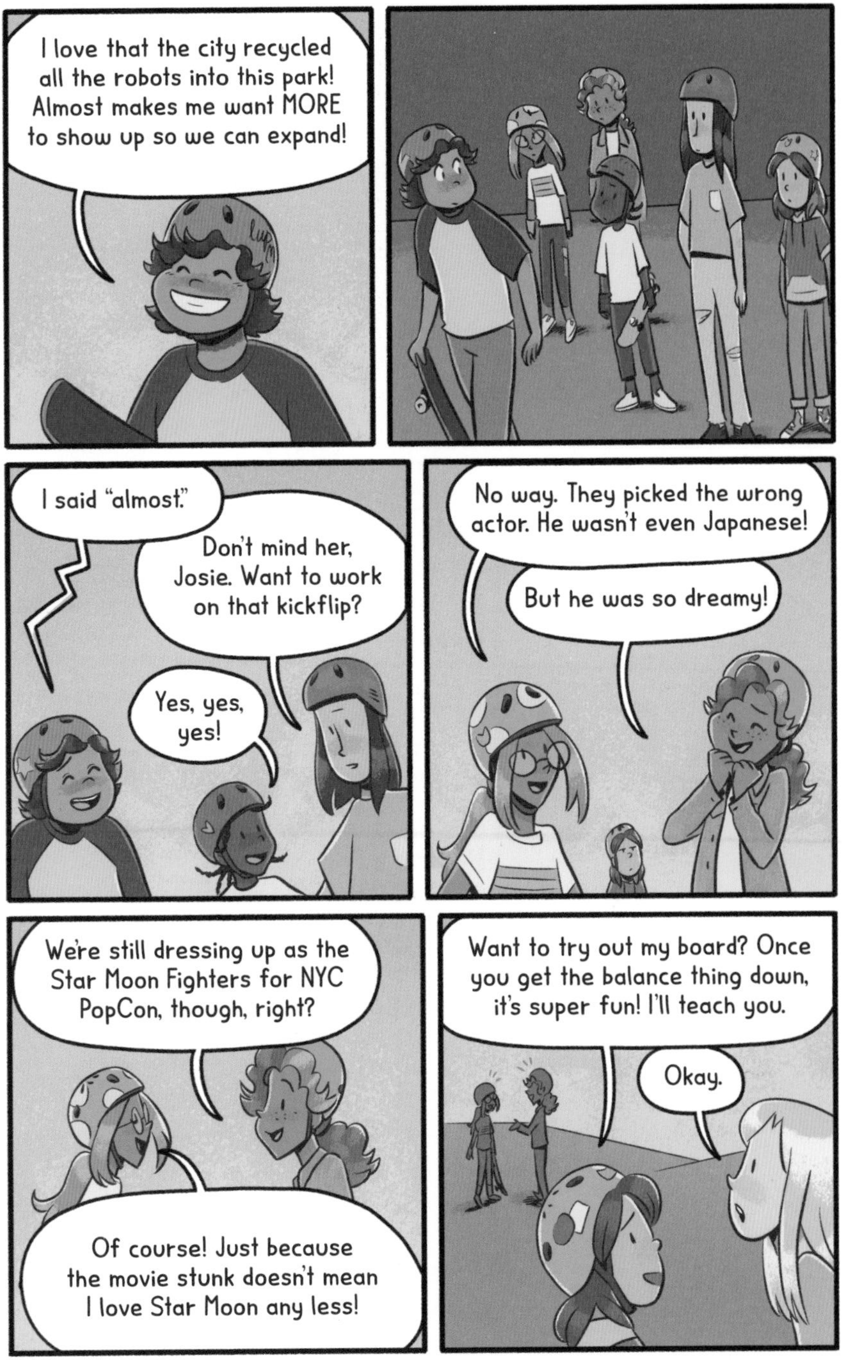
I love that the city recycled all the robots into this park! Almost makes me want MORE to show up so we can expand!
I said "almost."
Don't mind her, Josie. Want to work on that kickflip?
Yes, yes, yes!
No way. They picked the wrong actor. He wasn't even Japanese!
But he was so dreamy!
We're still dressing up as the Star Moon Fighters for NYC PopCon, though, right?
Of course! Just because the movie stunk doesn't mean I love Star Moon any less!
Want to try out my board? Once you get the balance thing down, it's super fun! I'll teach you.
Okay.

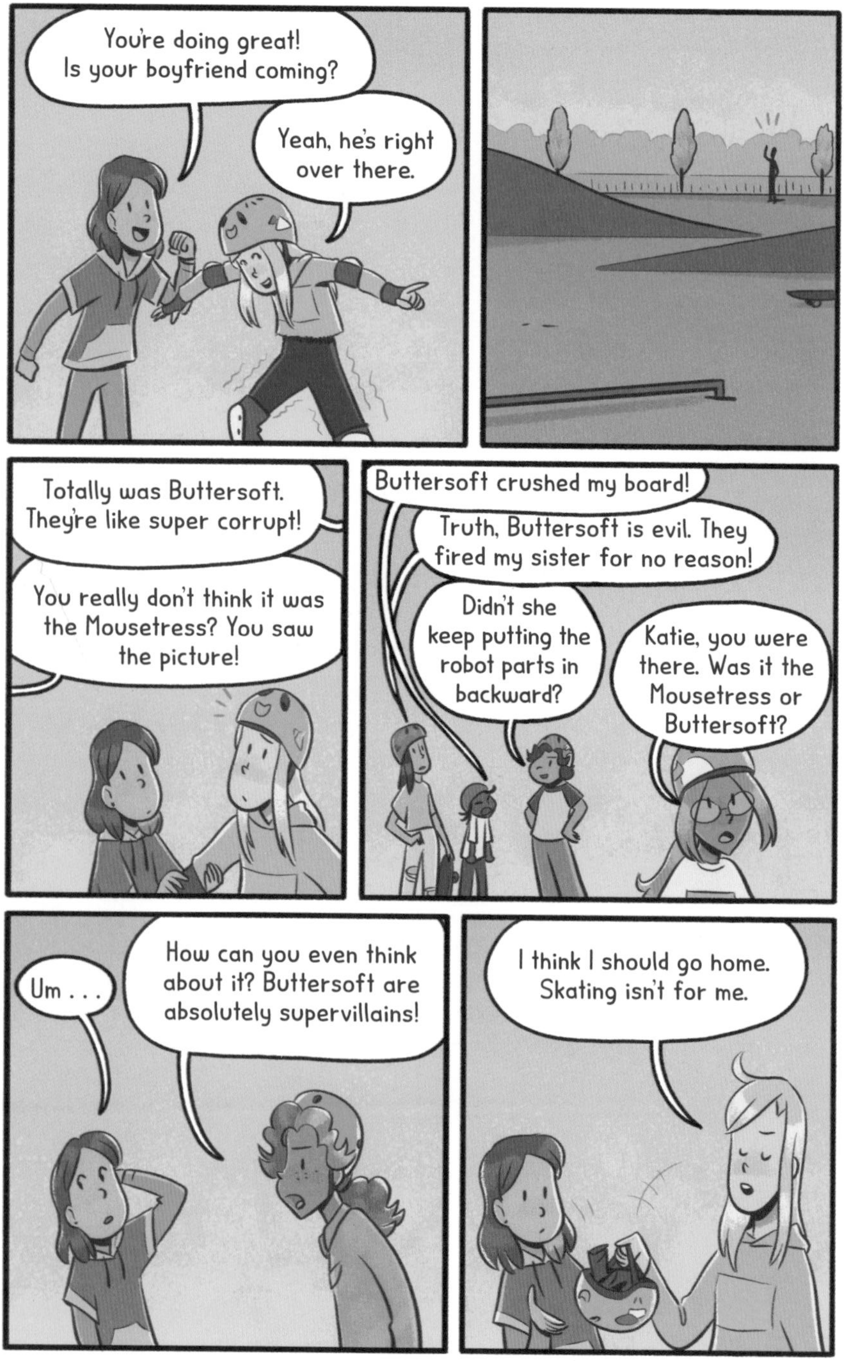
You're doing great!
Is your boyfriend coming?
Yeah, he's right over there.
Totally was Buttersoft. They're like super corrupt!
You really don't think it was the Mousetress? You saw the picture!
Buttersoft crushed my board!
Truth, Buttersoft is evil. They fired my sister for no reason!
Didn't she keep putting the robot parts in backward?
Katie, you were there. Was it the Mousetress or Buttersoft?
Um . . .
How can you even think about it? Buttersoft are absolutely supervillains!
I think I should go home. Skating isn't for me.

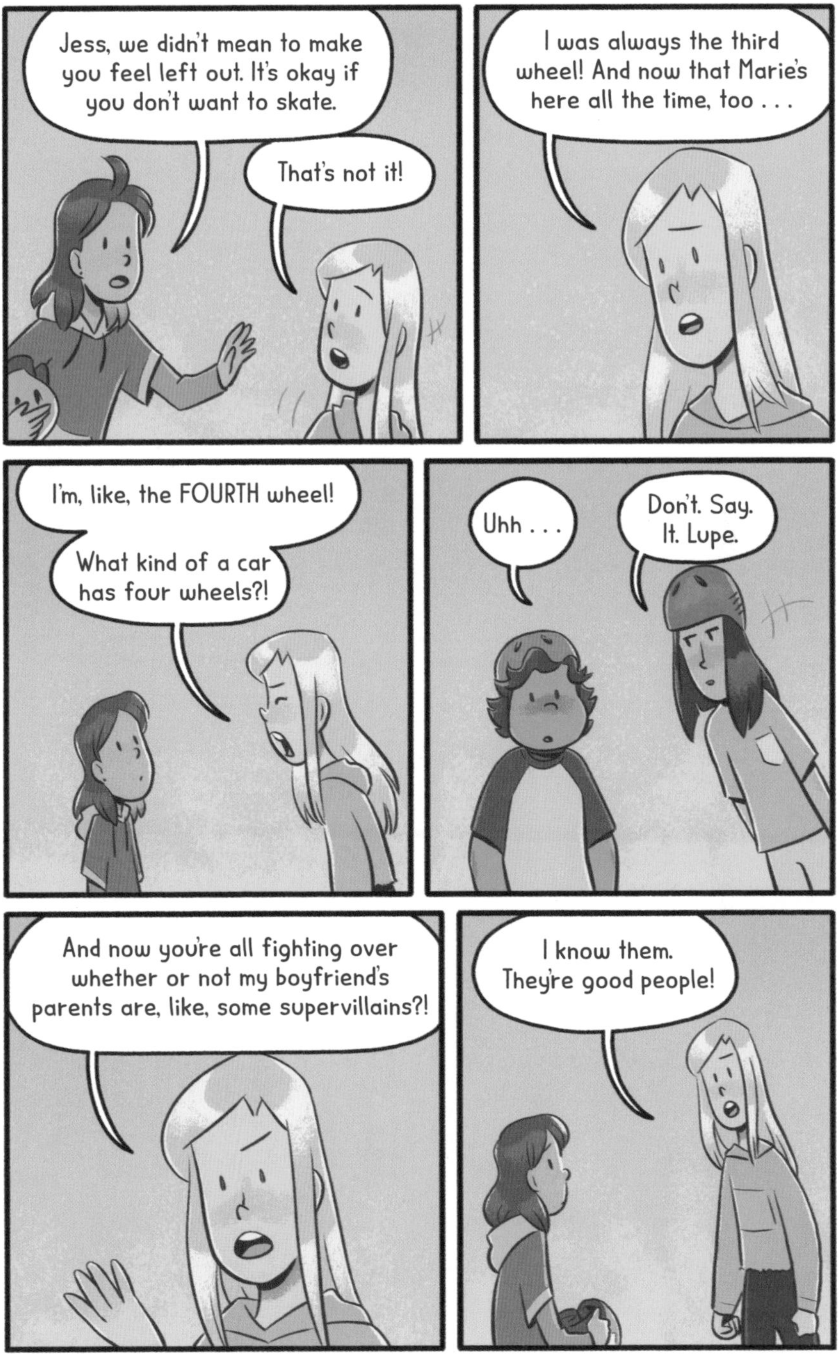

Jess, we didn't mean to make you feel left out. It's okay if you don't want to skate.
That's not it!
I was always the third wheel! And now that Marie's here all the time, too . . .
I'm, like, the FOURTH wheel!
What kind of a car has four wheels?!
Uhh . . .
Don't. Say. It. Lupe.
And now you're all fighting over whether or not my boyfriend's parents are, like, some supervillains?!
I know them. They're good people!

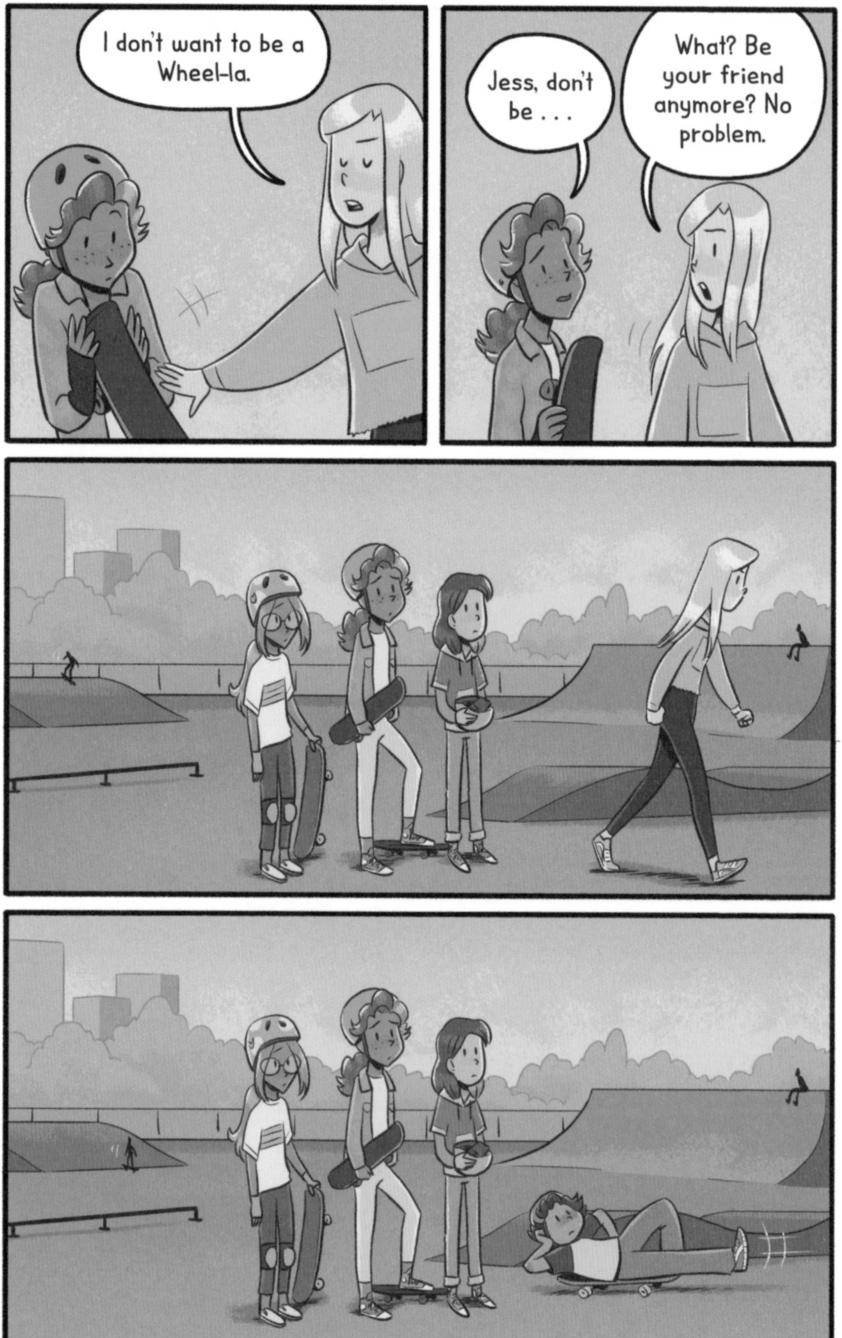
I don't want to be a Wheel-la.
Jess, don't be . . .
What? Be your friend anymore? No problem.

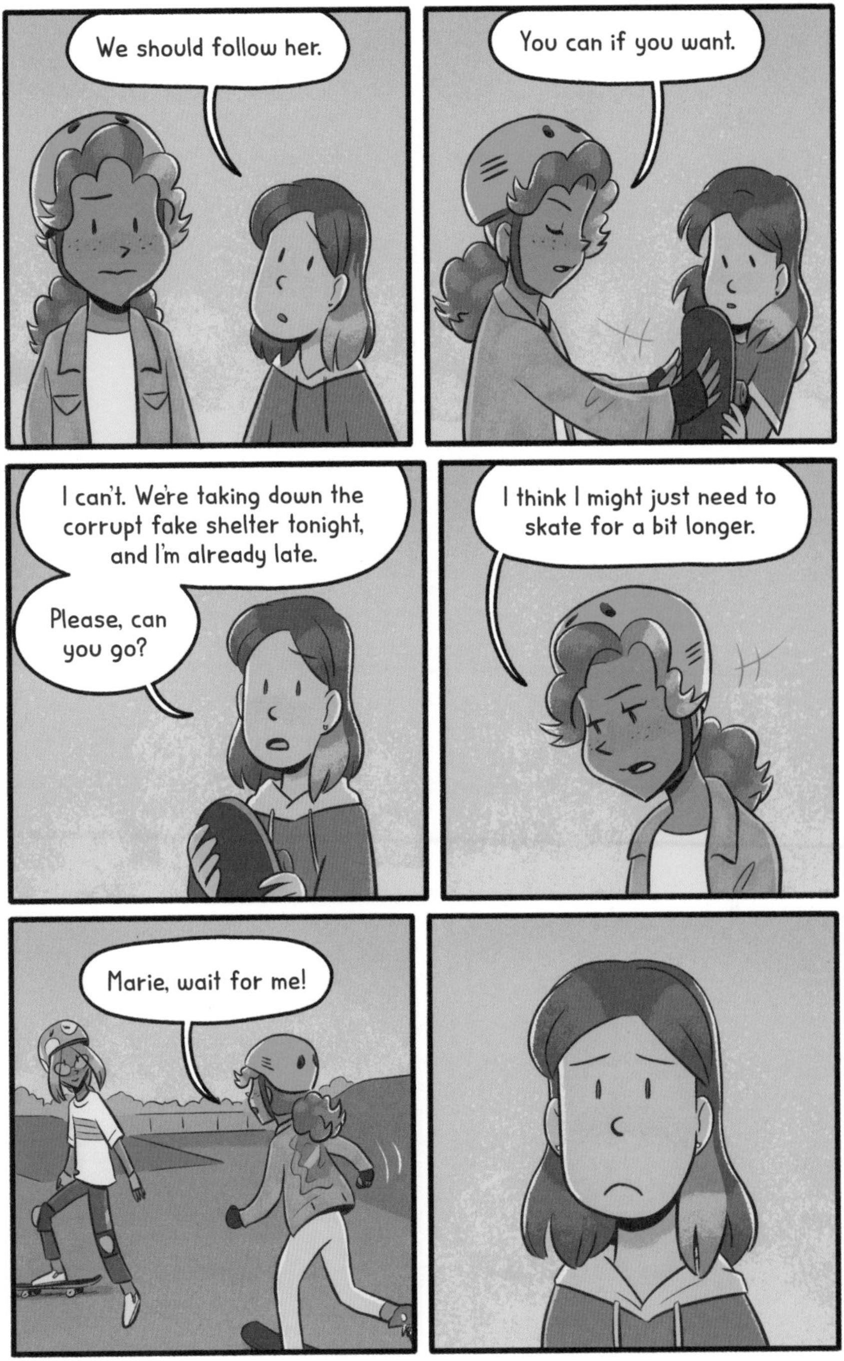
We should follow her.
You can if you want.
I can't. We're taking down the corrupt fake shelter tonight, and I'm already late.
Please, can you go?
I think I might just need to skate for a bit longer.
Marie, wait for me!

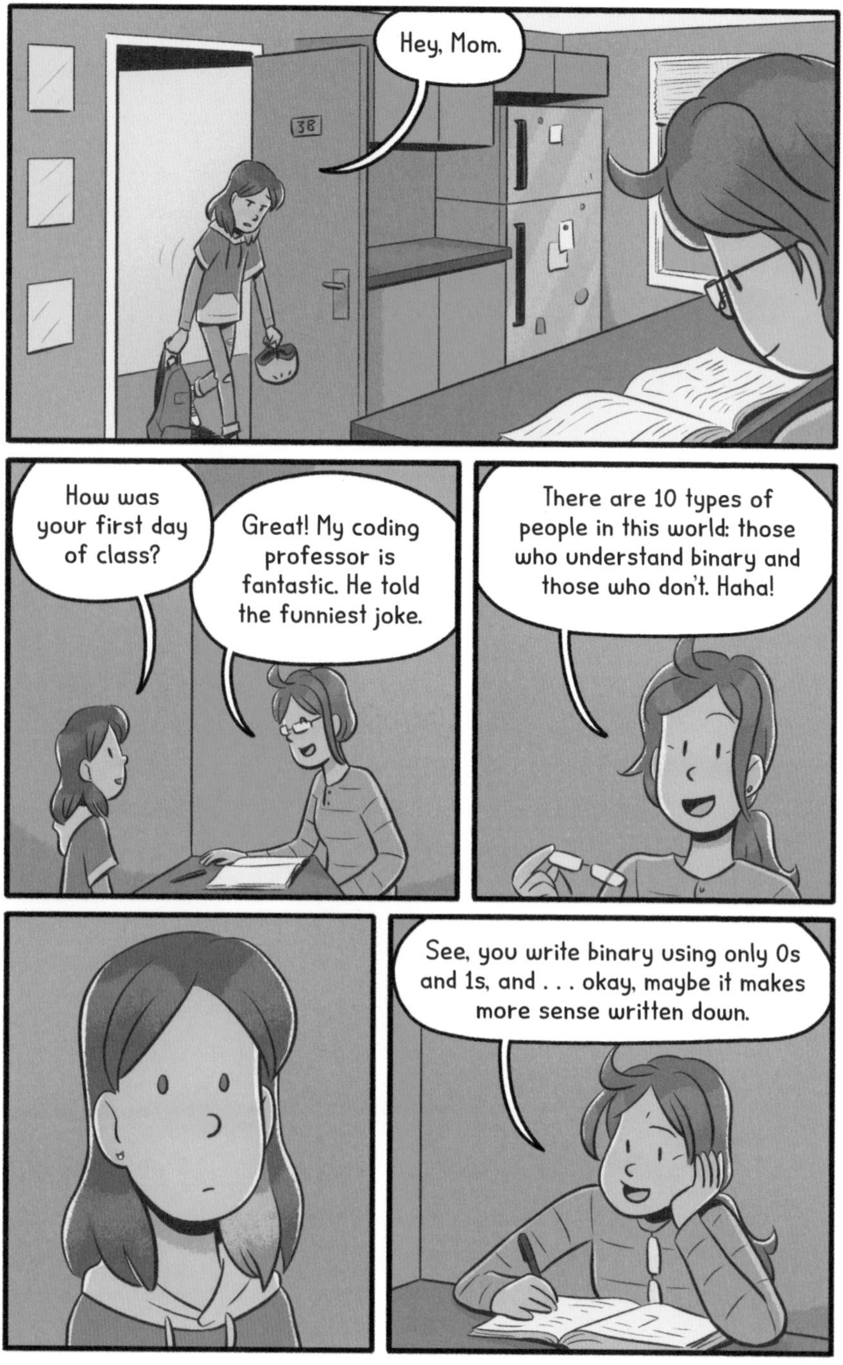
Hey, Mom.
How was your first day of class?
Great! My coding professor is fantastic. He told the funniest joke.
There are 10 types of people in this world: those who understand binary and those who don't. Haha!
See, you write binary using only 0s and 1s, and . . . okay, maybe it makes more sense written down.

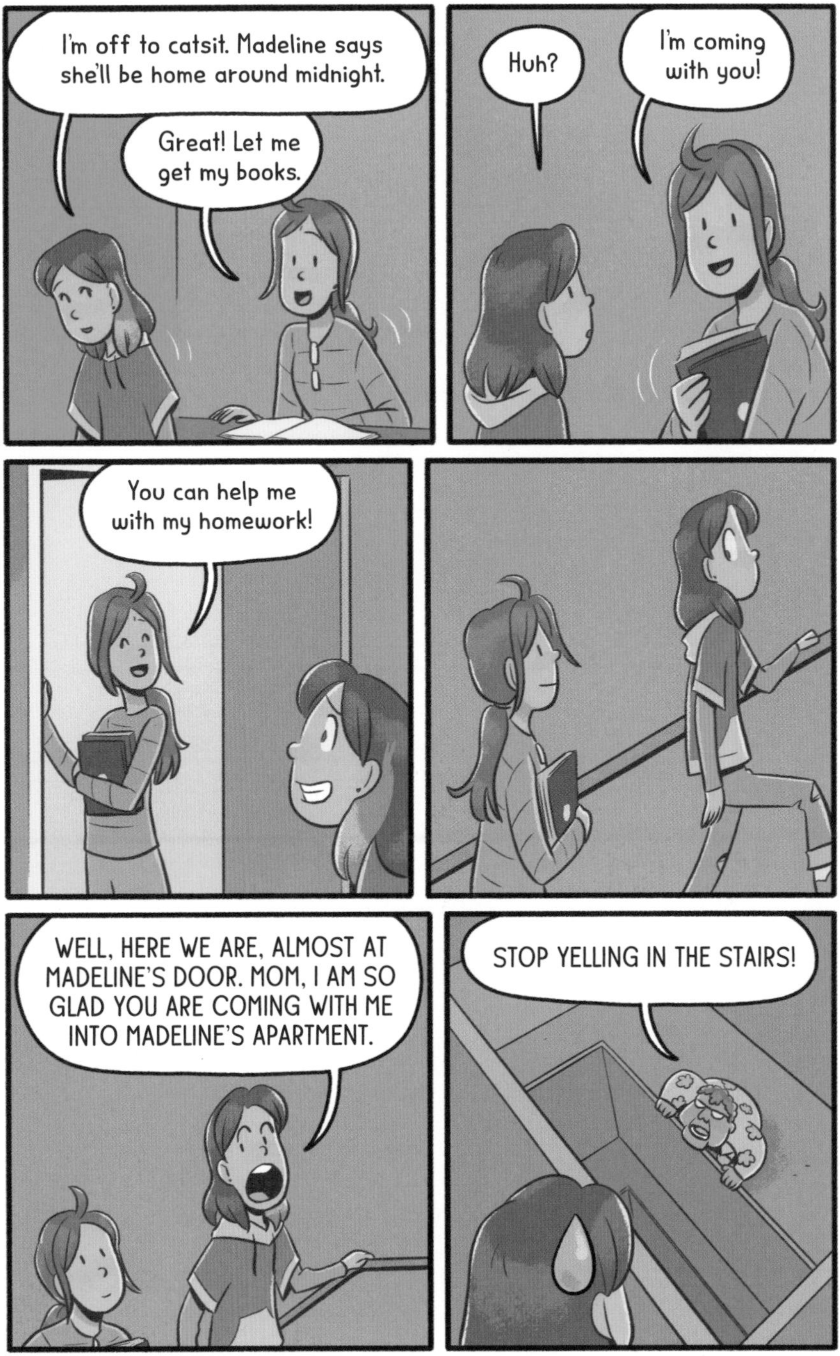
I'm off to catsit. Madeline says she'll be home around midnight.
Great! Let me get my books.
Huh?
I'm coming with you!
You can help me with my homework!
WELL, HERE WE ARE, ALMOST AT MADELINE'S DOOR. MOM, I AM SO GLAD YOU ARE COMING WITH ME INTO MADELINE'S APARTMENT.
STOP YELLING IN THE STAIRS!

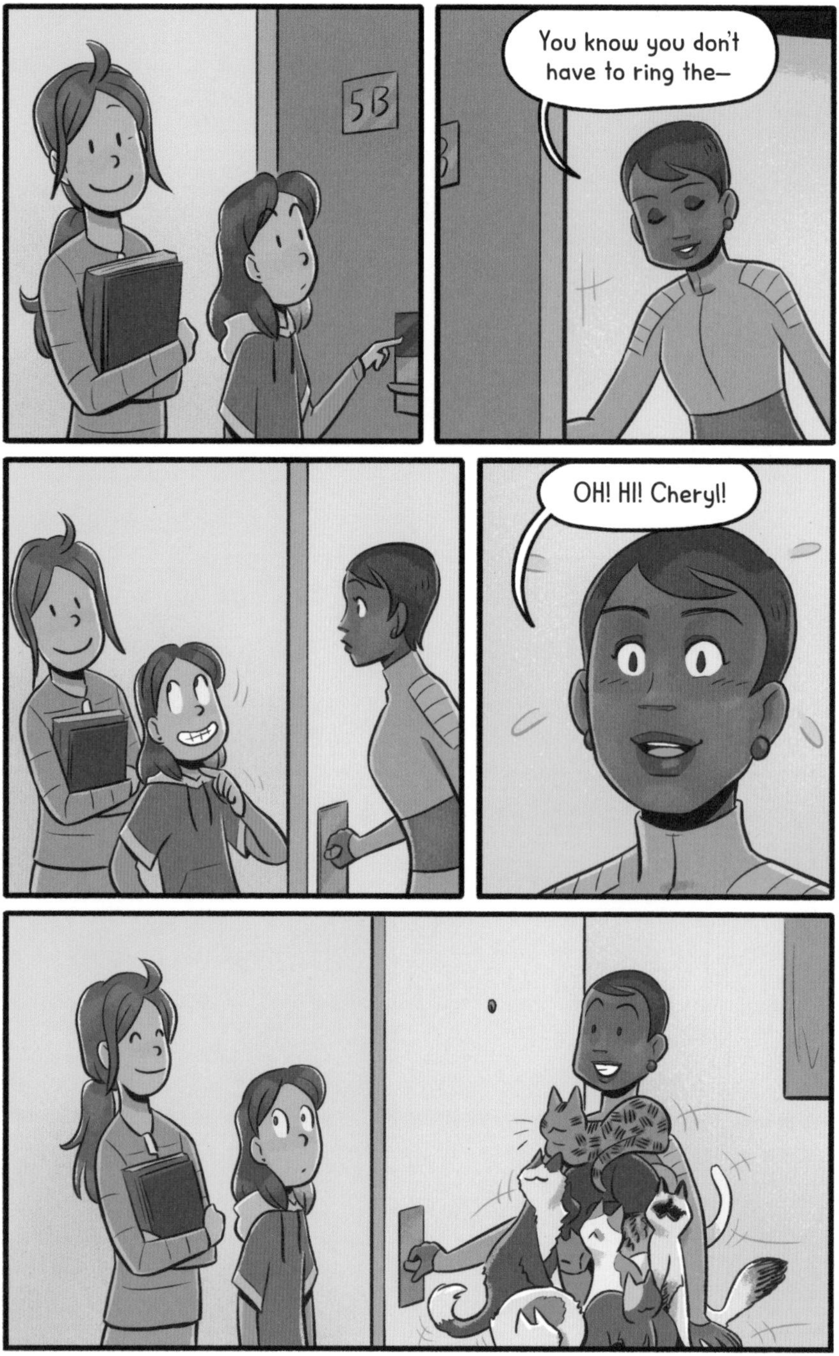
5B
You know you don't have to ring the—
OH! HI! Cheryl!

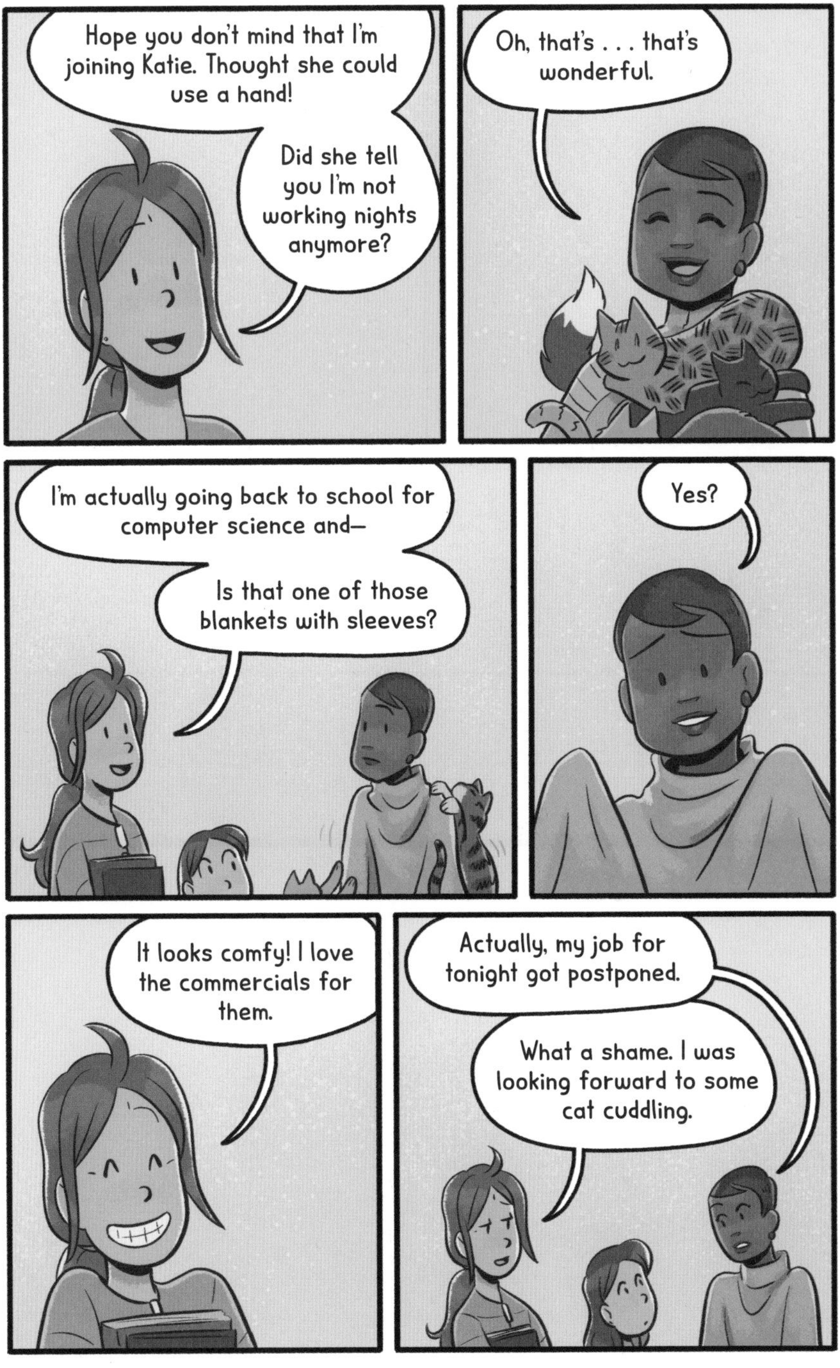
Hope you don't mind that I'm joining Katie. Thought she could use a hand!
Did she tell you I'm not working nights anymore?
Oh, that's . . . that's wonderful.
I'm actually going back to school for computer science and—
Is that one of those blankets with sleeves?
Yes?
It looks comfy! I love the commercials for them.
Actually, my job for tonight got postponed.
What a shame. I was looking forward to some cat cuddling.

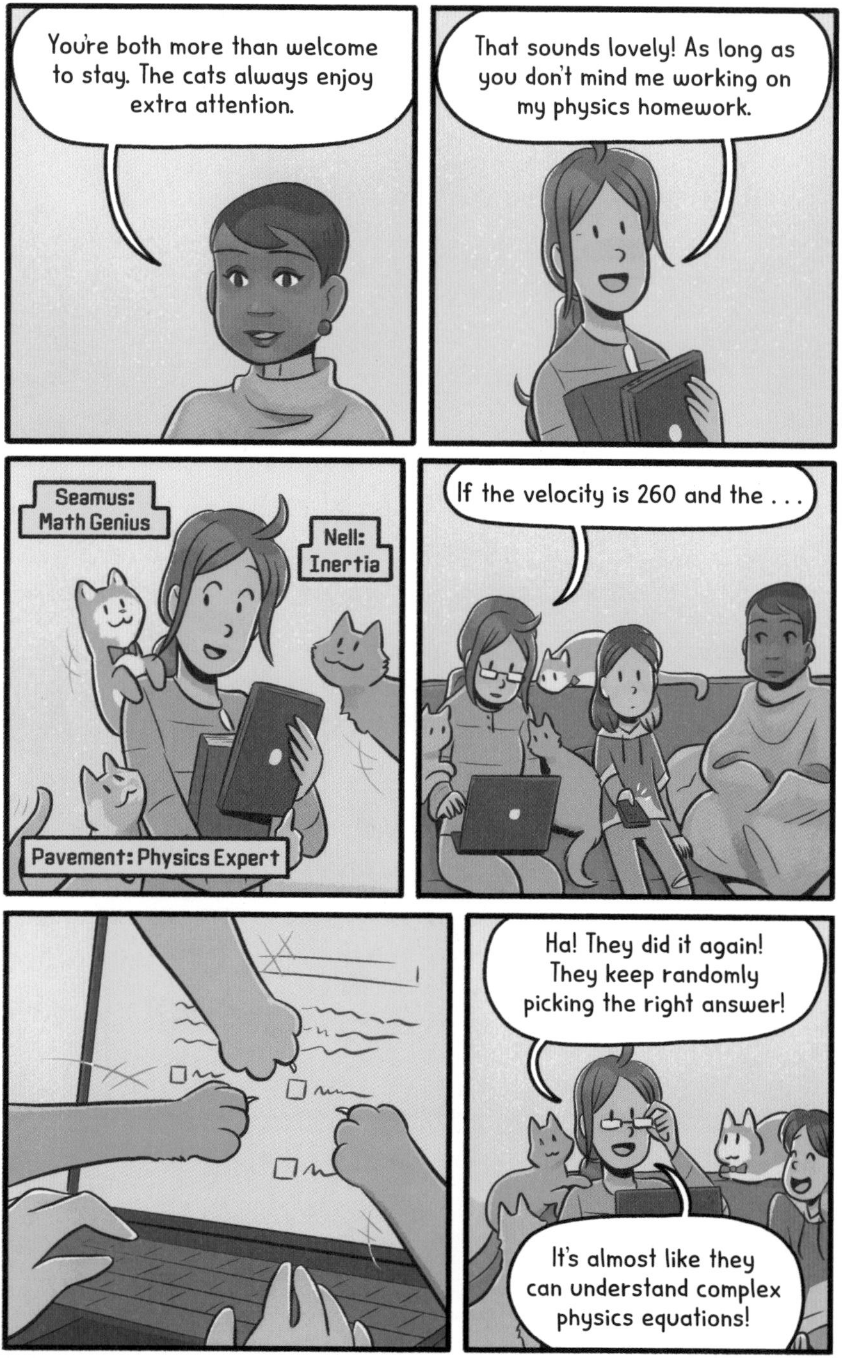
You're both more than welcome to stay. The cats always enjoy extra attention.
That sounds lovely! As long as you don't mind me working on my physics homework.
Seamus: Math Genius
Nell: Inertia
Pavement: Physics Expert
If the velocity is 260 and the . . .
Ha! They did it again! They keep randomly picking the right answer!
It's almost like they can understand complex physics equations!

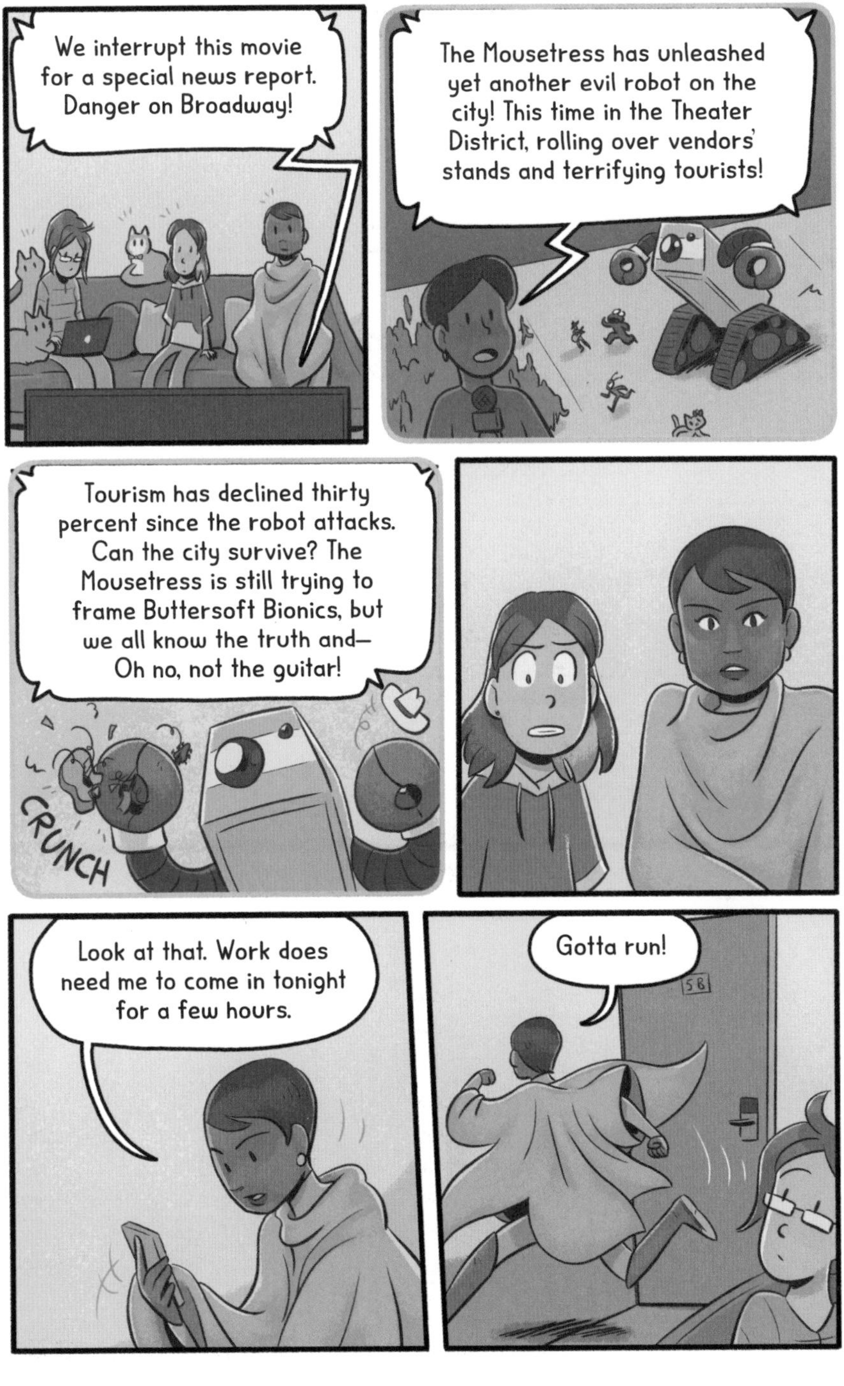
We interrupt this movie for a special news report. Danger on Broadway!
The Mousetress has unleashed yet another evil robot on the city! This time in the Theater District, rolling over vendors' stands and terrifying tourists!
Tourism has declined thirty percent since the robot attacks. Can the city survive? The Mousetress is still trying to frame Buttersoft Bionics, but we all know the truth and— Oh no, not the guitar!
CRUNCH
Look at that. Work does need me to come in tonight for a few hours.
Gotta run!
5B

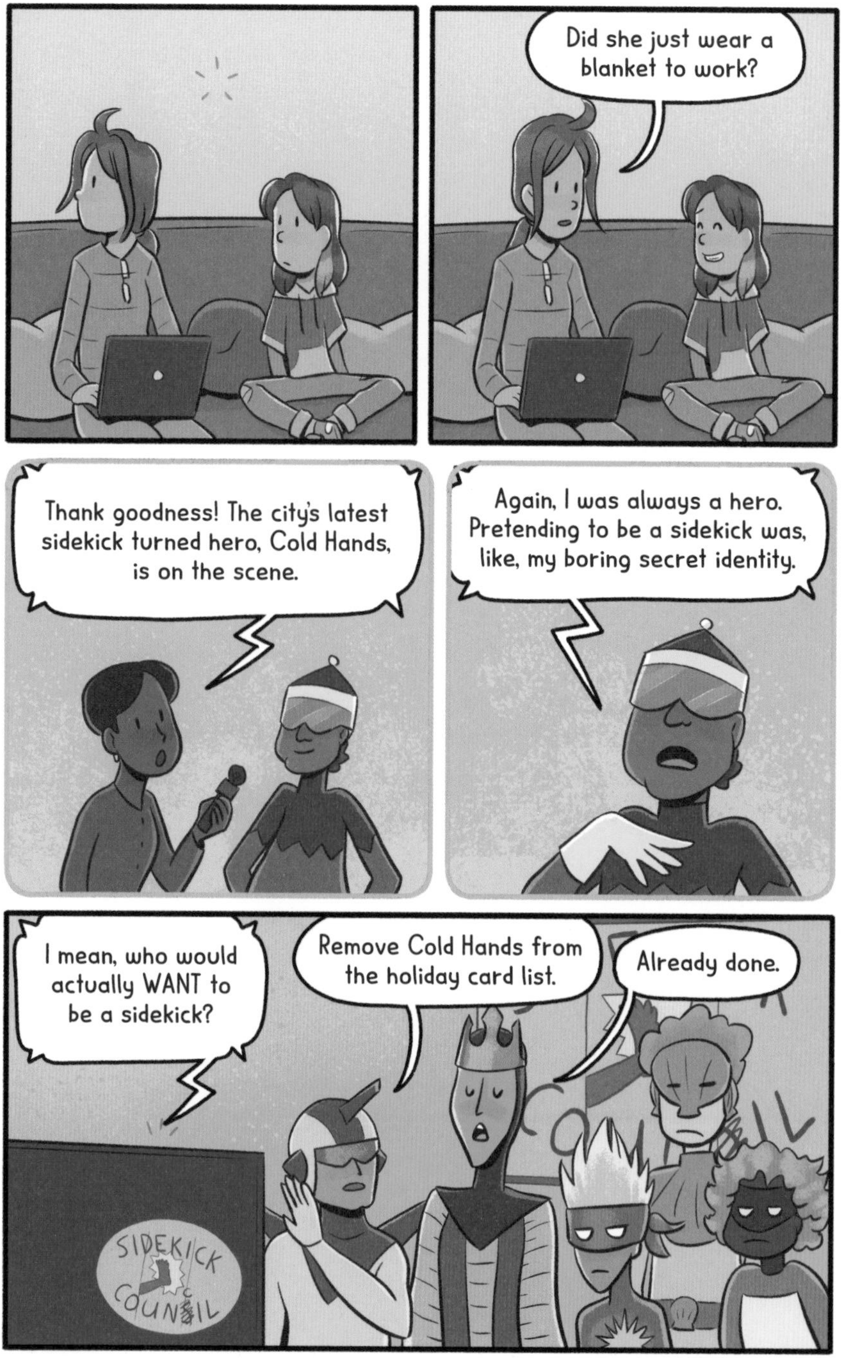
Did she just wear a blanket to work?
Thank goodness! The city's latest sidekick turned hero, Cold Hands, is on the scene.
Again, I was always a hero. Pretending to be a sidekick was, like, my boring secret identity.
I mean, who would actually WANT to be a sidekick?
Remove Cold Hands from the holiday card list.
Already done.
SIDEKICK COUNCIL

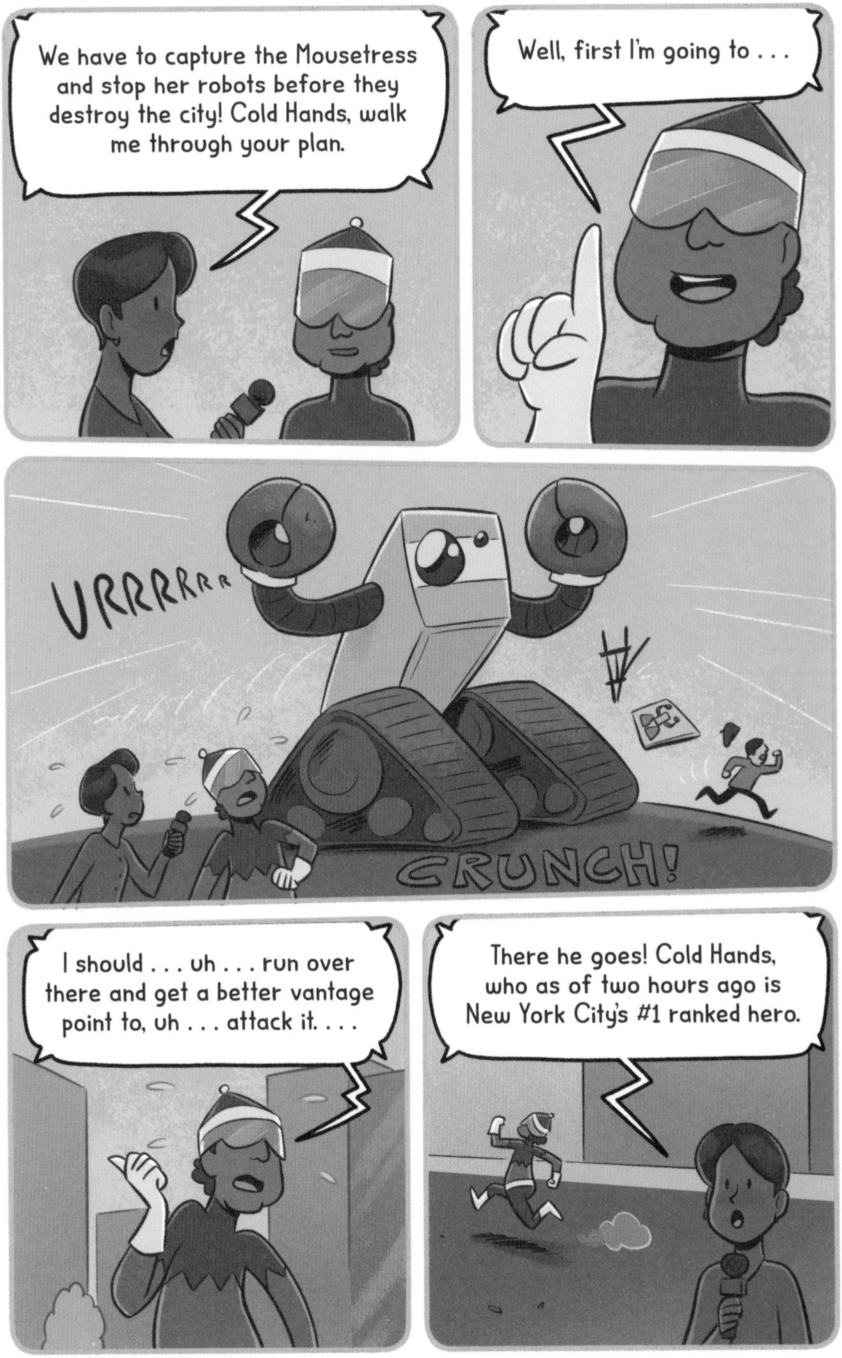
We have to capture the Mousetress and stop her robots before they destroy the city! Cold Hands, walk me through your plan.
Well, first I'm going to . . .
URRRRRR
CRUNCH!
I should . . . uh . . . run over there and get a better vantage point to, uh . . . attack it. . . .
There he goes! Cold Hands, who as of two hours ago is New York City's #1 ranked hero.

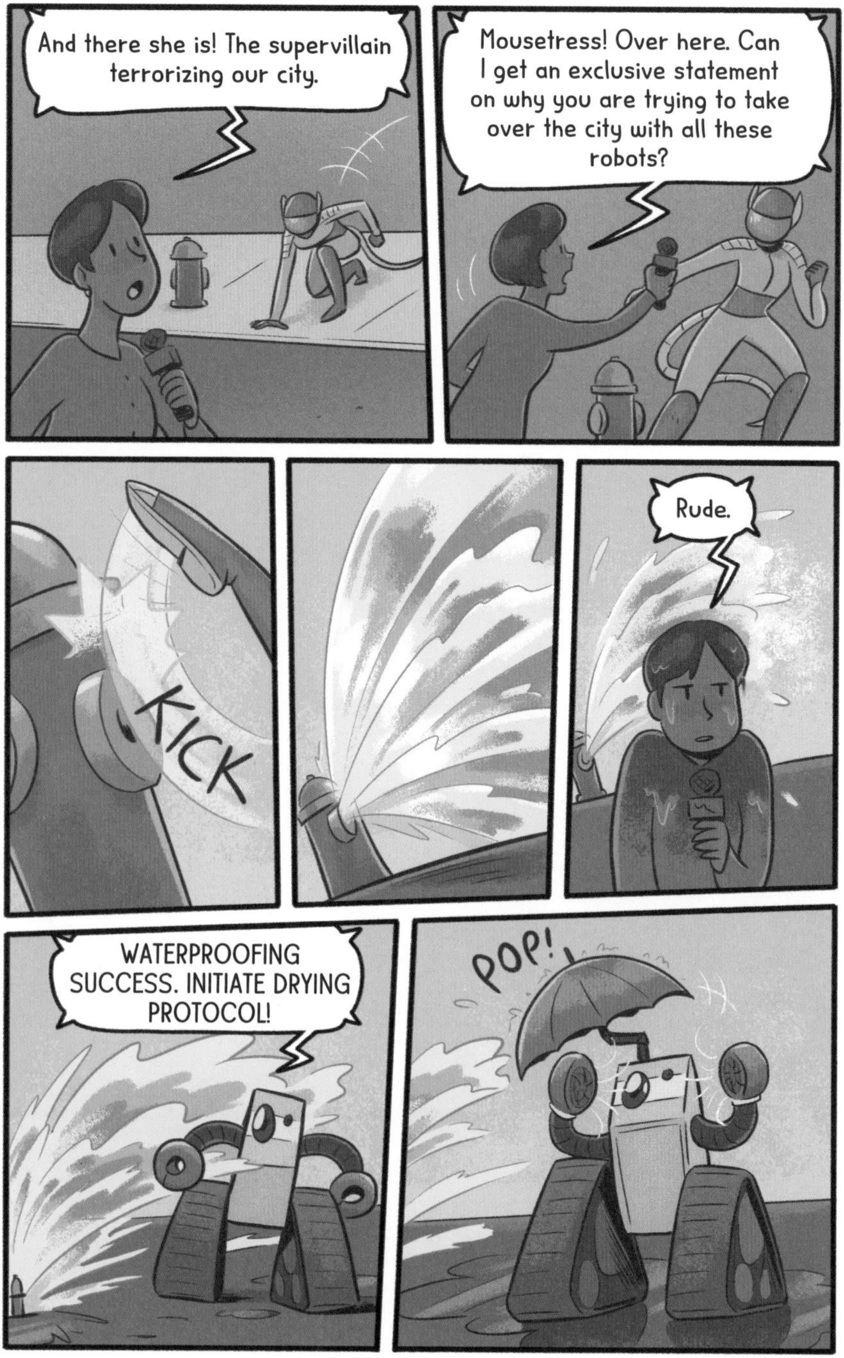
And there she is! The supervillain terrorizing our city.
Mousetress! Over here. Can I get an exclusive statement on why you are trying to take over the city with all these robots?
KICK
Rude.
WATERPROOFING SUCCESS. INITIATE DRYING PROTOCOL!
POP!

Pepper, Wicket.
All yours.

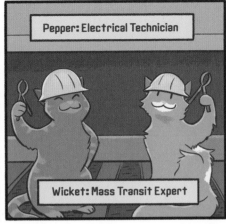

Pepper: Electrical Technician

Wicket: Mass Transit Expert

NOW!

BZZZT

BZZZZT

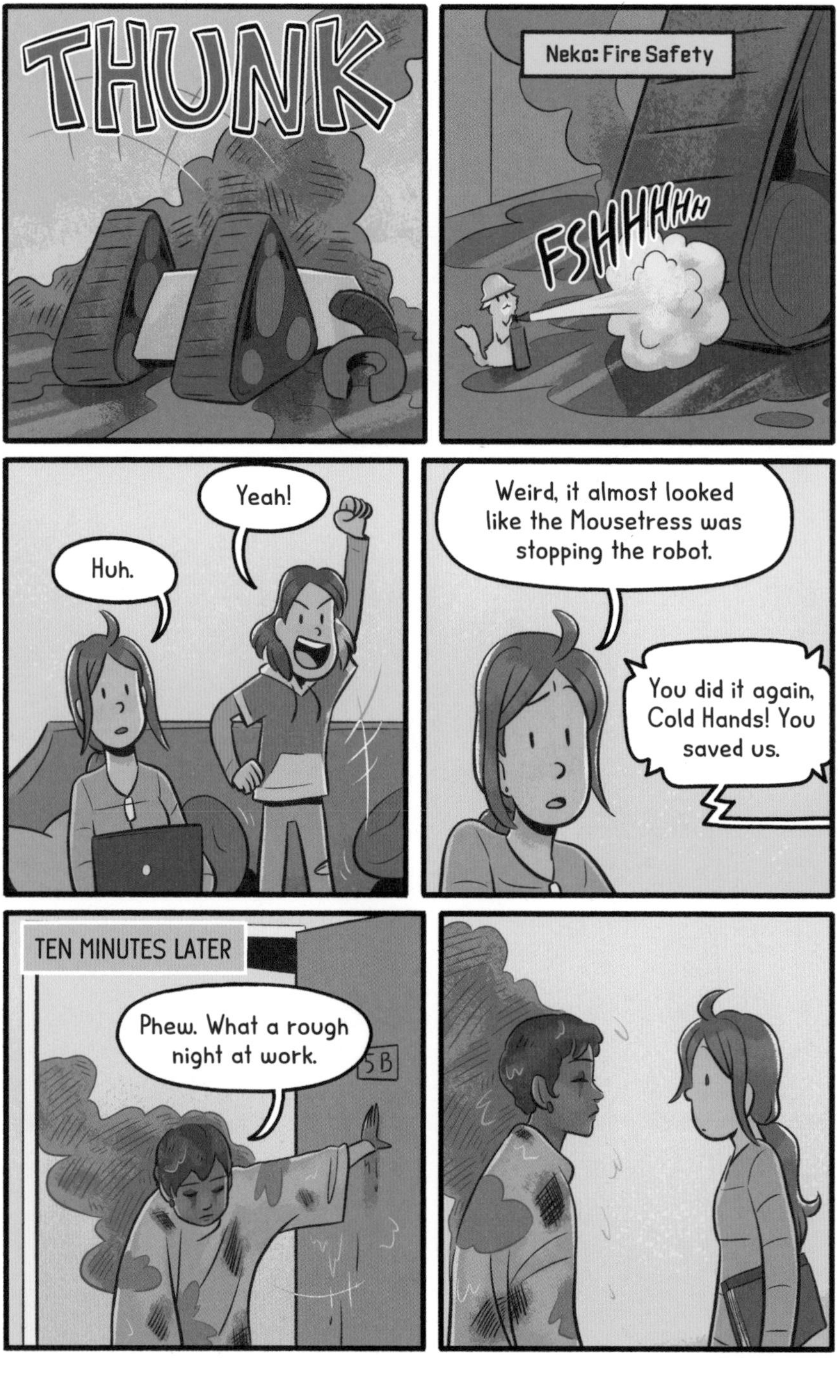
THUNK
Neko: Fire Safety
FSHHHHH
Yeah!
Huh.
Weird, it almost looked like the Mousetress was stopping the robot.
You did it again, Cold Hands! You saved us.
TEN MINUTES LATER
Phew. What a rough night at work.
5B

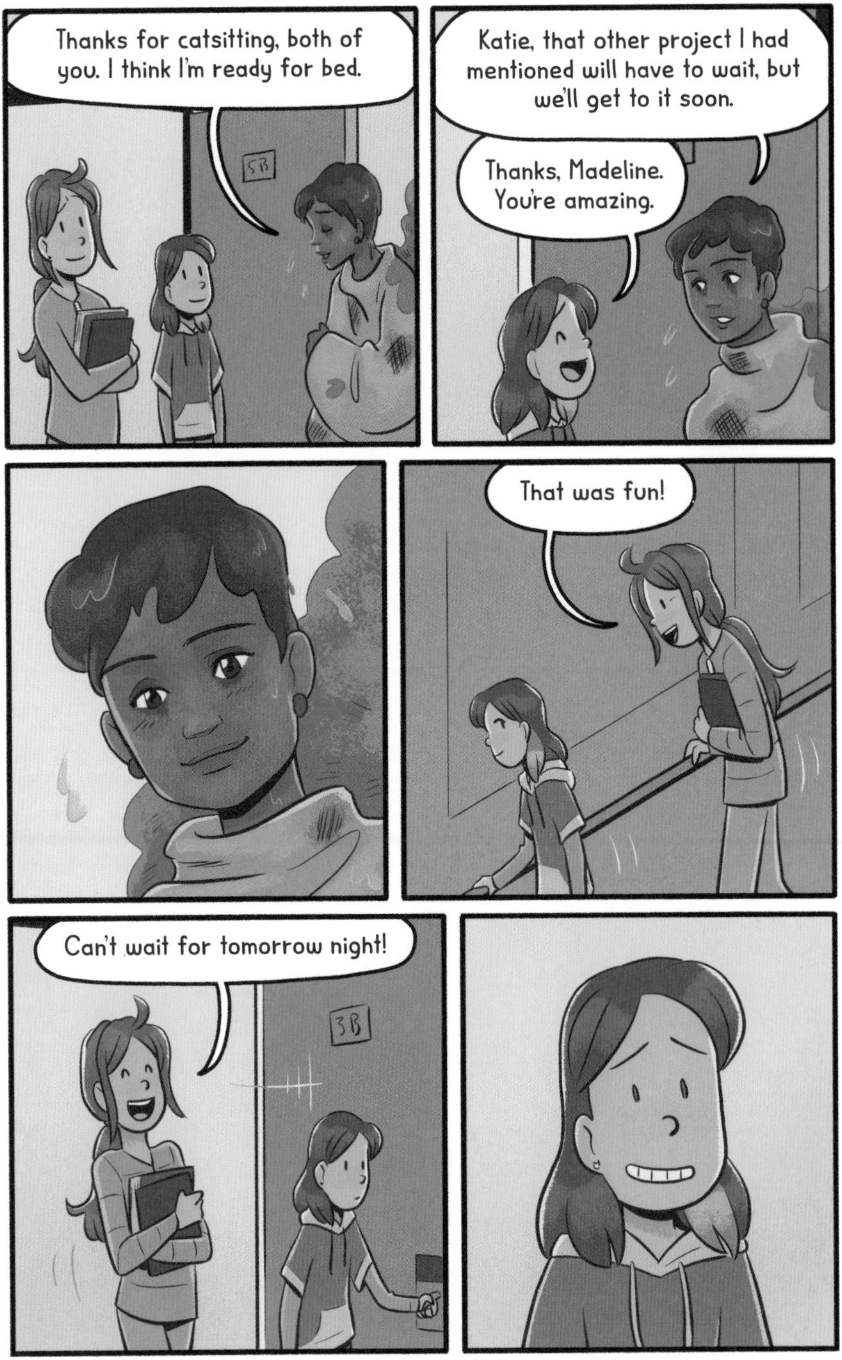
Thanks for catsitting, both of you. I think I'm ready for bed.
Katie, that other project I had mentioned will have to wait, but we'll get to it soon.
Thanks, Madeline. You're amazing.
That was fun!
Can't wait for tomorrow night!

CHAPTER EIGHT

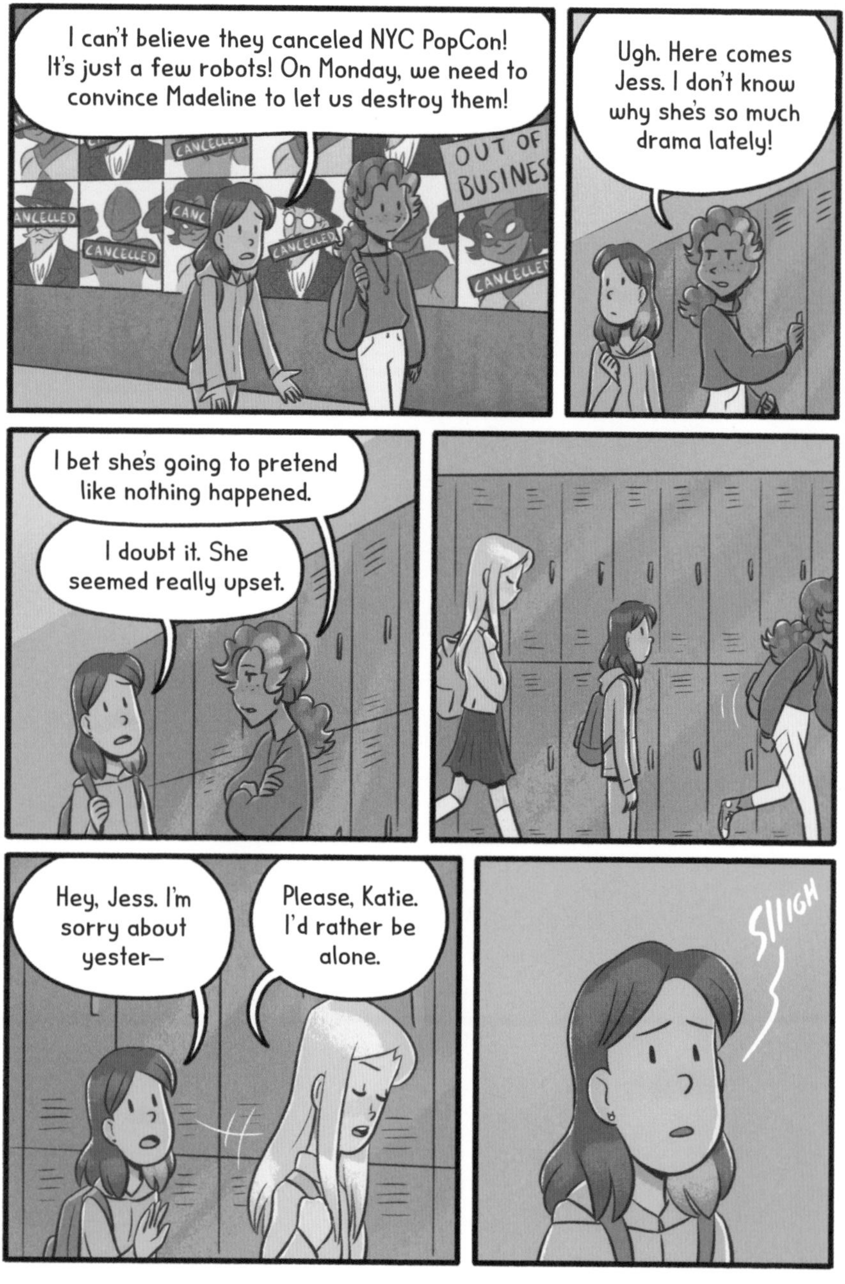

I can't believe they canceled NYC PopCon! It's just a few robots! On Monday, we need to convince Madeline to let us destroy them!
CANCELLED
OUT OF BUSINES
Ugh. Here comes Jess. I don't know why she's so much drama lately!
I bet she's going to pretend like nothing happened.
I doubt it. She seemed really upset.
Hey, Jess. I'm sorry about yester—
Please, Katie. I'd rather be alone.
SIIIGH

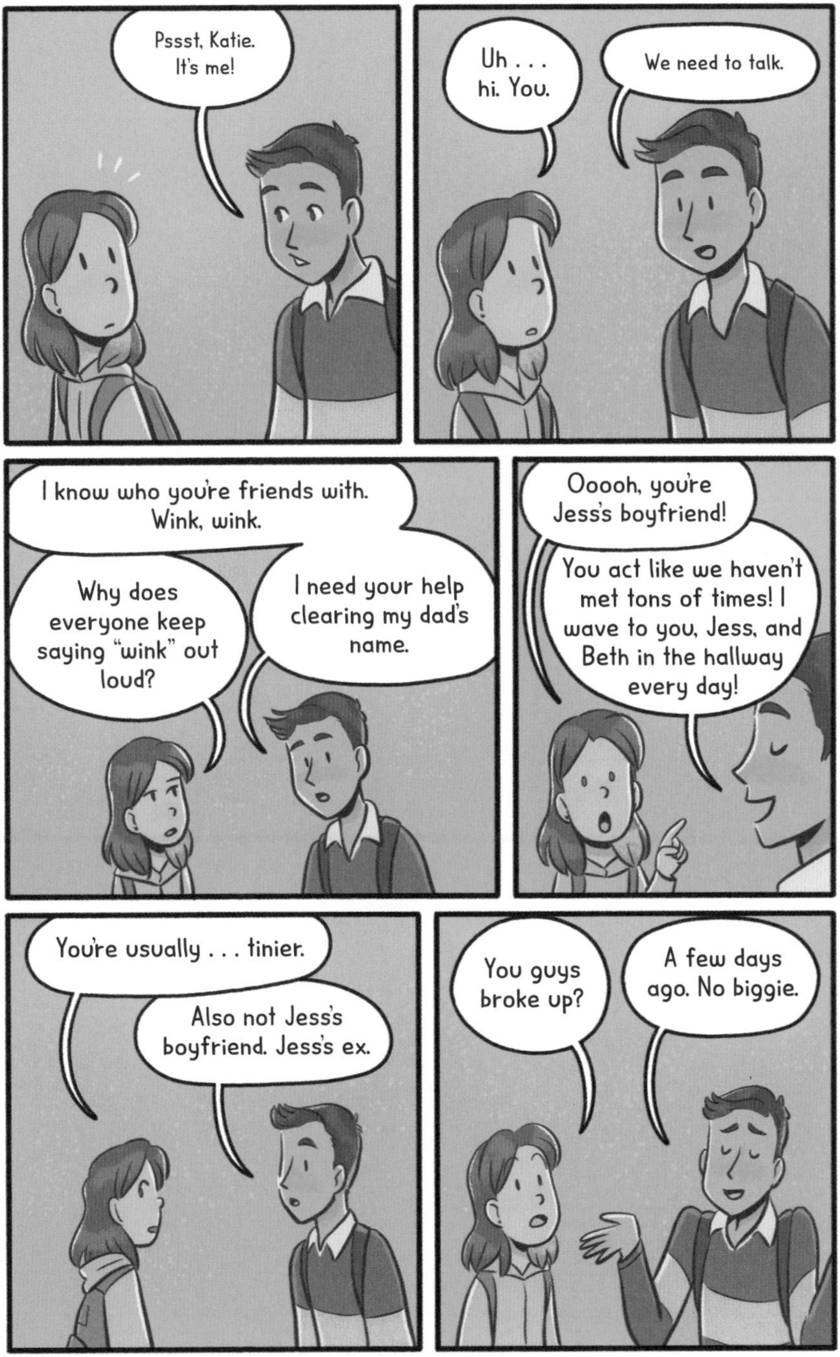

Pssst, Katie. It's me!
Uh . . . hi. You.
We need to talk.
I know who you're friends with. Wink, wink.
Why does everyone keep saying "wink" out loud?
I need your help clearing my dad's name.
Ooooh, you're Jess's boyfriend!
You act like we haven't met tons of times! I wave to you, Jess, and Beth in the hallway every day!
You're usually . . . tinier.
Also not Jess's boyfriend. Jess's ex.
You guys broke up?
A few days ago. No biggie.

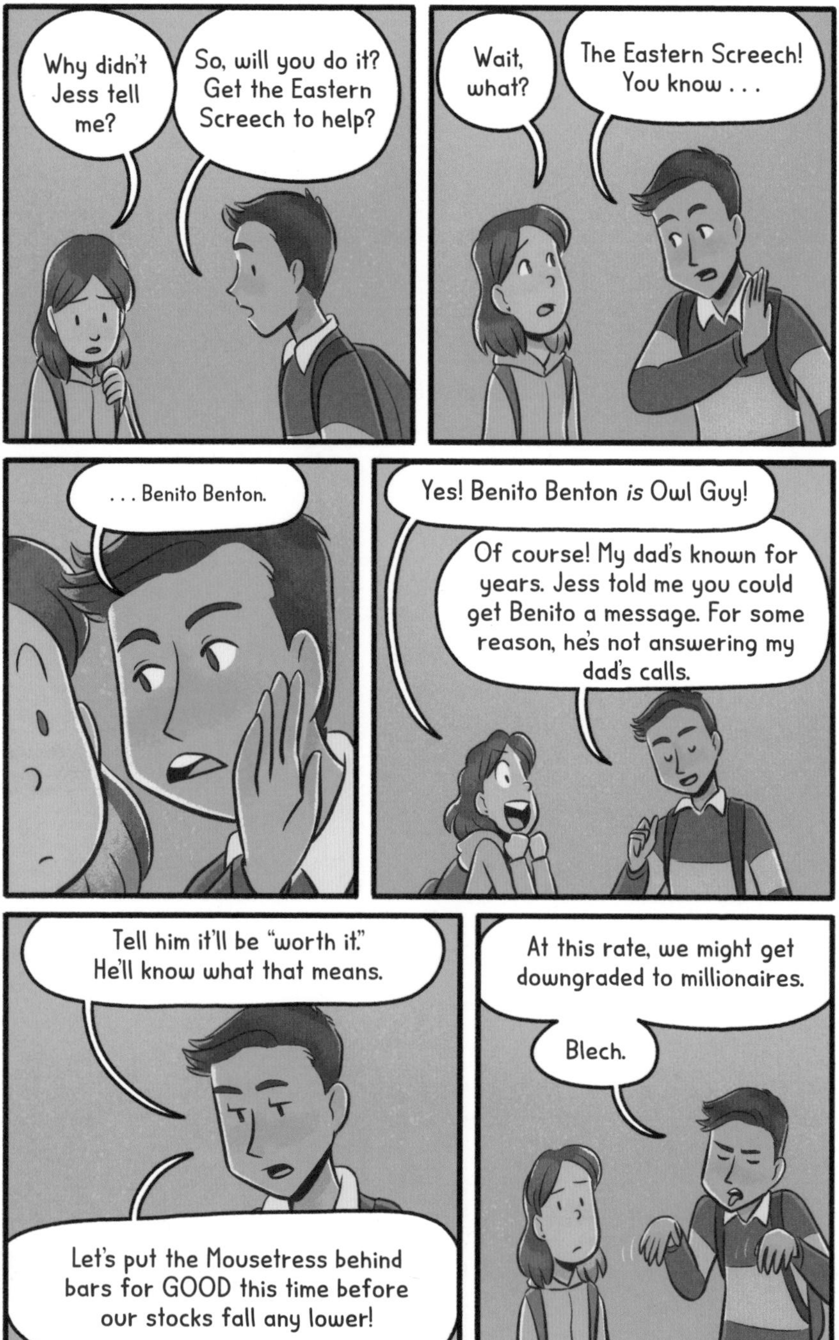
Why didn't Jess tell me?
So, will you do it? Get the Eastern Screech to help?
Wait, what?
The Eastern Screech! You know . . .
. . . Benito Benton.
Yes! Benito Benton *is* Owl Guy!
Of course! My dad's known for years. Jess told me you could get Benito a message. For some reason, he's not answering my dad's calls.
Tell him it'll be "worth it." He'll know what that means.
Let's put the Mousetress behind bars for GOOD this time before our stocks fall any lower!
At this rate, we might get downgraded to millionaires.
Blech.

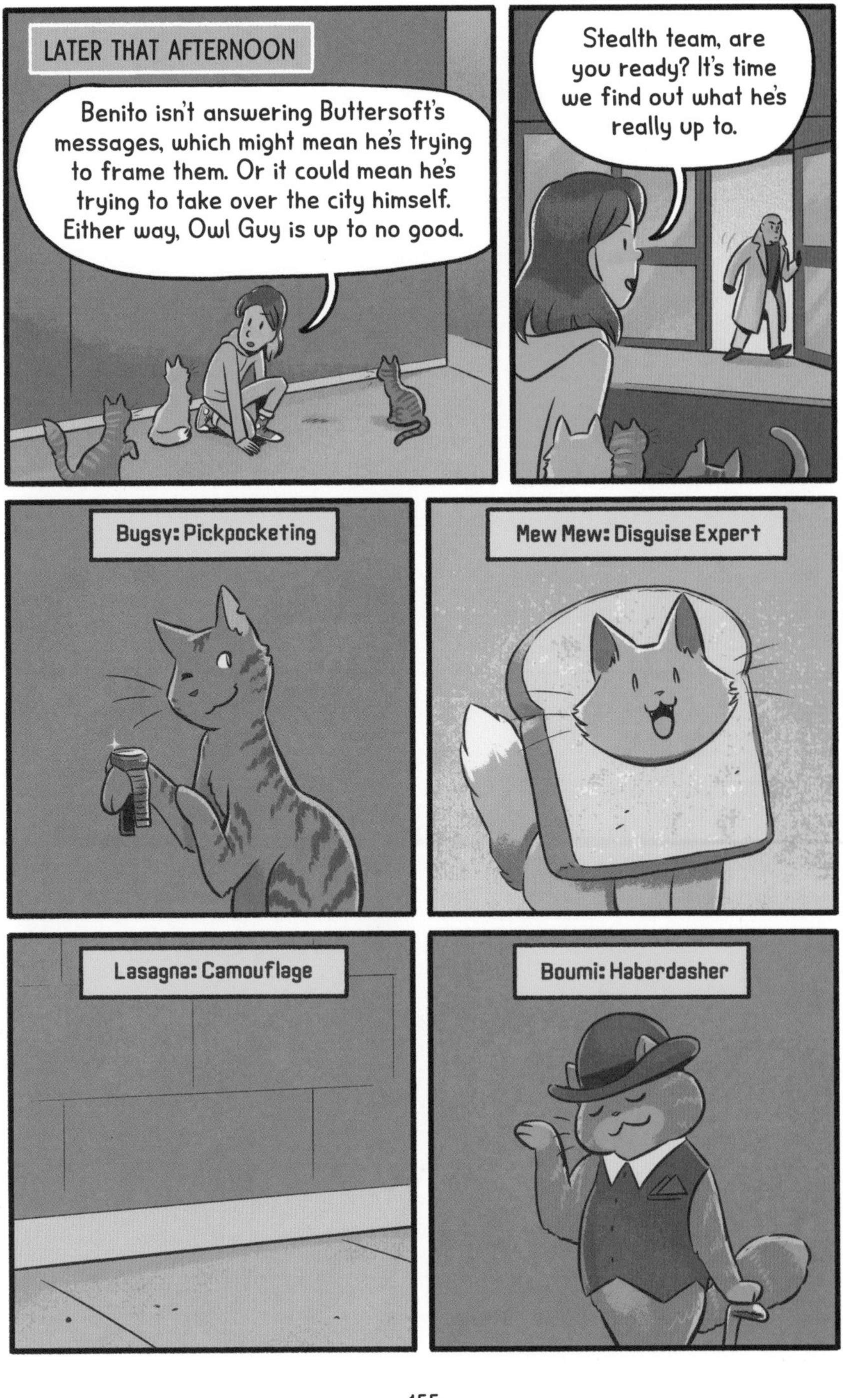

LATER THAT AFTERNOON
Benito isn't answering Buttersoft's messages, which might mean he's trying to frame them. Or it could mean he's trying to take over the city himself. Either way, Owl Guy is up to no good.
Stealth team, are you ready? It's time we find out what he's really up to.
Bugsy: Pickpocketing
Mew Mew: Disguise Expert
Lasagna: Camouflage
Boumi: Haberdasher

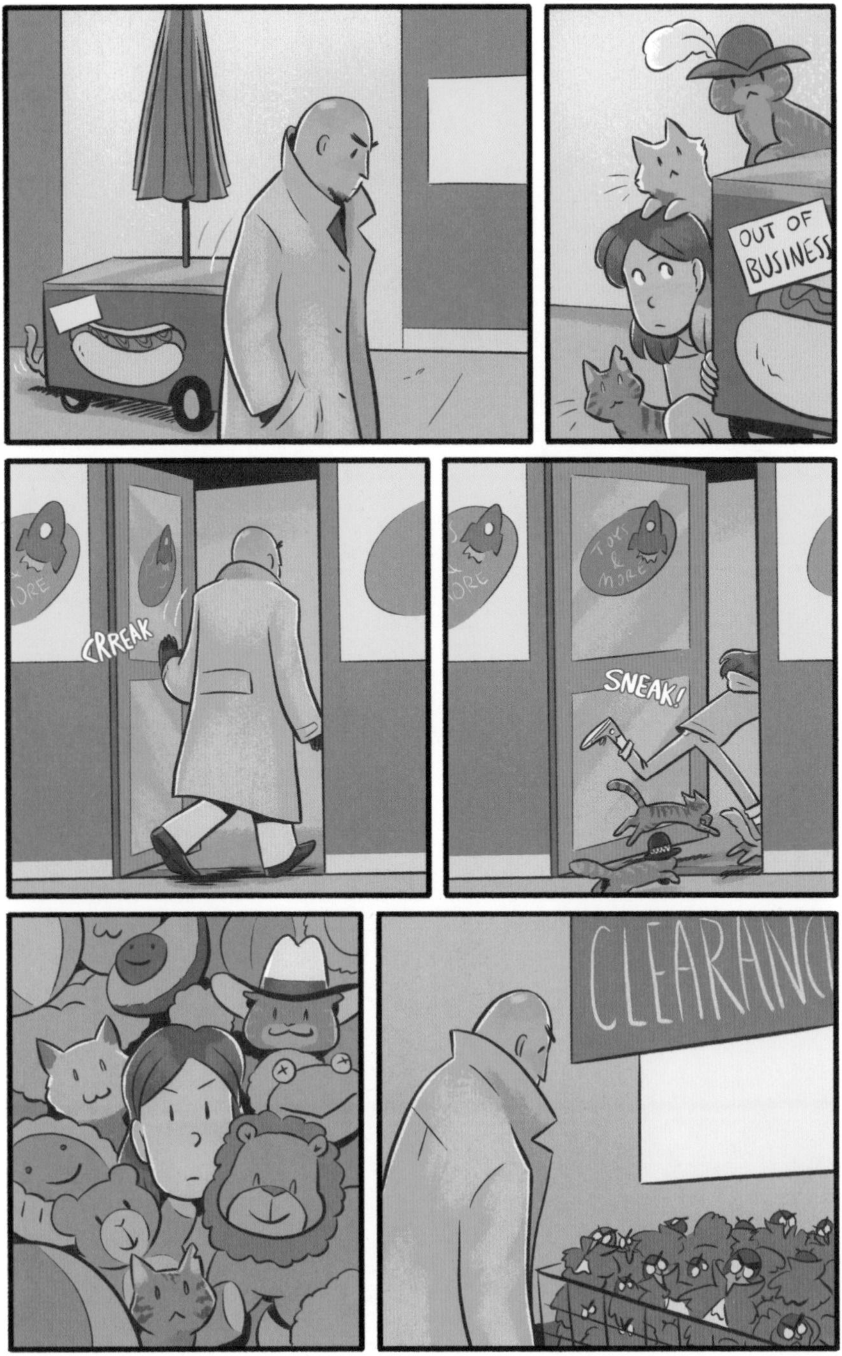

OUT OF BUSINESS
TOYS & MORE
CRREAK
SNEAK!
CLEARANC

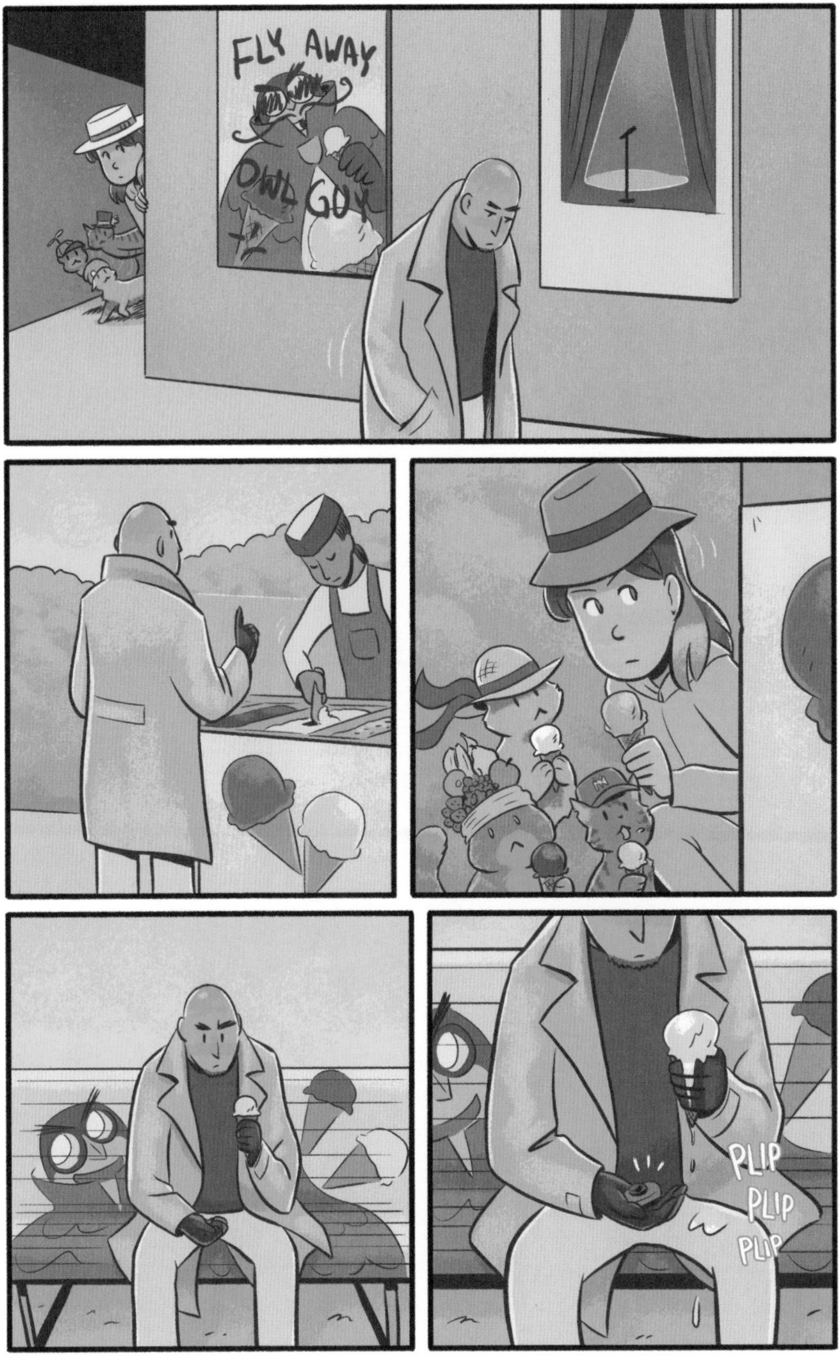
FLY AWAY
OWL GUY
PLIP
PLIP
PLIP

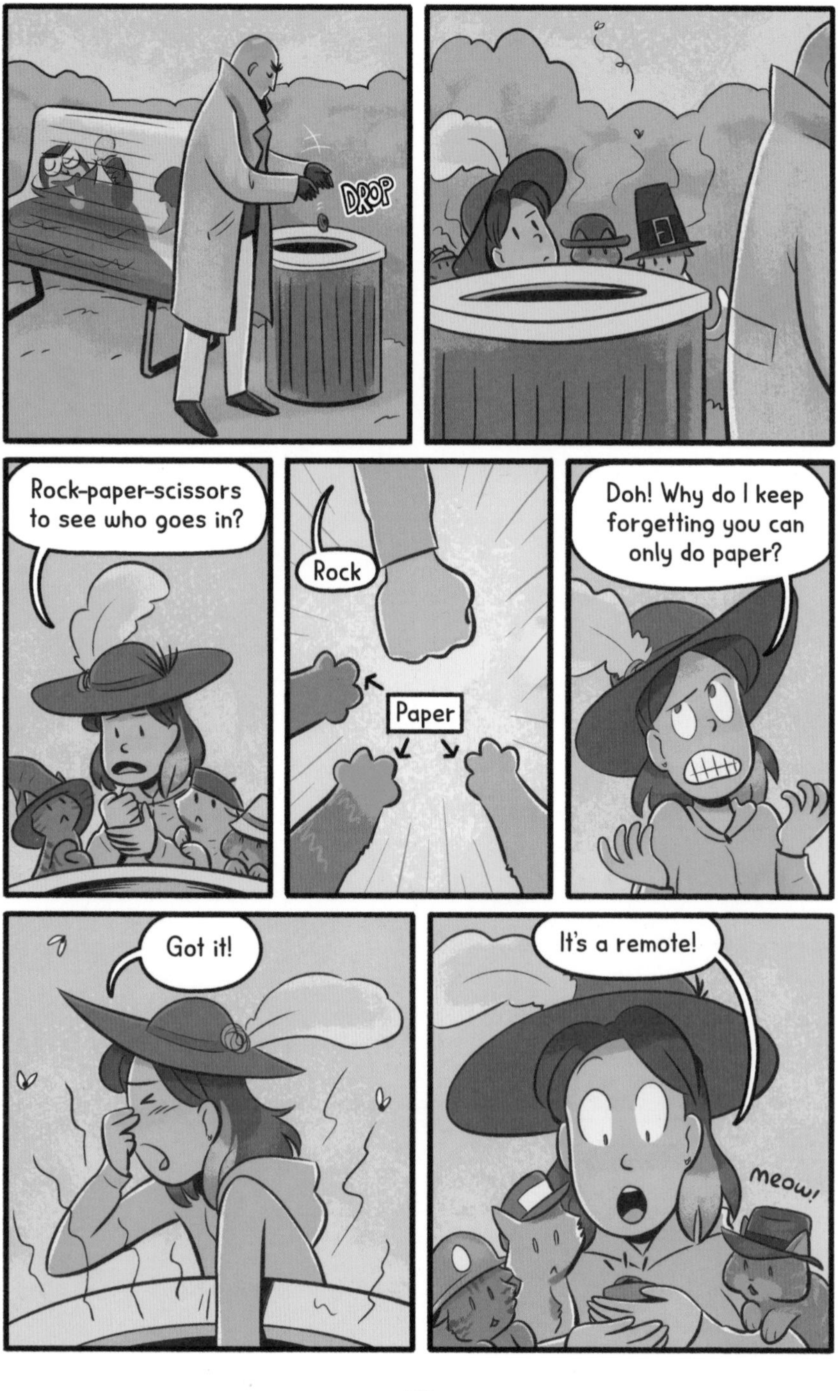
DROP
Rock-paper-scissors to see who goes in?
Rock
Paper
Doh! Why do I keep forgetting you can only do paper?
Got it!
It's a remote!
meow!

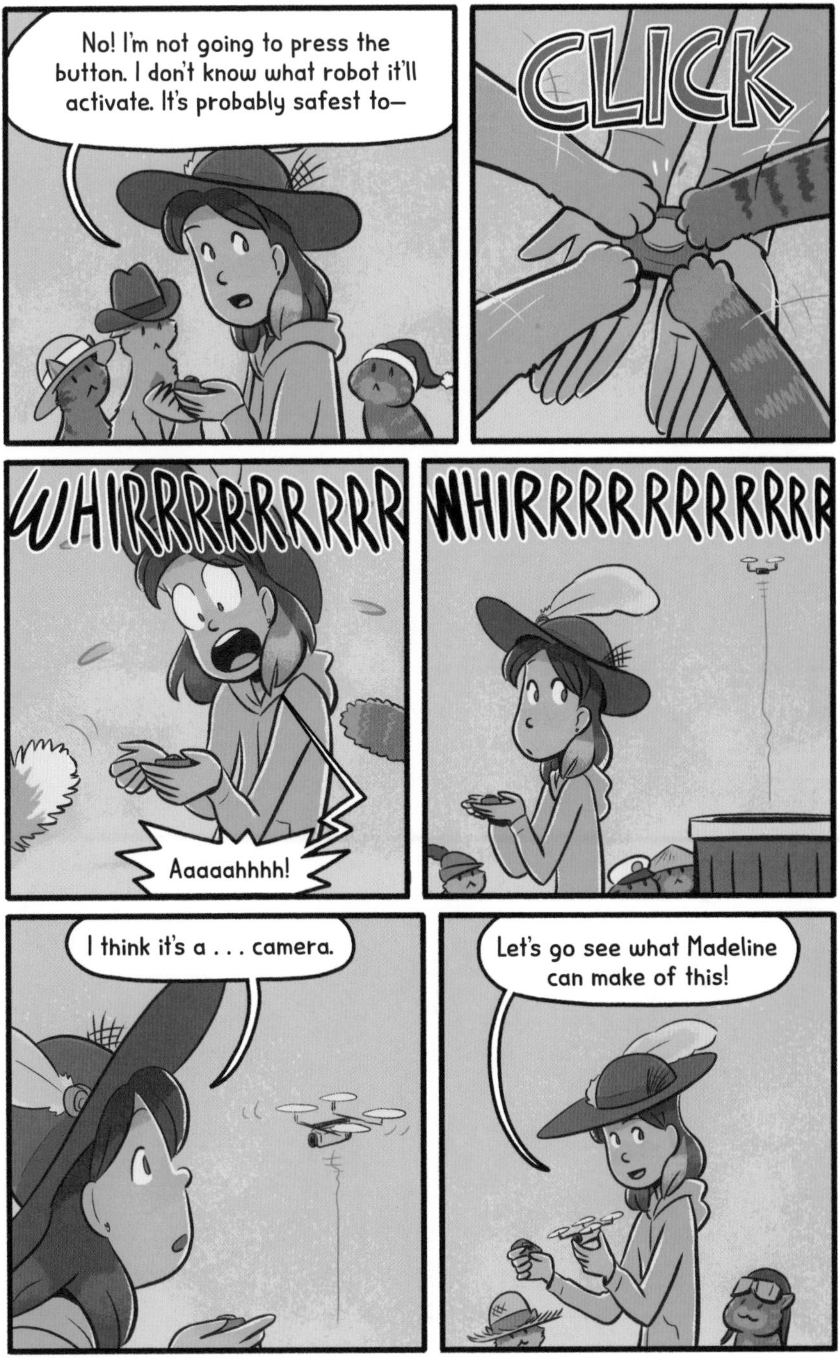
No! I'm not going to press the button. I don't know what robot it'll activate. It's probably safest to—
CLICK
WHIRRRRRRRRR
Aaaaahhhh!
WHIRRRRRRRRRRR
I think it's a . . . camera.
Let's go see what Madeline can make of this!

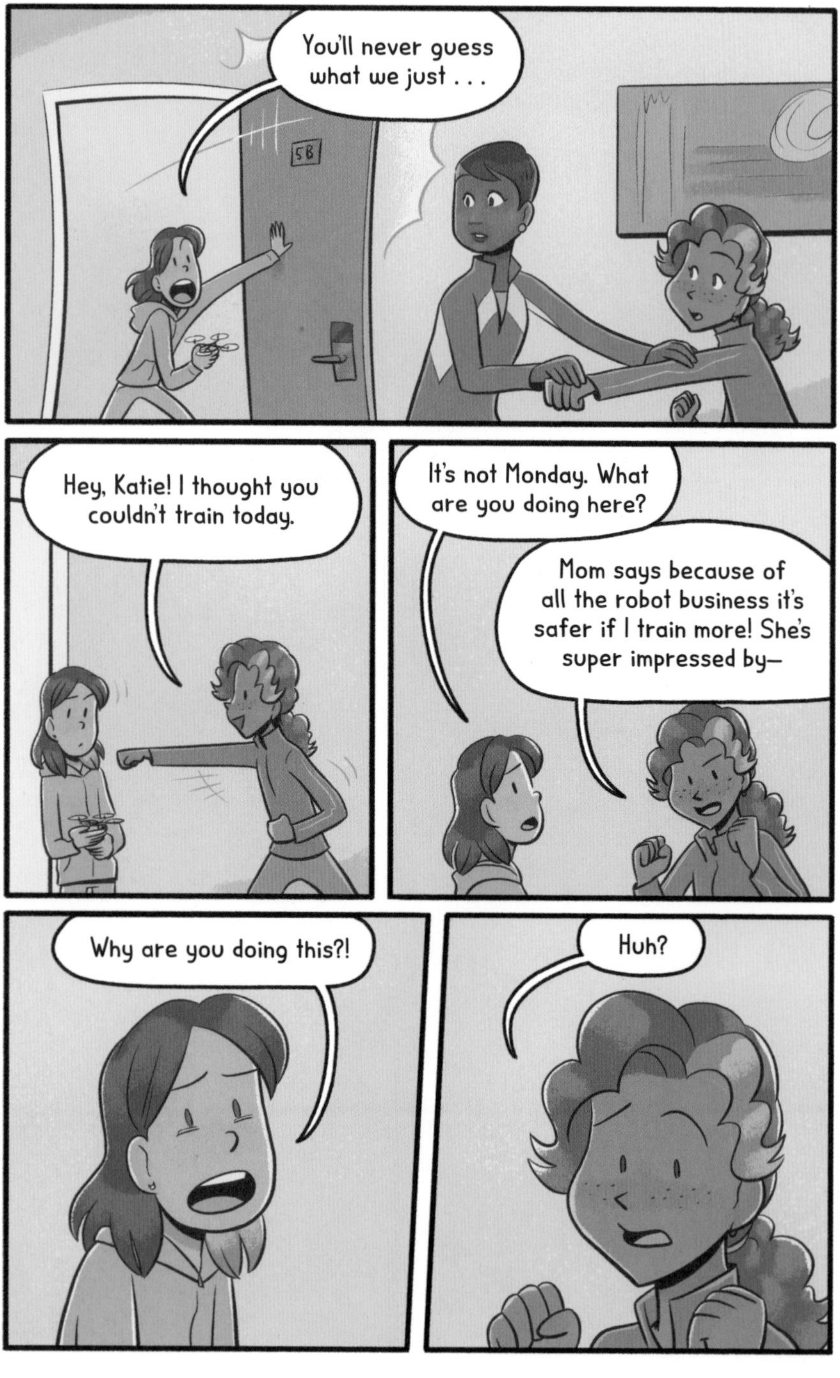
You'll never guess what we just . . .
5B
Hey, Katie! I thought you couldn't train today.
It's not Monday. What are you doing here?
Mom says because of all the robot business it's safer if I train more! She's super impressed by—
Why are you doing this?!
Huh?

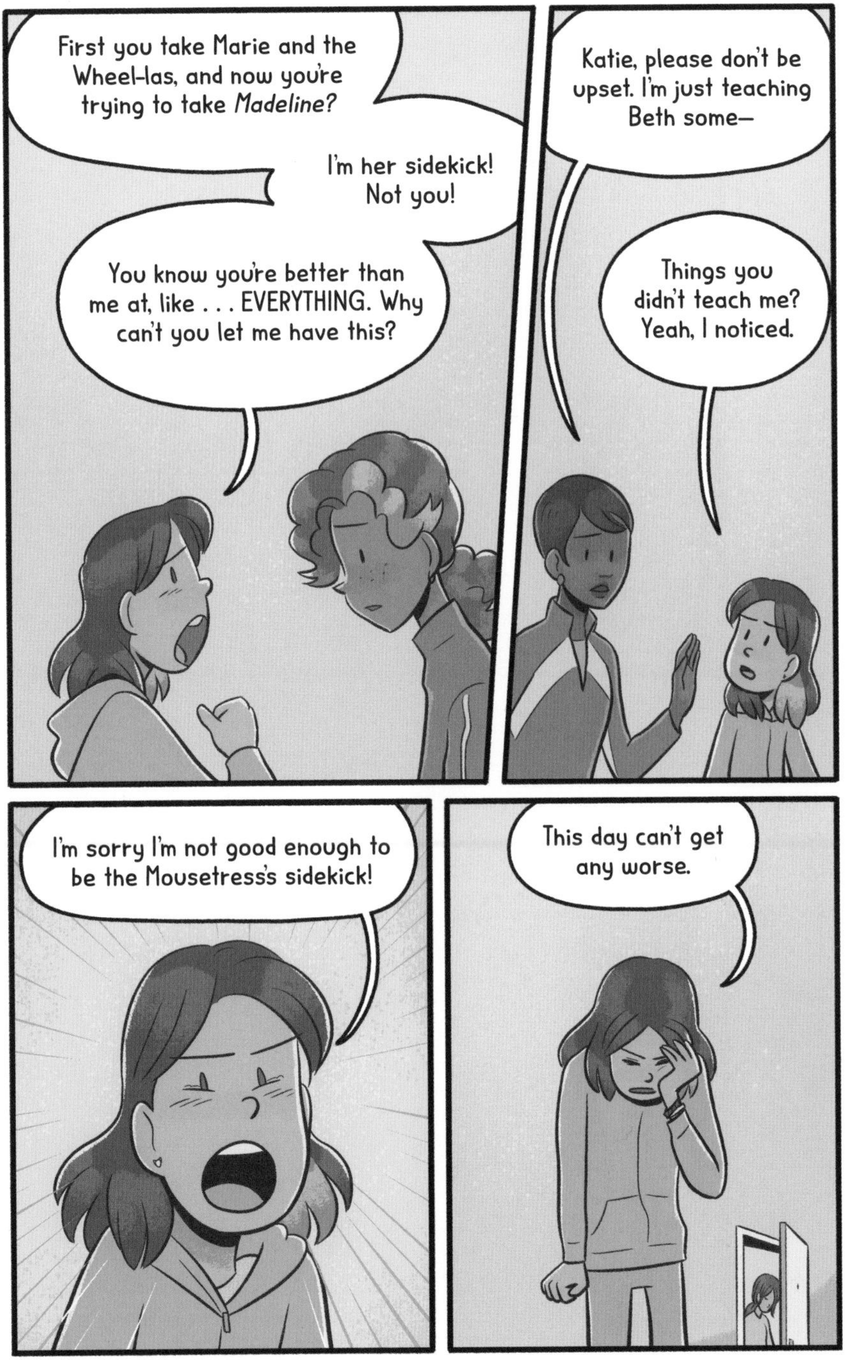
First you take Marie and the Wheel-las, and now you're trying to take *Madeline*?
I'm her sidekick! Not you!
You know you're better than me at, like . . . EVERYTHING. Why can't you let me have this?
Katie, please don't be upset. I'm just teaching Beth some—
Things you didn't teach me? Yeah, I noticed.
I'm sorry I'm not good enough to be the Mousetress's sidekick!
This day can't get any worse.

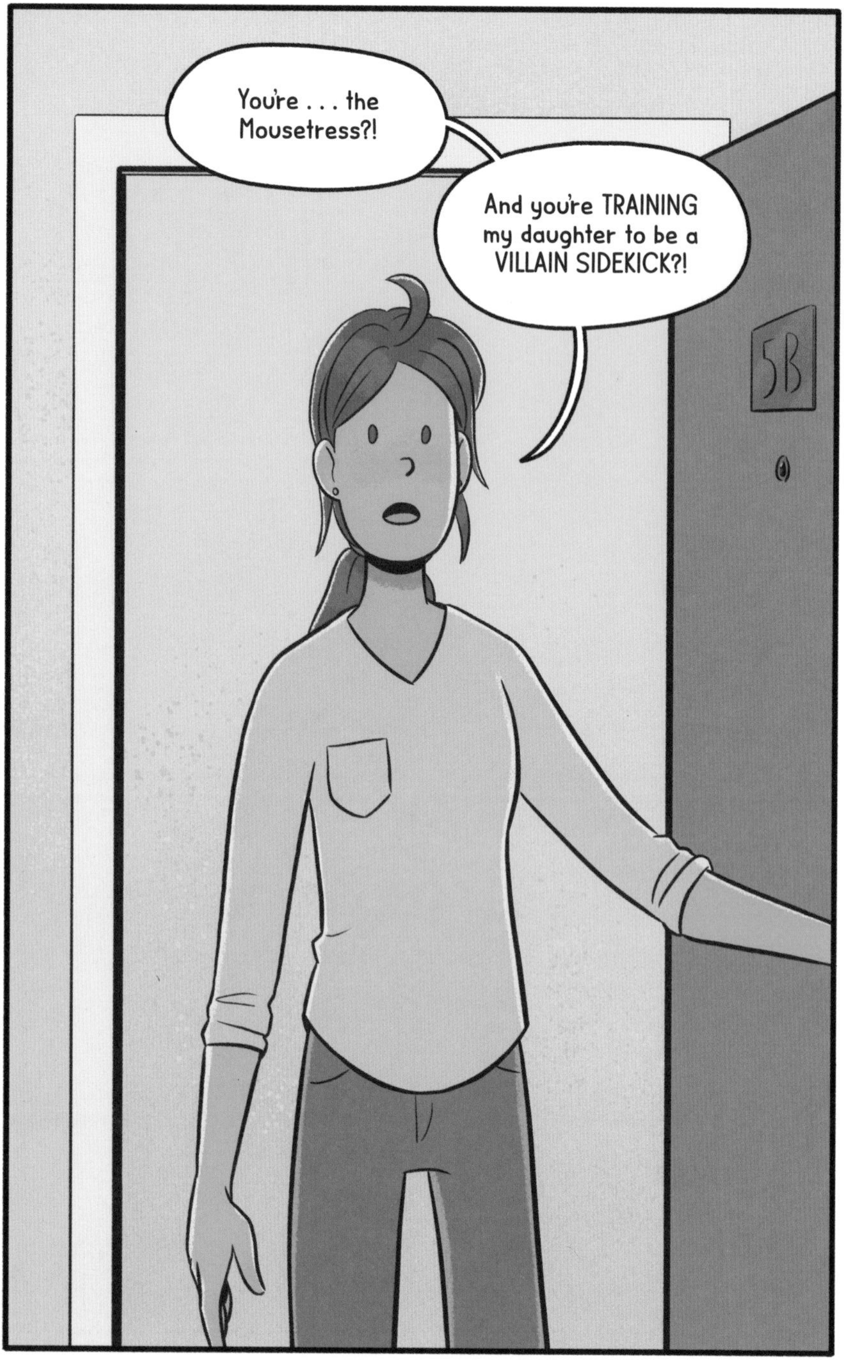
You're . . . the Mousetress?!
And you're TRAINING my daughter to be a VILLAIN SIDEKICK?!
5B

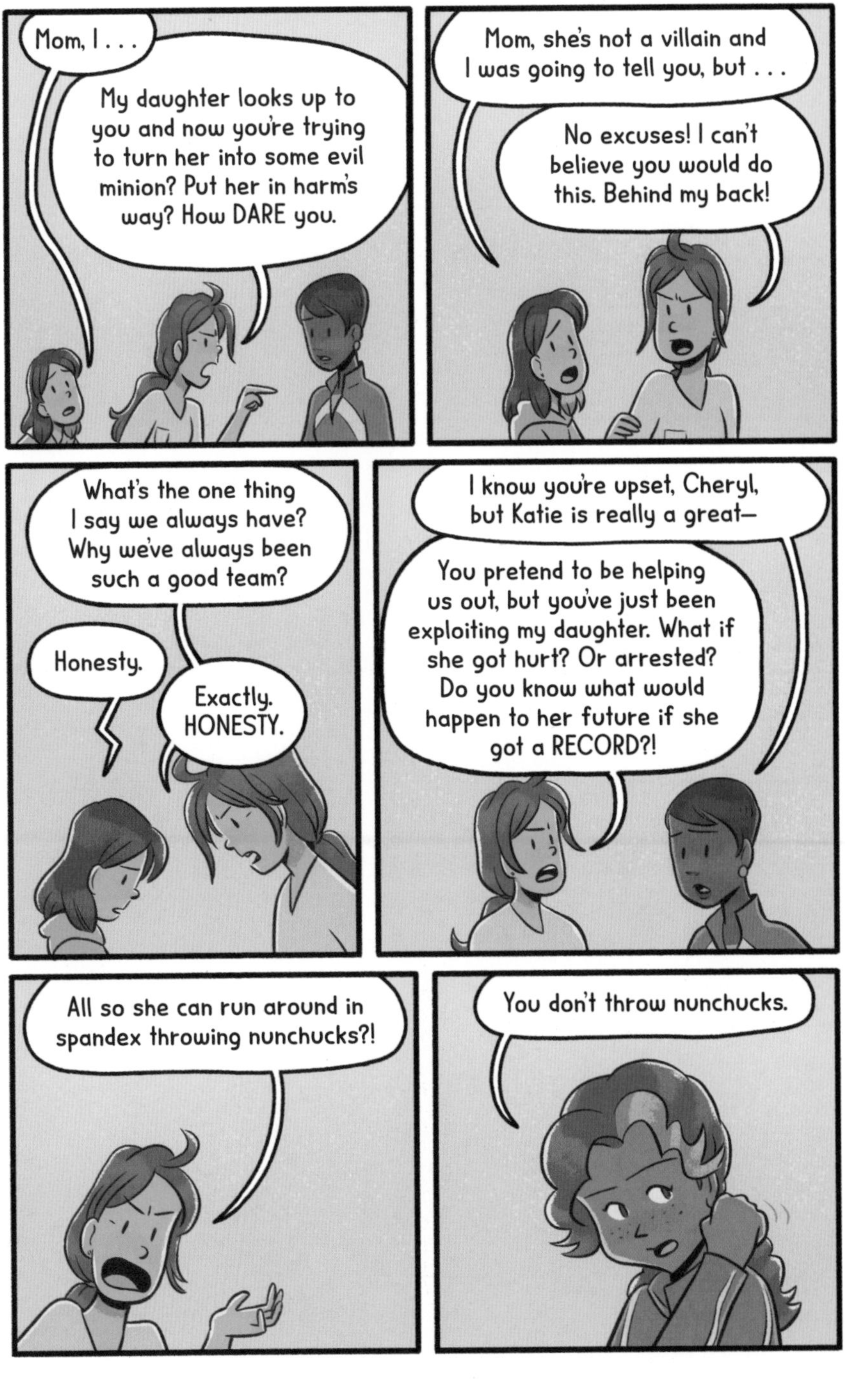
Mom, I . . .
My daughter looks up to you and now you're trying to turn her into some evil minion? Put her in harm's way? How DARE you.
Mom, she's not a villain and I was going to tell you, but . . .
No excuses! I can't believe you would do this. Behind my back!
What's the one thing I say we always have? Why we've always been such a good team?
Honesty.
Exactly. HONESTY.
I know you're upset, Cheryl, but Katie is really a great—
You pretend to be helping us out, but you've just been exploiting my daughter. What if she got hurt? Or arrested? Do you know what would happen to her future if she got a RECORD?!
All so she can run around in spandex throwing nunchucks?!
You don't throw nunchucks.

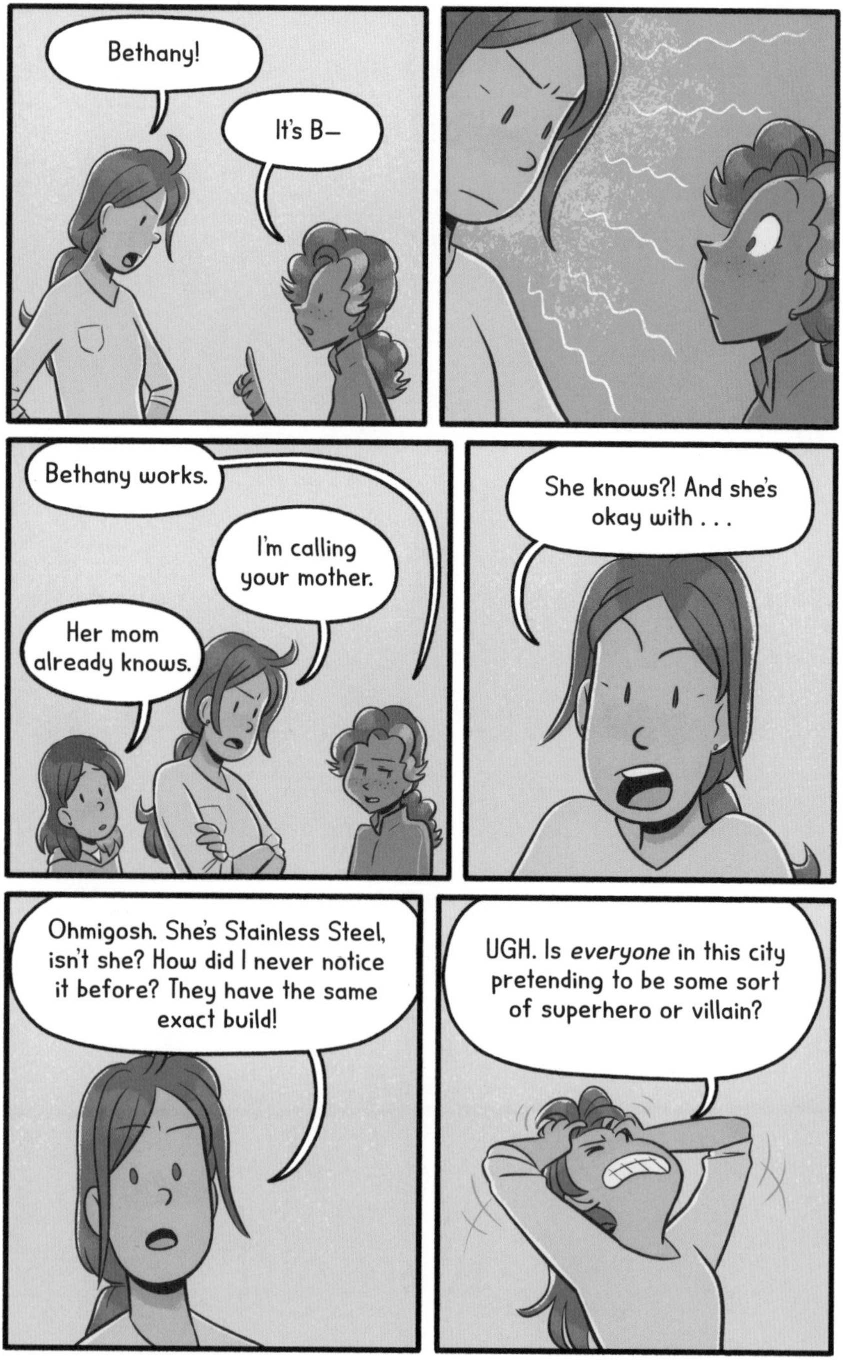
Bethany!
It's B—
Bethany works.
I'm calling your mother.
Her mom already knows.
She knows?! And she's okay with . . .
Ohmigosh. She's Stainless Steel, isn't she? How did I never notice it before? They have the same exact build!
UGH. Is *everyone* in this city pretending to be some sort of superhero or villain?

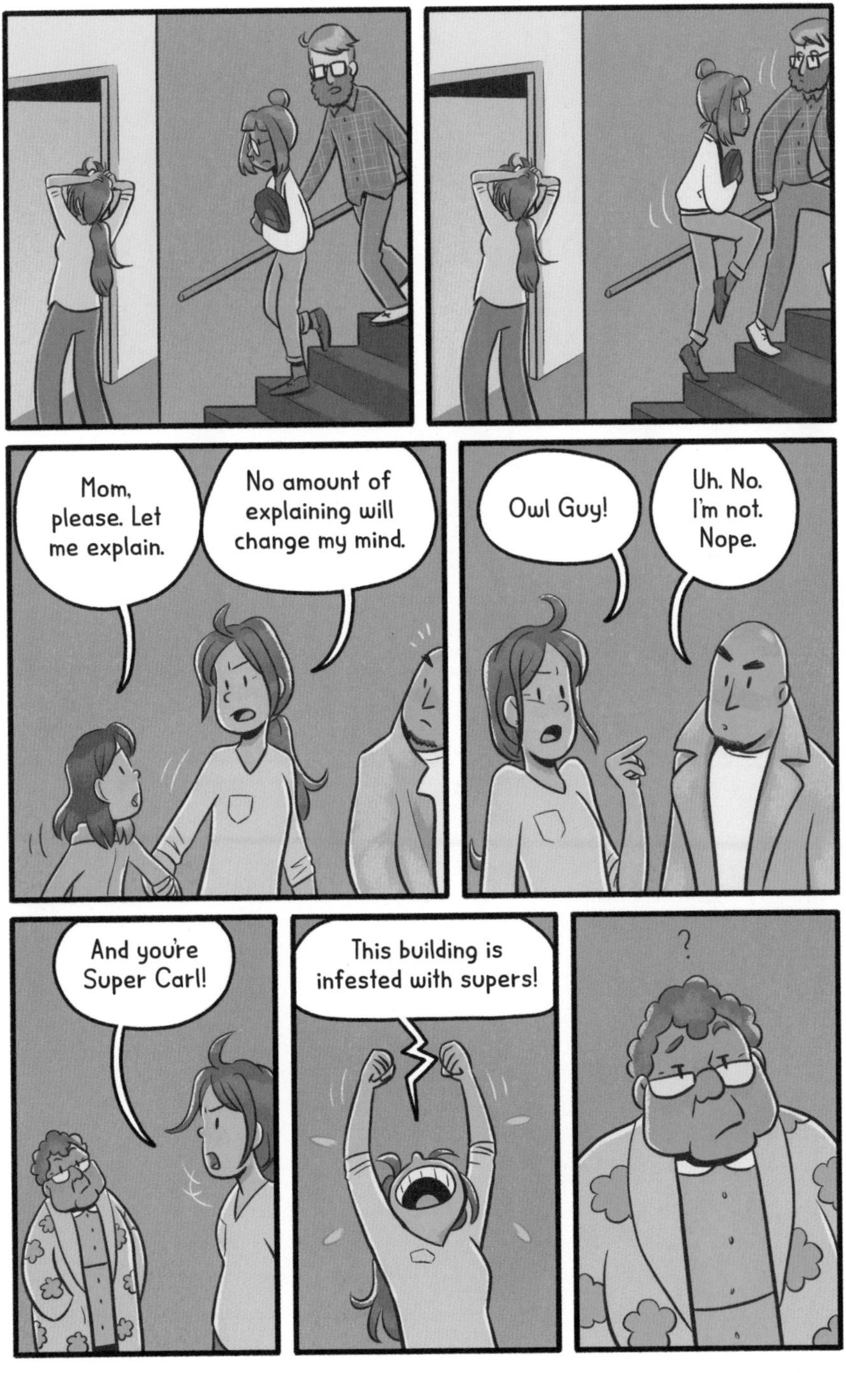
Mom, please. Let me explain.
No amount of explaining will change my mind.
Owl Guy!
Uh. No. I'm not. Nope.
And you're Super Carl!
This building is infested with supers!
?

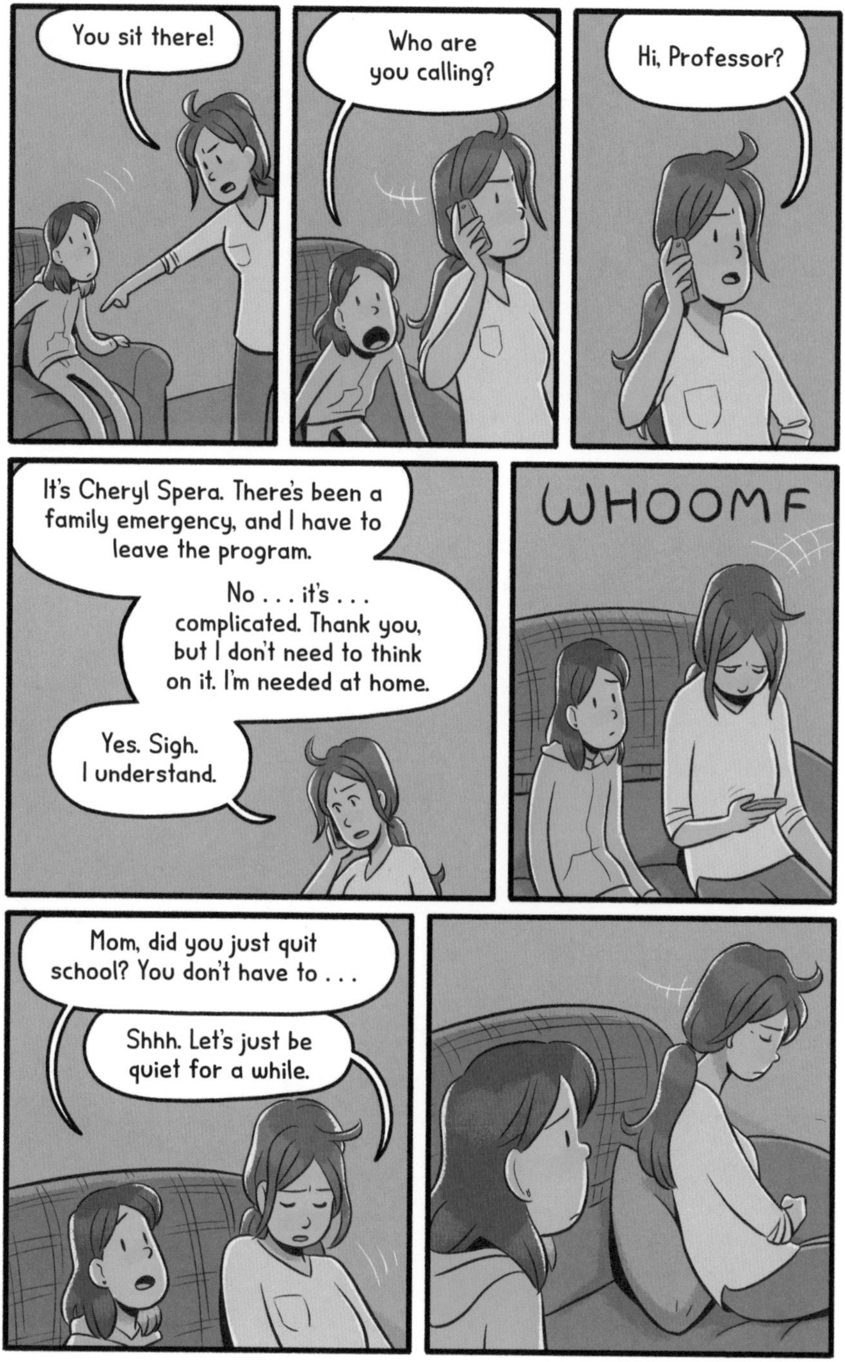
You sit there!
Who are you calling?
Hi, Professor?
It's Cheryl Spera. There's been a family emergency, and I have to leave the program.
No . . . it's . . . complicated. Thank you, but I don't need to think on it. I'm needed at home.
Yes. Sigh. I understand.
WHOOMF
Mom, did you just quit school? You don't have to . . .
Shhh. Let's just be quiet for a while.

CHAPTER NINE

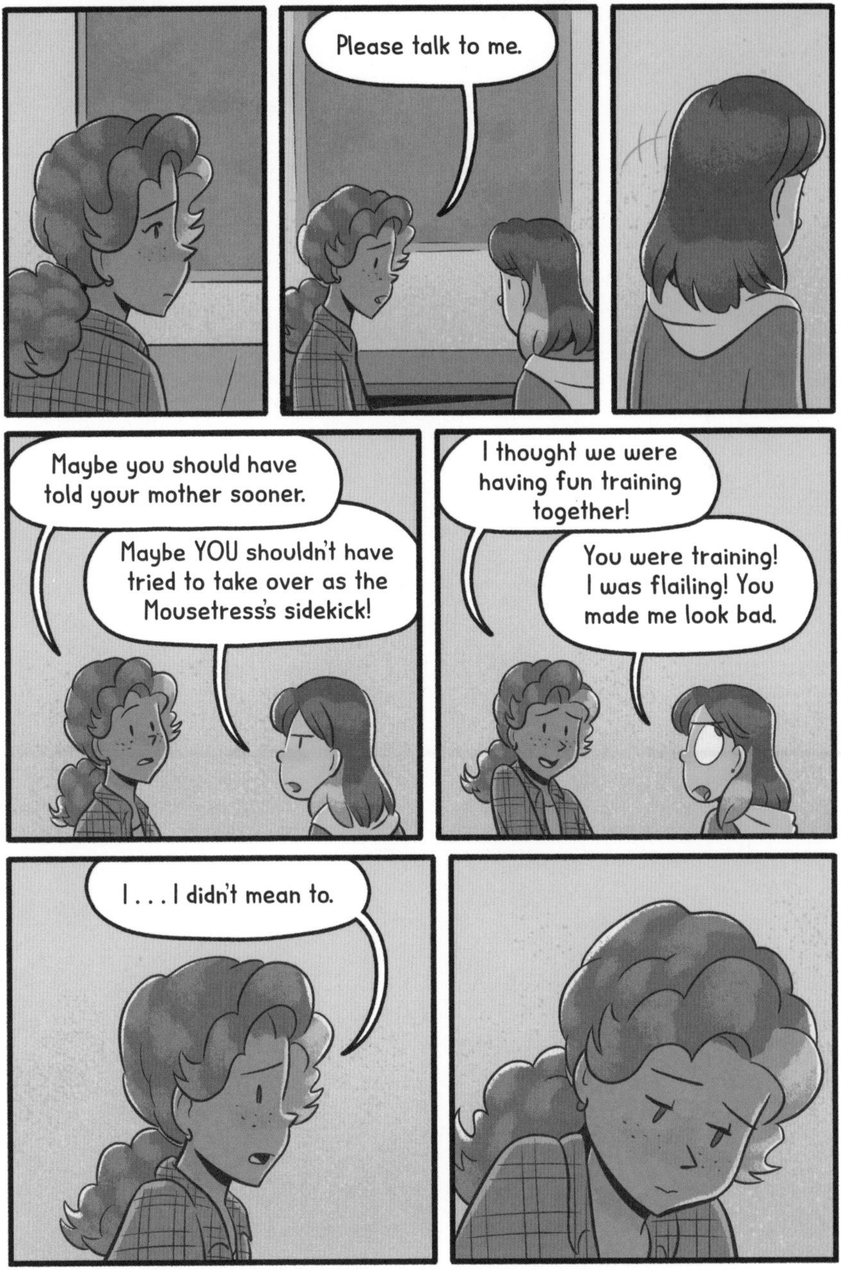

Please talk to me.
Maybe you should have told your mother sooner.
Maybe YOU shouldn't have tried to take over as the Mousetress's sidekick!
I thought we were having fun training together!
You were training! I was flailing! You made me look bad.
I . . . I didn't mean to.

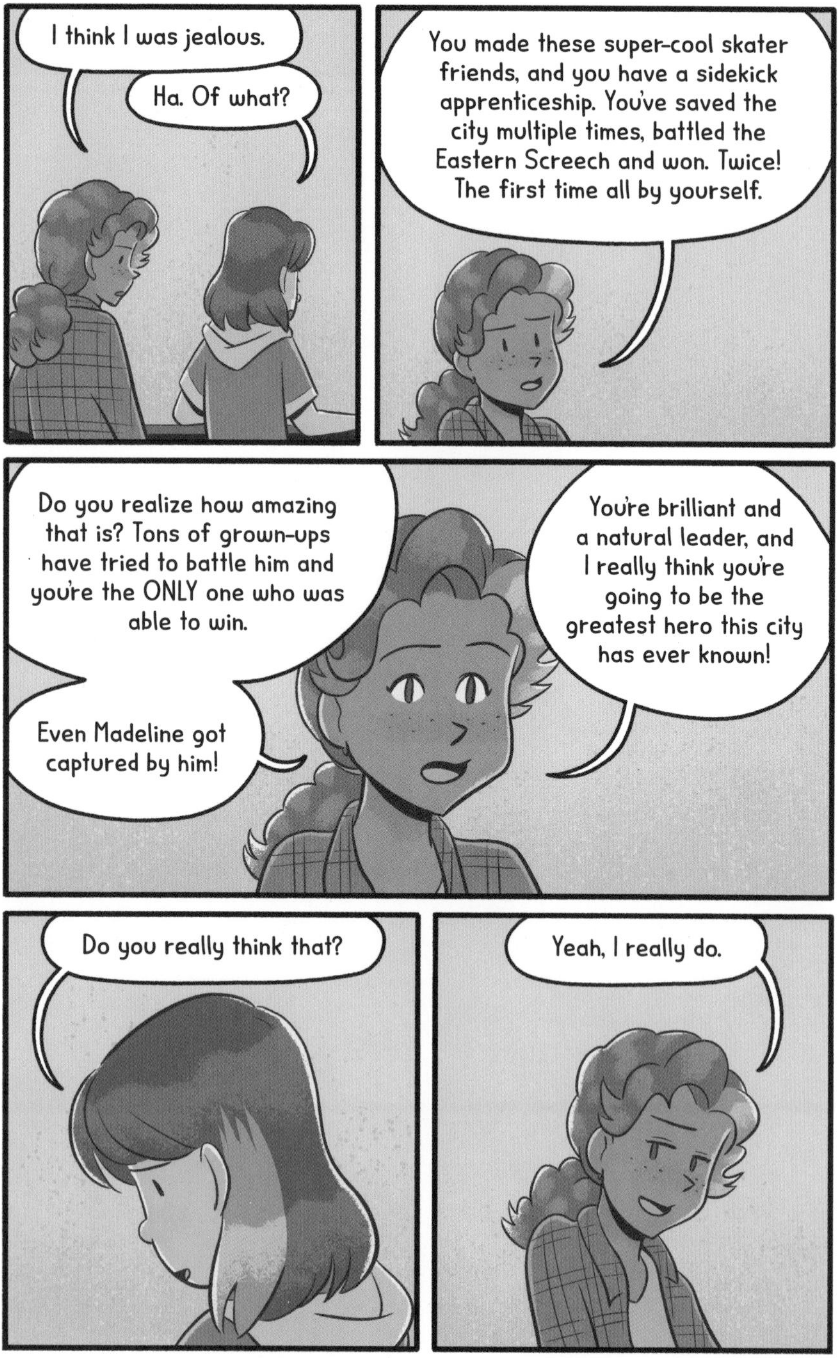
I think I was jealous.
Ha. Of what?
You made these super-cool skater friends, and you have a sidekick apprenticeship. You've saved the city multiple times, battled the Eastern Screech and won. Twice! The first time all by yourself.
Do you realize how amazing that is? Tons of grown-ups have tried to battle him and you're the ONLY one who was able to win.
Even Madeline got captured by him!
You're brilliant and a natural leader, and I really think you're going to be the greatest hero this city has ever known!
Do you really think that?
Yeah, I really do.

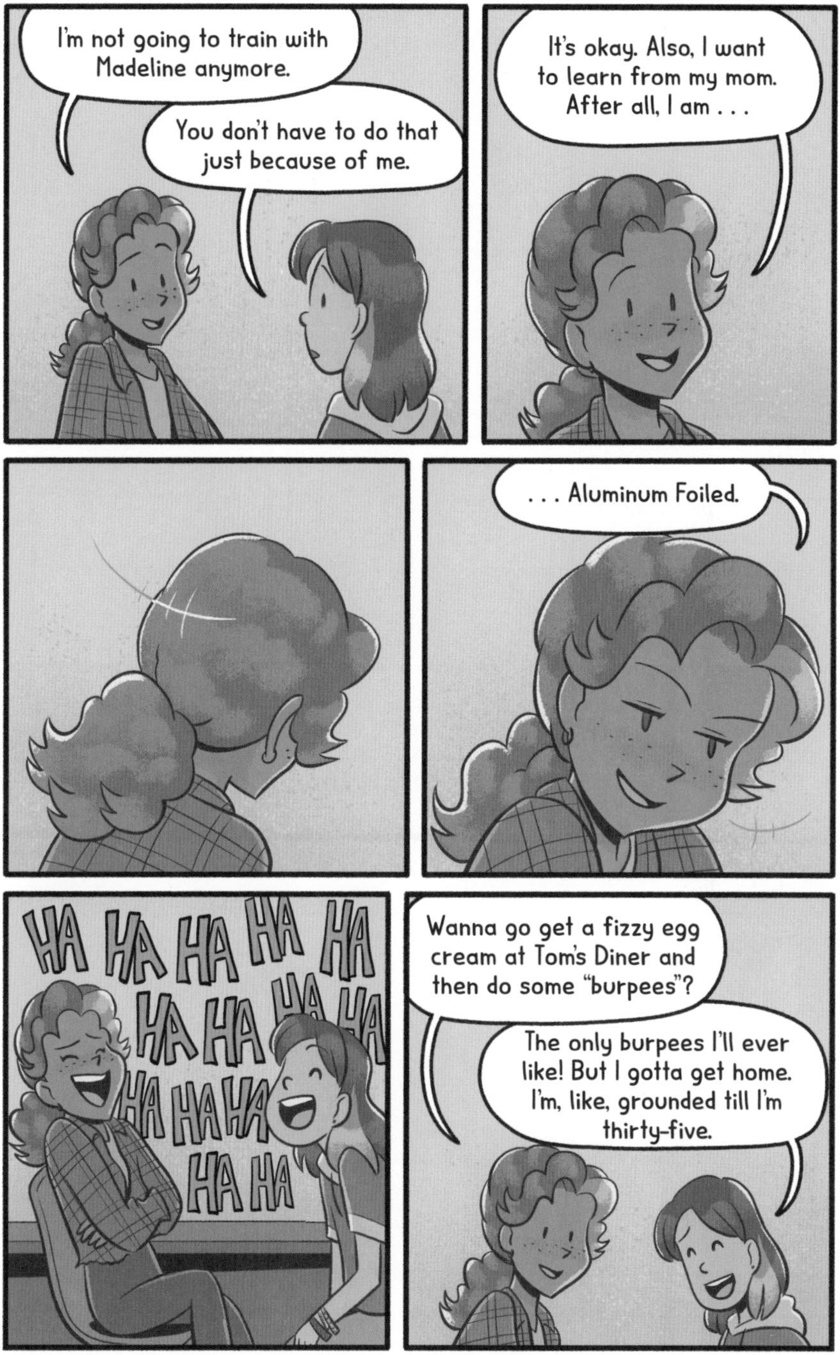
I'm not going to train with Madeline anymore.
You don't have to do that just because of me.
It's okay. Also, I want to learn from my mom. After all, I am . . .
. . . Aluminum Foiled.
HA HA HA HA HA HA HA HA HA HA HA HA HA HA HA
Wanna go get a fizzy egg cream at Tom's Diner and then do some "burpees"?
The only burpees I'll ever like! But I gotta get home. I'm, like, grounded till I'm thirty-five.

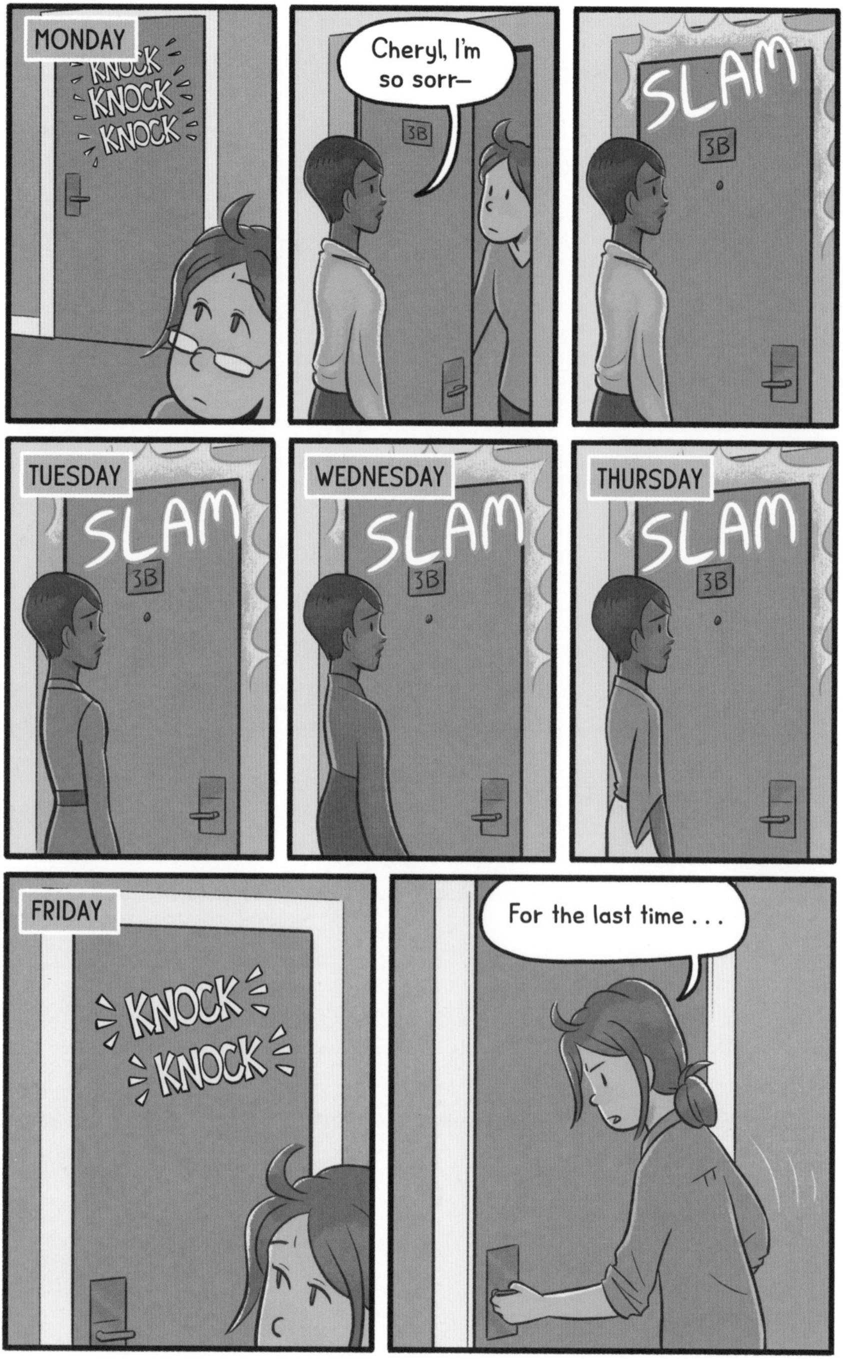
MONDAY
KNOCK
KNOCK
KNOCK
Cheryl, I'm so sorr—
SLAM
TUESDAY
SLAM
WEDNESDAY
SLAM
THURSDAY
SLAM
FRIDAY
KNOCK
KNOCK
For the last time . . .

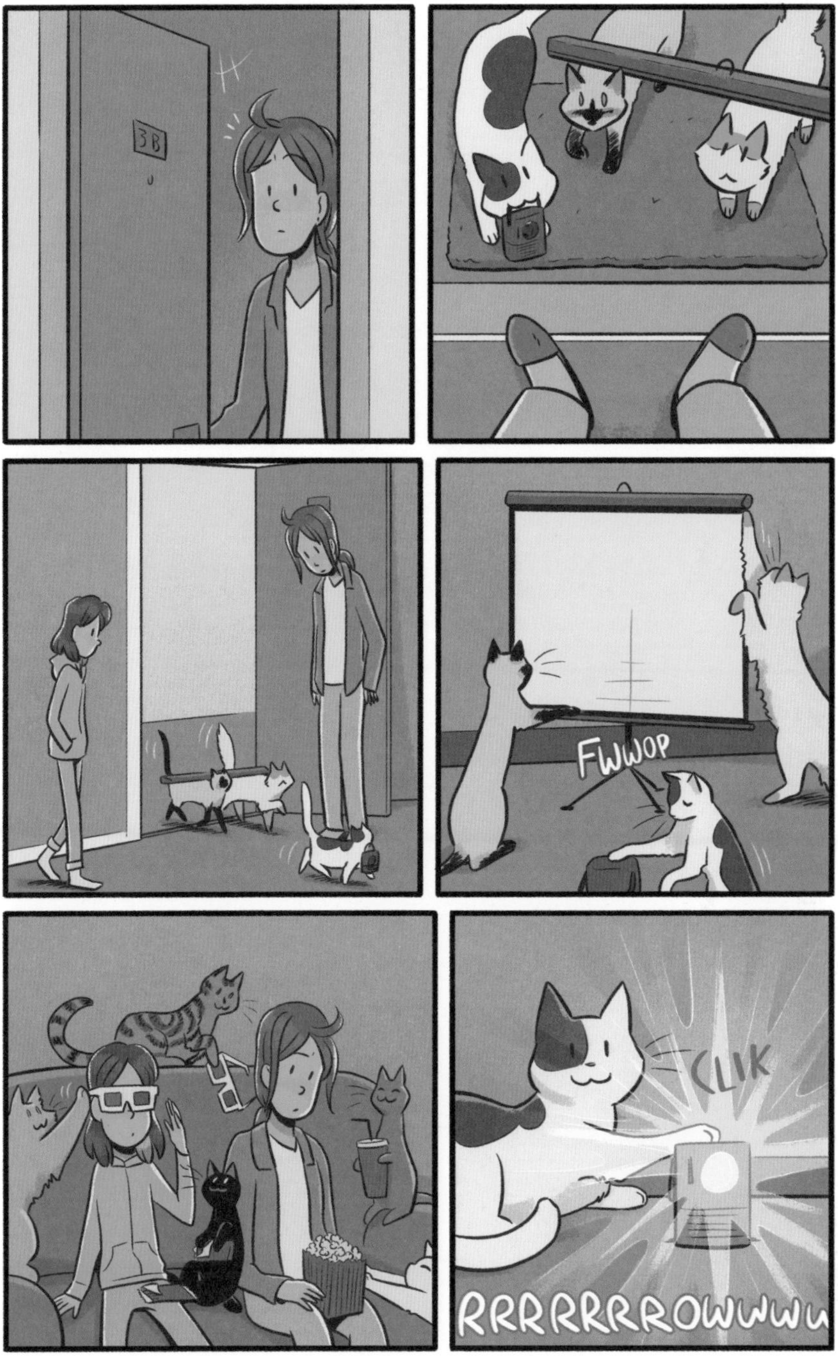
3B
FWWOP
CLIK
RRRRRRROWWWU

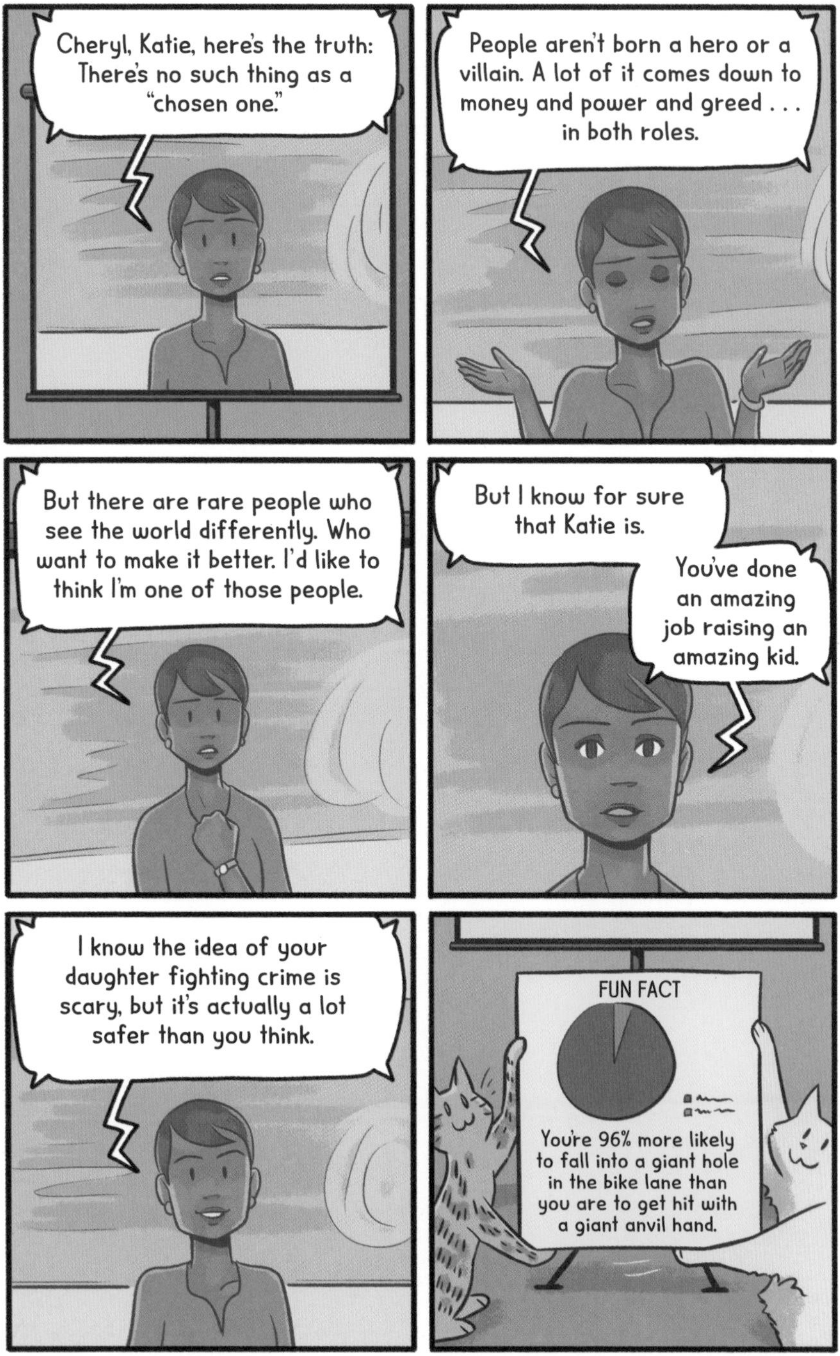
Cheryl, Katie, here's the truth: There's no such thing as a "chosen one."
People aren't born a hero or a villain. A lot of it comes down to money and power and greed . . . in both roles.
But there are rare people who see the world differently. Who want to make it better. I'd like to think I'm one of those people.
But I know for sure that Katie is.
You've done an amazing job raising an amazing kid.
I know the idea of your daughter fighting crime is scary, but it's actually a lot safer than you think.
FUN FACT
You're 96% more likely to fall into a giant hole in the bike lane than you are to get hit with a giant anvil hand.

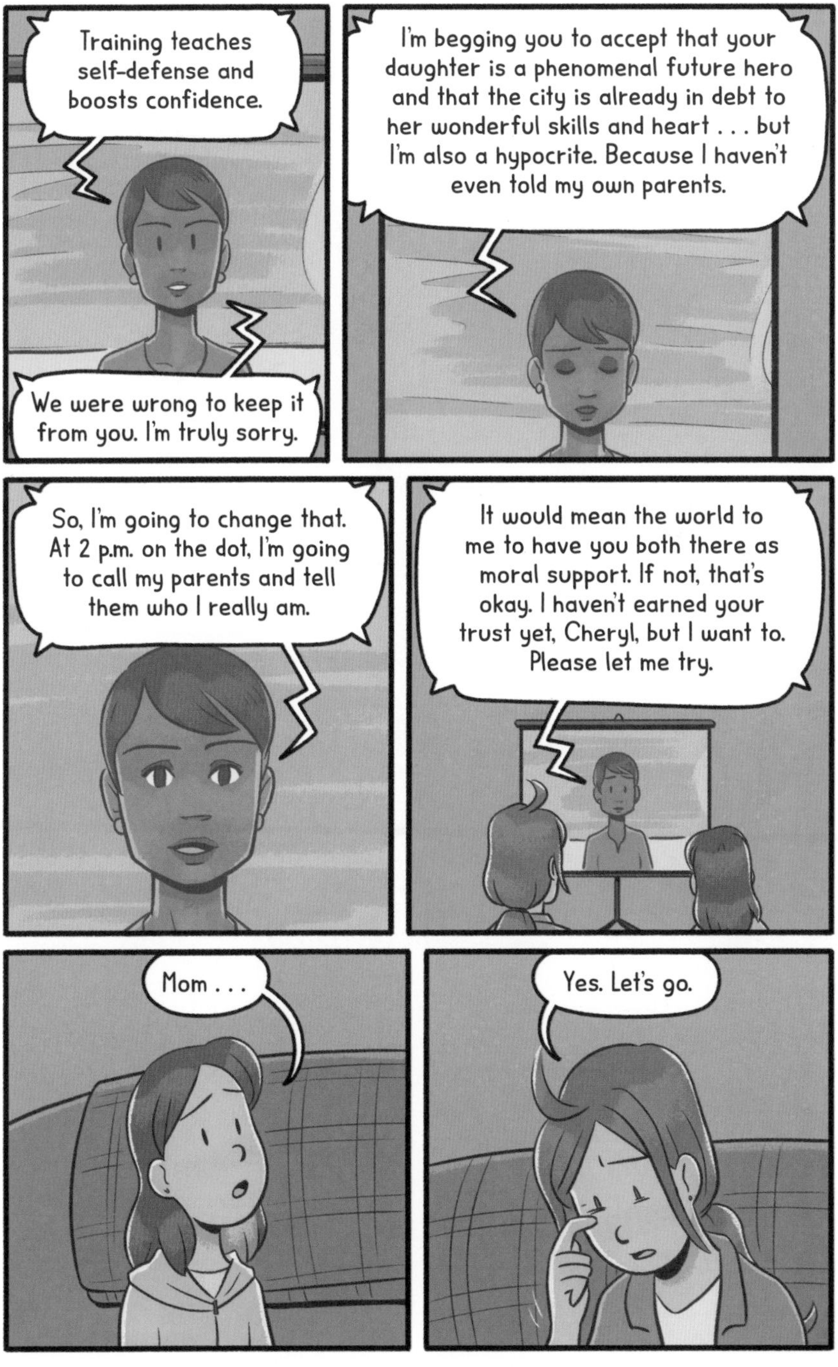
Training teaches self-defense and boosts confidence.
We were wrong to keep it from you. I'm truly sorry.
I'm begging you to accept that your daughter is a phenomenal future hero and that the city is already in debt to her wonderful skills and heart . . . but I'm also a hypocrite. Because I haven't even told my own parents.
So, I'm going to change that. At 2 p.m. on the dot, I'm going to call my parents and tell them who I really am.
It would mean the world to me to have you both there as moral support. If not, that's okay. I haven't earned your trust yet, Cheryl, but I want to. Please let me try.
Mom . . .
Yes. Let's go.

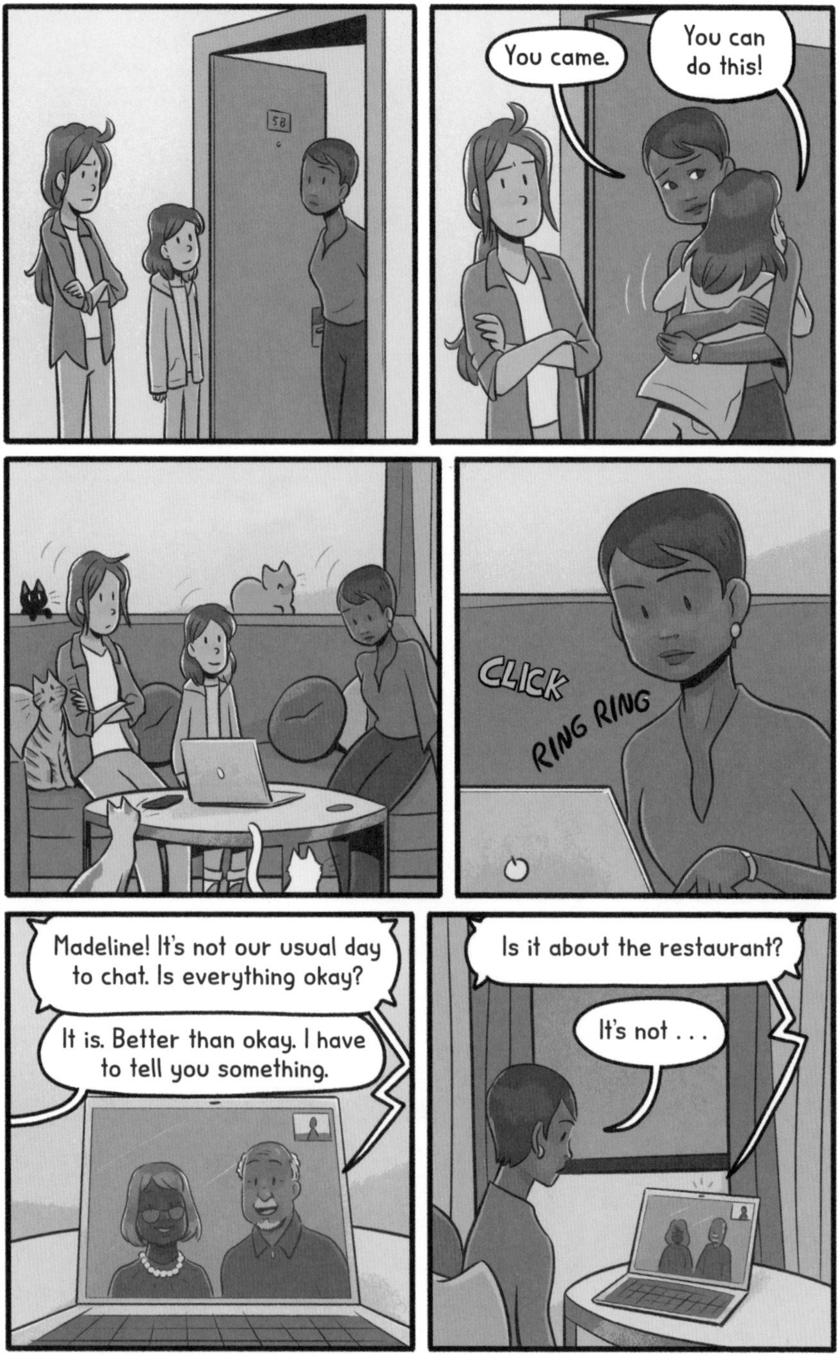
You came.
You can do this!
CLICK
RING RING
Madeline! It's not our usual day to chat. Is everything okay?
It is. Better than okay. I have to tell you something.
Is it about the restaurant?
It's not . . .

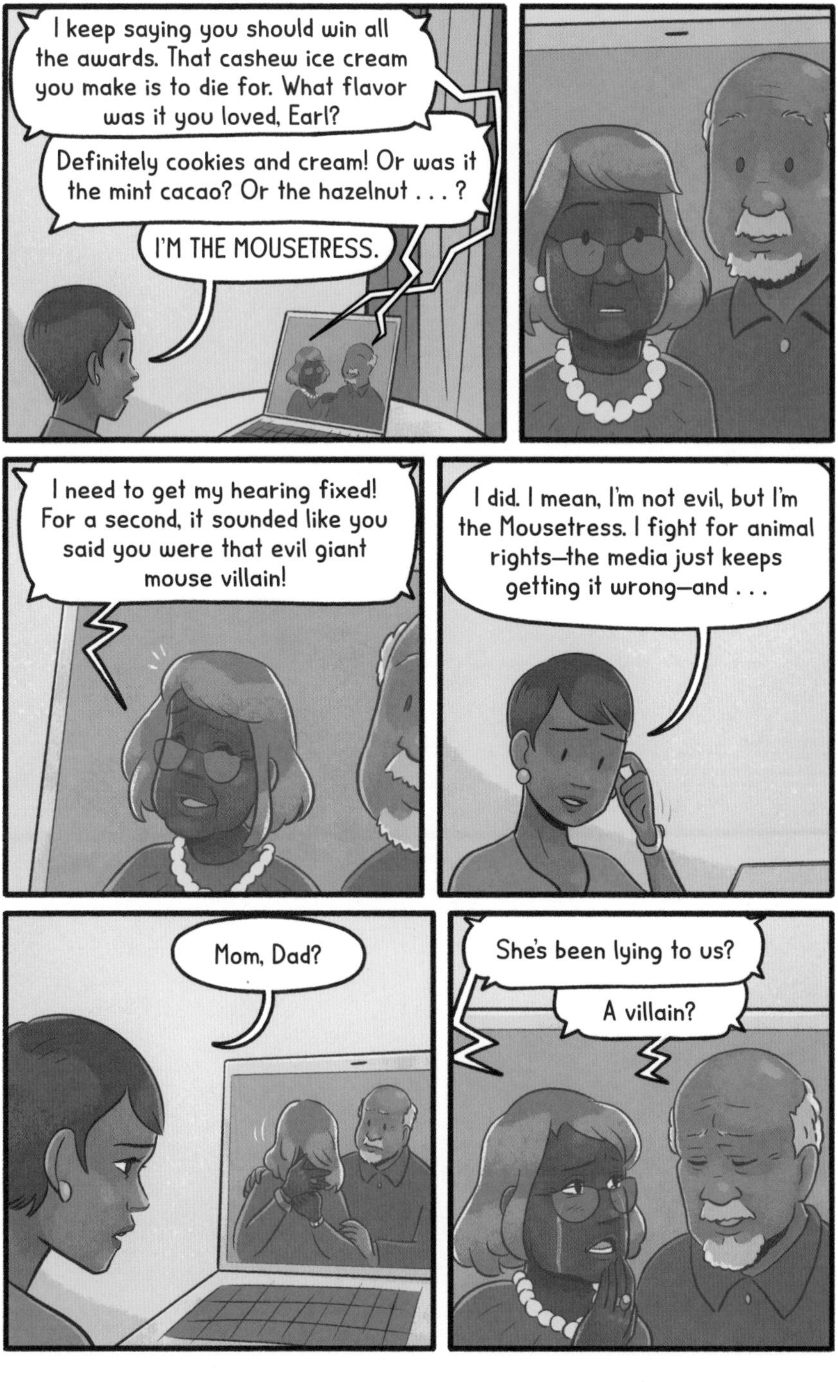
I keep saying you should win all the awards. That cashew ice cream you make is to die for. What flavor was it you loved, Earl?
Definitely cookies and cream! Or was it the mint cacao? Or the hazelnut . . . ?
I'M THE MOUSETRESS.
I need to get my hearing fixed! For a second, it sounded like you said you were that evil giant mouse villain!
I did. I mean, I'm not evil, but I'm the Mousetress. I fight for animal rights—the media just keeps getting it wrong—and . . .
Mom, Dad?
She's been lying to us?
A villain?

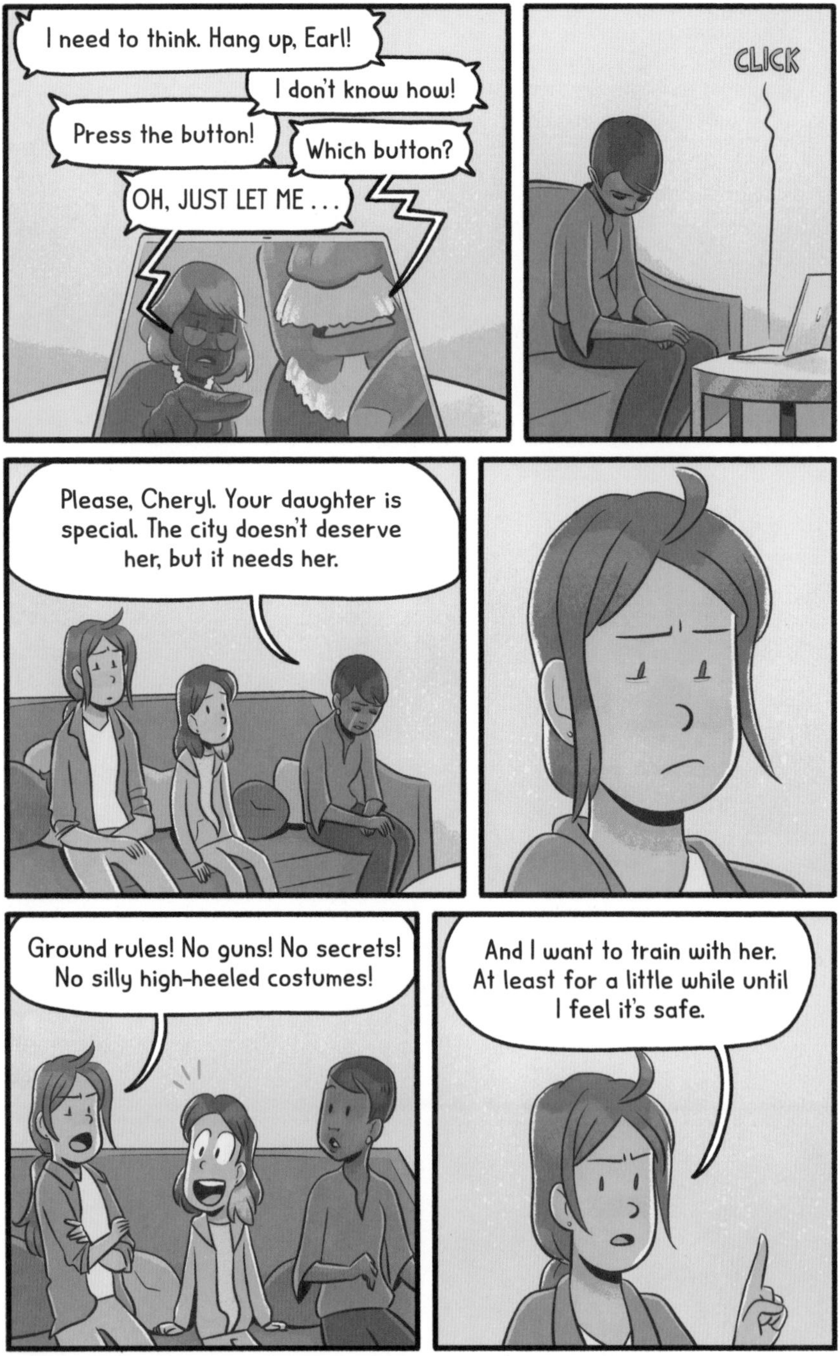
I need to think. Hang up, Earl!
I don't know how!
Press the button!
Which button?
OH, JUST LET ME . . .
CLICK
Please, Cheryl. Your daughter is special. The city doesn't deserve her, but it needs her.
Ground rules! No guns! No secrets! No silly high-heeled costumes!
And I want to train with her. At least for a little while until I feel it's safe.

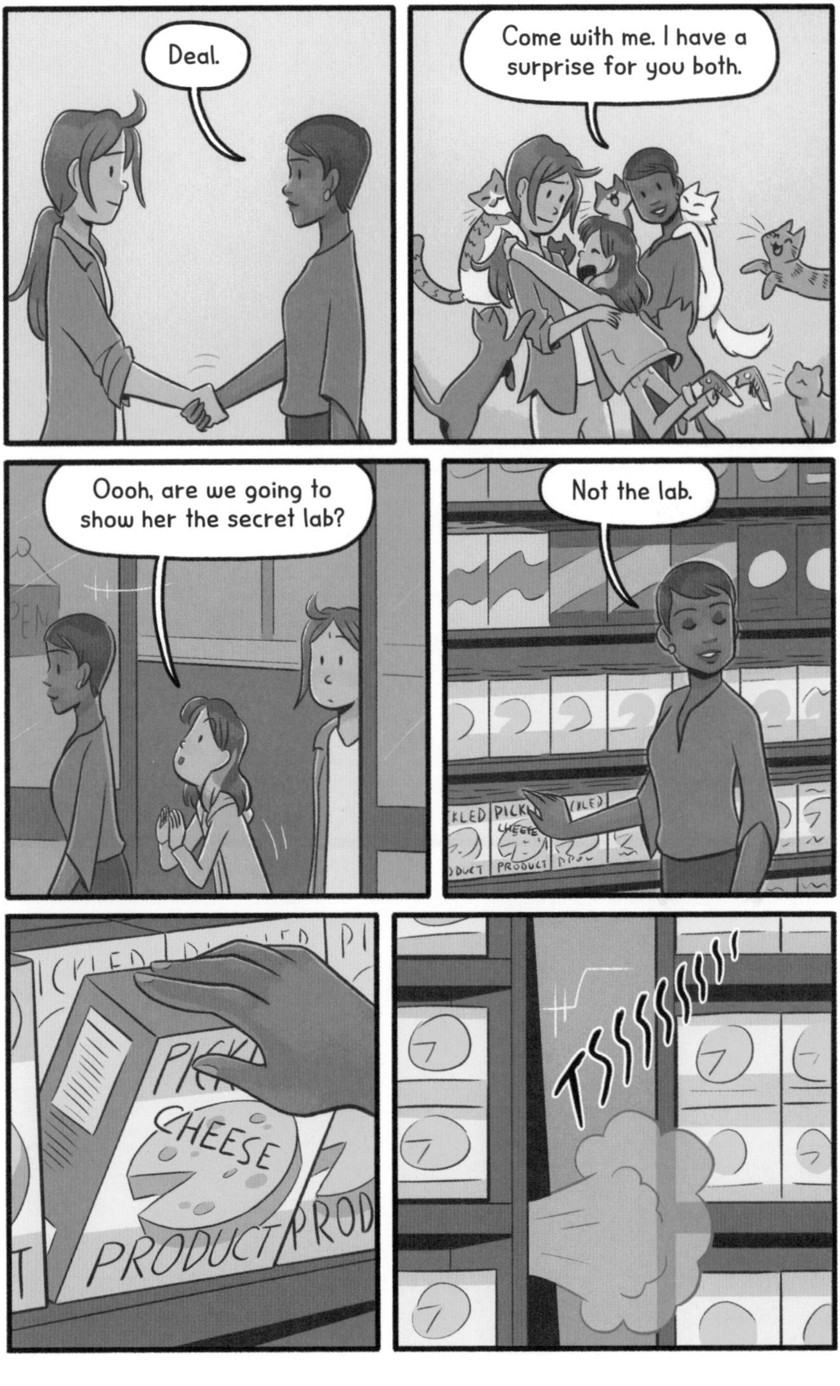
Deal.
Come with me. I have a surprise for you both.
Oooh, are we going to show her the secret lab?
Not the lab.
PICKLED CHEESE PRODUCT
TSSSSSSS'

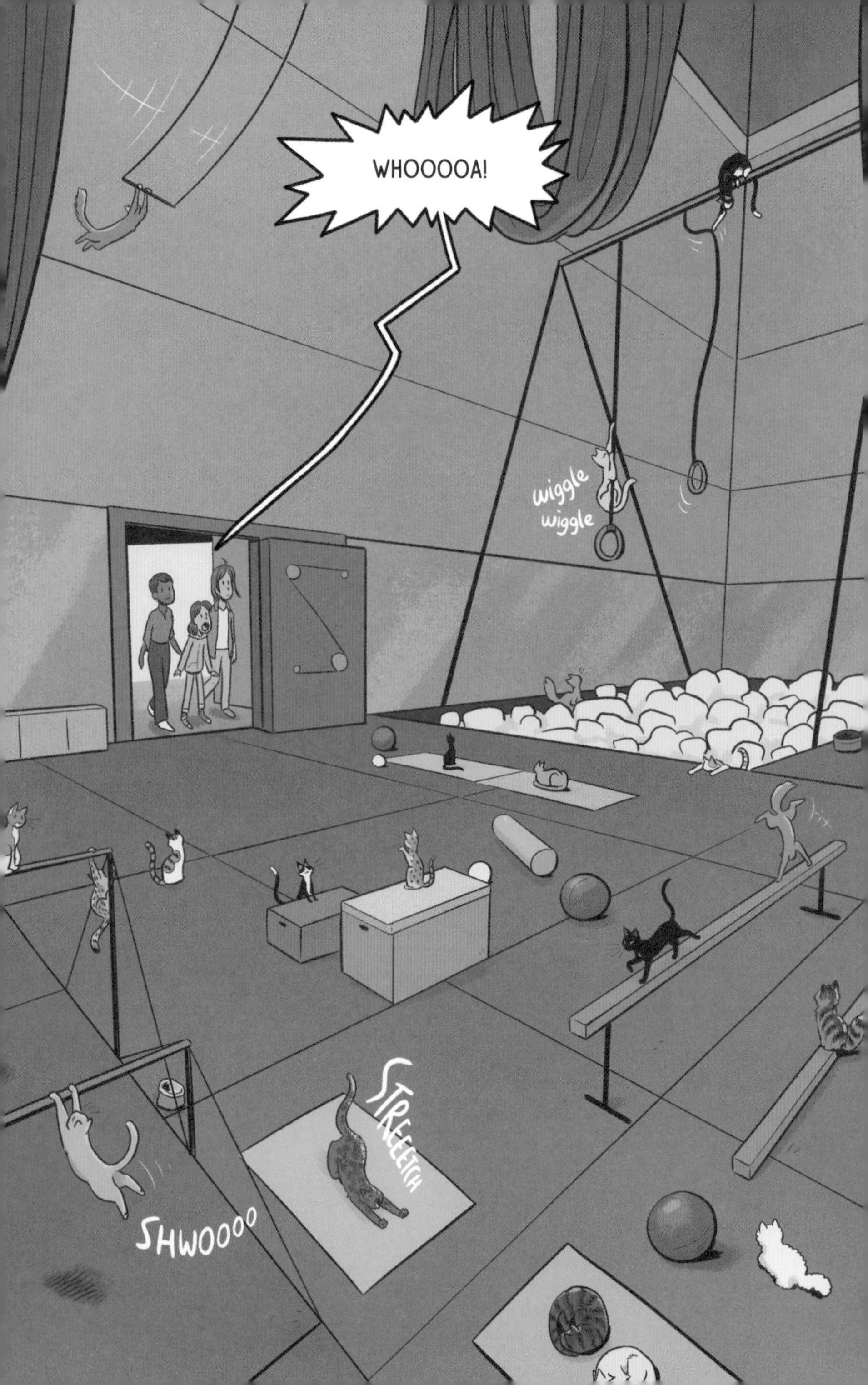
WHOOOOA!
wiggle
wiggle
STREEETCH
SHWOOOO

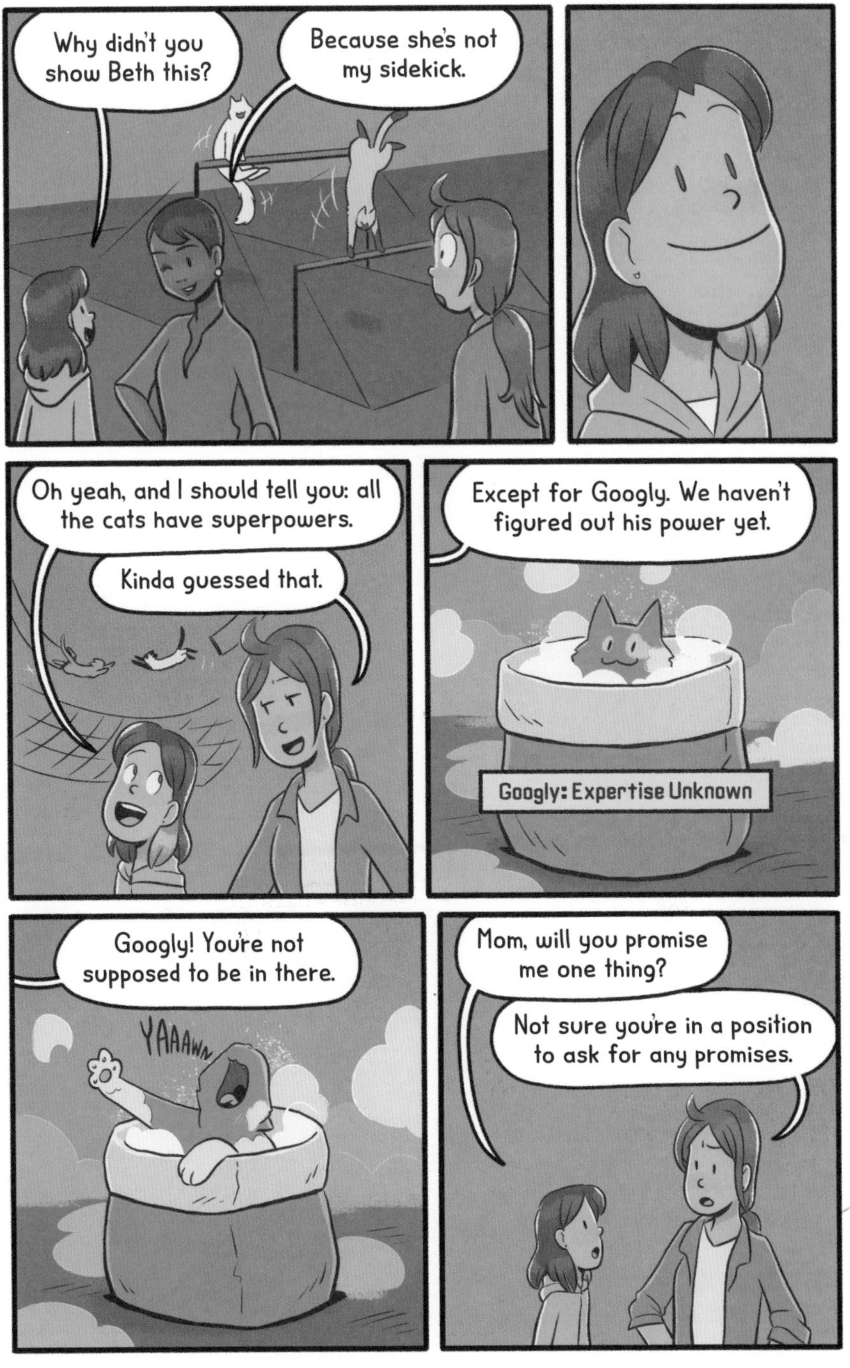
Why didn't you show Beth this?
Because she's not my sidekick.
Oh yeah, and I should tell you: all the cats have superpowers.
Kinda guessed that.
Except for Googly. We haven't figured out his power yet.
Googly: Expertise Unknown
Googly! You're not supposed to be in there.
YAAAWN
Mom, will you promise me one thing?
Not sure you're in a position to ask for any promises.

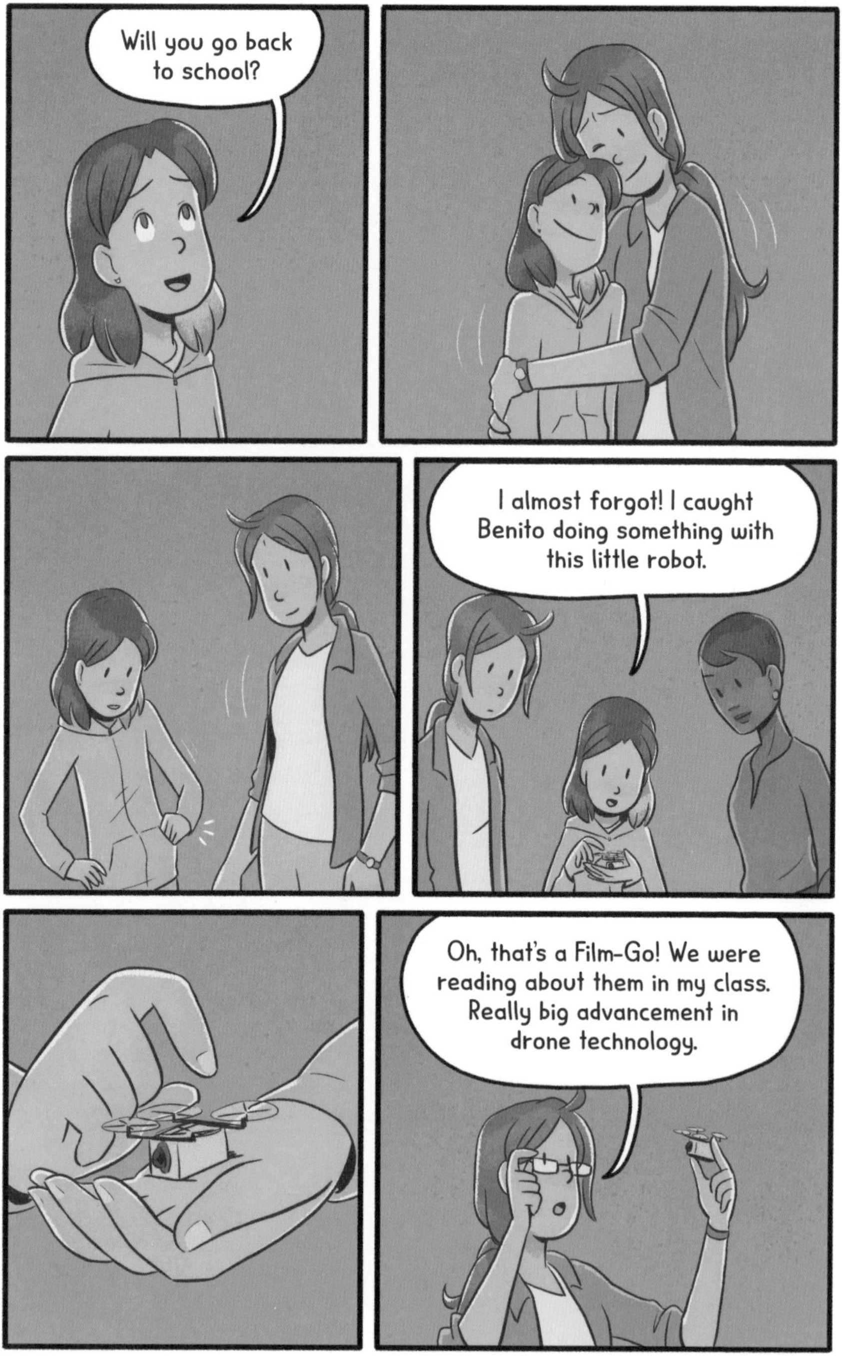
Will you go back to school?
I almost forgot! I caught Benito doing something with this little robot.
Oh, that's a Film-Go! We were reading about them in my class. Really big advancement in drone technology.

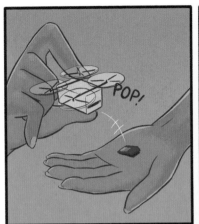

Let's see what Benito's been up to.

Is it on?

I think it's on.

Eastern Screech Files Number 72.

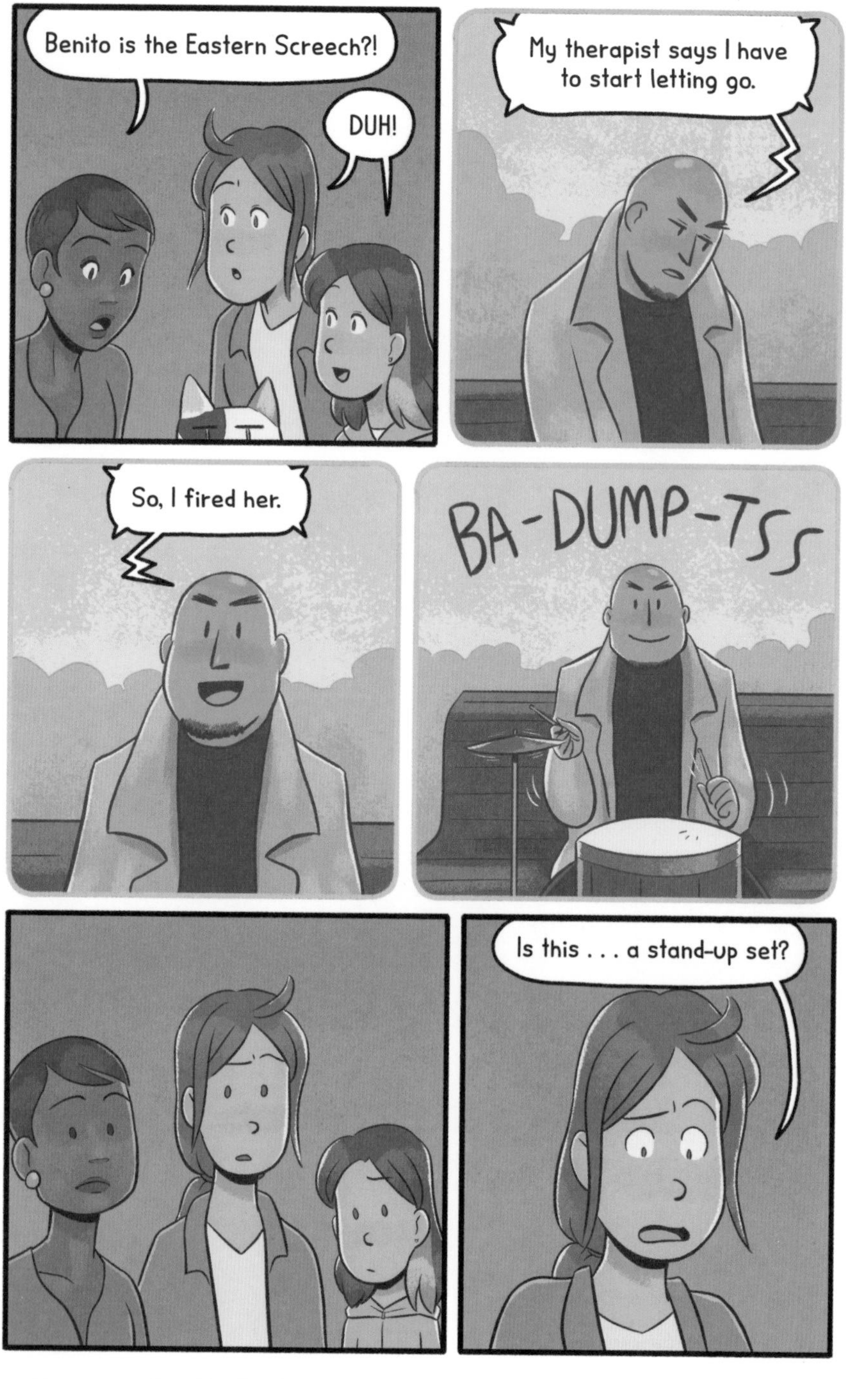
Benito is the Eastern Screech?!
DUH!
My therapist says I have to start letting go.
So, I fired her.
BA-DUMP-TSS
Is this . . . a stand-up set?

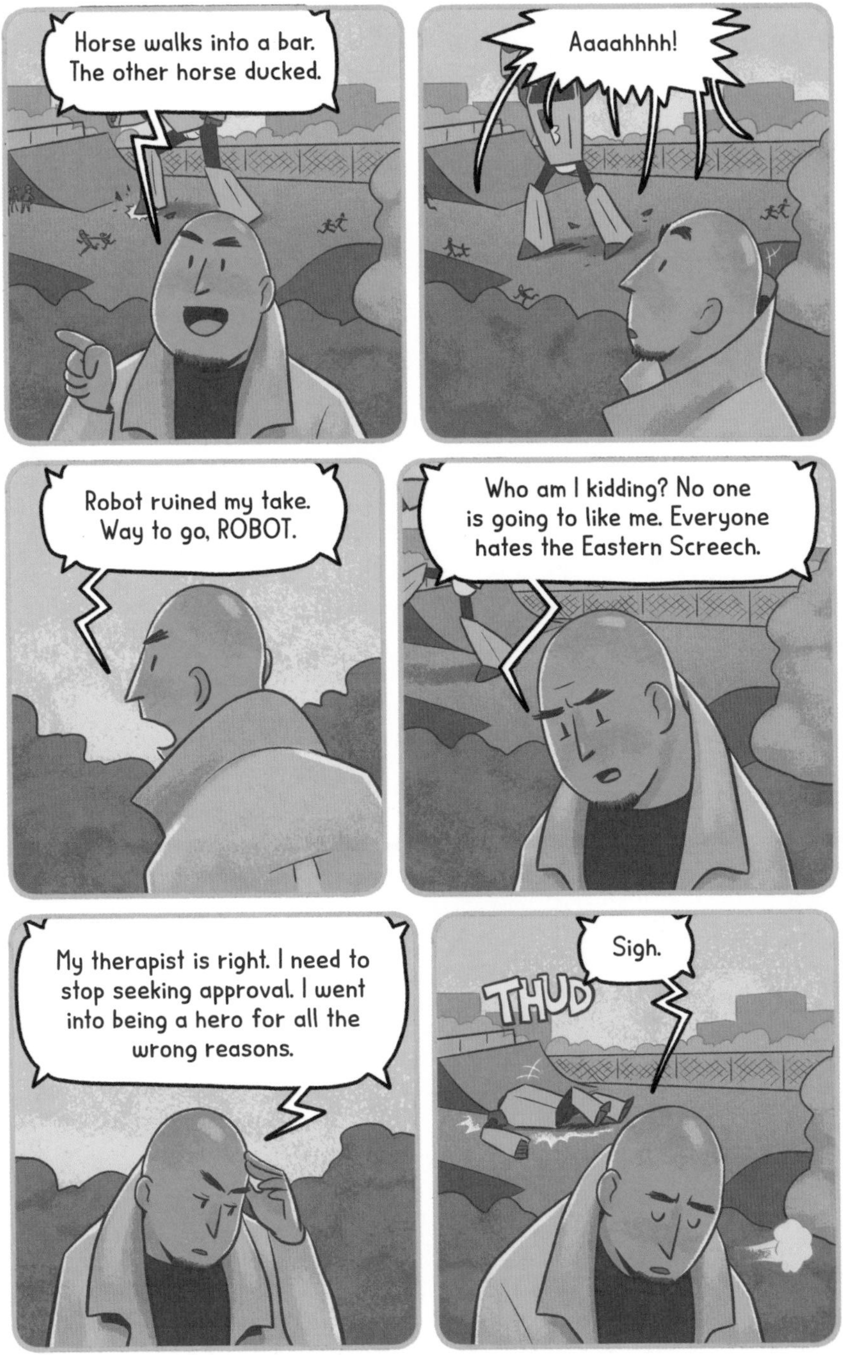
Horse walks into a bar. The other horse ducked.
Aaaahhhh!
Robot ruined my take. Way to go, ROBOT.
Who am I kidding? No one is going to like me. Everyone hates the Eastern Screech.
My therapist is right. I need to stop seeking approval. I went into being a hero for all the wrong reasons.
THUD
Sigh.

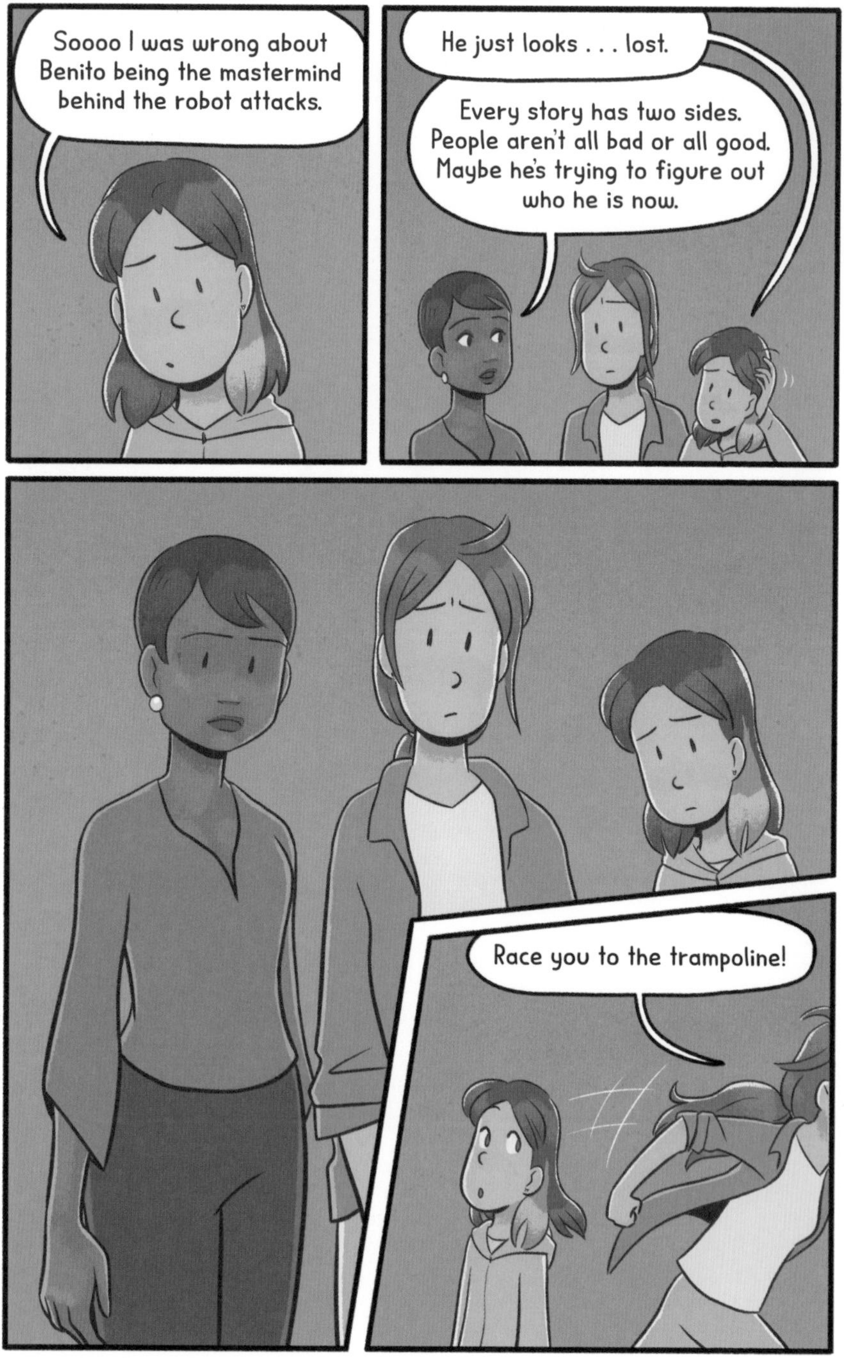
Soooo I was wrong about Benito being the mastermind behind the robot attacks.
He just looks . . . lost.
Every story has two sides. People aren't all bad or all good. Maybe he's trying to figure out who he is now.
Race you to the trampoline!

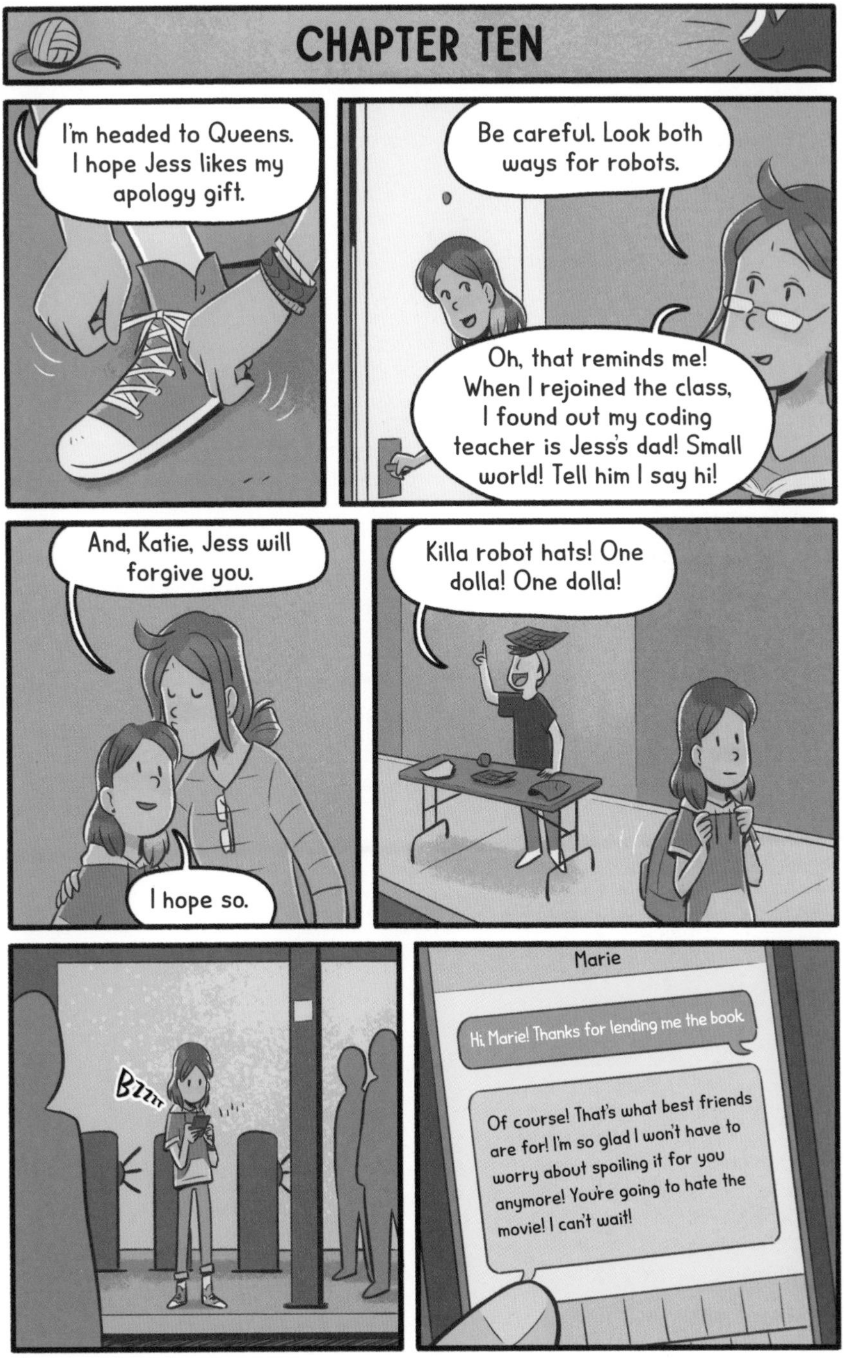
CHAPTER TEN
I'm headed to Queens. I hope Jess likes my apology gift.
Be careful. Look both ways for robots.
Oh, that reminds me! When I rejoined the class, I found out my coding teacher is Jess's dad! Small world! Tell him I say hi!
And, Katie, Jess will forgive you.
I hope so.
Killa robot hats! One dolla! One dolla!
BZZZT
Marie
Hi, Marie! Thanks for lending me the book.
Of course! That's what best friends are for! I'm so glad I won't have to worry about spoiling it for you anymore! You're going to hate the movie! I can't wait!

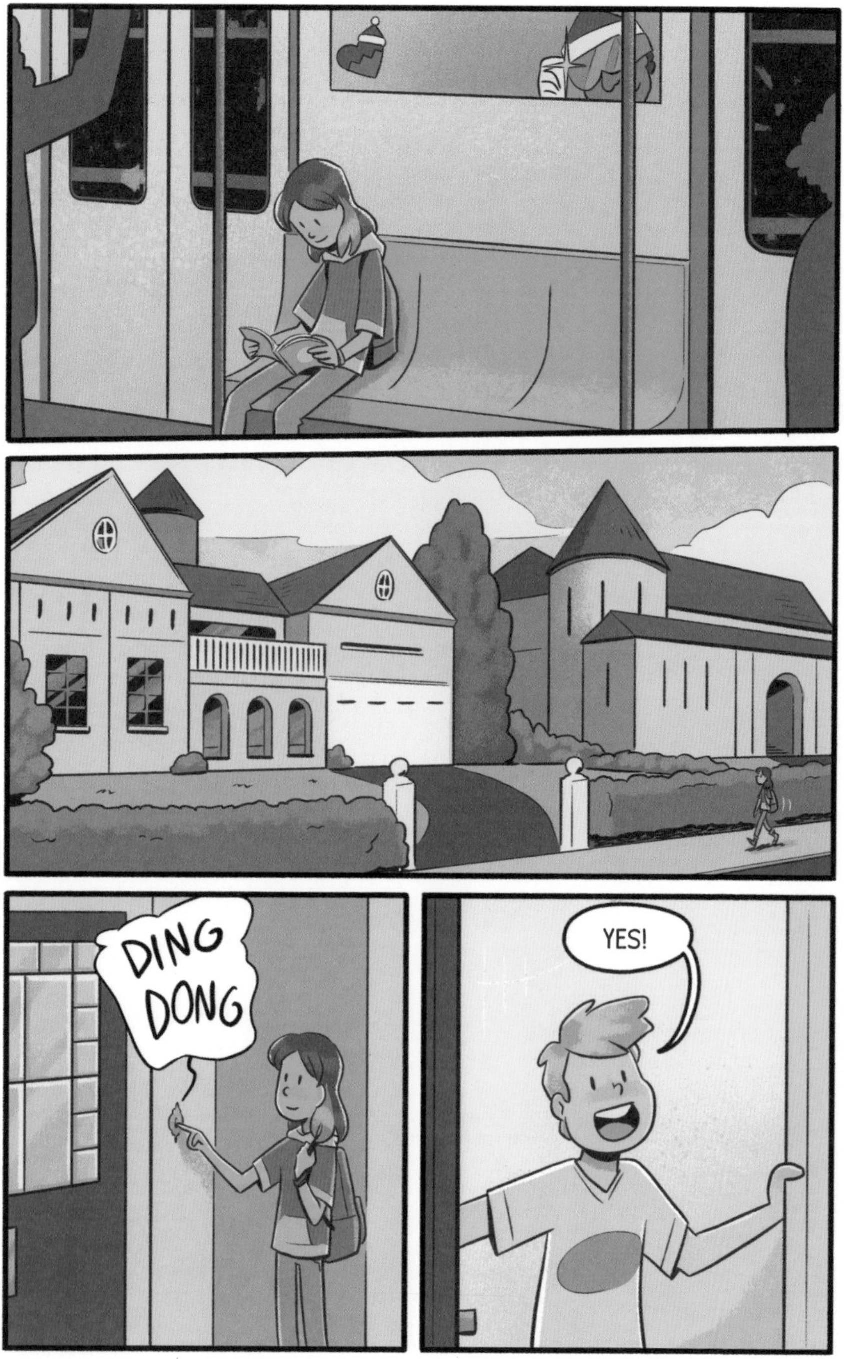
DING DONG
YES!

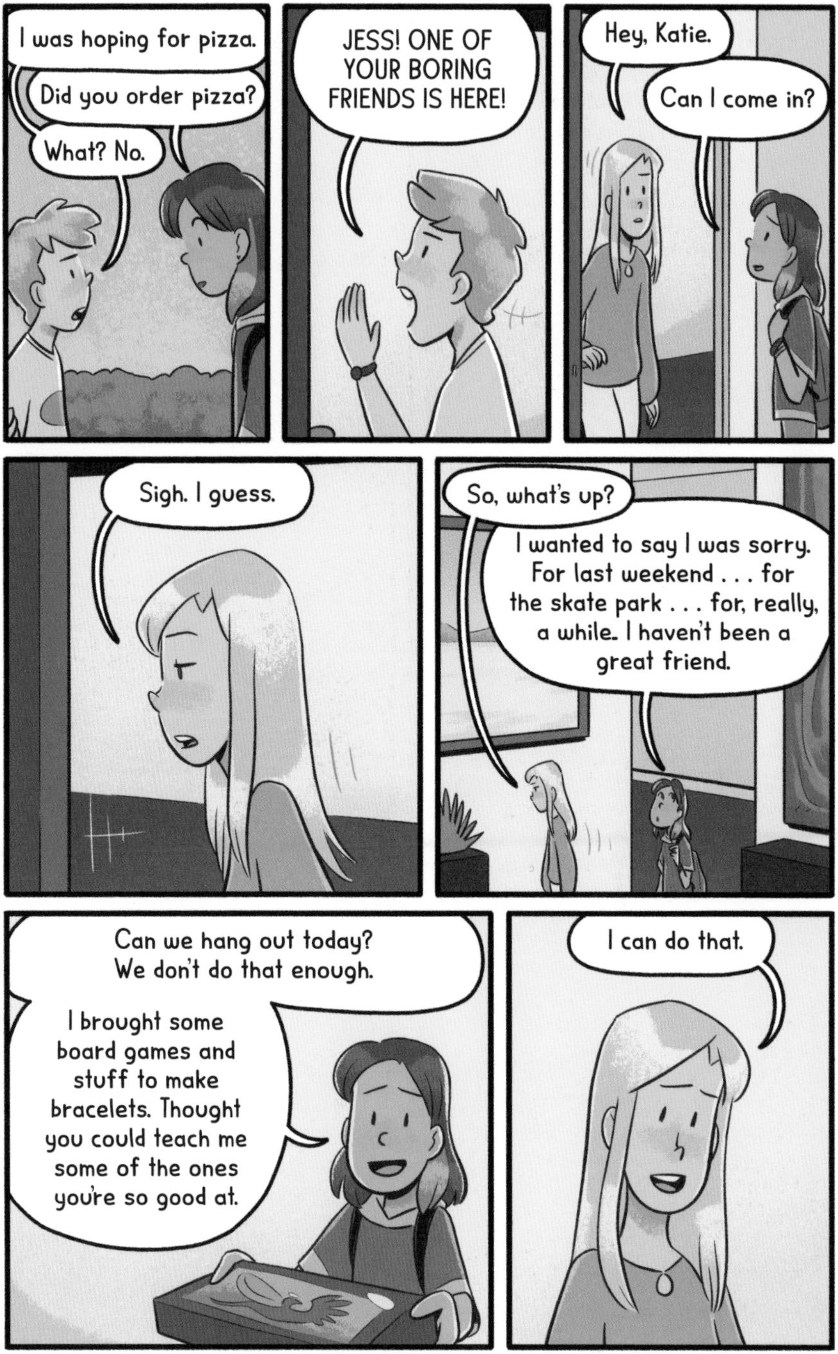
I was hoping for pizza.
Did you order pizza?
What? No.
JESS! ONE OF YOUR BORING FRIENDS IS HERE!
Hey, Katie.
Can I come in?
Sigh. I guess.
So, what's up?
I wanted to say I was sorry. For last weekend . . . for the skate park . . . for, really, a while. I haven't been a great friend.
Can we hang out today? We don't do that enough.
I brought some board games and stuff to make bracelets. Thought you could teach me some of the ones you're so good at.
I can do that.

Yeah, I mean, I was upset when he broke up with me. But he was always rambling about stocks and bonds, and I held his hand once . . . so gross! It was like holding a fish!

Ewww!

Good riddance!

And speaking of good, that bracelet looks fantastic! You keep saying you aren't athletic, but that takes some serious coordination!

Huh. You're right. It's not bad!

Here. It's for you.

Good thing, because I was making this one for you! It matches your shoes.

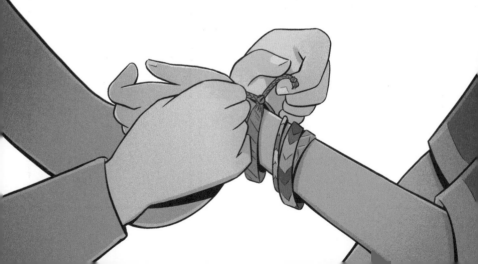

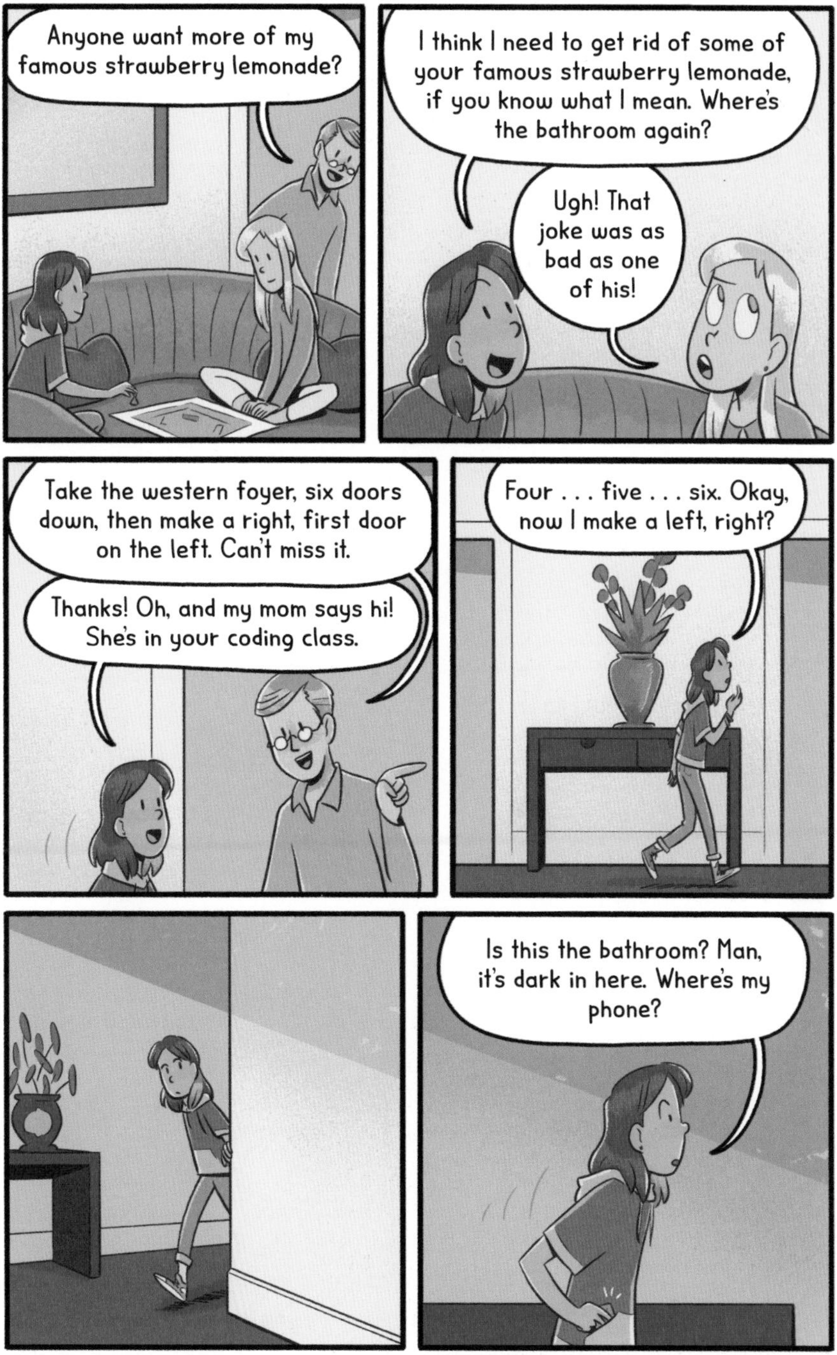
Anyone want more of my famous strawberry lemonade?
I think I need to get rid of some of your famous strawberry lemonade, if you know what I mean. Where's the bathroom again?
Ugh! That joke was as bad as one of his!
Take the western foyer, six doors down, then make a right, first door on the left. Can't miss it.
Thanks! Oh, and my mom says hi! She's in your coding class.
Four . . . five . . . six. Okay, now I make a left, right?
Is this the bathroom? Man, it's dark in here. Where's my phone?

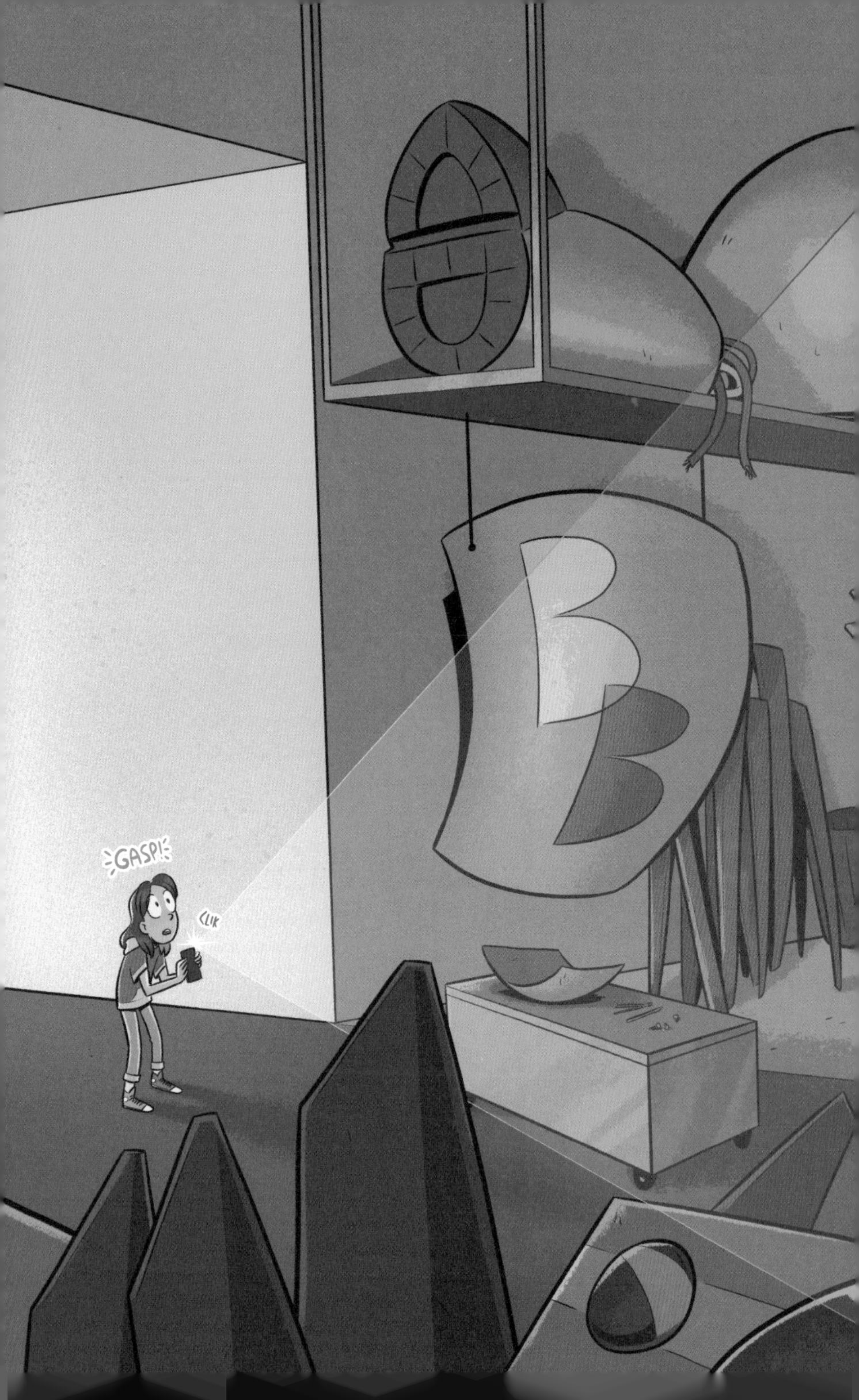
GASP!
CLIK

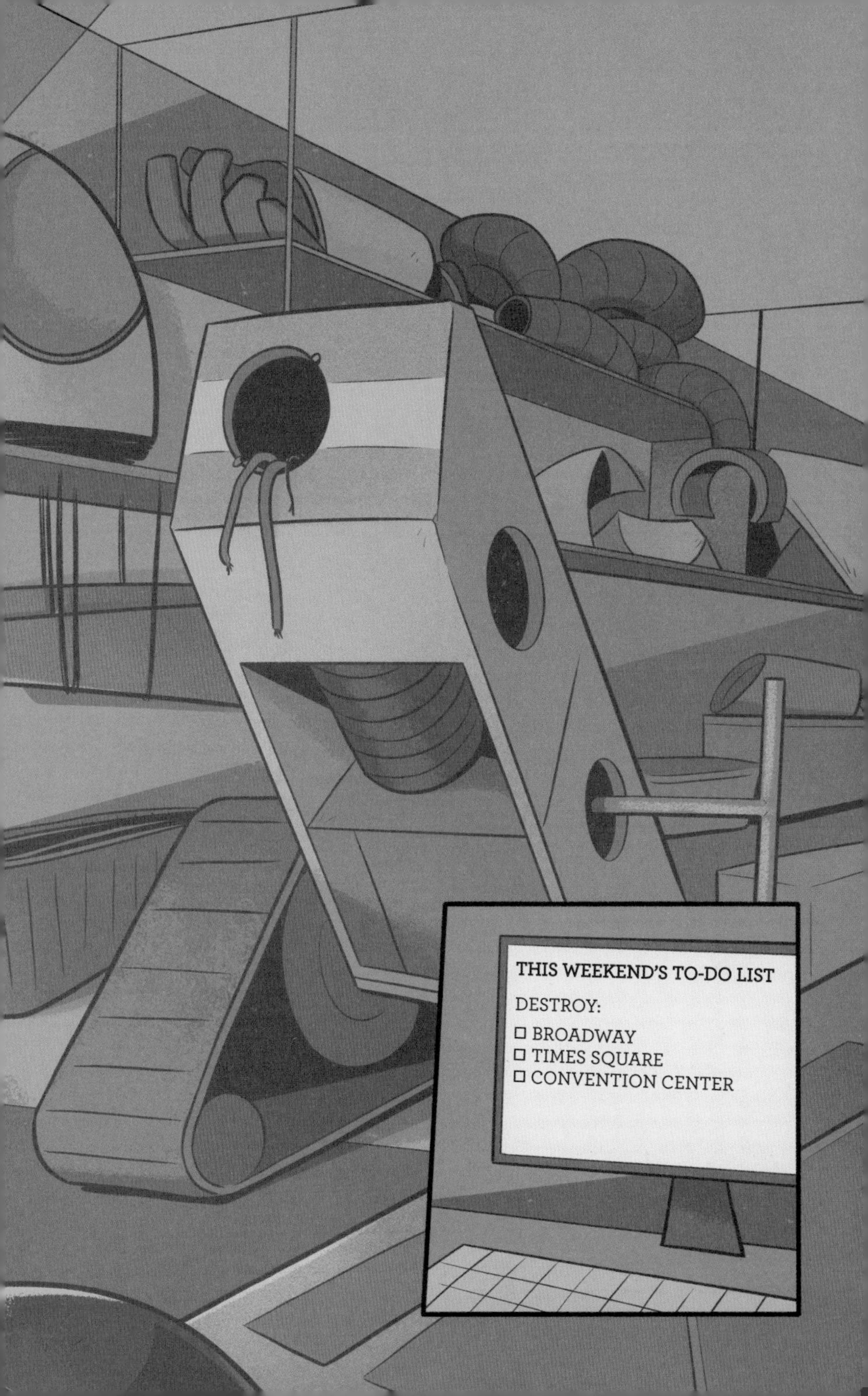
THIS WEEKEND'S TO-DO LIST
DESTROY:
☐ BROADWAY
☐ TIMES SQUARE
☐ CONVENTION CENTER

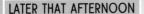

CHAPTER ELEVEN

LATER THAT AFTERNOON

Are you sure?

2,000% sure! Robots of every size! And there were plans on a screen of all the places they are going to attack!

I can't believe it. Professor Winchell, a supervillain.

There they are. Just like we thought. Both fired by Buttersoft. And even weirder ... they were both original founders.

What do we do? Jess's parents are nice! They're just trying to frame Buttersoft—who is actually doing worse things.

Maybe they aren't really going to destroy all those places?

But people got hurt. Those cyclists and businesses. Can't we tell them we know? Ask them to stop?

It's always best to start with communication. The Mousetress should pay them a visit.

But if they're really supervillains, are they going to listen to another villain? They know the Mousetress can't call the police.

You're right, Katie. I need a disguise.

Mew Mew: Disguise Expert

Curly: Expert Seamstress

Boumi: Haberdasher

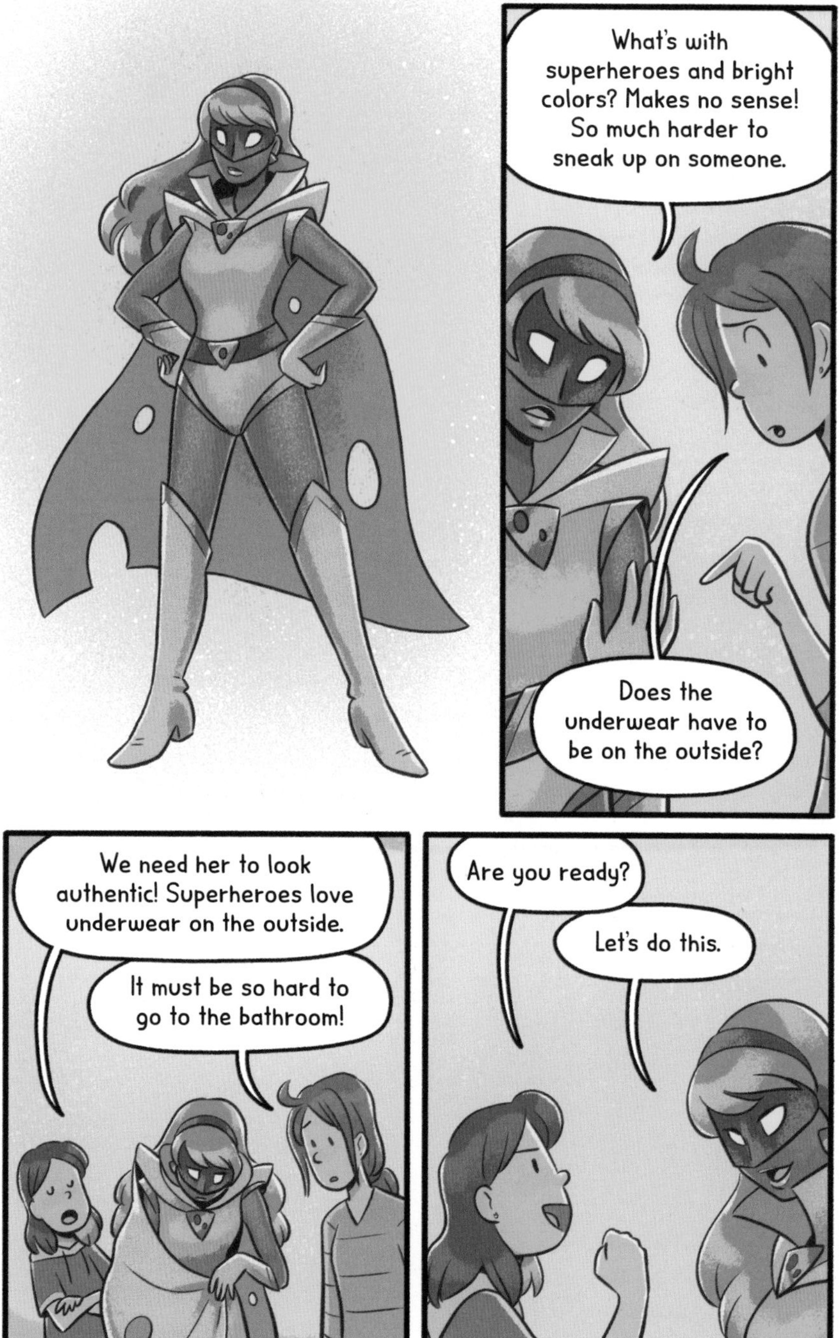
What's with superheroes and bright colors? Makes no sense! So much harder to sneak up on someone.
Does the underwear have to be on the outside?
We need her to look authentic! Superheroes love underwear on the outside.
It must be so hard to go to the bathroom!
Are you ready?
Let's do this.

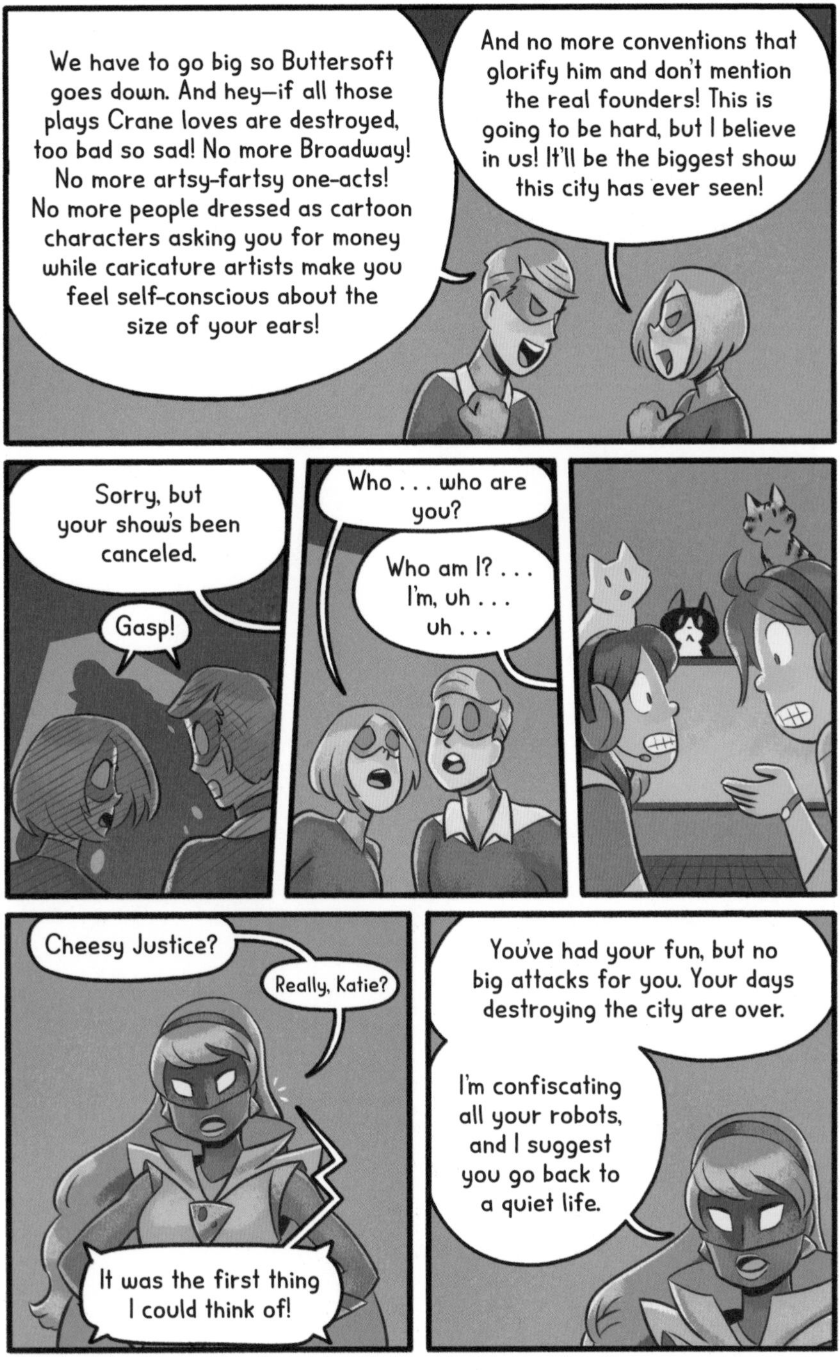
We have to go big so Buttersoft goes down. And hey—if all those plays Crane loves are destroyed, too bad so sad! No more Broadway! No more artsy-fartsy one-acts! No more people dressed as cartoon characters asking you for money while caricature artists make you feel self-conscious about the size of your ears!
And no more conventions that glorify him and don't mention the real founders! This is going to be hard, but I believe in us! It'll be the biggest show this city has ever seen!
Sorry, but your show's been canceled.
Gasp!
Who . . . who are you?
Who am I? . . . I'm, uh . . . uh . . .
Cheesy Justice?
Really, Katie?
It was the first thing I could think of!
You've had your fun, but no big attacks for you. Your days destroying the city are over.
I'm confiscating all your robots, and I suggest you go back to a quiet life.

Okay.

Okay? Phew, that was a whole lot easier than I thought it might be.

They're all yours.

Muahaha!

WRRRRRRRR

WRRRRRRRR

Oh, honey! Was that a new maniacal laugh? I love it!

I've been practicing!

WRRRRRRRRRRRRRRR

DESTROY HER! AND THEN DESTROY THE CITY!

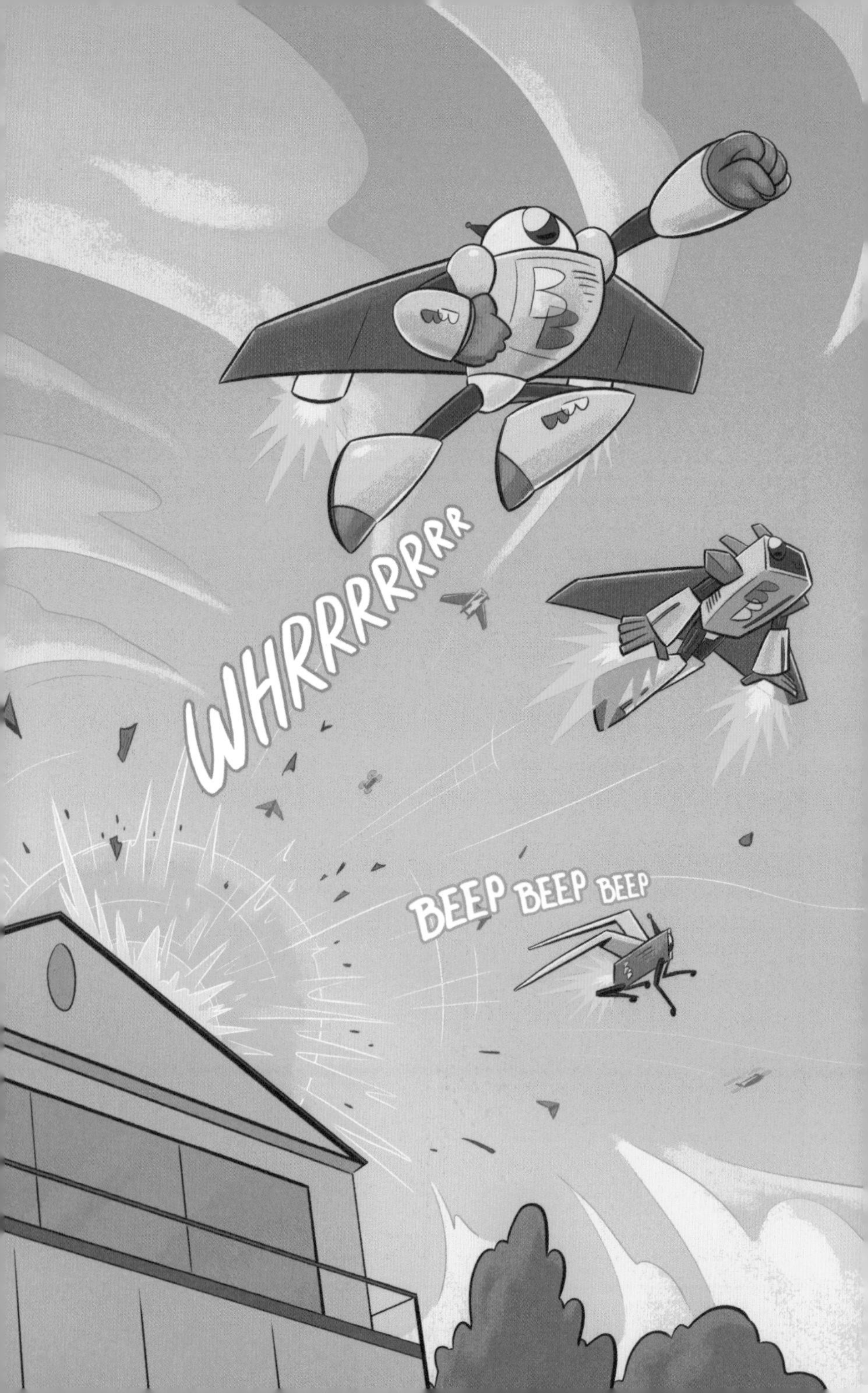
WHRRRRRRR
BEEP BEEP BEEP

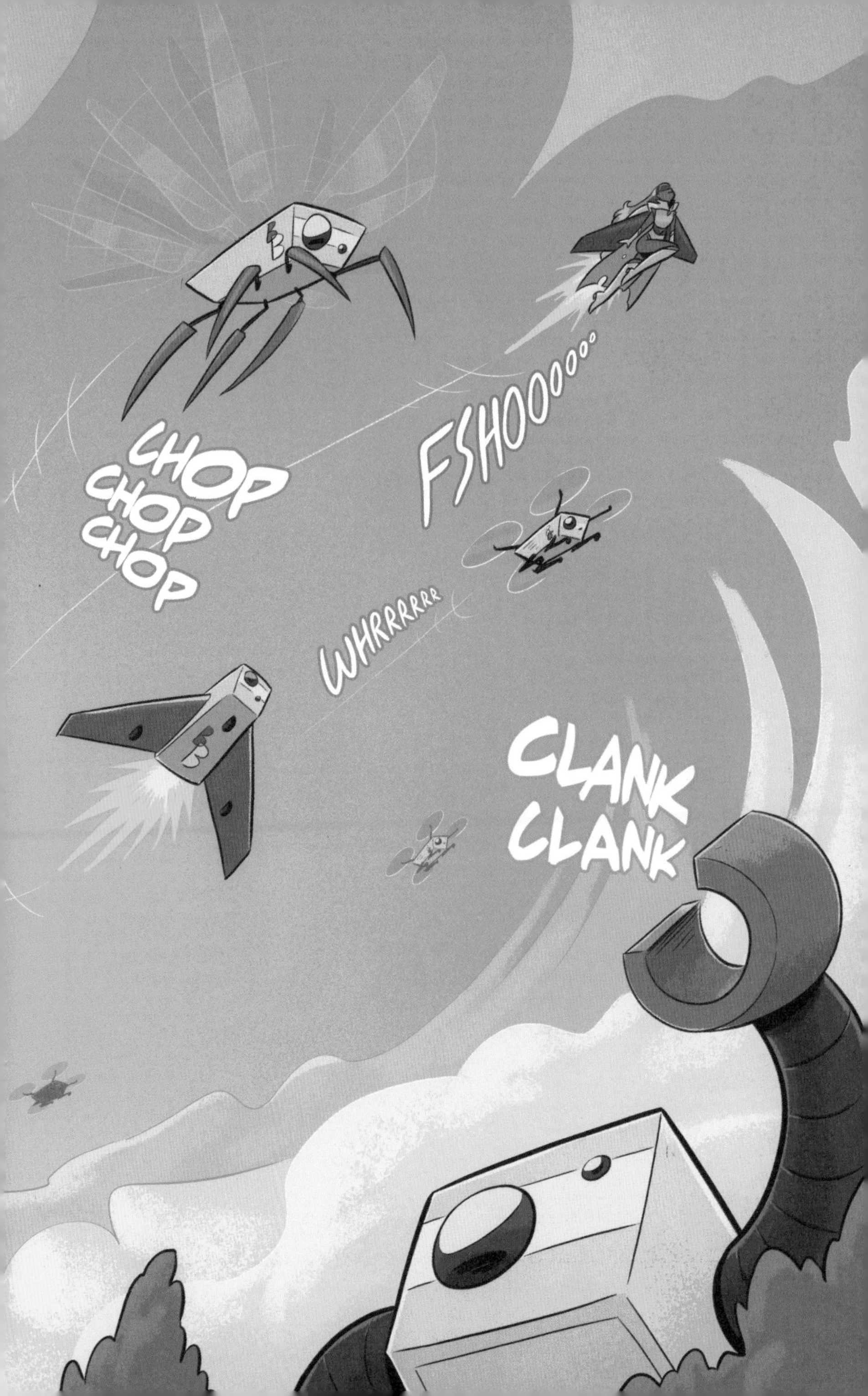
CHOP
CHOP
CHOP
FSHOOOOOO
WHRRRRRR
CLANK
CLANK

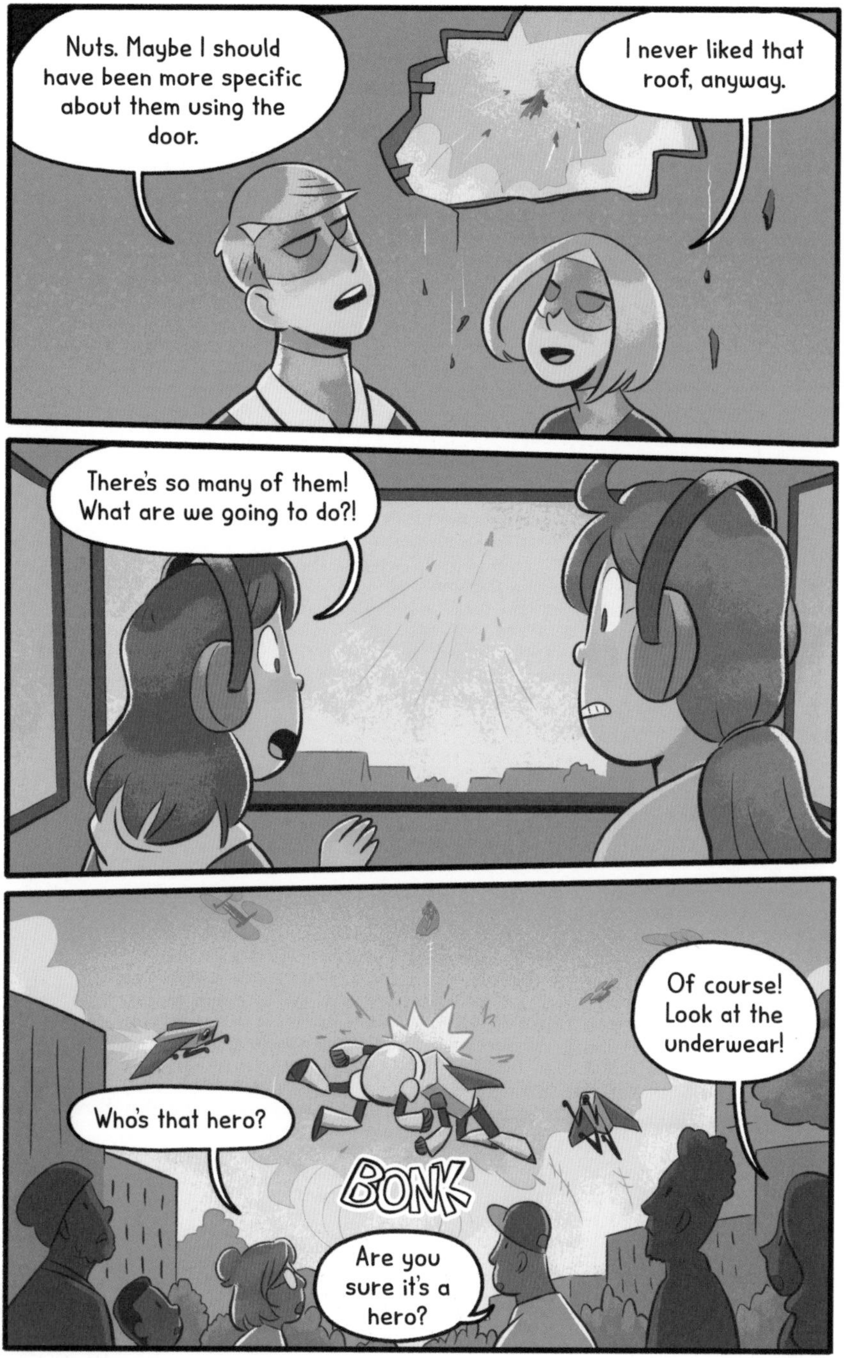

Nuts. Maybe I should have been more specific about them using the door.
I never liked that roof, anyway.
There's so many of them! What are we going to do?!
Who's that hero?
Of course! Look at the underwear!
BONK
Are you sure it's a hero?

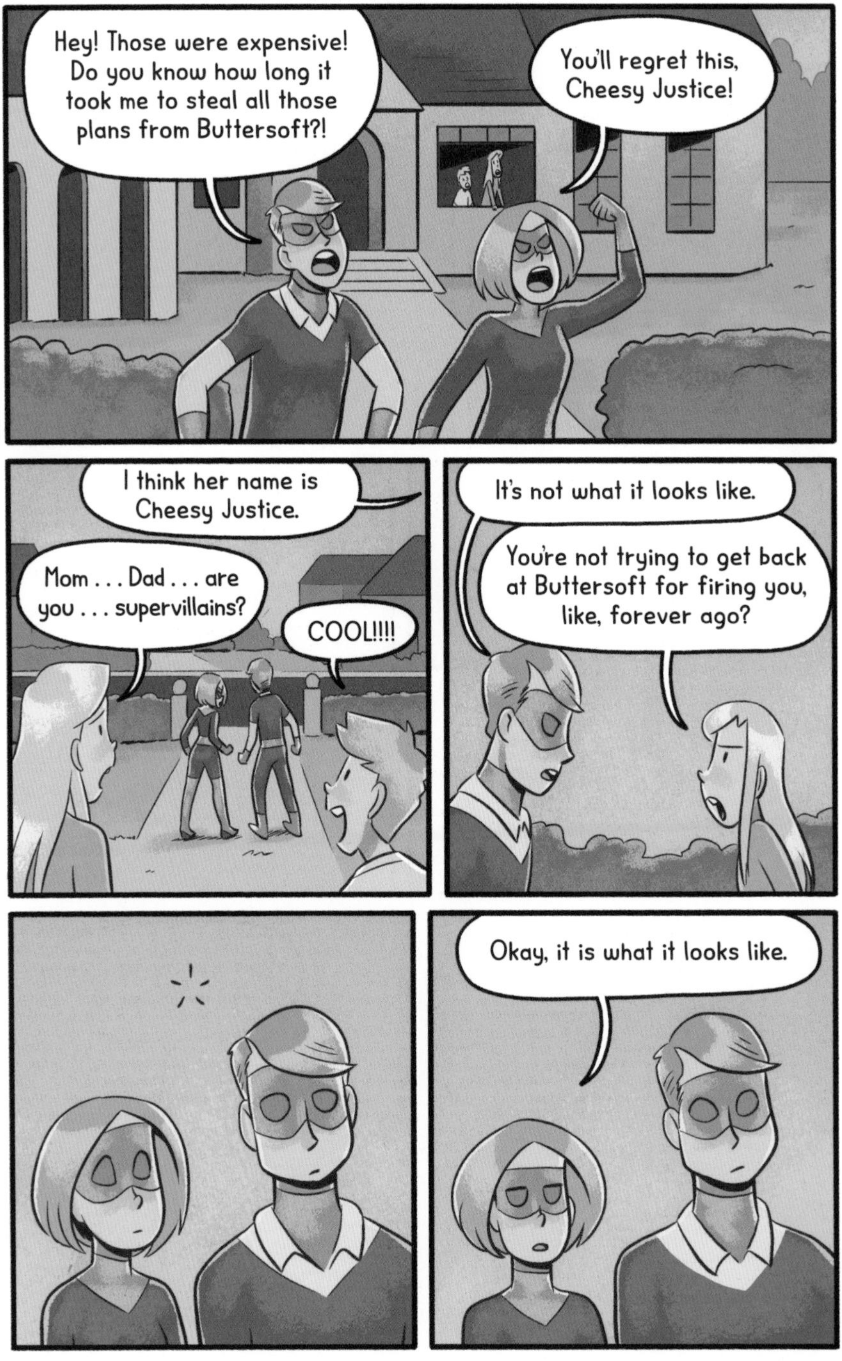
Hey! Those were expensive! Do you know how long it took me to steal all those plans from Buttersoft?!
You'll regret this, Cheesy Justice!
I think her name is Cheesy Justice.
Mom . . . Dad . . . are you . . . supervillains?
COOL!!!!
It's not what it looks like.
You're not trying to get back at Buttersoft for firing you, like, forever ago?
Okay, it is what it looks like.

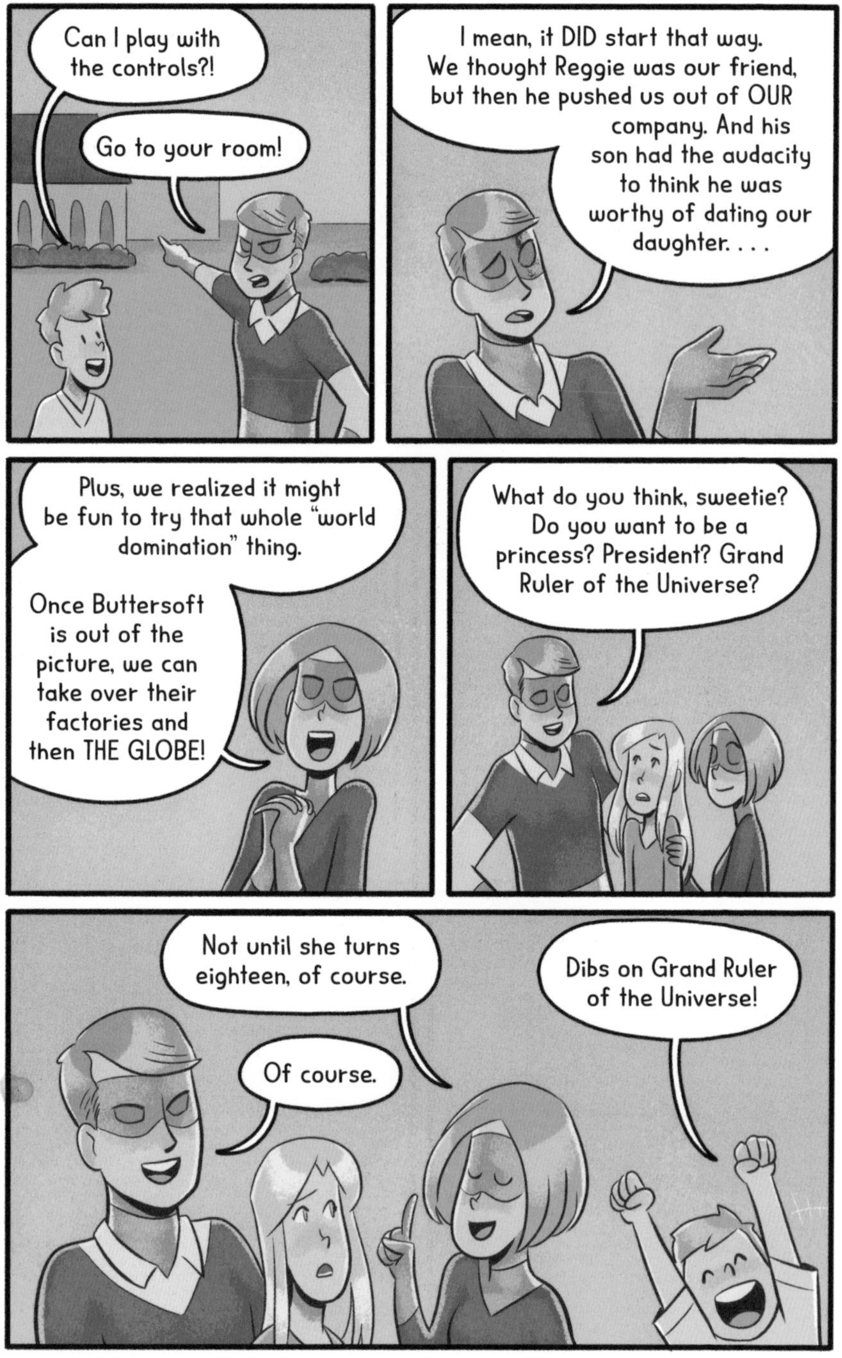
Can I play with the controls?!
Go to your room!
I mean, it DID start that way. We thought Reggie was our friend, but then he pushed us out of OUR company. And his son had the audacity to think he was worthy of dating our daughter. . . .
Plus, we realized it might be fun to try that whole "world domination" thing.
Once Buttersoft is out of the picture, we can take over their factories and then THE GLOBE!
What do you think, sweetie? Do you want to be a princess? President? Grand Ruler of the Universe?
Not until she turns eighteen, of course.
Of course.
Dibs on Grand Ruler of the Universe!

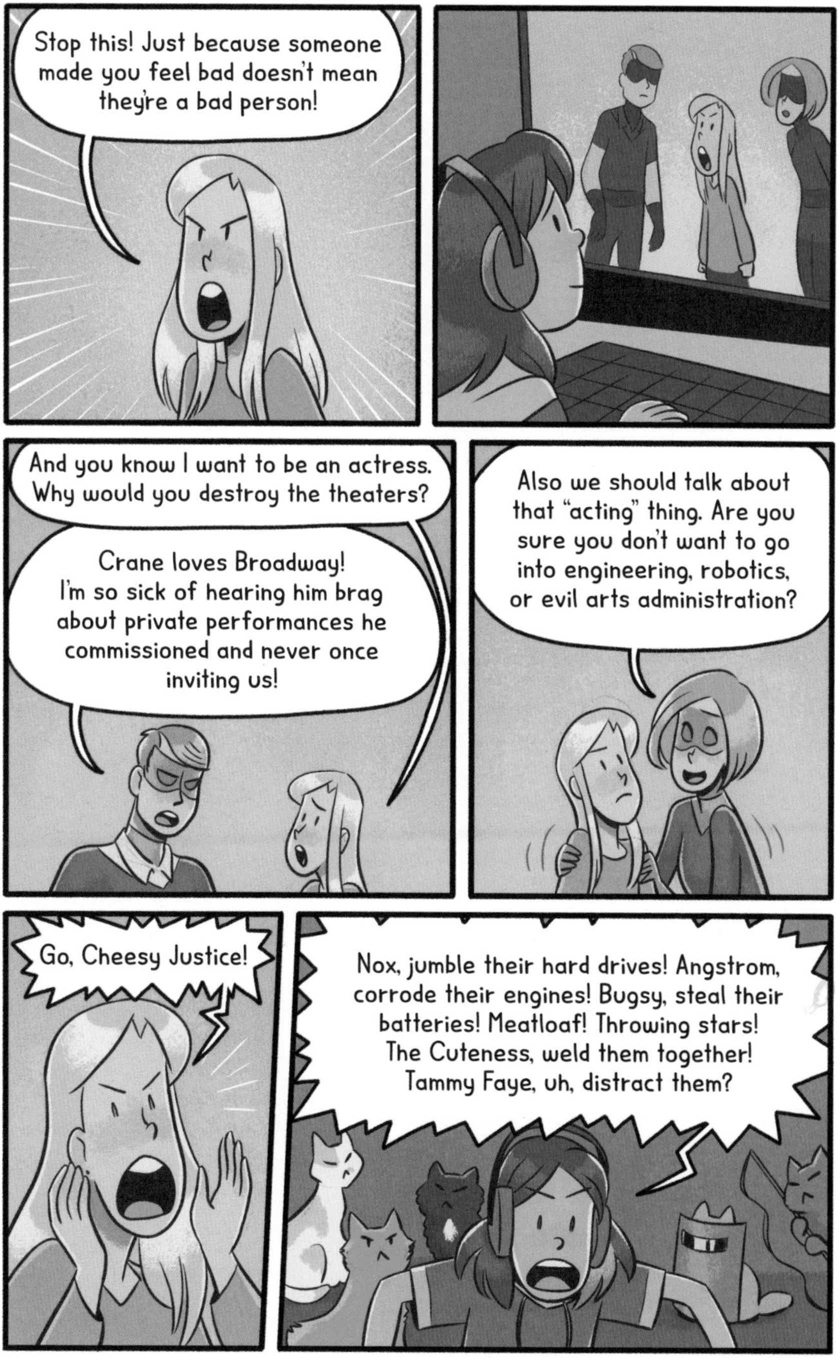
Stop this! Just because someone made you feel bad doesn't mean they're a bad person!
And you know I want to be an actress. Why would you destroy the theaters?
Crane loves Broadway! I'm so sick of hearing him brag about private performances he commissioned and never once inviting us!
Also we should talk about that "acting" thing. Are you sure you don't want to go into engineering, robotics, or evil arts administration?
Go, Cheesy Justice!
Nox, jumble their hard drives! Angstrom, corrode their engines! Bugsy, steal their batteries! Meatloaf! Throwing stars! The Cuteness, weld them together! Tammy Faye, uh, distract them?

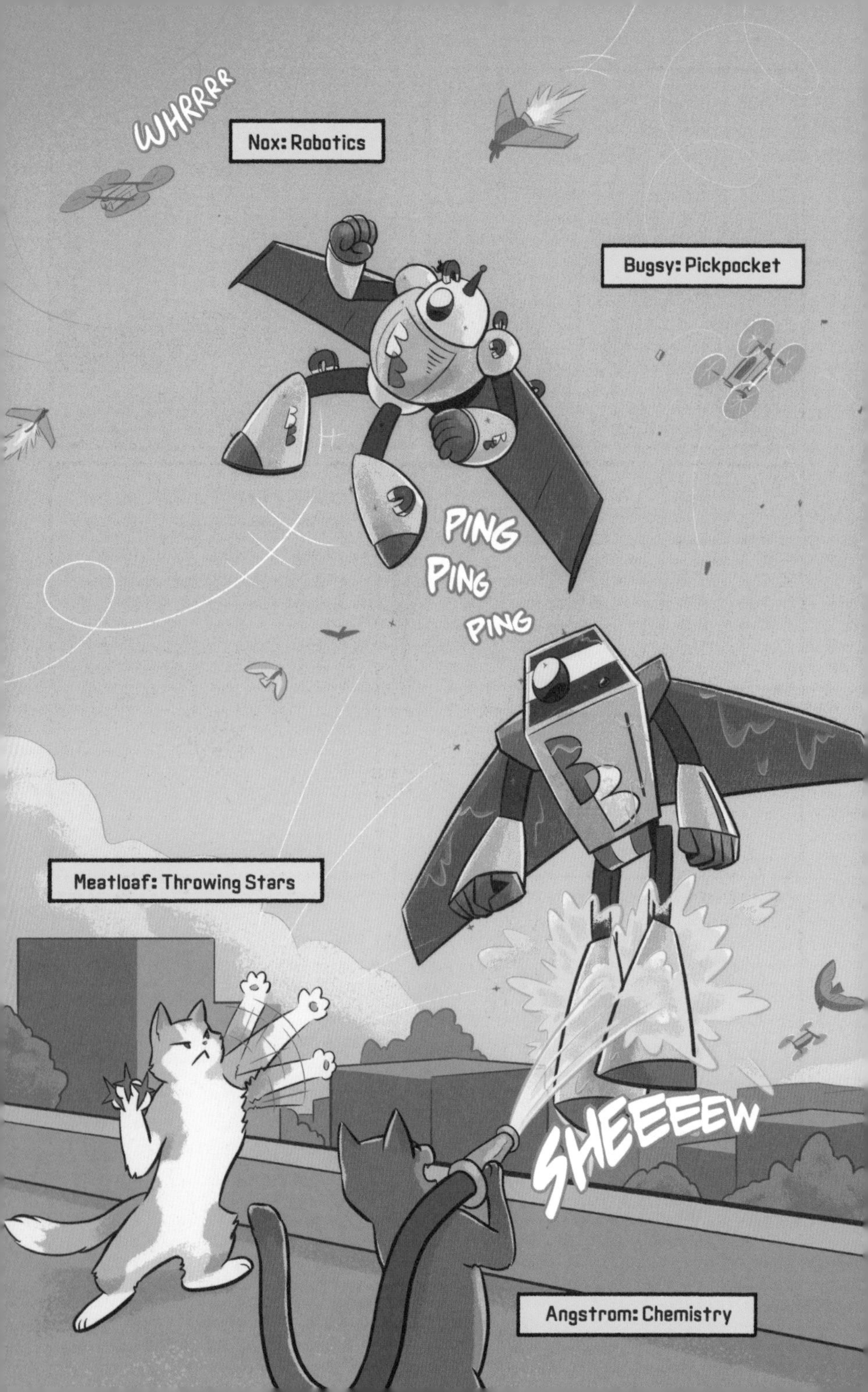
WHRRRR
Nox: Robotics
Bugsy: Pickpocket
PING
PING
PING
Meatloaf: Throwing Stars
SHEEEEW
Angstrom: Chemistry

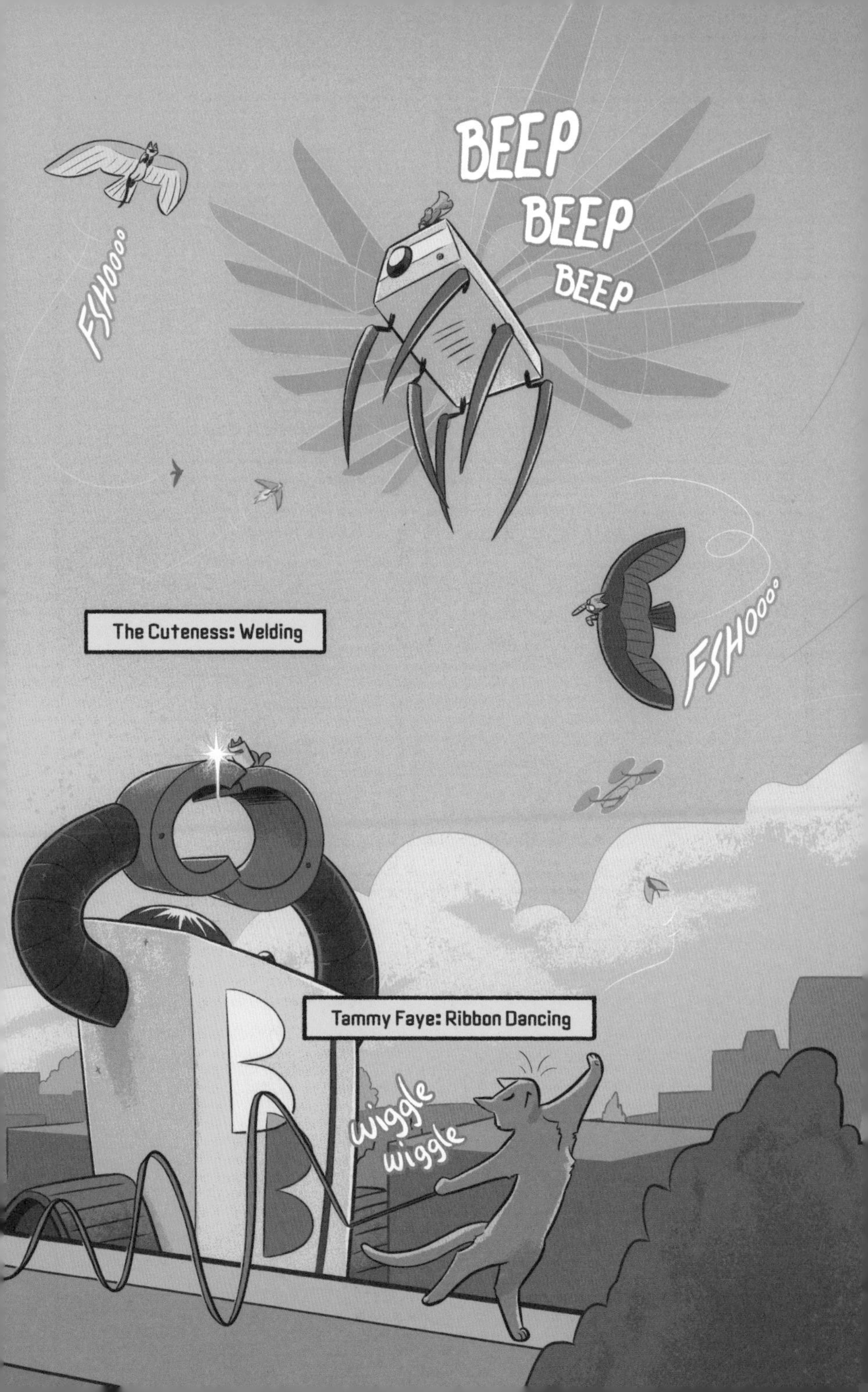
BEEP
BEEP
BEEP
FSHoooo
The Cuteness: Welding
FSHoooo
Tammy Faye: Ribbon Dancing
wiggle
wiggle

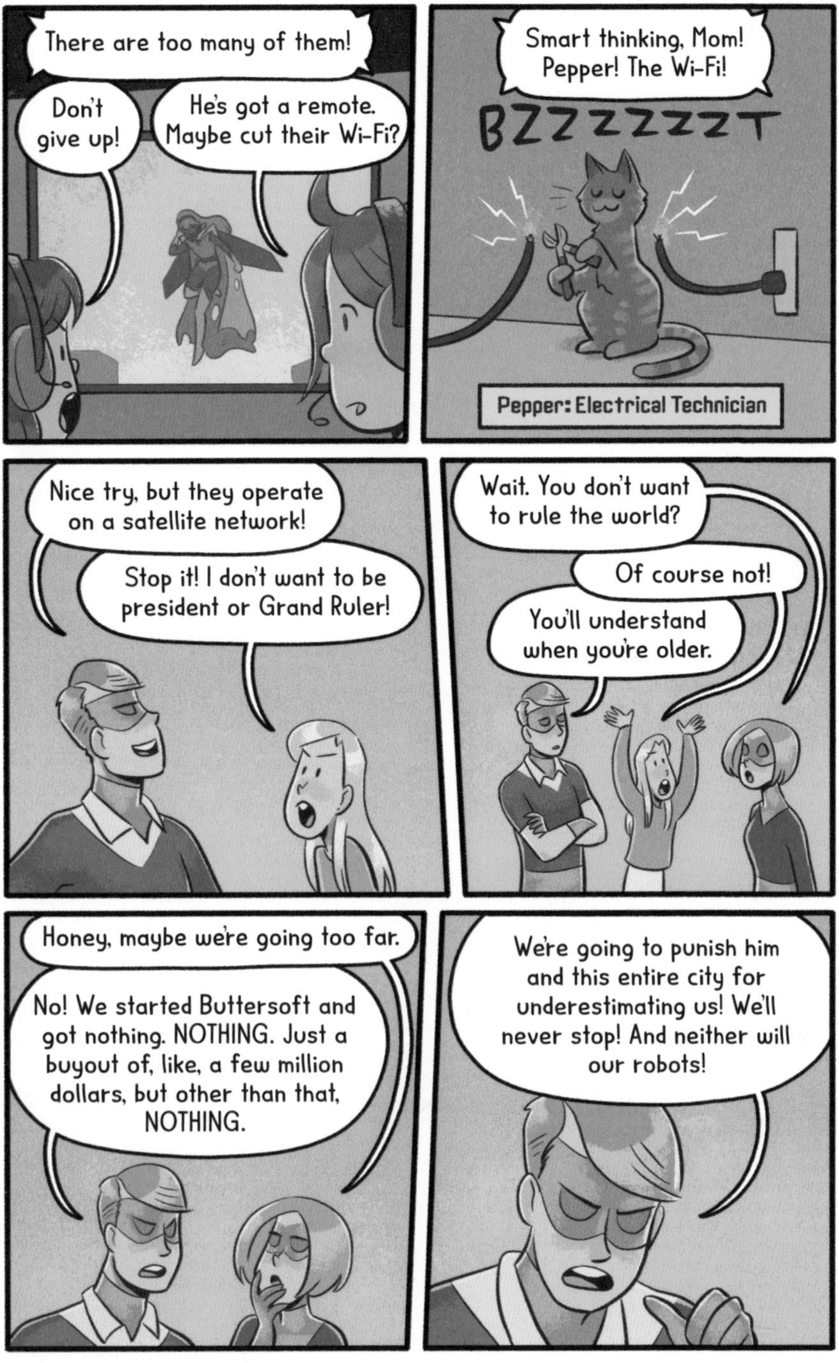
There are too many of them!
Don't give up!
He's got a remote. Maybe cut their Wi-Fi?
Smart thinking, Mom! Pepper! The Wi-Fi!
BZZZZZZT
Pepper: Electrical Technician
Nice try, but they operate on a satellite network!
Stop it! I don't want to be president or Grand Ruler!
Wait. You don't want to rule the world?
Of course not!
You'll understand when you're older.
Honey, maybe we're going too far.
No! We started Buttersoft and got nothing. NOTHING. Just a buyout of, like, a few million dollars, but other than that, NOTHING.
We're going to punish him and this entire city for underestimating us! We'll never stop! And neither will our robots!

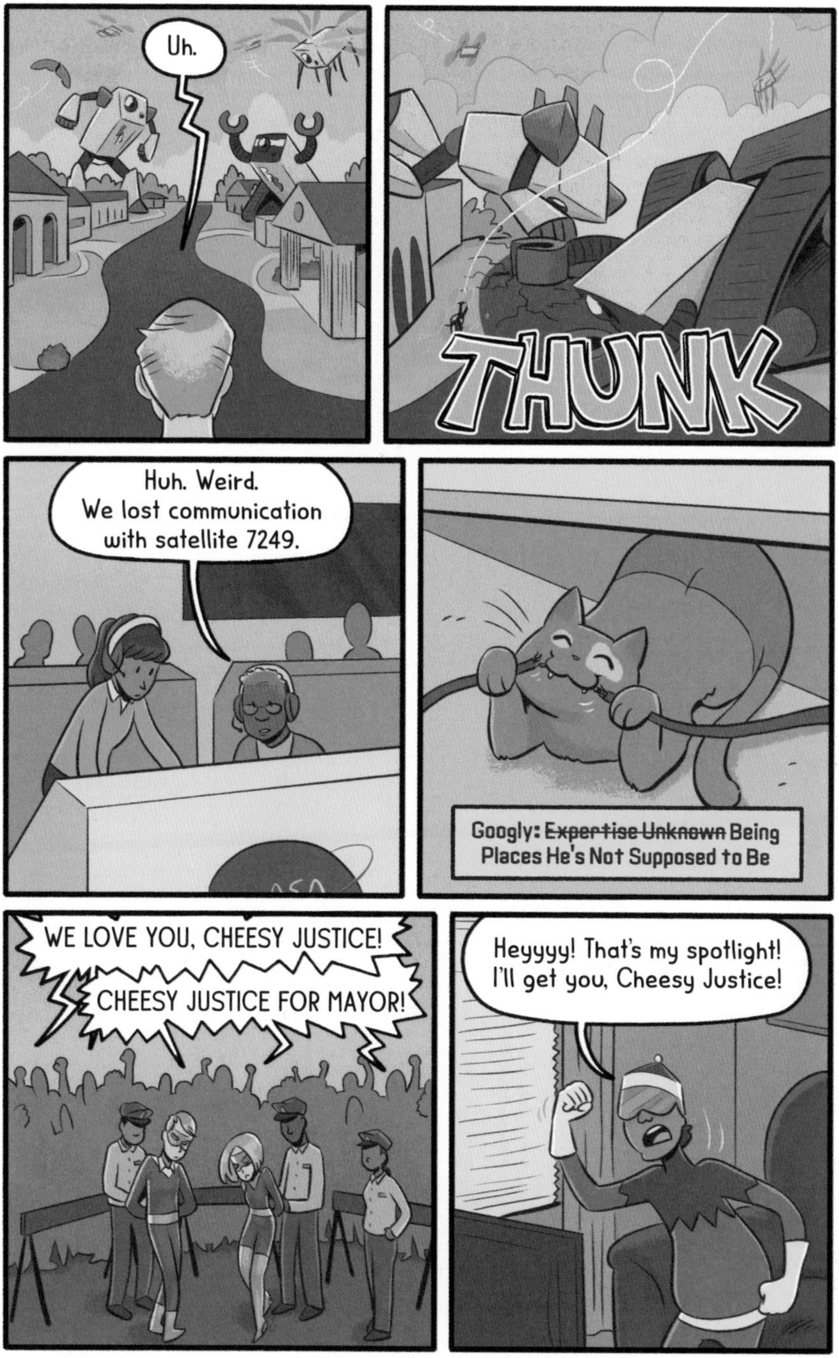
Uh.
THUNK
Huh. Weird.
We lost communication
with satellite 7249.
Googly: ~~Expertise Unknown~~ Being Places He's Not Supposed to Be
WE LOVE YOU, CHEESY JUSTICE!
CHEESY JUSTICE FOR MAYOR!
Heyyyy! That's my spotlight!
I'll get you, Cheesy Justice!

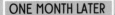ONE MONTH LATER

Are you doing okay?

At least they didn't actually destroy much more than our own roof and a few hot dog carts, but it didn't help that the judge was a *Cats the Musical* fan.

I barely know the cousins I'll be living with.

Chicago might be nice?

I should be more upset, but I'm still in shock.

I can't believe my parents were supervillains.

Though, come to think of it, they did start getting issues of *Maniacal Monthly.*

I guess now I have to become one, too. Spend all my time training and avenging them and destroying Cheesy Justice and the Mousetress so that they'll rue the day they crossed my family.

Muahahahaha!

Just kidding.

I think.

Not many colleges offer a degree in super villainism with a minor in theater.

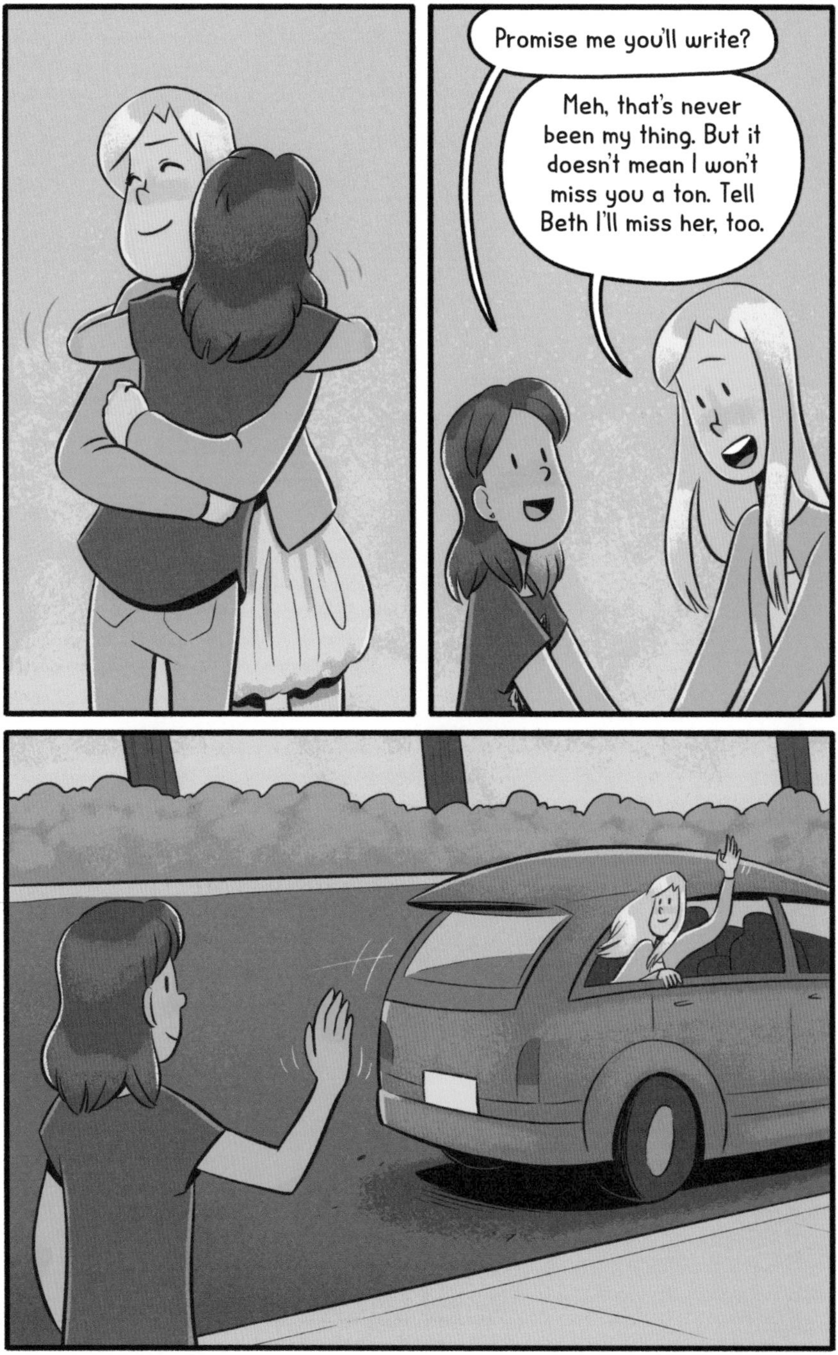
Promise me you'll write?
Meh, that's never been my thing. But it doesn't mean I won't miss you a ton. Tell Beth I'll miss her, too.

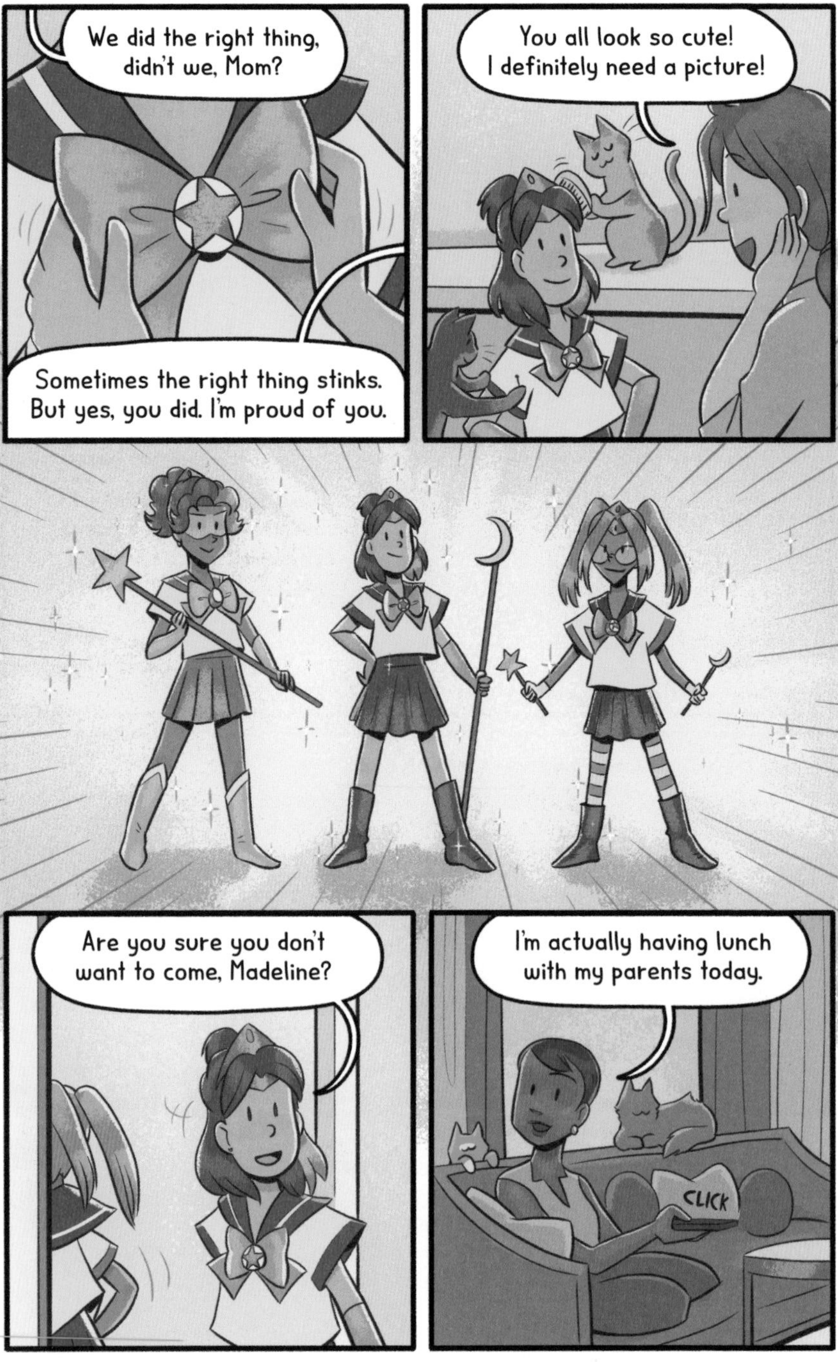
We did the right thing, didn't we, Mom?
Sometimes the right thing stinks. But yes, you did. I'm proud of you.
You all look so cute! I definitely need a picture!
Are you sure you don't want to come, Madeline?
I'm actually having lunch with my parents today.
CLICK

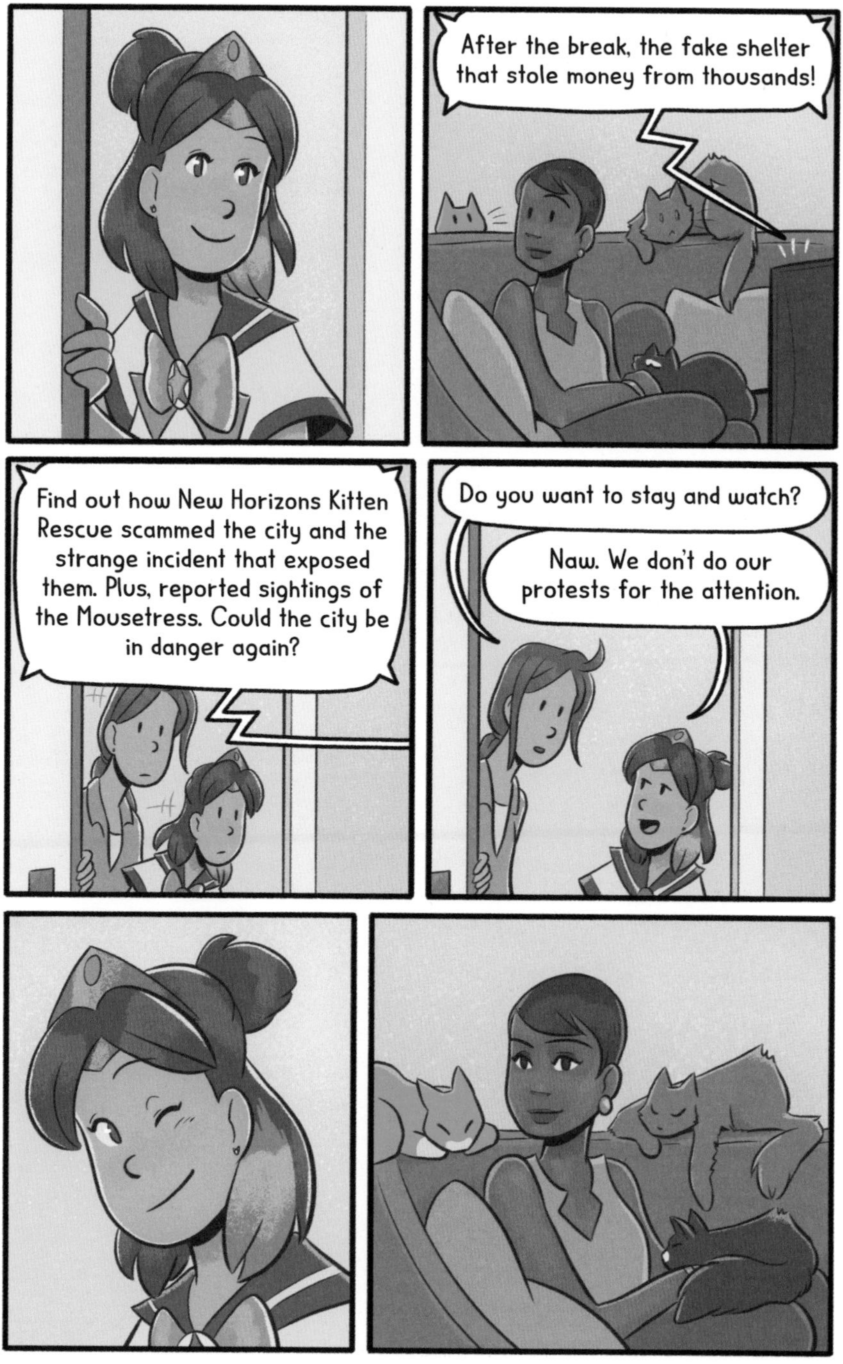
After the break, the fake shelter that stole money from thousands!
Find out how New Horizons Kitten Rescue scammed the city and the strange incident that exposed them. Plus, reported sightings of the Mousetress. Could the city be in danger again?
Do you want to stay and watch?
Naw. We don't do our protests for the attention.

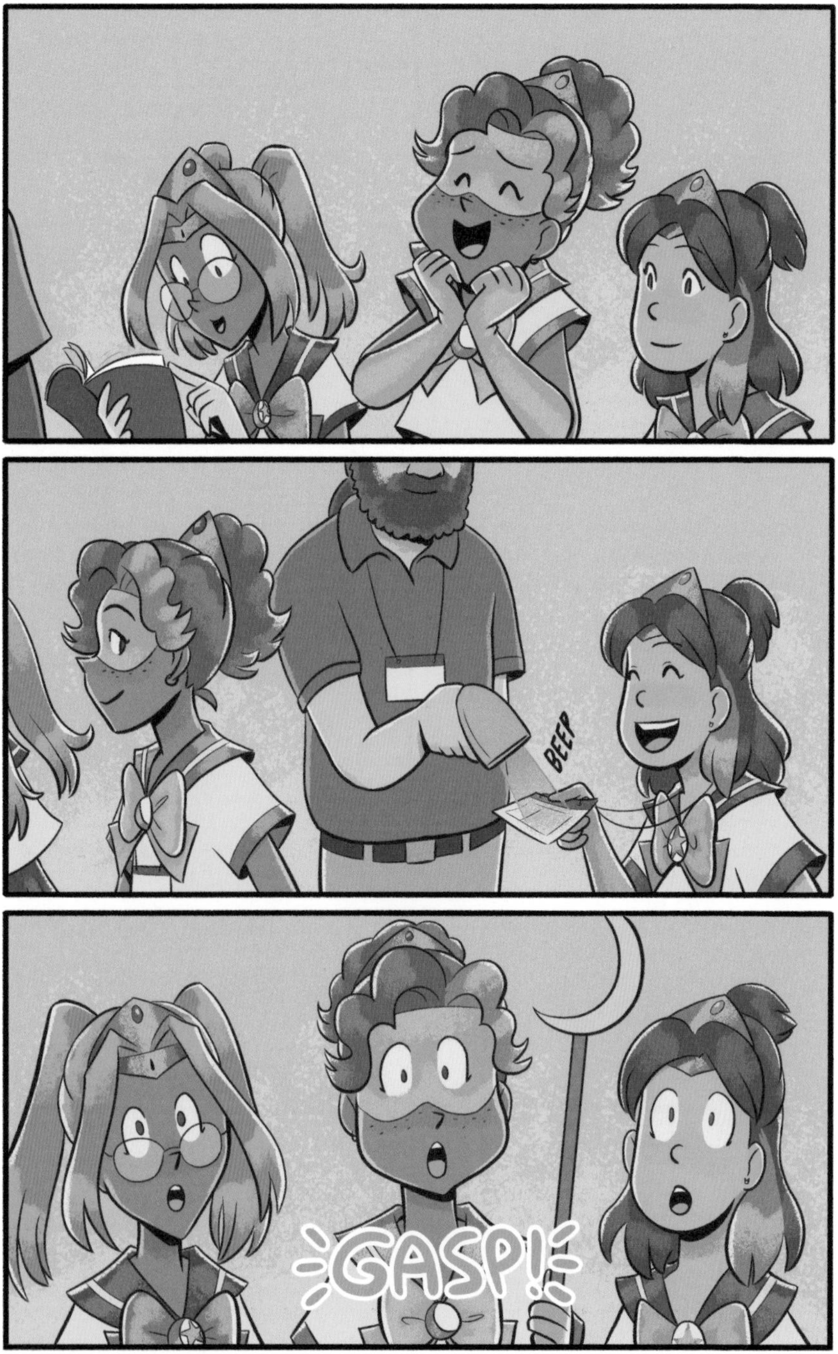
BEEP
GASP!

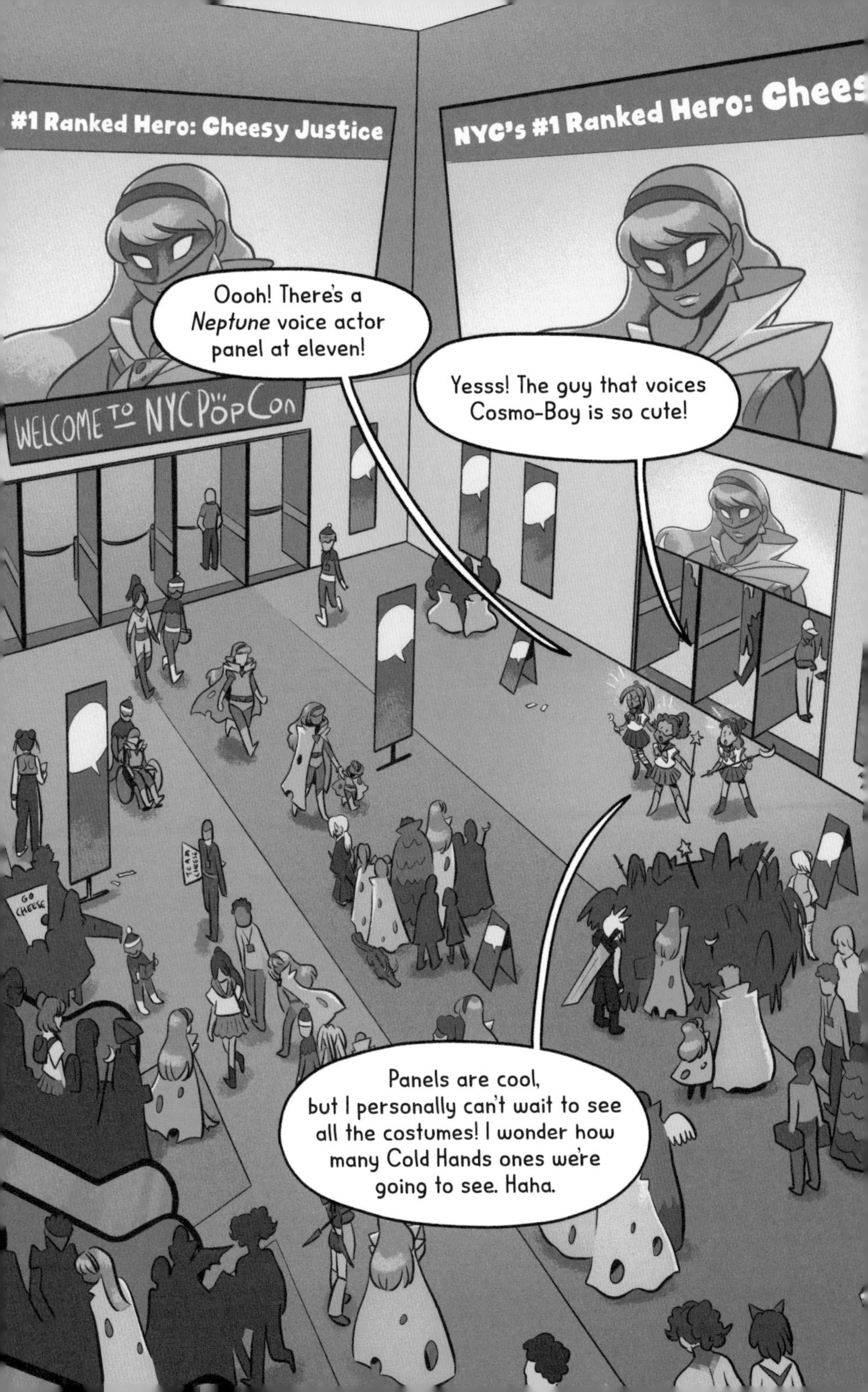
#1 Ranked Hero: Cheesy Justice
NYC's #1 Ranked Hero: Chees
WELCOME TO NYC PopCon
Oooh! There's a *Neptune* voice actor panel at eleven!
Yesss! The guy that voices Cosmo-Boy is so cute!
GO CHEESE
TEAM CHEESE
Panels are cool, but I personally can't wait to see all the costumes! I wonder how many Cold Hands ones we're going to see. Haha.

Some Heroes Have Capes . . .
. . . Katie Has Cats!

KATIE THE CATSITTER
Colleen AF Venable
Stephanie Yue
KATIE THE CATSITTER
BEST FRIENDS FOR NEVER
Colleen AF Venable
Stephanie Yue
KATIE THE CATSITTER
SECRETS AND SIDEKICKS
Colleen AF Venable
Stephanie Yue
Collect them all!

And don't miss

Katie the Catsitter
The Purrfect Plan

coming in 2024!

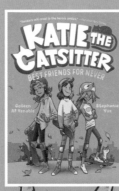

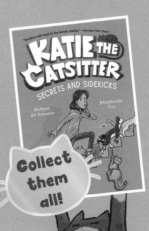

Sketch Pad!

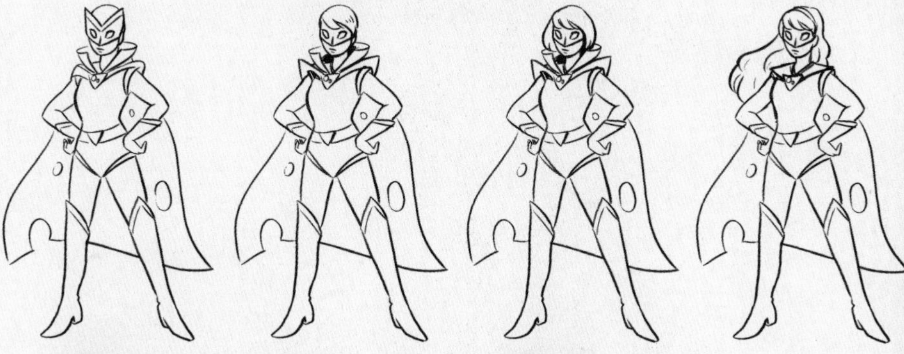

STEPH:

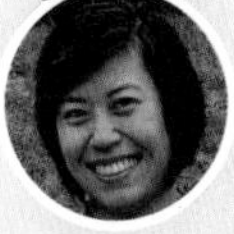

"I wanted the Cheesy Justice costume to be ridiculous and completely different from the Mousetress's more practical gear. Her costume kind of makes me crave a grilled cheese sandwich, so I think it worked out."

COLLEEN:

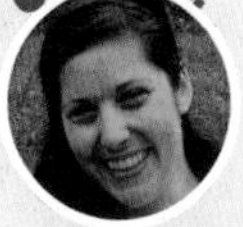

"Underwear on the outside will ALWAYS make me laugh, but that cheese cape Steph drew is next-level hysterical."

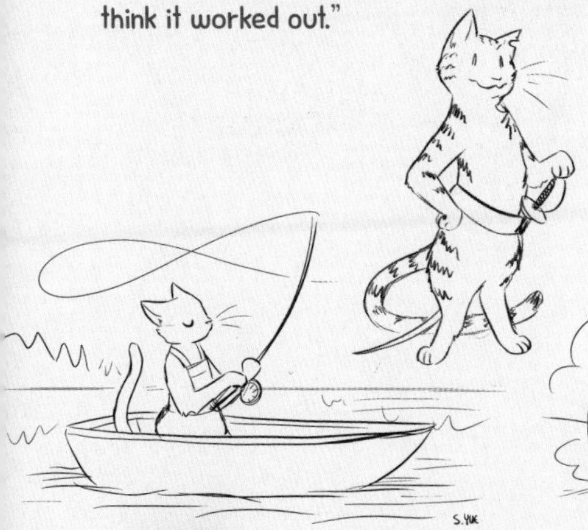
S.YUE

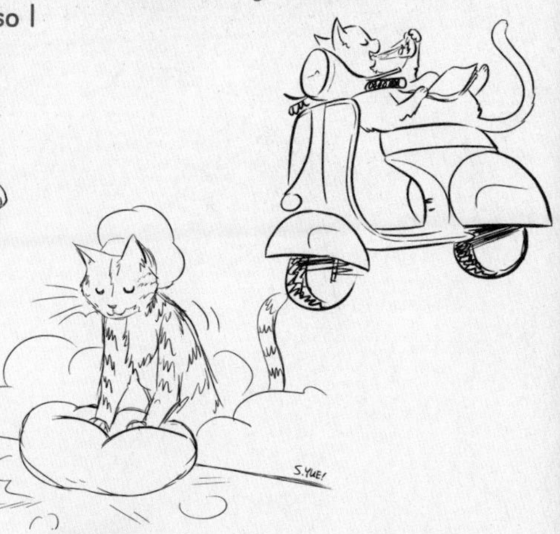
S.YUE!

COLLEEN:

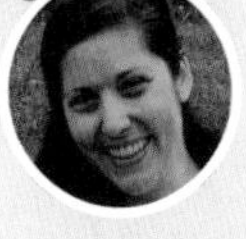

"I love that there's never anything that's too goofy or kick-butt that Steph can't draw! It's almost a challenge to come up with a cat talent that she can't make look super cool."

STEPH:

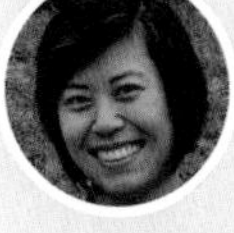

"When Colleen tells me the name of a new cat, the first thing I do is laugh, probably, because the cat has a funny name. Then look up the reference. If it's something I'm not familiar with, I can learn something new!"

MEET STEPH AND COLLEEN!

We send each other funny cat pics and make cheesy puns all the time. That counts as collaboration, right?

The only thing more fun than making books is making books with a friend! I LOVE collaboration!

Colleen AF (Ann Felicity) Venable is the author of many books for kids and was longlisted for a National Book Award for her YA graphic novel debut, *Kiss Number 8*. Colleen splits her time between Brooklyn, New York, and an old house in Western Massachusetts that she's rebuilding with friends. When she's not writing books, she can be found working at animal rescues, failing at imitating bird calls, and getting very excited when she spots a frog. Visit Colleen online at colleenaf.com and @colleenaf.

Stephanie Yue is the illustrator of several picture books and chapter books in addition to Katie the Catsitter, and she was the colorist for *Smile* by Raina Telgemeier. Steph travels the world by motorbike and spent the past year and a half converting a Sprinter van into a full-time mobile studio. She's currently drawing the next Katie the Catsitter from all over North America, and eating and climbing all the things. Visit her online at stephanieyue.com and on Twitter at @quezzie.

COLLEEN

Zodiac sign: Capricorn

Fave food: Soft-serve ice cream with sprinkles

Things you may not know:

- I'm SUPER good at making friendship bracelets and can finish one in under five minutes!

- I can build robots! Well, tiny robots using a coding language called Arduino. NOTE: I don't let them try to take over any cities.

STEPH

Zodiac sign: Scorpio

Fave food: Salt 'n' vinegar chips, french fries, noodles, tacos . . . I could never choose—I love all sorts of food!

Things you may not know:

- I may not be very good at skateboarding, but I used to Rollerblade and roller skate and even played roller derby! I played on the Mob Squad with Providence Roller Derby. Turns out, I'm not great at doing tricks or making pretty shapes, but I'm a natural at dodging hits and knocking people down.

- I was super lucky as a kid to go to Space Camp. We built rockets, did simulations, and tested out all sorts of equipment. It was everything I dreamed it would be. I still wear a U.S. Space Camp pin on my jacket.

How to Make a Friendship Bracelet

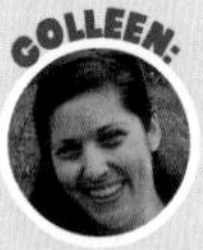
COLLEEN:

There are two ways I made friends growing up—well, three if you include my ***charming*** personality.

1. I loved black jelly beans and would trade ALL the other colors for those delicious licorice ones no one else ever wanted.
2. So. Many. Friendship. Bracelets. I was like a little factory! My hyperactive nature meant I could make them faster than anyone else. You could always tell who my friends were because they'd be covered in them, along with a thousand lanyard key chains.

Here's one of my favorites! It's called the Candy Stripe Bracelet. (Note: It is not edible . . . unless you are using rope candy . . . um . . . okay, I might need to make that someday!)

Step 1:

We're going with Katie/Beth colors, so cut two 36-inch strands of your best bright pink and teal thread.

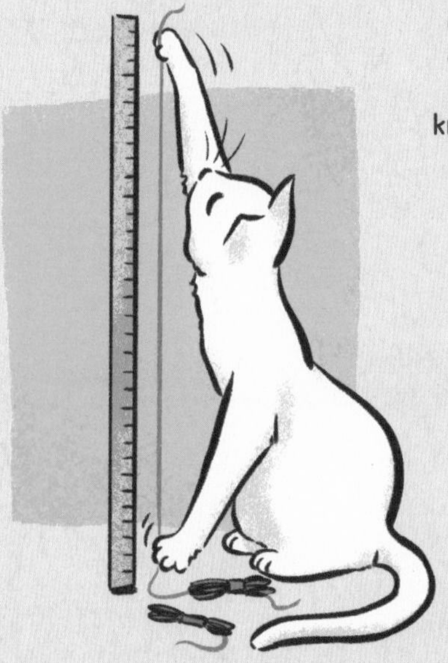

Step 2:

Fold them in half and tie a knot near the folded-over part. Now you have eight threads! I like my stripes nice and bold, so make sure the four pink threads are on one side and the four teal are on the other. This will make thick blocks of each color. Feel free to experiment with other ways, too! Use a safety pin or tape the knot to a table to keep the strings in place.

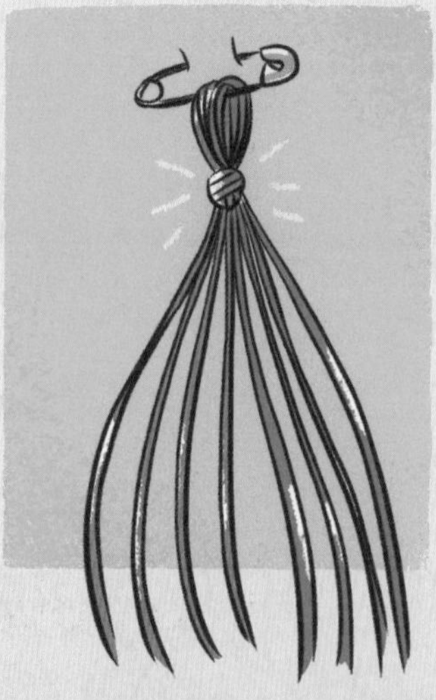

Step 3:

Step 3 is THE FOUR in all caps . . . or at least I always thought of it that way. Take the string at the far left, and make a "4" shape over string number 2 next to it.

Step 4:

Then put the end through the 4 shape you just made. Do this twice.

Step 5:

Now take that same string and make 4s on the third string twice, then the fourth string twice, and the fifth . . . Keep going until you get to the end of the row at the eighth string! Now your left-most string is all the way to the right!

Step 6:

Repeat steps 3, 4, and 5 with the new string all the way to the left, with two knots at every string it passes, ending on the right again. You'll start to see the diagonal pattern emerging! Keep going!

Step 7:

When the bracelet is long enough, tie a knot in the end and cut off any excess thread! FRIENDSHIP!

TAKE A TOUR OF STEPH'S MOBILE LIVE-WORK STUDIO!

HOW IT STARTED

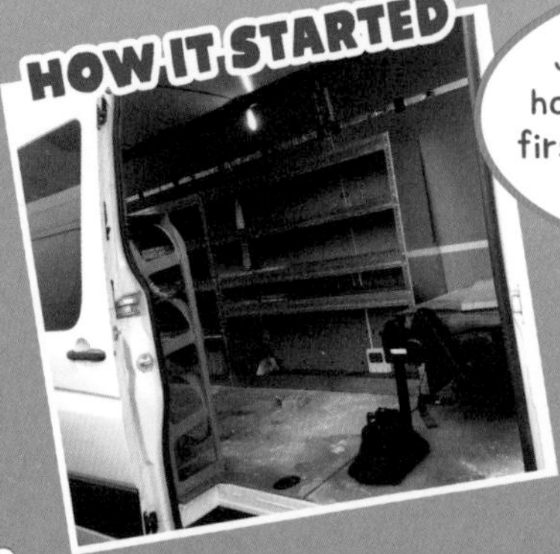

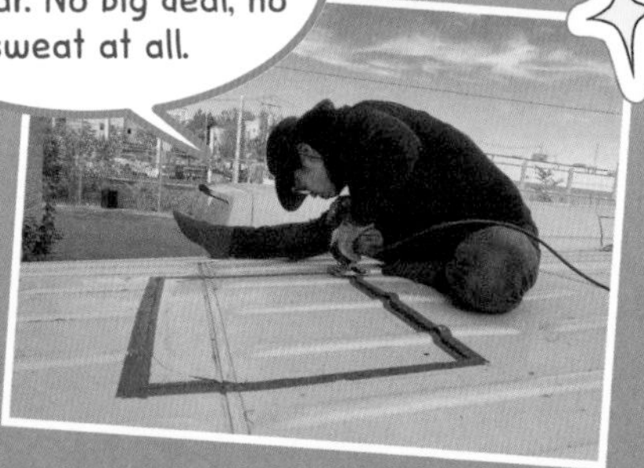
Just cutting a huge hole in the roof of my first car. No big deal, no sweat at all.

HOW IT'S GOING

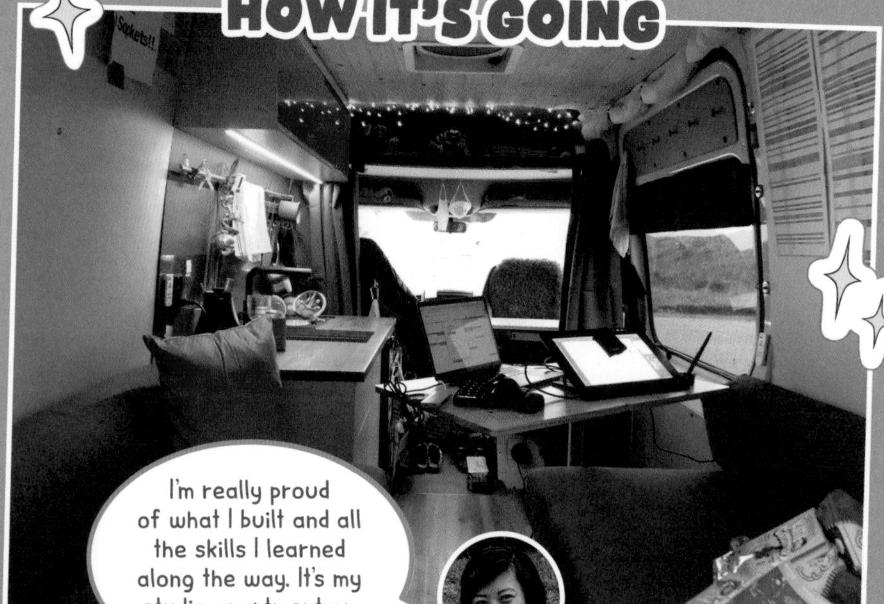
I'm really proud of what I built and all the skills I learned along the way. It's my studio apartment on wheels!